NOBODY IS SAFE

The Quill Point Chronicles 3

NOBODY IS SAFE

OCTOBER KANE

Published By: 4 Horsemen Publications, Inc.

4 Horsemen Publications, Inc.
PO Box 417
Sylva, NC 28779
4horsemenpublications.com
info@4horsemenpublications.com

Cover & Typesetting by Autumn Skye
Edited by Charles Miano

Library of Congress Control Number: 2025935564

Paperback ISBN-13: 979-8-8232-0856-7
Hardcover ISBN-13: 979-8-8232-0857-4
Audiobook ISBN-13: 979-8-8232-0859-8
Ebook ISBN-13: 979-8-8232-0858-1

For the readers of spooky tales
and epic adventures.

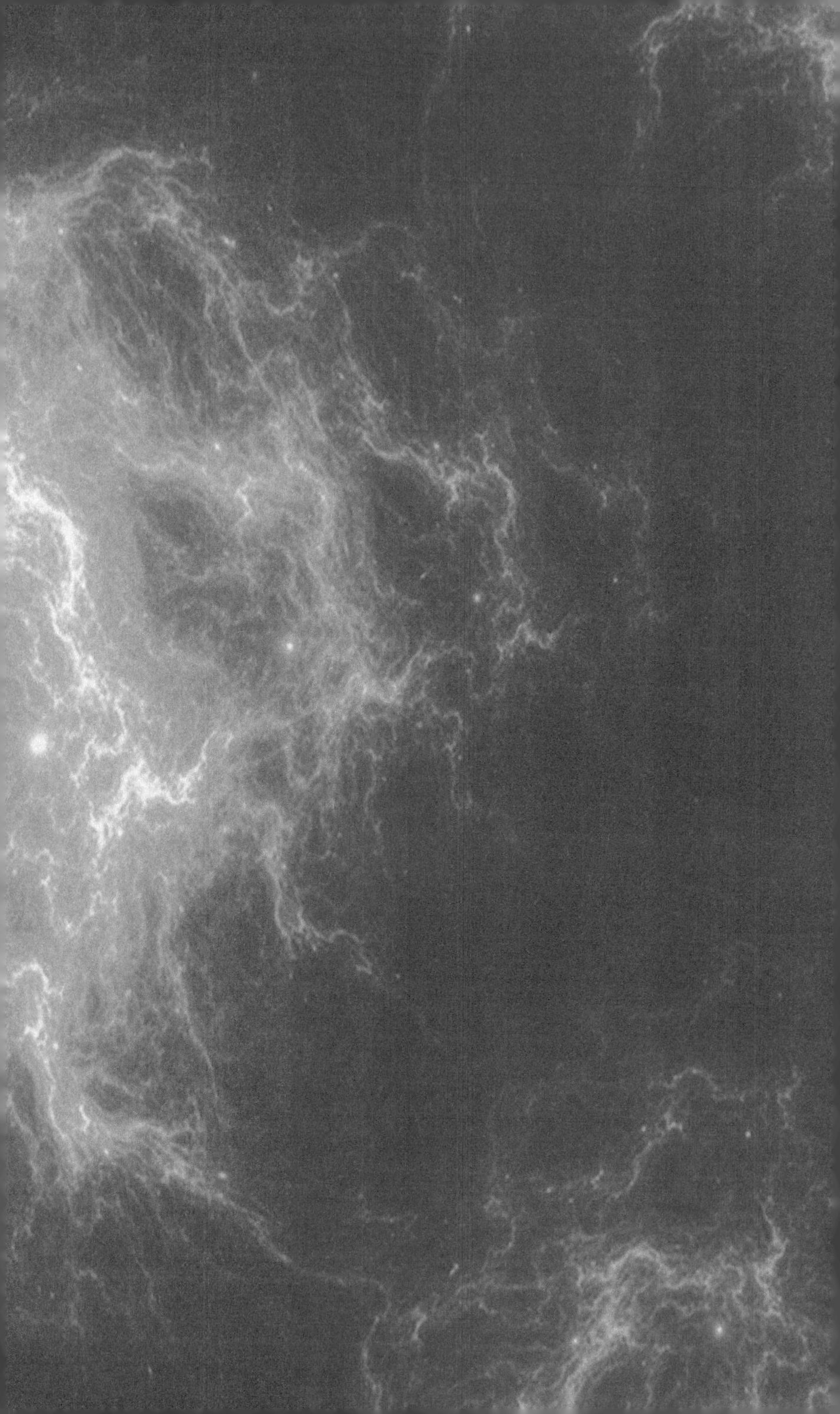

ACKNOWLEDGMENTS

It's funny. In the last book's acknowledgments, I said it was the most complex piece of fiction I'd ever attempted. I was wrong. This one is way more complex—and the next one will likely be even more so. And the writing of a book this complicated takes a support system. Without my friends and family, I never would've had the wherewithal to attempt something like this. Writing is a solitary activity and—in my case—an intense, challenging one. And I'm so glad that I have people who are there whenever I emerge from typing.

TABLE OF CONTENTS

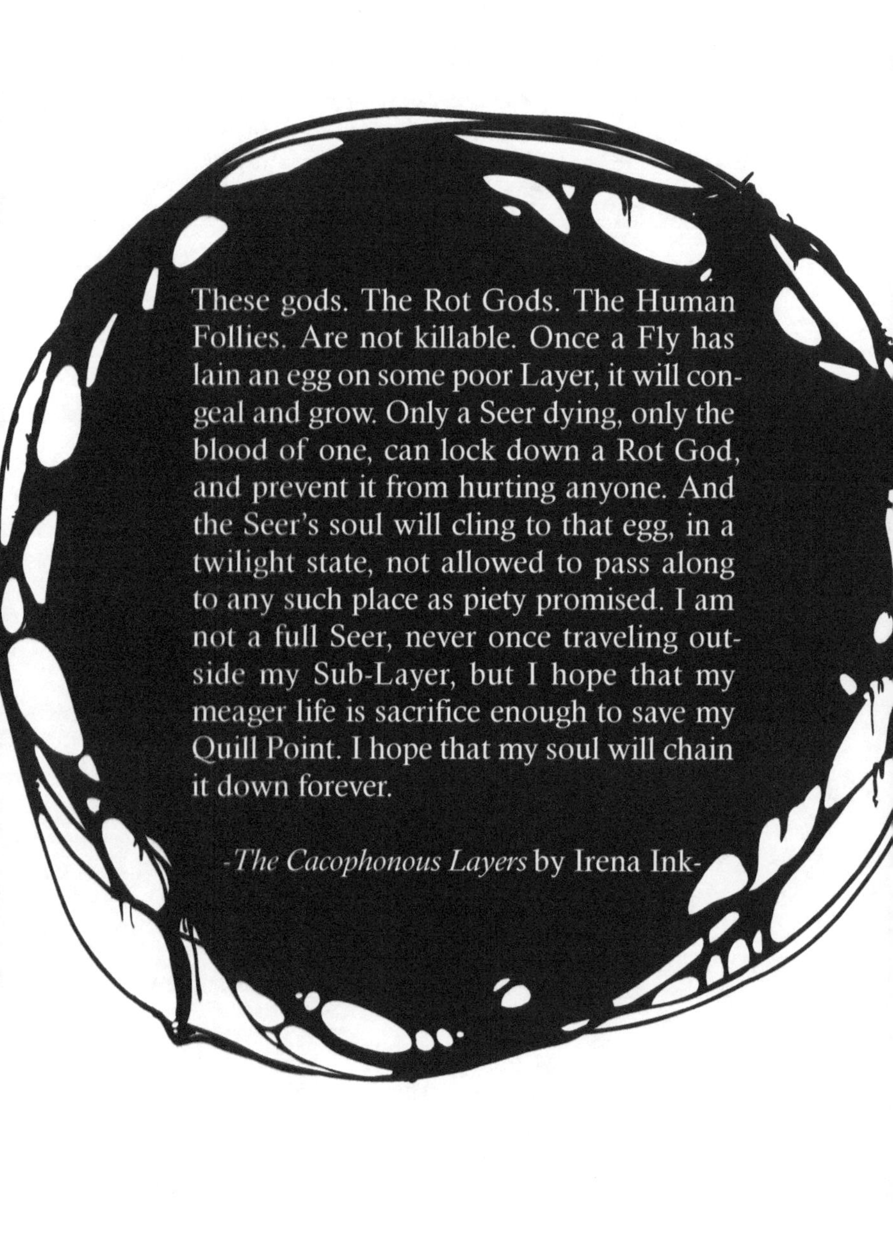
These gods. The Rot Gods. The Human Follies. Are not killable. Once a Fly has lain an egg on some poor Layer, it will congeal and grow. Only a Seer dying, only the blood of one, can lock down a Rot God, and prevent it from hurting anyone. And the Seer's soul will cling to that egg, in a twilight state, not allowed to pass along to any such place as piety promised. I am not a full Seer, never once traveling outside my Sub-Layer, but I hope that my meager life is sacrifice enough to save my Quill Point. I hope that my soul will chain it down forever.

-The Cacophonous Layers by Irena Ink-

Prologue

I RENA INK LOCKED *THE CACOPHONOUS Layers* inside a safe in the recently constructed court-house. The safe was the strongest she could get without her brother noticing the expenditure. There was only one key for the safe, and it would be passed down to each mayor of Quill Point. Only they would know what lay below the town—and why no one should ever go into that chamber.

Someone knocked on the door behind her.

"Come in," she said, already knowing who it was.

The door opened slowly, and Teagen Kelly peeked inside. Teagen was a shy and short man, with barely socially acceptable long blond hair. He had pale white skin and wore a blazer over a nice shirt and pants. His long hair always had the remnants of some art project, telling of his latest exploits.

"Am I interrupting anything?"

"Yes," Irena said with a smile. "But don't let that stop you."

Teagen nodded and opened the door the rest of the way. He had a series of papers tucked under his arm. "I've brought sketches of it before I do the finishing touches."

"Oh, thank you," Irena said. She gestured toward her desk. "You can leave it there. I need to see my brother about something."

Teagen stared at her, his mouth hanging open slightly.

Irena glanced back at him, and then at her arm. She had just lazily pointed over at her desk—

Oh, dammit.

Slowly, so slowly it irritated her, Irena lowered her arm back to her side. She'd long given up on keeping it a secret from her brother, but that was the first time in a while she'd made an error and moved as a Seer and not a Layer-Linked person.

"It's rude to stare," she said quietly.

"I'm sorry miss, I just … do you play some sort of sport?"

"Tennis," Irena lied. "It's good for circulation and even I need something to calm myself down after such long days."

"Right, yes," Teagen said, and didn't move.

Irena gave him an awkward smile and gestured—slowly—toward the desk again.

Teagen blinked and nodded. He walked over to the desk and deposited the papers. "Well, you must be a great challenge for anyone who plays against you."

"Yes, well, we all have our hobbies," she said.

"I suppose … well, then, the top few papers have the sculpture. I've already ensured that my team has started on the paintings you requested. You can find that in the papers, as well."

"Thank you, Teagen, thanks so much. Will I need to do anything more to handle this?"

He glanced at the papers. "Well … uh … no, not at all, miss. Not if you're satisfied with the plans presented. We'll do everything from here on out."

Irena let out a small sigh. Despite already knowing what she would have to do—for this town, for this Layer, for these people—her pulse thrummed so hard. She could measure in weeks, months perhaps, how much longer she could afford to be alive.

She glanced over at the illustration. At least her visage would live on somewhere.

"Excellent. You have been one of the best artisans I've ever met, Teagen. Thank you for all of this."

"That's … why thank you," Teagen said, nodding his head. "It's been an honor to sculpt you, Ms. Ink."

Irena nodded. She gestured for him to leave the room with her, and they both walked in silence. Over time, as she'd become more and more acclimated to being a Seer, to having a Sub-Layer, she found it harder and harder to be around other people. Teagen had a quick, almost nervous gait most of the time—and he was moving so slowly toward her.

After they were in the hallway for a moment, Irena cleared her throat. "I do need to get to my brother now, Teagen. But, again, thank you so much for all you've done. My name may be immortalized in those statues, but I do hope that history recalls all that you have made and will make."

Teagen smiled, but then it wavered. "Miss, is everything alright? I don't mean to invade your privacy, but you sound—I don't quite know. But … I hear something, and

I wouldn't be a proper person if I didn't enquire. You are … getting on in age."

Irena Ink gave a curt nod, slightly annoyed at the comment. "It's going to be fine, Teagen. There's more to founding a town than I can explain, but I will make sure that Quill Point lives on for so long that it *will* be in every history book."

"You will be right next to them in those books," Teagen said.

She smiled at him. "Thank you."

He seemed about to say something else, but Irena gave him a gentle shake of her head.

"I really do need to go, Teagen." She placed her hand on his shoulder, trying not to instantly shatter every bone there. "Once again, thank you."

He nodded, but his eyes widened.

Oh, I may have still done that too hard, Irena thought.

But she still walked aways as fast as would seem plausible. There was a Fly egg beneath her, still growing and feeding off the rot of greed and corruption that stained what had been forested land. It was a festering tick, eager to soar into other dimensions.

And Irena had to deal with the human who brought it down upon them all.

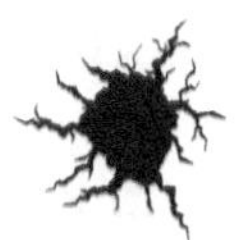

At the end of a day, Paxton liked to stand in the garden behind his and Irena's shared home and look at the birds that flocked to the feeders. Neither of the siblings had ever bothered to find someone to wed, and though they were both well off enough to have their own homes, it didn't seem logical to let Paxton be alone for too long.

Irena stood silently at the door to the garden, watching as her brother scribbled down information.

Irena had once loved her brother in the automatic ways of family, and even been on board for the development of Quill Point. He'd pitched it as legacy. Irena had seen it as something that could help people. A small town for those who needed a more peaceful place than the boom and wind of Chicago. A place where, god-willing, she might have found a home to cultivate.

But then she'd seen the painting, and nothing else had mattered for the longest time. Those sights and sounds of The Cacophonous Layers—the infinite expanse of dimensions and the space between them—made any town, any person, any dream, tiny and unworthy compared to its machinations.

And wouldn't you know it, her own brother brought one of the worst beings in the Layers to their doorstep.

"Paxton?" she said, keeping her voice level.

Paxton spun around, his eyes a little bloodshot. His blond beard snarled.

He placed the pencil between the pages of his book and snapped it shut. "Yes, sister?"

"Have you not been sleeping, Paxton?"

"Huh," Paxton said, more a sound than a word. "Sleep would be a lovely luxury, but no. I haven't been finding it very easy as of late."

Irena kept her face calm, even as thoughts churned in her stomach. Justice. Morality. It demanded this.

That didn't make it any easier.

"Why is that?" Irena asked.

"It is a lot, making a town," Paxton said. "Lots of paperwork—not that you would understand."

"I understand plenty," Irena said, walking slowly toward him.

Paxton subtly backed up. "What is it that you want, sister? I'm busy recording this lovely—"

He looked behind him, and the bird had flown off.

"—well, I *was* recording a bird."

"There are more important things lately, Paxton," Irena said.

She walked a little closer. She was counting in her head, counting how many seconds, if even that, this was going to take.

Paxton scrambled backward, bumping into the tree. Little orange leaves drifted down around him. A walnut pinged against the ground with a hard plop.

"Something has been different about you lately," Paxton said. "I don't understand it, what has become of you, but I really would like you to step back from me."

Irena had planned the words in her head for so long. Had thought of what she should say as she put this Layer right. And it had all been tainted with the harshest of emotions.

"Paxton, I almost wanted to exonerate you of guilt for what you've done. How could you know the metaphysical ramifications of what you've been doing in this town? How could you possibly know the secrets of the Layers?"

"What the devil are you on about?" Paxton said, sneering. "I've been letting you indulge in whatever this has been, but what could you blame me for?"

Irena cast her hands to either side and opened portals in the fabric of reality. It was impossible for a Seer to travel through their own portals—at least not without a certain material she hadn't found on this Layer—but it still let in the sounds.

The sounds of Rot God infected Layers. The ones on the brink of full collapse, their populations howling out as survival became a game where the rules were defined by unemotional nightmares. Irena's expression grew even more severe, and the air around her shined with a kaleidoscope of colors.

Paxton covered his ears with his hands.

"What—what is *this*?" he screamed.

Irena tried to deliver her words calmly. She was a judge now.

"I wasn't going to blame you for what you brought down on us, Paxton—but then I thought, and I thought, and I realized that your crime was greed enough to bring a god of such things to our doorstep."

Paxton darted to run around her.

The idea that he could outrun an angry Seer was comical.

Irena closed the portals and darted to stand in front of him again.

"Men like you, brother, though I hate that I am related by blood to a man like you, they assume that money supersedes. That money shields and clears guilt. That the production of money is worth more than the human cost. I *hate* The Rot Gods and all they do, but they do form a litmus test of sorts—"

Paxton tried to hit Irena. She reflexively caught his arm. She hesitated for a second, then flexed her fingers a little.

The forearm consists of two parallel bones with some space between them. Paxton's no longer had any space between them, and the shrapnel of it shredded hundreds of muscle strands.

It produced a sharp, double-echoed snap.

Paxton screamed so loud, but Irena kept speaking, unsure of how the words kept flowing out of her with such force and vigor.

"They are born of human sins so festering and wrong. Things allowed to rot for such a time that it attracts an insectile unholiness born of a dead god's corpse. And if the actions of a man, be it my brother or not, bring such horrible fates down, then I am not one to defy what is justice."

Irena released his broken arm, and Paxton dropped to the ground, still howling with pain. Any second now, someone would surely come to investigate the sounds. This was a small town—or would be. Someone would hear all of this.

"Who am I to claim executioner?" she continued. "But if not me, who will end all of this before it does what it has done to a thousand, million, billion other Layers? I declare you guilty, Paxton. I declare it now."

One hand opened another portal.

The other made a fist and hit her brother's neck. It was painlessly fast—he deserved that much. Blood and teeth exploded out of his mouth. His eyes, two colors, just like hers, lost the spark of life. Paxton's body flew off into the rapidly opening portal at such a speed that it sent tufts of hair off from the sheer force.

The world on the other side of the portal was in a Layer that had been destroyed long ago by The Being That Knows Every Violence. It had been reduced to a fiery wasteland by a series of strange weapons that released a horrible, deadly gas that ignited on contact with the air. Paxton's corpse was already burning.

In a rapid shift of motion, Irena caught the flying teeth. She formed a slipstream of wind to funnel the errant hairs. She sent it all through the portal. Then she let it close.

Irena took a second to breathe. Tears were streaming down her face. That had been much harder than she imagined.

She noticed it a moment later. He dropped it at some point: his book. One of the three documents he maintained. She picked it up. Irena gave a bitter chuckle.

"I guess it's good this didn't go with him," she said. "History will want records. It always does."

Off in the distance, she could hear the pounding pulse of people running to investigate the sound. She smoothed out her blouse, making sure that no blood had gotten on her. For one more week, a month perhaps, six at the most, she was a politician, and she would lie. She would get them to believe something else. She would tell them she'd gotten hurt or seen a rat. It was too easy to lie to people who underestimated her.

And when someone asked what had happened to Paxton, she would bring forth another lie. Her brother, she would tell people, had traveled out of Quill Point after its founding, and had left it to her to handle matters. And she would eventually pass the role over to someone else that the citizens voted to elect. And then, with the first mayor in place, she would cut open her own throat and bleed herself dry below the courthouse, so the god egg may never hatch.

And with that sacrifice, time would pass. Civilization would expand. Quill Point would become a town. And this Layer, Irena Ink hoped with all her soul, would never draw the attention of another Fly.

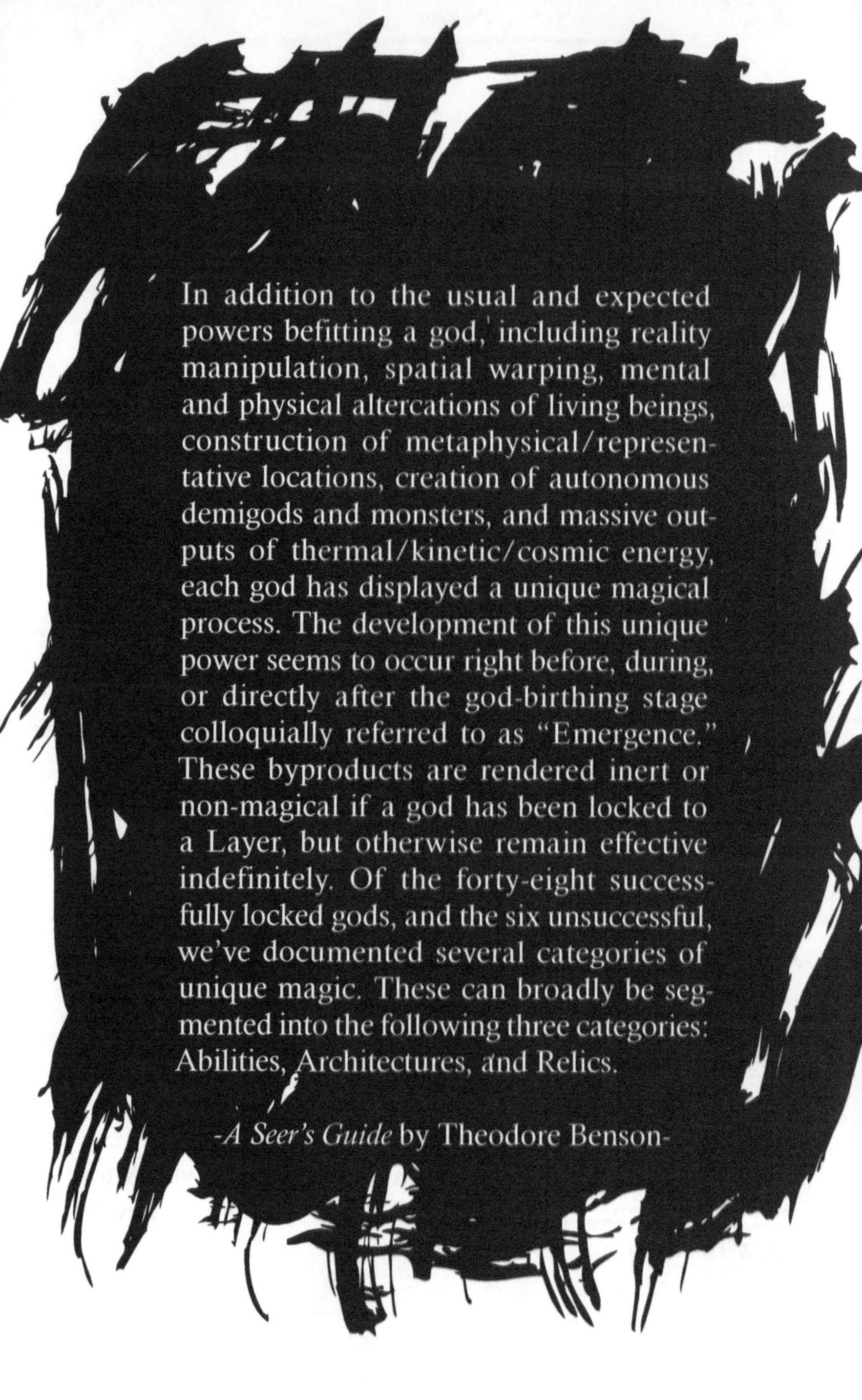

In addition to the usual and expected powers befitting a god, including reality manipulation, spatial warping, mental and physical altercations of living beings, construction of metaphysical/representative locations, creation of autonomous demigods and monsters, and massive outputs of thermal/kinetic/cosmic energy, each god has displayed a unique magical process. The development of this unique power seems to occur right before, during, or directly after the god-birthing stage colloquially referred to as "Emergence." These byproducts are rendered inert or non-magical if a god has been locked to a Layer, but otherwise remain effective indefinitely. Of the forty-eight successfully locked gods, and the six unsuccessful, we've documented several categories of unique magic. These can broadly be segmented into the following three categories: Abilities, Architectures, and Relics.

-A Seer's Guide by Theodore Benson-

Part 1

Quill Point Is Hiring

Chapter 1

CHUCK WAS BACK IN WHAT WAS LEFT OF Quill Point, Illinois. After a very long time trapped in a hellish house sitting in the middle of a forest of dead bodies, he was back in the town where he grew up, started his comic book business, and witnessed the sky change when everything started.

He wasn't much in a condition to celebrate being back. For several reasons. The night sky was still wrong—no stars. It was still colder than it should've been. But, more immediately perceived, his body was sore, his head cloudy, from likely a concussion, and the rush of what had happened before flitted in his mind.

Around him were his friends, allies, and one friend's corpse.

He glanced at Aoife's dead body, and then back away again. Her head was missing a chunk, her skull broken open. He hadn't seen which monster had done that—he'd been briefly unconscious after being flung across a room, and then almost choked to death—but all three of the things in that house were capable of it.

At some point, they would need to figure out a funeral for her. He would need to have a funeral for a *lot* of people. His heart ached that he'd never gotten chances for so many. Including his previous best friend, Patrick.

Chuck checked on Cassie next.

She was covered in blood—so much of it. It coated her wispy blond hair, sticking it to her scalp. But considering she wasn't screaming, and was breathing normally, and seemed conscious, if exhausted, it didn't seem to be much of *her* blood. She'd carried Aoife over the wall, made sure that, even in death, she wouldn't be trapped in that place. Chuck briefly thought about all of that too much.

He glanced at Grace and Declan next. They were close together, just as when Chuck had met them. In his head, Chuck couldn't imagine them apart. Platonic soul mates. Maybe that was also how they saw themselves.

Declan was crying—with relief, with shock, difficult to tell—and Grace was holding him.

So, they seemed okay enough.

Peter, though. Peter was a concern. He'd been sick before. He'd drunk the water down in that fetid place. Now he was unconscious, unmoving. And bleeding—for sure, some of his own blood. His nose was snapped to the side, and a worrying breathing noise accompanied a trickle of red. Chuck supposed it was good he was breathing at all.

But they needed to do something. Every moment, Peter could get worse.

Chuck took a long breath. He wanted to have another moment of calm, even if it was false calm. But he had to be the leader again. One of his own was injured.

And thinking on it for a moment, there was very little chance that they'd totally escaped all the monsters this town had to offer. Even if Peter was okay—they needed to move.

"Everyone…" he started, "everyone…"

Cassandra's eyes snapped to him. Chuck couldn't help but feel a surge of gratitude. Cassandra had his back, always. They hadn't even known each other before Murder Sky—just two people living in the same town—but he couldn't imagine facing things without her.

Peter didn't stir. Declan and Grace didn't look over. They were busy examining the *many* scratches on Declan's arm.

"Hey!" Cassandra snapped.

Grace stiffened and turned. Her eyes were a little dazed. "What?"

Cassandra gestured her head toward Chuck.

Grace looked over. Declan did too, after a moment.

"I know we just made it out," Chuck continued. "But we need to get Peter to somewhere."

Declan glanced at Peter, and the shock in his eyes seemed to fade a little. "Oh … fuck. Yeah, that sounds like a good idea."

"Where should we go?" Grace asked.

Chuck was about to answer. Then he paused. Grace hadn't told him everything about what had changed—but she'd told him that the hospital had burned down in his absence.

"Uh, well, actually … Grace?" Chuck asked.

"Yes?"

"Do you think the tent area would have medical supplies?"

"I mean … probably," Grace responded. "I mostly stayed in the Ink Well Diner. I wasn't around the firepit much. I'd assume they'd have some."

"I think I heard there was a stockpile of bandages," Declan chimed in.

"Okay," Chuck said. "That's something. But … dammit. So, I know the … I don't remember that fucking title of theirs … whoever The Mayor of Quill Point has as his soldiers….?"

"'Mayor's Men,'" Declan whispered.

"Yeah, 'Mayor's Men,'" Grace confirmed.

"Right. Them. Are they going to be a problem?"

"Only if they see us," Declan said. "Then yes. They will absolutely be a fucking problem."

Chuck winced. "How likely is that?"

"Pretty likely," Declan said. "They do rounds sometimes. And it'll be hard to stop gossip from spreading."

"Okay," Chuck said. "Alternative plans, then."

"Could we go to that diner you work at?" Cassandra chimed in.

Chuck nodded along with the idea. "Right. That might work. I know you were … attacked there, Grace. But is the Ink Well Diner workable now? Can we go there for a while?"

Declan grabbed Grace's hand, seemingly instinctually. She didn't look down as she squeezed back.

Grace shook her head. "No, I don't think so."

"You think they'll still go there?" Cassandra asked.

"No, it's … they were going to take all of the food," Grace said. "It's been at least a day. They'll probably have taken everything, even what little medical stuff I had."

Chuck thought for a moment. There was a lot of danger in every choice, it seemed. But there were actually multiple ticking clocks to deal with, not only for Peter but for all of them. Chuck could feel how dry his lips were. The human body could only survive without water for a very short time.

"Okay," Chuck said. "So, which is better then? Campsite or Ink Well, or should we try something else? We need to decide now."

Grace shook her head. "Okay, let's just go to the diner. I bet they didn't take my mattress—we can at least give Peter somewhere to lie down."

"Okay, good. Also—does anyone have medical experience? Like, anything?"

Chuck looked at three crestfallen faces.

"I ... know how to handle some allergic reactions," Grace said. "But no. Not really."

Chuck nodded. He had expected as much. He really wished his phone worked. Any information about what to do would be helpful. He supposed they could go to the library for medical information—but that was on the other side of town, and he had no idea what state it would be in after all his time gone.

"Okay ... we'll do what we can," Chuck said. "We made it this far, right?"

"Right," Cassandra agreed.

But he could hear it in her voice too. Chuck hadn't expected to win that fight down in that house. It felt like a fluke. Death had been the expected eventuality—and had occurred. And now, the threat felt different, more overpowering. You couldn't fix an injury like Peter's by attacking it.

"Right," Chuck echoed. "So, let's just go a little further."

Wordlessly, Cassandra went and scooped up Aoife again. A surge of emotional pain went through Chuck.

Aoife and he had argued—but she was part of the group stuck on that wooden shore. They'd had days' worth of talking. He knew her like he knew a family member.

Chuck wiped away a tear that had formed and promised himself that he would let himself cry more later. That he would grieve Aoife. But for now, he needed to save her caretaker, her dad. She would've wanted it that way.

Chuck leaned down to grab him.

"Here, let me help," Grace interrupted, moving to take his legs.

"Thanks."

Chuck looped his arms underneath Peter's armpits. Grace grabbed his legs. Together, they lifted him up. Chuck tried to make sure his head stayed up high as much as possible. It was an injury much more severe than a nosebleed, but he assumed some of the same theories applied.

Chuck and Grace both turned sideways, so they could better see where they were going. The diner wasn't that far of a walk, and, even after so long, Chuck knew where it was.

Everybody in Quill Point knew about the Ink Well Diner.

CHAPTER 2

THE INK WELL DINER WAS NOT AS CHUCK remembered. They didn't even make it inside. Way before they would've gotten to that door with its crappy electronic bell, they had to stop.

The Mayor's Men had claimed it.

And before their party, or maybe during it, they'd done some serious damage.

All the windows that Chuck could see were smashed. The alternating party lights from inside reflected off the jagged edges. Several booths lay on the ground outside, ripped away from their home.

And on the wall of the building, declared in massive lines of what seemed like acrylic paint, were the words:

The Mayor Owns This Building.

"Those fuckers," Grace said very quietly. "That's *my* diner."

"Quiet," Chuck instructed. "We don't know if they can hear us."

It seemed unlikely though. The music blaring from inside the building was loud enough to drown out the conversations happening inside, let alone from around a hundred feet away. But the Mayor's Men were still clearly trying to talk to each other. Shouts and yells punctuated the drowning beat, mixing into a cacophony.

"Guess we'll have to try the bonfire," Cassandra whispered.

Chuck frowned. Seeing this, he didn't like the odds. The Mayor really had taken over since he'd last been in town. Their best bet might be to find a place to hide, and then send a few people to scout and scavenge.

That's how you lost Ike and Evelyn.

Chuck let out a calming breath. He couldn't afford to think like that. There was learning from mistakes—and there was being frozen by them. If that plan didn't have a good track record, he'd think of something later. But it was difficult to quell grief once it started. People had died. His heart rate was rising. Panic was settling in, clouding, electric.

Cassandra shot him a look of concern. No, perhaps something a little more forceful than concern.

We need you right now, the look said.

Despite everything, that worked. Chuck focused on that. Other people had always been the thing to keep him steady. He started the comic book shop for himself, for his dreams and passions. But he kept it *alive*, kept it running, fought through the difficulties of being an entrepreneur, because it was—for some of his customers—one of the only safe places they had. He couldn't deny them that.

He gave her a half shake of his head.

Okay. I'm okay, was what that said.

She nodded and waited for whatever he had planned.

But before he could say anything, before he could propose a plan, the front door to the diner banged open. A flash of red and green lights hit the ground outside the door. Two Mayor's Men walked out—and for a moment, Chuck could see a crowd of about twenty dancing across the open Ink Well Diner floor.

"Shit, fall back," Chuck warned.

He didn't have to say it twice. Declan and Cassandra both scrambled. As soon as Chuck started moving, Grace followed along, carrying Peter.

They moved to a collection of stalled cars. A large truck and two minivans had all frozen right by each other. They went behind those, and moved down the slight slope of the road, into the grass.

"Put him down for a minute," Chuck instructed. "We need to figure out a new plan."

Grace lowered Peter's legs down gently, and Chuck did his best to do the same with his head. Chuck wished the grass was in better shape. It was pointy and full of weeds, but it was still better than placing him down onto the road.

Once they had him settled, Chuck moved to the side a little and looked out.

The Mayor's Men hadn't followed—or noticed, thank god. The two of them were standing against the side of the building. One of them was smoking. With the door closed and the party lights gone, the glow of his cigarette looked extremely bright.

Chuck didn't know either of their names. He knew their faces—at some point, living in Quill Point, you saw everyone's faces. But they weren't past customers of his store or immediate neighbors.

They were dressed mostly identically, the one smoking with a red shirt on, the other a gray button-up. They both wore blue jeans. The one smoking looked older and had sunburned white skin and brown hair. The younger one was sipping from a can of soda and had pale white skin. The younger one kept looking at the older one, but only when he wasn't likely to notice.

Grace moved alongside Chuck and lifted her head to look.

"Oh, them," she said after a moment.

"You know them?" Chuck asked.

Grace rolled her eyes. "I had to deal with a lot of Mayor's Men when I was running the diner. The guy smoking is named Wyld. I don't know the other one's name. He was new. He mostly followed around the others."

Chuck shook his head. "Goddamn, The Mayor took over a whole town this quickly, huh?"

"I'm starting to think he's working with the supernatural," Grace said.

Chuck nodded. "So am I. The forest is full of monsters. There's no reason that they can't just swarm in and kill us. This is part of some bigger plan. I'm actually starting to think the only reason we had search parties that first night was so that Murder Sky could happen."

Grace breathed hard but didn't say anything. Chuck glanced over. She had her hands in tight fists.

"We'll find a way to fix this," Chuck said. "We did it before."

"I just can't believe all of this sometimes," Grace said. "I don't like to stop and think about it, but this is all … just impossible."

Chuck nodded. He looked over at the rest of his team. They all looked beyond exhausted. They'd literally just finished a battle with demonic monsters.

"I know," Chuck said. "It really is."

"...so what now?" Grace asked.

"Not sure yet. But at least there's one thing going right for us."

"What?" Grace asked incredulously. "What could possibly be good about this situation?"

Chuck didn't answer that question. Instead, he asked, "About how many Mayor's Men are there in the town?"

"I ... what?"

"How many guys does The Mayor have working for him?"

Grace took a second. She muttered a few names under her breath before answering. "I don't know for sure, but I think it's around twenty or twenty-five. Maybe as many as thirty."

"Then it's even better. I think all of them are at that party—or almost all of them," Chuck said. "So, at least they aren't anywhere else."

"That's ... fair."

Chuck nodded to himself. This was the only way forward now—use every moment of luck they could to their advantage. Maybe, if they were especially lucky, they could avoid all the Mayor's Men for days.

CHAPTER 3

THEY WERE NOT LUCKY.

They hadn't made it far at all before voices carried on the breeze. As the music faded into the background, and they made their way toward the bonfire, Chuck had only just stopped looking behind him every few moments. But then the new sounds flowed in from the front. Boisterous, argumentative voices.

And before Chuck could call out a quiet warning to his group—those new voices stopped.

And then several of them started talking again.

"Oh, wow, they really didn't get far at all. Looks like we don't need the others' help. Maybe we can go to the party, after all."

"Liam, shut the fuck up. We have a job to do."

Chuck looked over at Grace, panicking. There was no way they could drop just drop Peter now. There was no way any of them could outrun another set of pursuers.

Six Mayor's Men walked closer, fanning out.

"The Mayor sent us to find you," another one of them said.

This one, Chuck knew personally.

Hunter. He had brown hair, a pinkish complexion, and was wearing a fairly generic tee shirt and tan pants. He looked normal, as he remembered him. There was a look in his brown eyes now though. Cold. Not anything like the secretly nerdy kid who played in tournaments on the weekends.

And then the others walked closer—and Chuck recognized all of them.

Wyatt. He was a big white guy with big, muscular arms.

Liam. A shorter, pale white kid, wearing a too-big army jacket and fingerless gloves.

Tristan. His hair cut short; his skin white. He was wearing a tee shirt for a horror franchise Chuck vaguely knew about.

And, finally, Jax and his brother, Jack. They were only two years apart—Jax, the older one.

Jax had pale white skin, blond hair, and brown eyes. He smelled strongly of some cologne.

Jack had brown hair, was a little taller, and had several tattoos on his arm.

"The Mayor sent us to find you," Hunter repeated. "Well, some of you. He's asked for Declan and Grace to meet him. We're here to assure that they do."

The Mayor's Men all surrounded them in a circle. They closed in.

"Whoa, is that a dead body?" Liam asked, pointing at Aoife. "Did you guys kill her?"

"No, you fucks!" Cassandra yelled back. "Your people did."

"Shut up, Liam," Hunter said. "It has nothing to do with us."

"Well, not anymore, clearly."

"This doesn't have to take long," Hunter said, ignoring him.

He stepped closer, eyes locked on Grace. And then Declan stepped in front of Hunter. Declan put his arms out. Despite everything, everyone seemed to freeze for a moment.

"You…" Declan started to say, before having to take a steadying breath. "You stay the fuck away from us."

Hunter regarded him for just a second. Then, so quick it made Chuck jolt, Hunter took out a fold-out baton, and—with a metallic clack—readied it.

"My orders were clear," Hunter said calmly. "Not only are you requested, but you've committed several crimes, Grace and Declan. I'll inform you of them later. But I *will* use this—if I have to."

"Whoa, that was quick," Liam commented. "We just got those things. You're excited to bash some heads in, aren't you, Hunter?"

Wyatt took out his baton. "Him and me, both. The Mayor gave us them to use for a reason."

Hunter glanced back at both of them, his face unchanging. "We have a job to do—please be professional about this."

"There are no companies or businesses anymore," Tristan commented.

Hunter didn't even deem that worth a response. He turned back to the group, to Declan, to Grace. "Ready to go?"

"They're not going anywhere with you," Chuck said as calmy as he could. But holding up Peter was making his arms ache, and his heart was pounding away in his chest.

Declan took a step back. "Uh … yeah … we're not. Fuck you. I fought off … I fought off…"

Declan trailed off but still stood firm.

This can only go badly, Chuck thought. He gestured to Grace. And the two of them, once again, started to lower Peter to the ground. They'd just finished when there was a whacking sound. Almost like wind hitting the side of a wall. The noise wasn't that loud, all told, but it seemed to echo through the night.

Grace yelled. Cassandra did too.

Chuck turned to see Declan hit the ground and bounce once. A thin line of blood was dripping from the wound on the side of his head. He didn't get up.

Grace yelled again and ran forward. If nothing had stopped her, she would've smacked Hunter in the face. In any other situation, she probably would've broken his jaw.

But she didn't get that far. Tristan and Liam, standing on either side of Hunter, stepped in. Tristan caught her arm and spun her slightly. Grace's feet went out from under her, and if Liam hadn't caught her—she would've hit the ground.

Chuck took one step forward to help and found the remaining three Mayor's Men standing in front of him. The brothers, Jax and Jack—without Chuck noticing— had readied their batons. Wyatt hadn't bothered with his.

"Hi there," Jax said. "Nice to see you again."

"Yeah—it's been a while," Jack added.

Chuck froze. He looked between the three of them, then looked past them to Declan.

Hunter stood over Declan's unconscious body. He flicked the baton, hard, toward the ground, clearing off the blood. Then he collapsed it back down.

"I had simple instructions," Hunter said. "I'm doing my job. Remember that you all made this happen. It didn't have to be so complicated. But we're done here now. We'll be taking these two to where they need to be. And … Jack? Jax?"

"Yes, boss?" Jax said with a grin.

"Whatcha need?" Jack added.

"I don't want these others following us, getting in the way. Stay with them for a little while. Do not hurt them … unless it's necessary."

"Sure," Jax said.

"I mean it," Hunter said, his voice actually sounding angry. "I will tell The Mayor if you do anything that I feel wasn't necessary to getting this done."

Jack nodded. "Got it."

Jax took a second, but then also nodded. "Got it as well."

"Good," Hunter said. "Stay with them until there's no chance they'll follow us. Then feel free to go to the party."

"Oh, come on!" Liam said. "Why do they get to—"

Hunter shot him a look. And it was enough that time. Liam went quiet.

Chuck glanced around—and each of his friends. He couldn't think of anything he could do. They were out-numbered and certainly out-armed. Unlike the monsters in the house, there wasn't some trick to this.

They only *just* saved themselves.

Hunter took a long breath. He collapsed the baton and put it back on his hip. "Wyatt, pick Declan up. Let's go."

Wyatt walked forward and swung the unconscious Declan over his shoulders. It didn't seem to be difficult for him.

"Got it."

And Liam, Wyatt, Hunter, and Tristan all walked off. Taking two of Chuck's people with them—to who knew what, and who knew where. The group of Mayor's Men took a turn almost immediately and quickly disappeared from view. Chuck could hear Grace yelling for a lot longer.

Chapter 4

THE BROTHERS JACK AND JAX MADE Chuck and Cassandra sit on the ground and paced around them, batons at the ready. Chuck kept glancing at Peter. It was way too long without someone helping him, but any attempt to even check on him made Jack or Jax glare with open malice. The blood had stopped flowing from Peter's nose—but Chuck didn't know if that was a good or bad thing.

But even if it was a good thing, it didn't matter.

It had all gone to shit, yet again.

That had been the order of the day for Chuck ever since Patrick got snatched into the sky, his blood flying behind him. Ever since he and Cassandra had run into the forest as that cabin exploded.

Fuck, ever since the sky *changed*.

The machinations of whatever was happening in Quill Point had spread to everything—and followed them to each new place or plan.

But thinking about that too long wasn't going to help.

At least Grace and Declan were likely okay. Chuck initially assumed that was wishful thinking on his part, but it made more and more sense that they would be currently unharmed.

Unless they were being led off to be fed to monsters.

But why not do the same to him and Cassandra?

So, no.

Whatever The Mayor wanted couldn't be *good*, but it couldn't be death. Chuck held onto the hope that they still had time to find Grace and Declan, to save them, before *whatever* new bad thing happened.

"How much longer do you think we need to wait?" Jack asked aloud, breaking the long silence.

"Not much longer," Jax replied. "A few minutes should be enough. And then we can leave these two with their corpses."

"Fuck you," Cassandra said.

"Why are you doing this?" Chuck added, glancing at their batons. "Don't you get that this is ... horrible? Cruel?"

The brothers looked at one another—and for a second, just a faint second, Chuck saw a flicker of green energy on them. A little radioactive glow.

And the thought, fully formed, popped into Chuck's head.

Something magical is altering their personalities.

"It's the end of the world," Jax said. "And we're in charge."

Jack nodded along. "That works for us."

Cassandra looked between the two of them. Chuck could tell she had plenty of swears, insults, and more she *could* level at them. But she didn't. She just crossed her arms and glared at them.

Chuck didn't say anything either. There wasn't a point to it. He couldn't think of any way they could escape—even if they managed to evade the brothers, they couldn't without leaving Peter behind.

So, instead, Chuck was now working on a new theory.

He'd been thinking of the monsters and Mayor's Men as completely separate problems, but maybe there was some overlap now.

Certainly, Jax and Jack weren't acting like he knew them.

He'd met them a few years ago. Jax and Jack had once been patrons of his shop. He'd even liked them at first. They liked comic books and dabbled in a few games—but he'd been forced to kick them out pretty quickly. As soon as they started spending money, they seemed to think consequences weren't as real for them. They'd been frequently rude, made "jokes" about his customers, sometimes to their faces, and generally made the experience of the shop worse.

The brothers had been pissed when he'd told them to find another shop, but they had, ultimately, left and hadn't returned.

But now, they were unperturbed by violence, almost blasé about Aoife's corpse. The brothers had watched Hunter hit Declan so hard that he'd dropped unconscious.

Unless they'd hidden away all of that malice from Chuck, playing as nice, perhaps because society forced them to be, this was a massive step up in cruelty, in lack of empathy. Unless they were incredible actors, that weird green energy was altering them somehow.

It was an odd thing, that magic, though.

So far, all the magic that Chuck had witnessed operated within a metaphor. The climate change house had been very clearly based on various aspects of climate change. But the monsters had been based on the worst versions of greedy businesspeople—which was a slightly broader topic.

It was possible whatever was happening to the Mayor's Men was an even more diluted form of that.

"So, are you just going to be in charge then?" Chuck asked.

Jack stopped and tilted his head. "The Mayor is in charge. But yes—we'll be ruling for him. He can't oversee everything."

"I like to think of it like knights," Jax added. "The Mayor is the new king, and we're his lords, overseeing the land he owns. When the world ends, it'll be a new age, where the powerful rule."

"And will you get riches too?" Chuck asked aloud.

Jack smiled. "Well, that's the bonus, isn't it?"

Jax laughed. He went over and leaned against his brother. "It's going to be a blast."

Chuck looked between the two of them—and the green light flashed again. He couldn't tell if it was the same brightness as before—or even worse.

What happens when…

Chuck didn't finish the thought. He had a feeling he wasn't going to enjoy learning the answer to that question—even if, ultimately, he had a feeling he absolutely *would* learn the answer.

"But before then," Jack said. "We've got a party to get to."

Jax smiled. "You could follow us, but I don't think you'd enjoy it very much."

Jack collapsed his baton—then Jax did. Without looking back, the brothers strode off into the night, toward where Chuck had just been.

Chuck sat on the ground for another moment, expecting a trick. But the brothers kept walking.

Soon enough, he couldn't see them.

Chuck immediately moved over to check on Peter.

CHAPTER 5

HE LOOKED MOSTLY THE SAME: VERY sick. Pale, thin. Peter had ingested some of that maybe-poisonous, *definitely* caustic water down in the basement of the house, and he'd never recovered. Down in that hell, it had ripped him apart.

Now, somehow, it had gotten worse.

A large collection of blood had dried on his face. It had gotten on his shirt, on his chin, mouth, and everywhere around his broken nose. Everywhere else not covered in blood had the look of dried sweat or dehydrated skin. It had been hours since Peter had any water.

Chuck reached out to gently nudge his arm. He didn't want to wake him up too forcefully—but if they didn't need to carry him anymore, that would be ideal. Chuck nudged him once. Then twice.

Then Chuck noticed.

Even staring at the nose, it hadn't jumped out at him. He had just assumed. But Peter's mouth and nose weren't moving. They didn't slightly shift, flare, or twitch.

Chuck put his hand on his chest.

Nothing.

On his stomach, then. He would feel the air lift it. Chuck waited for even the smallest motion of his body. Any sign. Waiting for—

"Oh."

Time stretched out. He vaguely could tell Cassandra was behind him, but to turn and look would take an infinity of moments. The signals that traveled down Chuck's limbs seemed to be syrupy, slow.

Still, infinitely slowly, he put both his hands over Peter's chest, and, still, over what felt like decades, Chuck leaned forward for better leverage. He couldn't quite recall what he was even trying to do. What the point of it was.

You start back up the heart.

He did the compressions, unsure of the pattern needed. Did them for minutes. Cassandra didn't interrupt. The world didn't throw new horrors at them. Where they were, Quill Point sat, cold and empty, full of dead cars and abandoned patterns of life.

It felt different this time.

Chuck had lost so many people at this point. And they'd all died in horrible ways. But either he'd only learned later, after the fact, that it had happened, or it had been a distinct *moment.* Patrick had been alive, standing by the window, and then yanked into the sky.

Peter had died right next to him, quietly.

Chuck had looked over at his friend, laying there, and worried about him—and how many of those looks had been at a person beyond his help? Was there a window, lost in the sea of avoiding Mayor's Men, where he could've done something?

Cassandra remained quiet. She sat next to Chuck and stayed next to Chuck. He didn't need to look to know she was there—that she wasn't going to move from that spot.

And he was so glad he wasn't alone.

It felt to him like the world was blurring at the edges a little. That what was happening was happening somewhere else, to someone else. Through a screen. It felt like his vision was focusing, then un-focusing, every few moments.

We just made it out.

Chuck let his head drop. He put his hands on both sides of his head and tried to breathe evenly.

"Take one minute," Cassandra said quietly.

"W-what?" Chuck asked. His voice, too, like someone else's.

"Five, if you need it."

"What are you talking about, Cassie?"

She looked at him. And Chuck could see the anger, sadness, grief, so much more plastered across her face. It was so obvious to him. So clear. From the moment that house exploded, and they ran into the woods, they'd been teammates—and, as far as he knew, they'd never hidden emotions from one another.

And this was the face she made when she was holding back everything—because it needed holding back.

"We need to have a plan," Cassandra said, her voice cracking, "but we can't… we need to be… we need to be sure it's a good plan. We have people we need to save. So, take five minutes. I wish I could give you more."

An ache ran through Chuck's chest. It was there in every moment, even if he didn't always acknowledge it. There, in every second, he had to consider the scale of what had happened already. Cassandra's words invited it in.

"What about … what about you?" Chuck managed to say.

"Just make sure I get my five minutes at some point."

Chuck let out the faintest, weakest laugh, and then let his head drop again.

Aoife died. Peter died. Grace had been dragged away. Declan had been hurt so badly and then also taken away—just after they'd saved him from the abattoir monster.

Chuck let tears fall—and gasps escape. He let the emotion of loss overtake any concentrated thoughts. It was a sickening thing, grief. Like a nausea that also curled around the soul. It was a mountain of stone, grief. Destroyed most often by slow erosion.

Five minutes wasn't enough. But it would have to do.

CHAPTER 6

FIRST, CHUCK AND CASSANDRA DECIDED how the funeral would go. It wasn't much of a conversation. They didn't have time for it to begin with. But they would manage one.

Then, they did their best to prepare it as they discussed their other plans. They did not have shovels. What they did have was a large amount of loose foliage.

Back before Murder Sky, when the storm started, it had knocked over so many trees. No one had bothered to clean up afterward.

Chuck gathered a few branches underneath his arms. His head still hurt with that special sort of headache crying often causes—but Cassandra had been right to have him take those minutes. It made him feel the smallest bit less overwhelmed. In the smallest of optimistic news, the pain of his possible concussion was fading.

"So, our main two options—" Chuck started to say, and then coughed from how dry his throat was.

"You okay?" Cassandra asked immediately, picking up a large collection of leaves.

"I'm not choking," Chuck managed to reply.

"Okay," Cassandra said. "That's good."

"Yeah … yeah."

So, I assume one of the plans is to try to locate where they took Grace and Declan?"

Chuck nodded, then cleared his throat. "Yes."

"And does the other one involve getting water?" Cassandra continued.

"It didn't."

"It should," Cassandra said.

Chuck sighed. He dropped off the collection of twigs he'd found next to Aoife, gave her a quick glance, and then went back to grab more.

"Yes, it should," he eventually said. "Maybe we should make that our first priority."

"Do you think the faucets in any of the buildings are still working?"

"I don't know," Chuck admitted. "Resources are a problem. I don't know how much that includes water. Quill Point has a reservoir—but it's been weeks since we left. It could be gone by now."

"Blotter Lake?"

"Too far away to matter," Chuck said quickly. "And The Mayor's dumped enough shit in it."

"Some other natural water source?"

"I'm not going anywhere near the forest wall again," Chuck said. "And that's the only other place where there had been a river."

"Yeah … I agree," Cassandra said. "Let's not do that."

Chuck glanced at the forest wall, so far away, and a shiver went up his spine. The climate change house had probably reformed. They knew the abattoir monster was still around. He hoped that The Lobbyist, The Monopolist, and The Oil Baron were at least well and truly dead. That the house would at least stand empty.

"What was your other plan?" Cassandra asked.

"Well, it's similar to the original. Go to the bonfire—like I think we should've at the beginning—but there's even more than that."

"What?" Cassandra asked immediately.

"…I don't know if it would work."

"Tell me anyway," Cassandra said gently.

Chuck turned to glance at her. She looked back, held his gaze for a moment, then placed more of the leaves in a pile. They almost had foliage enough for what they wanted to do.

"I … we are *so* outnumbered," Chuck said. "Even if we did catch up to Grace and Declan—it would go the same as before."

"Probably worse," Cassandra said.

"Yeah, quite possibly. We can't win that kind of fight. We can't win any of these fights. The Mayor … he's got effectively an army. But it's not *that* many people, compared to how many people are in this town."

"You think we can depose him?" Cassandra asked.

"He is acting like a tyrant," Chuck replied. "I think the only way this town is going to survive what's happening to it is to band together."

"I agree," Cassandra said. "I … yeah, I agree."

"I'm sure we're not the only ones thinking about it."

"Probably not," Cassandra replied.

"But they don't know … what's out there. How bad it is. And then there's something I think is *about* to happen. Some kind of … another big magical event."

"Great," Cassandra said, her voice dripping with sarcasm. "What is it?"

"The Mayor's Men have some kind of magic glow on them."

"Oh?"

"It's hard to see. It's not individually that important, I don't think. It's maybe some kind of mind-altering magic. But I bet they *all* have it. And I think The Mayor's planning something—well, I mean, we *know* he's planning something, but, between him ordering his army to capture people, the glow, the symbolism of the climate change house … it's going to be something big. Something horrible."

"Lots of people are going to die," Grace said with extreme finality.

"Yeah."

"Is it climate change again?"

"I think … I'm not sure what the theme of it will be. But I bet it's metaphysical, again. I think that's just how this magic works."

"Makes as much sense as anything else," Cassandra said.

"Yeah. So we *need* to go to the bonfire. It's where a lot of people in the town are, apparently. If we're going to depose the Mayor's Men and their leader, we need them. We need them to find Grace and Declan too. We just fucking need them."

"And," Cassandra added, "they also might have water."

"That too."

Cassandra took a long breath. She picked up another set of twigs and then wiped at her forehead. "I can't wait for that."

Chuck frowned. "Wait, can you?"

"What?"

"Wait—for water? Can you make it that long? Are you doing okay?"

Cassandra reached up to her lips. Even Chuck could see they were chapped, cracked. She winced when she touched a spot. A thin trickle of blood flowed down from her lips.

"Well, uh, depends," she said. "Do we … uh … know how far away it is?"

Chuck almost answered and then realized that he didn't quite have an idea of it. Only the general direction. Only that it wasn't the way the Ink Well Diner was.

"Shit," Chuck said very quietly, then a little louder: "I don't. Did Grace mention where it was?"

"No … but she did mention a bonfire."

Chuck immediately turned to check the horizon. It was well and truly nighttime, so the light should carry for a long while. Even still, it took a moment for him to spot a faint orange glow off in the distance.

"That way," Chuck said, and pointed.

Cassandra turned to look. "Fuck, that's far away."

"Yep."

"After this, then?"

"Yeah," Chuck said, turning back. "Yeah. I wish we didn't have to do this so fast. It's not right. They don't deserve it. They deserve metals."

They deserve proper graves.

Cassandra was quiet for a moment. When she spoke, her voice cracked a little

"I wish I didn't fight with her so much," Cassandra said.

Cassandra's eyes were getting misty now. Chuck knew she hated it when people saw her cry, so he looked away.

"It was a bad situation," Chuck said. "It was stress."

Cassandra let out a sigh. "I know. But still."

"Yeah."

They'd laid them next to each other. Father and daughter. Wordlessly, they placed the plant matter around the two bodies. A ring of sticks—the only coffin they'd get. Some plants for decoration; it should've at least been flowers.

The speech was next.

During some of their direst moments, when the raft had been lost, and it seemed like Aoife, Chuck, Peter, and Cassandra would all die in that hell basement of starvation, they talked about what they'd wanted from their lives—what they thought their lives would've been like before the world ended.

It had felt, then, like making sure their dreams could be mourned. That they wouldn't disappear the moment their owner died.

Cassandra and Chuck stood there.

And they knew those dreams.

"Aoife. She wanted to be a photographer," Chuck said.

"Peter. He was going to eventually launch a career making carved furniture," Cassandra said.

"Goodbye," Chuck said.

"Bye," Cassandra said.

CHAPTER 7

CHUCK KEPT HIS GAZE ON THE FAINT orange glow as they walked. Watching as it got brighter and brighter. It blurred occasionally from his tears—but it remained a marker. The top of a bonfire, beautiful in a way, flickering out its warmth on the perpetually cold Quill Point. If it wasn't for that slight glow, it would've felt like they were walking through an endless night, full of endless cars, and endless chances for Mayor's Men to attack.

Then, rolling forward, arrived something. Something that didn't bode well—and was worse than the Mayor's Men. It was the supernatural, once again.

The orange and red tendrils that had been the warning before Murder Sky were suddenly present, despite it being nighttime.

They *stretched down* to the ground.

Chuck stopped in his tracks, his mouth falling open.

Cassandra walked slightly forward but slowed after only a few steps. Her knees looked like they might buckle. Chuck certainly didn't feel like he could quite stand.

"Holy fucking shit," Cassandra said quietly.

Chuck still couldn't get himself to say anything. What he knew of Murder Sky…

He'd missed the worst of it. They'd already been sealed away in the strange world of the trees.

But Grace had tried to explain it. Something overtook the whole damn sky. She'd tried to get across the scale of the event with a few words—but it would've taken so much more to explain it.

Chuck understood now.

It was happening far away, further than the bonfire and the camp, but it was growing.

The tendrils weren't just descending, either. They were forming shapes. Twisting into massive formations. One he could see, off to the right, formed layers of rectangles—

—a building. That was a *building*. A several-story tall thing currently only made of lines. But it was clear that, once the blueprint was finished, it would turn into a—

It reminded him of something.

The house was made of magic. When it was falling apart, it wasn't a real house. This magic … it makes places for its own uses. What the fuck kind of buildings are these going to…?

He took an involuntary step back, even though the tendrils hadn't yet reached him. The tendrils just kept building things. And taking up more and more of the sky.

Before Chuck could consider running, there was a flash of lightning, then an orange tendril arced downward and zipped several feet above his head. It went as a jagged line, clearing a great distance.

Even from where Chuck stood, he could tell that contact with that tendril would be extremely lethal.

He followed it with his gaze—and couldn't help but think it was going…

A second line dropped straight down from the sky. It fell fast, right at the same spot that the other was flowing toward. It could be a coincidence, two in the same spot, but Chuck couldn't imagine that it was doing anything other than seeking his friends.

Is it also looking for bodies?

There wasn't time to examine that. He darted to Cassandra.

"We have to go," Chuck yelled.

"*Where?*" Cassandra yelled back.

"I don't—"

A sound closest to an airplane screaming by overhead drowned out Chuck's words. He turned to look.

A large golden orb flew across the sky, low and fast. Electricity crackled across it. It zipped toward somewhere else in the town. A moment later—

Explosion. A golden inferno rushing to the sky. Chuck's hands went to block his head, but all that happened was a wave of heat that then sharply stopped.

Chuck gasped. He didn't know what it meant—but there was no version of it that was a *good* thing.

Especially not with sudden voices yelling out from several directions.

"It's almost time!"

"It's almost here!"

Cassandra looked around in a panic. The same emotion in Chuck was currently making him freeze. How was all of this happening at *once*? Was this the end of the world? Was that golden flame about to let loose some god or demon?

"Holy shit… holy shit…" he found himself repeating over and over.

"Chuck!" Cassandra screamed.

Death was the only word in Chuck's head when he looked at what Cassandra was seeing.

Beings, monsters, zipped, blitzed, moved impossibly fast across the landscape—across the night. Between the dead and abandoned trucks, vans, cars. Around trees. New nightmares for a town full of them.

Chuck could almost see one of the monsters clearly, even at that distance. A mouth full of column teeth, sharp at the ends. Strange, blood-soaked patches across their arms.

And, amongst them, a familiar, strong scent of cologne.

Jax? Chuck thought. *No, not just him. The Mayor's Men!*

"Find them all!" another voice yelled. "Greed's new world is upon us!"

In response, at least twenty voices started chanting.

"Greed! Greed! Greed!"

Chuck wanted to freeze again. He was reeling still—but Cassandra was with him. There was no question in his mind that the Mayor's Men would kill them on sight. No question at all. If he didn't think of something *right then*, all the fighting, the loss, wouldn't even matter.

More and more figures moved like optical illusions. They swept by the buildings, appearing at different doors. Breaking those doors down. Some disappeared into the buildings, no doubt searching each. Any second, Chuck and Cassandra would be noticed—if they weren't already.

Chuck looked around desperately. "We need to hide."

"Where?"

"I don't know." Chuck felt tears—of terror and frustration—well up in his eyes. "I don't know."

Cassandra looked around again, and then her eyes went wide. "Oh, my god. The cars. The cars! Are they locked?"

A jolt shot through Chuck. The cars had just been obstacles before. Dead things left about. The blurs of Mayor's Men weren't focused around any he could see. He'd almost stopped paying attention to the cars as well. But—

A sound like rushing flames sprung up. Only it wasn't flames. Or snapping bones. It was a laugh masquerading. It could only be the Mayor's Men cackling.

Chuck desperately grabbed the door of a large truck, pulled—and almost fell over. It wasn't locked. The door swung open, revealing the backseat.

"In here," he whispered. "Hide in here."

Cassandra rushed over and dove into the backseat. She pulled herself all the way across and curled up into a ball at the far end. Chuck was bigger than her, but still closed the car door, and jammed himself into the narrow space.

He kept his head down as low as he could—so nothing should've been obviously visible. If one of the Mayor's Men decided to look inside, examine the car, they would see them. And they would likely be dead very quickly.

Chuck's pulse thrummed in his ears. He tried to hold his breath as much as he could. Cassandra was so quiet he was worried about her—but couldn't easily turn to look. Any motion would be a risk.

Through the tinted windows, Chuck could vaguely see things happening. The flashes of red and orange tendrils. Buildings were springing into existence.

The sounds were much worse.

Mayor's Men moved nearby. Some even stopped to talk with each other—unaware of how close they were to finding them. Chuck couldn't place the second of the voices. But he knew one of them was Jax.

He might be the one leaning on the car door, making the vehicle shake slightly.

"I can hear … him. We serve a god now." Jax's laugh crackled. "I've never been this powerful."

"Did you see him on his throne?"

"No," Jax said. "But of course someone like him has a throne."

"Yes! Of course. I can see it. He has a form, here, on this … this world. Made of blood and bone and loss. He's going to change everything while he's here."

"And then?"

"He'll grace the cosmos."

Jax laughed again. So did the other one.

Chuck shrank back even more. Jax still sounded like himself. His voice, his inflection, all of it was as it had been. Whatever was done to the Mayor's Men, it hadn't fully changed them.

Can they be … saved? Chuck thought desperately. *Can we undo it?*

He had a feeling the answer was no. And there was something else important about what Jax had said. It wasn't as surprising to Chuck as it could've been. After all they'd been through, a god being the cause of everything wasn't all that much of a stretch.

The laughter died down.

"Have you gotten to kill anyone yet?" Jax asked.

"I haven't found anyone yet. But it would be so easy, wouldn't it?"

Chuck almost reacted. He could feel Cassandra shift next to him. She didn't make a sound though.

"Yeah," Jax said. "Yeah, it would be."

"We have to make them do things though," the other voice said. "The buildings—we can only kill so many at a time."

"I'm starting to hear that too," Jax said, his voice a little softer. "I guess we already murdered so many of them. This all won't work unless we're patient."

"Then we should get to it! Kill while we can!"

"Okay," Jax replied excitedly. "Okay!"

There was a faint sound that Chuck could only guess was the rush of air from super-fast monsters running off. Even if those two were gone though, he wasn't going to chance there being more of them.

He adjusted himself as best he could. There were no comfortable options.

Outside, the light was different. The light increased, casting larger and larger shadows across the two of them.

Chuck tensed up even more. He didn't know what each building would do, but he couldn't help but imagine climate change house after climate change house constructing themselves.

He was almost sure that Quill Point functionally no longer existed. No longer isolated to the forest, or any pocket of the town—but the effect *everywhere*. A god— likely of greed—was overwriting the landscape.

He couldn't imagine the myriad things that could *already* be happening to the people out in it. How many Monopolists, Oil Barons, Lobbyists, were born just then? How many more people would have their skulls—

Chuck was interrupted by the car moving. Not forward. Not by wheels. A screech rang out as it moved slightly—and then the whole car jolted and shot off in one direction.

CHAPTER 8

CHUCK TRIED TO BRACE HIMSELF AGAINST the nearest surface. It was like driving over potholes, only the entire road was made of them. He managed to bump his elbow, his knee, and his head against something in a matter of moments. It was hard to gauge, but the car must've been moving at least seventy miles per hour, if not more.

Despite everything, Chuck and Cassandra managed to stay quiet—even when the car stopped. And it stopped hard. The car seemed to tilt slightly, everything moving to a point, and then finally, with a jarring, leveling drop, the car stopped.

Chuck ended up on his back, staring at the fuzzy ceiling. He waited for something else to happen. Anything could, it seemed. But his best guess was that the sunroof was going to cave in. He could distinctly imagine a claw ripping through it.

That didn't happen though.

Instead, it got gradually warmer in that car.

A dry heat. Chuck was sweating. A horrible glare pushed through the window—the sun beating down.

Wait … wasn't it nighttime? Chuck thought.

Cassandra broke the silence with an incredibly quiet whisper. "What the fuck…?"

Chuck looked over at her. She looked back. Cassandra tilted her head to ask, *do we go outside?* Chuck, after a moment, nodded. He held up his fingers.

One. Two. Three.

They both sat up. Chuck had to cover his eyes. Yep, that was sunlight. It was the kind of sun Illinois only managed in the worst parts of summer. When the heat would get so bad that it felt like the pavement should crack.

He lowered his hand and looked out the window. Cassandra did the same.

He didn't know *what* he expected, but a sea of parking spaces—many of them filled with cars—was not it. The lot stretched as far as he could see.

"Where do you think we are?" Cassandra whispered.

"I don't know," Chuck replied. "But … the car moved here. Do you think *all* the cars are here?"

"Maybe not all of them," Cassandra said.

"Fair," Chuck said. "But a lot of them."

They kept looking around in silence. Chuck considered his options again. There weren't many of them. They could stay in the car. Or they could leave the car. And with how dehydrated they already were, it wasn't a good idea to risk heat stroke in a rapidly warming vehicle.

"Okay. We should get out," Chuck said.

"Don't have to ask me twice," Cassandra said.

She pushed on the doorhandle. The door stuck for a moment, but with another shove, popped open. She poked her head out.

"No evil monsters," she said. "At least, not any yet. We should be good."

"That's comforting," Chuck commented.

Cassandra stepped out and immediately winced. "Goddamn. I can feel it through my shoes. This is a fucking skillet."

"You okay?" Chuck asked.

"We might get blisters," Cassandra said. "But yes, I'm okay."

Chuck nodded, then followed Cassandra out. As soon as he stepped down, he could feel it too. The parking lot was sweltering. But, fortunately, not quite *painful* yet.

He looked around the lot again. It really did seem to go on forever. Just cars and—

"Were those there before?" he asked.

Cassandra looked. And frowned. "Um… I don't know. I didn't see them before now."

Just at a distance, where it faded into the heat haze of the parking lot, was a metal framework. The kind for dropping off used shopping carts. And then, as soon as Chuck made that connection, possibly *because* he made that connection, he could see occasional shopping cars haphazardly placed around. Extremely messily so. Some of them were on their sides. Some boxed-in cars.

Very slowly, one rolled toward them. Its wheel creaked. It was slower than even walking speed, but it didn't slow down. It didn't wobble. Chuck could almost imagine someone standing on the other side of it, pushing it along.

Chuck and Cassandra both backed away from it. It continued forward.

Chuck and Cassandra took a step to the right.

The cart slowly arced itself—the wheel giving another, somehow *angry*-sounding squeak—so that it was facing them again. It was almost imperceptible, but it appeared to be picking up speed too.

"Okay, that's a new one," Cassandra said.

"Yeah…" Chuck replied. "That's weird."

"We're not going to let it bump into us, right?" Cassandra said.

"Oh, absolutely not."

"Got a plan?" Cassandra asked.

"Working on it," Chuck said. "I don't know the rules yet."

"I'm guessing it gets faster and faster."

Chuck, despite himself, let out a small laugh. "Yep. I think you're right. But, besides that."

The cart, as if it could hear them, sped up a little more. It rolled with what could only be described as *intent.*

"Should we run?"

"Not yet," he said.

"Why?"

"Because I don't want to turn my back on it."

A slight squeak sounded again. But it wasn't from that cart. Chuck glanced to the side—and another cart was drifting in their direction. Then another. He couldn't keep track of all of them as they emerged from the heat haze.

The metal at the front of each cart seemed to bend slightly, warp slightly. Chuck couldn't help but imagine them smiling at him with metallic fangs.

And, right where someone pushing a cart would stand, was the faint—but getting less so—outline of someone. Heat haze taking on a distinct outline. They moved like unfinished stop-motion animation and blinked in and out of existence.

But they, too, were smiling.

"Oh," Chuck said, his heart rate rising. "I should have expected that."

"Run now?"

Chuck sucked in a breath. "Yes. Now."

He spun on his heels—and then immediately stopped. Despite the present danger, it was hard not to be surprised by an entire building not being where it had been.

A box store, from the look of it. A *massive* box store. Sitting in the center of that sea of a parking lot, with more carts drifting from every direction but one, sat *The Spire Market*.

The words were in giant letters, easily the size of a smaller building.

Chuck wanted to question that. He didn't have time to question it.

They both started running. As the building got closer, Chuck really hoped, at the very least, that the store had some water in it.

Chapter 9

CHUCK STOOD ON THE SIDEWALK AROUND The Spire Market, gasping for air. Cassandra had her hands on her knees, bent over. The demon carts had all sped up—closing in much, much quicker than he'd imagined. None had gotten to them, but the echo of the metallic rattle sang in his mind.

The carts—and their monster drivers—currently stood a few feet from him. Not a single wheel or foot on the sidewalk. But there were *rows* of them. Five at the most, three at the least. They crowded into each other, all the way up to the line.

"We'll go in," Chuck said breathlessly. "We'll go in."

The monsters nodded. Rolling backward, the carts and their owners dispersed. Some of them literally popped out of existence in the heat haze.

I wonder if there's a limit to how much can be created at one time, he thought. *Or it takes up some resources, maybe.*

"Are we really going in?" Cassandra asked. "Are we really doing this again?"

Chuck had the worst feeling of déjà vu. Those monsters couldn't follow them to the building. Like the abattoir monster. It seemed to be one of the default constructions the greed god worked with. Monsters on the outside—worse things on the inside.

Knowing that didn't make things better.

"No choice." Like Declan had said. That was also part of the other buildings' construction. No choice.

Chuck took one more breath, then glanced her way. "Yeah, for now."

"Fuck," Cassandra said, her voice cracking a little. "Fuck."

Chuck spun to see the doors. He didn't feel very hopeful—but he tried to push hope into his voice. "We made a lot of mistakes last time. We know the rules better."

"You know the rules can change, right?" Cassandra said.

"I do," Chuck said.

"Goddammit," Cassandra replied.

The doors, now that he was close to The Spire Market, appeared standard. Automatic sliding doors. Mats sat on the ground in front of each one. They all had the same spire-based logo.

Chuck took a step forward, and not only did the doors in front of him open but so did *all* the automatic doors. The inside was apparently air-conditioned.

Chuck glanced at Cassandra.

"Ready, Cassie?"

Cassandra stepped so that they were standing side-by-side. "*No.* Obviously. But, yeah, let's go."

CHAPTER 10

CHUCK WALKED THROUGH THE DOORWAY. He almost expected it to be like a portal. Or for the world to change again. But he supposed things were already so warped that there wasn't any point in that.

They passed through a small antechamber between the next set of automatic doors. To the right of them were even more shopping carts stacked and ready for some customers to use. Those didn't move—but Chuck found himself constantly glancing at them.

The second set of doors didn't all open—just the one they walked up to, and immediately the smell of bread washed over them. Not fresh bread though. Stale chemicals were doing a decent enough job of smelling like bread that it couldn't be anything else. Chuck tried to find its source and could only see a currently closed sandwich shop. It looked otherwise normal.

The Spire Market mostly *was* normal. It was huge, yes, but not that dissimilar from a normal department store. Except for a few notable exceptions.

Three stood out to Chuck.

The first was that it was tiered. Not the floor plan, but the shelves. They got taller the further back they were. All of it leading to the tallest thing in the store: a spire.

Not a spire. The ... what had Grace called it? The ... Prayer Spire.

She'd only mentioned that briefly too.

It was called the Prayer Spire because of how the bodies were around it. Thirteen bodies, to be exact.

Patrick and Ms. Daffodil's bodies were two of the thirteen Chuck remembered.

There was no reason to visit it. The odds it was dangerous were quite high, especially because of its ability to pull people in for hours. Or because there was a void-like formation above it. He still wanted to see his friends. Chuck pushed back down the grief that only had more fuel every hour.

The *second* weird thing was that the ceiling had a sort of supernatural bunting. The tendrils hadn't all repurposed themselves into buildings. These just were around the ceiling. They all went to the Prayer Spire in the back, to that odd change in the air right above it. So far, they'd not done anything.

And finally, thirdly, the door. Off to the far, far left—taking up a good chunk of the wall—was a door. It was completely out of place with the rest of The Spire Market. It was a circle and made of possibly real gold.

"We should check that out," he said absentmindedly.

"Sure," Cassandra said. "You don't think it'll try to kill us?"

"I'm not entirely sure about anything in here," Chuck said. "But that's a door. And it could be a doorway out. One without shopping cart demons."

"*If* it opens," Cassandra said.

"If it opens," Chuck amended. "We'll deal with that in a minute though…"

Toward the right back wall, opposite to the golden door, was not only what looked like water bottles but also a whole host of refrigerated drinks.

"There we go," Chuck said, pointing. "That should work."

"You think they have snacks too?"

"I bet they have chips."

"Are we assuming the food in this place is safe then?" Cassandra asked.

Chuck didn't respond right away. It was an easy enough question—but it was also a pivotal one. Not just for their immediate survival but going forward. It had more meaning to it. A type of magic that could warp reality, make the sun be out at night, create entire buildings at will, was *certainly* capable of killing them outright. But it hadn't. The water and food in the climate change house hadn't been poisoned. Maybe not in The Spire Market either.

And, further, the monsters didn't always just go for the kill.

The carts gave chase. But they effectively warned them about their presence beforehand. And they couldn't, seemingly arbitrarily, go into the store.

Why is it set up this way? Chuck mused.

"I think we don't have a choice," he said aloud. "But yes, I think the food is fine. But, *why?*"

"What? Why what?"

"Why is it fine?" he repeated.

Cassandra let out a long breath. "I see what you mean. But … I don't know. Isn't climate change bad for agriculture? Why would something made around *that* have edible food?"

"Why is it symbolic, at all?" Chuck muttered.

Cassandra turned to look at him, her voice had a slight edge. "Okay, Chuck—we can do this after we eat, and have water. We can do the whole speculate and analyze thing—but I *need* food. I especially need water. If we have to run again, I don't know if I'll manage."

Chuck nodded. "Okay, good point."

CHAPTER 11

C HUCK LEANED AGAINST THE GLASS door, feeling the even colder air from inside. He kept looking around, but nothing had happened yet. No monsters. No spontaneously generating objects. The only thing that had changed was a radio going on. It was playing boring, corporate music from speakers he hadn't yet located.

Cassandra was sitting on the ground next to him. She'd opened a large bag of chips. She took a handful, snarfed it down, and then picked up the water bottle and chugged it.

Chuck took a sip of his second water bottle. He couldn't explain how much he'd needed the first one. He'd eaten a bag of pretzels—partially for food, partially to recover lost salt—and his mouth was dry again. At least this time it was for a normal reason.

Cassandra tossed another plastic bottle across the floor. It bounced a few times.

"You know if you do that too fast, you'll just puke," Chuck said.

"Don't care. This is the first decent-tasting food in so fucking long."

Chuck remembered. They'd managed to find enough food to keep all of them alive—but it had been a fairly eclectic selection in the climate change house.

It was weird to him though, that the store not only had food—but seemingly its own brand. All the bottles, the chips, had the Spire on them. He couldn't imagine a marketing team of monsters debating the merits of the design—that was absurd—but, really, *all* The Spire Market, not just the branding, implied a deep understanding of the things being built. A level of thought went into this. It was downright contemporary.

Is that why the Prayer Spire took thirteen people? Was it getting a sample size of perspectives?

"Okay, spit it out," Cassandra said.

Chuck looked down at her. "What?"

"I have my food now. I have my water now. What were you saying about the weirdness of … everything? Spill your theory. Explain what you meant."

Chuck laughed slightly. "It's kind of the big metaphysics part of it."

"Yeah, well, that's still useful."

Chuck shrugged. "Okay, tell me if I'm not making sense."

"You know I will."

Another, almost normal laugh bubbled out of Chuck. It was goddamn nice to laugh. He kept looking around, expecting some kind of monster—maybe based around clothing racks or something—to run at them. And then there was the matter of Peter, of Aoife, of having lost them. Of not knowing if Grace and Declan were still alive…

He was so glad he had Cassandra with him. Chuck didn't know what would've happened to him without her.

"So," he began, "the magic changed everything, but didn't just kill us outright. Why?"

"It couldn't?" Cassandra offered.

"Do you really think that?"

"No, not really. It obviously can kill us."

"Right. So, why didn't it?"

Cassandra shrugged. She bit into another chip. She looked up at Chuck and arched her eyebrow. It meant: *well, go on.*

Chuck nodded. "So, obviously I'm just guessing—but I think this is a sacrifice thing. They can kill us, and they do kill us, but it's better for them if it's done within the bounds of the symbolism they're going for."

"Climate change?"

"Yes, that, but also what the Mayor's Men were talking about. Greed in general, I think."

"Then why are we in a department store?" Cassandra asked. "I don't directly associate that with greed."

"I'm not sure yet—but I have a few ideas. Besides, I have a feeling we'll know pretty quickly how this place connects to that concept, or, like, a sub-concept."

Cassandra was quiet for a moment. She stared ahead; her lips pursed.

"What do you think…?"

She didn't say anything else.

Chuck gave her a few more moments but was too curious to wait beyond that. "Yeah?"

"Sacrificing people for what?"

Now it was Chuck's turn to pause. He hadn't thought that far about it yet. He supposed sacrifice might be the wrong word for it. It implied the deaths were going *toward* something. It implied it wasn't just killing because it was an activity it did.

But this seemed like a lot of work for just that.

"I don't know," Chuck said frankly. "Maybe it's unknowable."

"To you?" Cassandra said. "I doubt it. You'll figure it out."

Chuck blinked. "Thanks."

"You're welcome," she said.

"No, but thank you."

Cassandra shrugged her shoulders. "I said you're welcome, Chuck. If it is possible for anyone to figure it out, you'll be the one to figure it out."

Chuck had a small smile but didn't say anything more. He wasn't sure she was right—but it was nice to hear.

He drank a little more water and leaned a little more on the glass door. Chuck wouldn't let himself truly *relax*. He wasn't sure he had relaxed since Murder Sky. But he did let himself rest a little.

He looked around the store more. Much more casually this time. He wasn't looking at anything specific. It was shelves of merchandise, all of them with the logo. It had tile floors. There wasn't anything odd about it—

"Oh … that might be important," he said.

"Breakthrough?" Cassandra asked. "Knew you would."

"I … guess…" Chuck said. "More a worry. Where is everyone?"

"You mean monsters?"

"Maybe…" Chuck was having trouble thinking of how to say it. "This isn't a house. It's a building meant for … lots of people. Shouldn't there *be* lots of people?"

"It's a good thing people aren't trapped in here," Cassandra commented.

"It is—but…"

Chuck tapped his foot a few times. He leaned his head against the cold glass. He hated when a thought wasn't quite formed. He knew he had it—somewhere— in his mind.

"Oh, there's something … something to this…"

"I'm sure you'll think of it," Cassandra said gently. "Just … wait a bit."

"Uh … fine," Chuck said. "Okay—well, we need to think about what we're going to do for now."

Cassandra balled up the empty chip bag and tossed it across the floor. She stood up and dusted off her hands. Then leaned against the spot next to Chuck.

"I had an idea for that," she said.

"Yeah?"

"Yeah. We might even be able to not sleep on a wooden floor next to fucking pollution."

"Then, by all means, let's go."

CHAPTER 12

THE EMPLOYEE LOUNGE—FOR EMPLOYEES Chuck hadn't seen yet—was a smallish room. Maybe the size of a cabin. The door had been unlocked. Past that, they only had to walk down a short, angular hallway to get to it. The floor plan consisted of a row of lockers for the back wall and two lacquered, basically picnic tables bolted to the floor. A selection of fold-out chairs lay to the side of one of the tables.

And then there was the counter, with a small fridge next to it. The fridge was quickly determined to hold nothing. But the counter had on it a comical number of coffee machines. They barely fit on it. Most of them looked brand new, but a few of them looked so used that it was a wonder if they even worked.

Chuck picked up one. It had the Spire logo on it.

If this is based on impressions, it's taking the whole 'needs caffeine to be productive' thing a little too literally, Chuck thought.

"Nothing in the lockers," Cassandra commented.

"Not surprised," Chuck said.

"Yeah, I'm not either."

Chuck gave the coffee machine one more close look, then tossed it to the side and turned back to Cassandra.

Time to make camp.

With minimal exploration, they found a collection of pillows and blankets. Also, some rugs. Cassandra started setting out little beds, of sorts, between the tables.

"Do you think I should lock the door?" Chuck asked.

"Probably not," Cassandra replied. "Anything that would want to get in is made of this place. It's not going to have any trouble. And, if those coffee pots are murderous, it'll just slow us down unlocking a door."

"Good call," Chuck said.

He walked over and examined the bed she'd made for him. Just looking at it made exhaustion flow over his brain. It hadn't been that long since they'd last slept— maybe a couple of hours—but the amount of things that had happened…

"What time do you think it is?" Chuck asked aloud.

"There isn't a nighttime here."

"Yeah—but, like, what *would* it be?"

Cassandra made a small noise in the back of her throat. "I don't … I really lost track when we're down in the basement. I'm not even sure what day of the week it is."

"Same," Chuck said. "But it had been nighttime when we popped out of the wall. It's probably still nighttime now."

"That sounds reasonable."

Chuck looked up at the light fixture. "Do you want me to turn off the light in here?"

"No … I'd rather you didn't."

"Okay. Do you want me to take first watch?"

"Yes … please."

Chuck nodded. He sat down on the table, letting his legs hang. "Okay, Cassie. You get some sleep. I'll wake you up in…?"

"Until you need sleep bad enough?"

"Sure," Chuck said. "Sounds good."

"Umm … goodnight, Chuck, I guess."

"You too."

A few moments of silence. Then Cassandra—her voice so damn tired—spoke up again.

"Do you think they're okay?"

"I hope so."

CHAPTER 13

CHUCK SAT IN THE ROOM, STARING AT the corner before the door. He shifted a little, trying not to make too much noise. Cassandra needed the sleep.

So did he, of course.

His mind kept wandering. His attention blurring at the edges. There was a lot to think about. He did hope that Grace and Declan were okay, but he was having his doubts now. The buildings greed made would want their sacrifices. Right that moment, they could be screaming, dying, lost to some symbolically horrible thing. The Monopolist could pull people apart. Who knew what new things were out there—

He tried not to think about that.

He wondered how many forms of buildings there were. The main two were warped, or created, he imagined, but how many variations of that were there? Greed was a broad topic, and if department stores were an option, then maybe so were restaurants and more niche stores.

Maybe bookstores. Maybe comic book shops.

He wondered if greed had overtaken his *own* shop. If Kraken Cards and Games still stood, somewhere. Would it have a real kraken, somehow? There were so many ways—

He tried not to think about that.

Chuck got up slowly. Cassandra didn't stir, as he walked around the bend. The door had a little glass window. He stood against the wall, right next to it, and peered out at the store's expansive floor.

It was too bright, he decided. Slightly more than any real store would be. The air conditioning was a little too cold, and the lights were too glaring.

When he and Cassandra had killed The Oil Baron— and when the climate change house was falling apart— he'd seen those strange bubbles. Globules might've been a better word. They were wrong. Simply wrong.

Rot and sickness and wrongness, he thought with a slight shiver. *That might be what evil magic looks like, actually.*

Likely, almost assuredly, the store was made of the same stuff. Everything around him. Like molecules made up the normal world.

And, like molecules, Chuck mused, *it's really hard to think about how they are the building blocks of creation.*

That meant the food they'd eaten was made of that. The ground on which he stood was, too. Maybe even the air he breathed. A whole new form of physics, technically. Did it obey the same rules? Would a microscope show something like atom chains? Or would it show smaller and smaller version of the same magical rot? Maybe, at some level, the magic was just made of the same stuff as everything else. That would be the least complicated.

He let himself think about that line of logic. It was the only subject that didn't make him feel deeply sad—just slightly disturbed.

He leaned a little more against the wall.

This is going to be a long night.

CHAPTER 14

AFTER GENTLY WAKING UP CASSANDRA, Chuck sat down in the middle of the pillows and blankets. He could still feel the floor—but it was better than it had been down in the basement.

"Are you sure you're good for a while?" he asked.

Cassandra shook her head gently. "Yes, Chuck. Get some sleep. Please."

"Okay," Chuck said quietly.

They'd had this argument—if it could be called an argument—before.

Chuck lay down, pulling the blanket up to his chest, and the soreness that had been there the whole time made itself known.

"Fuuuuck … I would really like to not fight fucking monsters for a little while—ideally, never again."

Cassandra chuckled, but her voice still sounded half-awake. She sat where he'd been sitting, and she leaned forward. She touched the bracelet on her wrist that her brother gave her. The brother that she didn't know if he was still alive. She didn't talk about that much. Chuck didn't ask about it much.

"Um … goodnight," Chuck offered.

"Night," Cassandra said simply.

Chuck closed his eyes. His circadian rhythm was all fucked up from everything, but even with the lights being on in a brightly lit store, even with it being a hot, sunny day outside, he hoped his body knew that it was actually the middle of the night. He told his body to relax—

It's the middle of the night.

His eyes snapped back open.

"The store is closed!"

Cassandra jolted and looked down at him. Her eyes were wide. "What? What the fuck?"

Chuck sat back up. All of tiredness fled for a moment, pushed away by the realization.

"It's *nighttime.* It's nighttime right now. And this is a *store.* It's based on a store. It's following the rules of a normal store. Like … like, people's impressions of one. The customers, the employees, *nobody's here* … because the store is *closed*!"

Cassandra got off the table and glanced at the door.

"So," she said, "that means in a few hours…?"

"This place is going to be full of monsters," Chuck concluded. "That's how this works."

"Knew you'd get it," Cassandra said with a soft, tired smile.

"I think I do," Chuck said. "I think … yeah … and … if it *is* following any of the old rules…"

"Then…?"

"*Then* … if this place is going to kill people—then, well, uh, okay, *either* the customers, *or* the employees are going to be … whatever this place's version of The

Monopolist is. And I guess … the other ones are going to be the sacrifices."

"How are they getting here?" Cassandra asked.

Chuck frowned. "I mean … through the front doors I guess…"

Cassandra got a look on her face, then suddenly clapped her hands together. "No. Not the *front* door."

Chuck couldn't help but let out a laugh in response. Because *of course*. What else would a golden door that big be for? Why include that in an otherwise contemporary department store, if not for people to walk into the store?

"Yes!" Chuck exclaimed. "We *are* getting better at this!"

"But what do we do with that?" Cassandra asked.

"Well…"

Chuck had a few ideas.

It depended on how it worked, exactly.

He was absolutely positive that, in the morning, a large group would walk through those golden doors. That much was clear.

But he didn't know beyond that.

And the rush of realization, of working out a problem, wasn't keeping him awake as well as it had a moment ago.

But the idea that he would go back to sleep *now* was nigh-instantly discarded. It likely wasn't going to happen in the next few minutes, but the shop could start to open at any time.

Chuck looked at the countertop, and the irony of his next idea was not lost on him.

"I think we need to wait by the door. How would you like a cup of coffee?"

Chapter 15

CHUCK PUT DOWN HIS MUG OF COFFEE on top of a shiny, metal garbage bin so he could pull the plastic off the curtain rod. They were in the home section of the store, right by the golden door, and he'd found a bin with tons of them. Most of the rods were oceanic blue. He held it up with one hand, feeling the heft of it.

Thinking for a moment, he practiced giving little feints, stabbing forward with the bulb placed at the end so that curtains wouldn't fall off.

"Having fun there?" Cassandra asked.

"It's way better than a plank of wood," he replied. "Way more reach."

"Give me one then," Cassandra said.

Chuck pulled out another one and handed it to her.

"Hopefully, we won't have to fight at all," Chuck added. "But this should work."

Cassandra nodded. "Do you think it'll be monsters or people through that door?"

"I'm happy that it might not be for sure monsters. But I have no idea."

Cassandra sighed and took another drink of her coffee. "Yeah, me neither."

She was on her fifth cup so far. It had taken them some time to find mugs, creamer, and coffee grounds. Even more time to find backpacks to fill with as much food as they could reasonably carry. The store had been a little more difficult to navigate than they'd initially thought. The landmarks were obvious—but the rest of the store felt like a dream labyrinth while walking through it. Objects blurred when they went by them until they didn't quite seem like real items. The arrangement of the aisles wasn't lines, but sharp turns.

Chuck picked back up his mug and took another sip. The smell of hazelnut was surreally pleasant. He'd only had two cups so far—and he wasn't sure he could handle more if he tried. But he kept sipping. The back of his head felt like it was more *open* somehow, and he was acutely aware that he hadn't blinked very much in the last few minutes.

But at least he was awake. If a torrent of monsters spilled out of that golden door, there would be little time to do much more than duck back into the shelves.

The golden door itself hadn't offered much. No information about its passengers, nor its operational timeline. As they got close to it, Chuck had worked out it was about as tall as a two-story building, and about as wide as four lanes of highway. The gold itself was unblemished—just extremely shiny.

There were lines though. Cuts. Marks that showed how it was likely going to open when it did open. And though Chuck knew it was made of magic, it still bugged him that it didn't make sense. There wasn't a mechanism or anything, but eight slices of it would have to pull back, overlap, somehow, for it to be an effective door.

He supposed he would learn soon enough.

"How much longer…?" he muttered under his breath. "How long until … hell?"

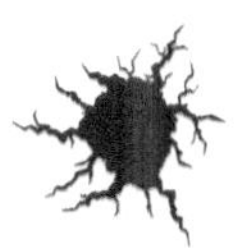

Several hours, easily four, as it turned out. Chuck and Cassandra were sitting in the fold-out chairs. Chuck was wired, but also still sleepy somehow—he'd ended up having an ill-advised fourth cup of coffee—when the door *clicked.* The smooth surface suddenly wasn't uniform anymore, and the segments stood out.

Cassandra sat up straight, grabbed her shower rod and backpack, and stood. Chuck did the same.

To different degrees, the metal popped out further. It reminded Chuck of a spiral staircase but on its side. Then, with loud chimes that put Chuck in mind of a dirge, the lowest step slid underneath the next lowest, and on it went, until there was only one pie-slice hanging, pointing downward.

A small trapdoor of some sort opened at the bottom of the circle—and the pie slice dropped perfectly, making a golden rectangle for the people to walk over.

"Oh, thank god," Chuck said.

Because it *was* people, not horrible monsters, that walked down the tunnel. Rows and rows of them. If the crowd was as big as Chuck thought it was, the store was being staffed by easily over five-hundred people. He recognized a few of them even. Toward the front of the crowd was Calvin, an older guy who started playing *PrecogKnights* during his retirement.

Chuck wanted to walk over to him but paused. Because it was people, yes, but they weren't quite acting like people would in this situation. No one was panicking. No one looked even perturbed.

They looked normal. Some of them chatted calmly. Others looked a little bored.

"What the hell…?" Cassandra muttered.

Chuck agreed with that assessment. It almost scared him more to see them fine than if they'd been panicking.

The first of the group was about to walk through the doorway, onto the store's linoleum. Chuck didn't know her name, but she was a middle-aged woman, with sun-tanned white skin, brown hair, and wore what looked like pajamas. Purple pants with a pink shirt.

As soon as she did pass through, a shudder wracked her shoulders. She blinked rapidly, glancing around in a panic. Pure fear quickly widened her eyes, quickened her breath.

"What is happening—what is—"

Before Chuck could do something—though he wasn't sure what it would be—the speaker system crackled to life, and a feminine voice played through the store.

"Hello new employees!" the voice said. "You work for us now. You have worked for us for a long time. You have been working for us for as long as you can recall. You are an employee—you are an employee—you are an employee—"

Chuck felt a sharp sense of vertigo. He almost fell over. Images of employee manuals and work procedures that only half made sense rushed through his head. The voice over the speaker hadn't stopped, exactly. It had continued and continued until it sounded more like a drill digging into a tooth.

A hand clapped him on the shoulder, and the sensation dissipated with a faint pop inside his head. Chuck, instinctually, put his hand on top of the one on his shoulder.

"Fuck—I hate that…" Cassandra muttered behind him.

Chuck turned to look at her. "I guess that trick still works."

"Yeah…" Cassandra said roughly.

"Are you okay?"

"I am okay enough. They're not though."

Chuck turned back to the woman—and all the others that had stepped into the store. The woman didn't look fearful anymore. But she also didn't look casual either. It was a slightly more difficult emotion to place, but every single other person passing into the store had it, so that made it somewhat easier.

Stress.

The kind that makes shoulders rise with irregular breaths. The kind that casts someone's gaze all over, like a murderer might emerge with an ax.

"Time for work," the feminine voice intoned. "Our customers are ready to have a wonderful shopping experience for the next eight hours of your ever-shrinking lives."

The crowd that had made it through the door dissipated with speed. Most of the "employees" practically *sprinted* to various parts of the store. The sound of that many feet hitting the ground was a dull roar.

The speakers let out a faint chuckle. Then started back from the beginning.

The same sensation pushed at Chuck's mind—but was as dull as before.

"Okay, we have to keep contact," Chuck said.

"Okay," Cassandra replied.

The next wave of people walked in. They went right from casual chatting to that overwhelmingly stressed look.

"We should adjust," Cassandra commented. "We can't fight like this."

Chuck nodded his head. "Yeah, you're right."

With a little maneuvering, they moved to stand side-by-side, each of them holding their weapons.

"Ready to go forward?" Chuck asked.

"Yep."

The crowd of people was still large enough—and their random running erratic enough—that it was going to be difficult to get to the golden door. But they moved forward.

Right in their direct path was a person.

He was a twenty-something with pale white skin, light brown eyes, and his blond hair severely cut short. He smelled strongly of wood smoke—like he'd been sitting by a bonfire in the last few hours.

He was on the stress part of the cycle.

They could've gone around, but Chuck squeezed Cassandra's hand in a message that meant *stop for a second.*

"What?" she asked.

"Do you think we can snap them out of it?" Chuck asked.

"I don't know. Maybe."

"We should try."

"They could attack us," Cassandra replied. "Do we want to take that risk?"

"We'll try something once. We'll keep a little distance. Be ready though. Take my weapon for a minute."

"…Sure."

Chuck handed the shower rod across his chest, and once Cassandra took it, he waved his hand in front of the guy's face.

"Hey! Hey there?"

To Chuck's surprise, the man looked directly at him. He still seemed extremely stressed but could clearly perceive Chuck being there. Rather than attack, he gave a forced smile.

"Hello," he said, his voice normal, heavy with a Chicagoan accent. "Welcome to The Spire Market. My name is Ian. How can I assist you today?"

Chuck blinked in confusion. But he rolled with it. This was, at the very worst, a good way to learn more about how this worked. At the very best, it could mean they could save people around the store.

"Uh, huh, Ian," he began. "Do you … know…?"

"Do you know you're in hell?" Cassandra chimed in.

"Uh, yeah, that?" Chuck said.

Ian blinked, and his face shifted a little. "I can help you with finding whatever you need."

Cassandra chimed in again. "We want to find a way for this not to be hell."

"Can you help us with that?" Chuck asked.

Ian let out a faint chuckle, and then his teeth started chattering. He tried to laugh a little more around it, but his shoulders were spasming. His left eye snapped closed, and he had to force it open again. Like ink against paper, a red blood mark grew across that eye.

Chuck and Cassandra both backed up.

"Uh, Ian…?" Chuck said. "You … okay?"

"I… I was… the sky was…"

Ian hugged himself. He stared at them, blood now pooling from his nose.

"You had a question? You had a question? You had a question—"

"Never mind," Chuck said quickly. "We… we got what we needed."

Ian breathed in hard through his nose, sucking back up the line of blood. The pool of blood in his eye shrank slowly, dragged in small lines toward his pupil, and then disappeared like it had fallen down a well.

"Great," Ian said brightly. "I hope you enjoy your shopping experience."

Chuck was staring at him. He wanted to scream. But he kept it away. He pushed it *down*.

His attempts to not react weren't entirely successful. One, because he was visibly shaking. And, also, because he jolted slightly when the speaker told everyone to get to work and Ian sprinted past them. The new employee booked it for the grocery section, his shoes a series of squeaks among the massive chorus of running people.

Chuck shook his head. Tried to calm his heart. He was breathing quite fast.

"Later," Cassandra said, squeezing his hand. "Later, okay?"

"Fuck," Chuck said. "I don't think … I don't think we can help them at the moment. This is … worse than I expected somehow."

"I know. Later, okay?" Cassandra repeated.

"Later. Yep. Got it. Yep. I'll take my five minutes later," Chuck said. "I want out of here."

They walked briskly forward again, and there *was* good news on that plan's front. The news in question was that the last group was done. The doorway had cleared.

And past it, the long pathway stretched off into an unforeseeable distance, lit by halogen lights that reminded Chuck too much of the abattoir monster's eyes.

Please let the tunnel not have some trick to it, Chuck thought. *Please, just go somewhere.*

The bad news—because of course there was also bad news—arrived a few hurried steps later. A series of noises came from the front of the store. Chuck turned in alarm.

He'd been right about there being a large influx of monsters. They might not have been from the golden door, but they had arrived. The automatic doors at the front of The Spire Market were open, and a mass of—easily more than fifty—creatures walked into the store.

The speaker above abruptly stopped playing its repeating messages. And instead, that same feminine voice gave a more personal announcement.

"Good, they're arrived. They are paying special premiums for this—the others will arrive later—so please allow them to feast upon your blood as they wish. And, as they do, will you two—yes, you two down there, I *see* you—please stop being alive? I have other people to murder."

CHAPTER 16

THE MONSTERS REMINDED CHUCK OF THE Lobbyist, though he didn't know their names instantly like he had with The Lobbyist.

They were dressed in three-piece suits that could've cost the same, if not more, than a year of rent. Garish, massive watches sat on all of their wrists.

Their faces didn't have mouths in the place mouths would normally be. Below, two blood-red eyes—no pupil, no irises, just red globes—were rips in their skin. And lamprey mouths were beyond each one.

"Please kill them," the speaker chimed above.

The customers' heads swiveled like owls, locking onto Chuck and Cassandra. Extremely quickly, from their garish watches downward, a film of bubbling gold coated their hands. They all blinked at the same time.

Then they ran at them.

Chuck let out a faint gasp. And started running. Cassandra was already moving to do the same.

And if they hadn't already been close to the exit, they would've had zero chances to escape. The customers weren't fast like the Mayor's Men had been after their transformation, but they were running full tilt.

As Chuck and Cassandra closed the distance between them and escape, the golden door—almost predictably—started to close. The golden slice moved back up under its own power. The trapdoor reset itself, and then the door began to unfold into its pieces.

Chuck felt more of that same magic push at his mind, but he and Cassandra successfully ran through the rapidly narrowing doorway. As soon as they were over the threshold, the sensation stopped—and a new one started.

It was less aggressive. Less aimed. It suggested that the tunnel was outside, that it was a quant walking path. They had nothing at all to be concerned about as they traveled through hell.

Isn't it nice to go to the business?

Chuck shook his head, even as he sprinted.

It's nice to not be murdered by fucking monsters.

The golden door closed with a metallic clang. The tunnel shook like an earthquake had passed through it. Another dirge chime rang out but was muffled somewhat.

The two ran for a few more moments, but then Chuck and Cassandra slowed slightly, still going forward.

Cassandra glanced backward. She gasped in alarm.

"Oh fuck," she said. "Stop. They're too fast."

Chapter 17

Chuck spun around quickly, still holding Cassandra's hand. And then immediately had to let go as he dodged to the side. A customer monster barreled past him, letting out a snarl.

As soon as Chuck lost contact with her, the tunnel turned into that outdoor walking path. It was like they'd been teleported.

But the monsters still looked like monsters.

Another of the customers rushed him. The gold on the customer's hand bubbled again, rising up into little spikes.

It swung.

Chuck countered with the shower rod in a wide arc, connecting with the side of the customer's arm. The rules of how the monsters interact with generated objects held true. The moderate blow was enough to send it completely off balance. It could barely keep its feet underneath itself. The lamprey mouths let out sharp screeches.

Chuck glanced over at Cassandra. She was doing even better than him. As far as he could tell, there were three monsters that had made it into the tunnel with them—and she'd injured the shoulder of one of them.

It had a lot of gold mixed with its blood. A syrupy red and yellow slime gushed from the wound.

It screamed so loud the skin around the lamprey mouths cracked, letting bleeding lines crisscross its face.

"Fuck you," Cassandra shot back.

A different scream sounded behind Chuck. And the one Chuck had just hit also raced at him.

Adrenaline crackled in his body.

Chuck stabbed forward the front of the rod. The rounded bulb smashed into the monster's stomach. For a split second, the monster folded over it—then its stomach cracked open like stepping on a gourd. And it went flying backward.

Chuck spun to face his other attacker—but not fast enough.

The other crashed into him. Chuck went down, smacking hard into the ground, the water bottles in his backpack digging into his spine. He only had enough presence of mind to hold up the rod in defense.

The monster's golden glove hit the center of the rod. And shattered it. There was a small explosion of shrapnel. Chuck's hands were thrown to either side, knocking away his weapon. He winced in pain from an open cut on his face, already bleeding.

The lamprey mouths all shrieked down at him, and the gloved hand went up for the kill.

Chuck kicked.

Human blows, without anything made by Greed, weren't nearly as effective. His kick made a hollow thud against the monster's chest and only pushed it back a little.

There was enough space for Chuck to roll to the side, scramble, then push himself to stand. Behind him was the violent crack of the glove hitting, shattering, crashing into the ground.

His gaze darted around for either piece of the weapon. "Cassandra?!" he yelled out.

Another lamprey scream.

"Alive," she answered, then grunted. "Alive right now."

On your own, Chuck thought.

He spied one of the pieces, ran forward, and scooped it up. The edge of it was sort of jagged. Not enough to really use as a spear or knife. He spun back to see the monster.

It was closer than he expected. Two steps away from him, and already swinging the spiked hand at his head. Chuck ducked under it, hearing the whoosh of air as it went.

Then the kick landed.

He didn't even see the monster shift, but its leg crashed into Chuck's stomach. It wasn't as hard as when The Monopolist had knocked Chuck off his feet—but it still very much hurt. His shoes skidded across the ground from the force, and he let out a strangled wheeze of pain.

"Chuck!" Cassandra called out.

Chuck tried to respond, but he couldn't quite get air into his lungs. He coughed and sputtered, taking steps backward as best he could.

The monster let out another shrieking cry and ran at him—

Cassandra's shower curtain hit the side of the monster's head and jerked its neck with a loud crack. A chunk of its chin fell away, blood oozing down.

The shower rod hit the ground with a clatter. It rolled slowly.

The monster wobbled, the lamprey mouths screaming. It clawed at the wound, seemingly trying to push the blood back up into its face, but it all oozed past its fingers.

Chuck let out a painful gasp, finally forcing air into his aching lungs. He felt lightheaded—but made an unsteady path to the weapon.

He picked it up. The shower rod felt almost heavy to him right then. He lifted it up as high as he could—

The monster moved slowly, its chin wound weeping blood—

Chuck brought it down in one strike. If it had been a normal shower rod against a human, it might've caused a mild concussion. For this monster, Chuck may as well have used a sword.

Or a hammer.

The lamprey monster's head dented inward and then split open. Chuck's blow went down to the neck before the rest of the monster fell to the ground.

Chuck stared in shock for a moment. His hands were coated with cold, gold-flecked blood.

"Fuck! Help!" Cassandra yelled in alarm.

Chuck turned, still holding the shower rod, and saw Cassandra trying to pin the final monster. She was clearly struggling to even hold the monster's non-weaponized arm behind its back, let alone avoid its aggressive swings.

Chuck's entire body was sore. Multiple muscles hadn't really recovered from previous fights, previous days.

But Cassandra was in danger.

He slung the shower rod over his shoulder and sprinted forward.

Cassandra waited until the last second. She dove her foot into the back of the monster's left knee with visual effort. Pain flashed across her face, but the move worked.

As the monster dropped, she let it go, stepping back. Chuck took a solid swing.

The monster's head shattered at about the same time it left its neck. A cascade of almost ceramic-like shards scattered across the tunnel's ground with a splatter of blood.

Chuck let the shower rod fall. He held out his hand for Cassandra. When she took it, the illusion dissipated again.

CHAPTER 18

CHUCK COUGHED AND THEN TRIED talking. "Okay … that was bad."

"Are you okay?"

He wheezed slightly. "That kick … really … fucking hurt."

"But are you okay, Chuck?"

Chuck ran his hand over his stomach. He didn't want to imagine how bad it was going to bruise. It didn't currently feel like any ribs were broken, but it was hard to tell.

"I … think so," Chuck said. "Where'd you learn that … uh … arm grapple thing?"

"I learned it in those self-defense classes I took," Cassandra replied. "I wasn't sure it would work on something like these things."

Chuck nodded. "I'm surprised it did at all."

"I mean … they can't be immune to everything not made of them," Cassandra said. "If we, like, hit them with a flamethrower, I'm sure that would do something."

"I don't know…" Chuck mused.

He poked the monster's corpse with his foot.

Even after everything, there still was so much he didn't fully know. These *were* monsters, but, like the shopping cart monsters, they weren't quite the same as The Monopolist or The Oil Baron. They didn't have individual names. They weren't as strong or apparently durable.

"We got to get going," Cassandra chimed in.

"Yeah…" Chuck said. "We really do. I hate to say it … but I think there's some kind of hierarchy here. These were nothing compared to the climate change trio. That voice on the speakers is probably much worse."

"And yet they still almost killed us." She picked up the shower rod. It had a pattern of gold and red blood on it. "And we only have one weapon."

Chuck looked down the long tunnel. It was a cave system of stone that didn't quite look like natural minerals. If the goal wasn't for people to traverse it, Chuck assumed it would go on forever. But it didn't seem to. It did curve away; it forked into two different paths. He had a few ideas of what they might find out in further modified Quill Point, but there was no way to know for sure.

So, they started walking.

After a few echoey steps, Chuck looked down at his hand. He still had a ton of that weird gold blood on him. But it had dried. Quite quickly dried. He rubbed his hand against his pant leg and it flaked away like golden confetti.

"Yeah, really, they were *nothing* like the last ones…" Chuck said. "There could be a whole taxonomy of monster types out there. Worse, weaker, better, deadlier. Who knows how many variations there could be?"

"Don't sound excited," Cassandra said.

"I'm not," Chuck replied. "Just … always trying to understand."

"I know," Cassandra said, a little more gently. "I know."

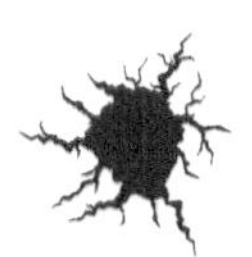

They walked in silence for a time, getting to the fork in the path. They stopped between the two. Chuck peered down right, and it didn't seem to have anything else but more tunnel. It curved off eventually. He peered down the left way. There was a bright light. Maybe sunlight, maybe the beam from some massive floodlight, maybe some nightmarish ritual of intense, glowing energy, but it was difficult to tell.

"Which way do you want to go?" Chuck asked.

"I guess left. I don't want to just keep walking in here. It's getting into my head more and more."

Chuck had noticed that too. The tunnel's visions of lovely outdoor locations never could quite get in fully, not when they were in physical contact, but it tried. Flashes of it would pass across Chuck's vision. He'd smell faint, floral scents and occasionally the sharper smell of cut grass.

"Yeah. I wonder if it's like this so that it has time to kick in for everyone."

"I hate that," Cassandra said.

"Do you think it's a wrong assessment?"

"No, I just hate it."

Chuck let out a faint chuckle but didn't add anything else to the conversation.

They took the left path, and, on a whim, Chuck glanced behind them. He wasn't *disappointed* that the tunnel hadn't wiped away all of his other options, but he was a little surprised. It just seemed likely that the place would pull something like that.

But no, just a tunnel.

He looked back a second time, a few moments later, just to be sure.

Yep, just a tunnel.

Neither of them said anything aloud about it, but they unanimously, almost at the same time, picked up speed as they got closer to the bright lights.

It was probably sunlight. But filtered in weird ways. The rays dappled the ground, maybe altered through glass, maybe clouds, maybe both and more—there was a hue to it that didn't seem quite organic.

Closer now, Chuck could see parts of it before they were outside, but not all of it. And as more and more of it fell into view, he felt a little like he was falling. Like he was tilting backward. There was a profound sense of vertigo, not just because of the buildings, and not just because he couldn't help but look up. His mind told him that what he was seeing wasn't real. Couldn't be real.

There's no way.

Even after all the things that had happened so far, nothing prepared him for Quill Point as it was now.

CHAPTER 19

THE LIGHT-ALTERING WAS CAUSED BY AN amber-colored, bug-like shell of a structure. The tunnel wasn't gone, just more transparent, and with many branching paths scurrying over city streets and cracked sidewalks otherwise congested with cars that didn't move—but did spew out continuous smog and the occasional irritating blast of complaining car horn. Far off from Chuck and Cassandra, at the edges of the tunnels' denser hubs, were a few pedestrians, none of them human, walking purposely somewhere. They were monsters. A creature that looked like a human nervous system but made of clay. Two patchwork people, walking side-by-side, with shifting blocks for faces. And quite a few of the lamprey-mouthed demons from before.

And they were in a city full of buildings that didn't make sense.

The tendrils that had been merely bunting in The Spire Market were the size of trains and draped across leaning, shining, metallic skyscrapers that defied all architectural laws and gravitational rules to *bend* toward one another. Upper floors would almost touch, with thin, dizzying, rail-less bridges connecting them.

And the sky?

What the *fuck* had happened to the sky?

The tendrils that had declared the beginning of the apocalypse, so long ago now, so many nightmares ago now, were down amongst the buildings. But the Earthly sights of puffy clouds, or the blue Illinois sky, were still taken away, perhaps eviscerated in the changing of reality.

Instead, was a star cluster expanse of latticework, an infinite cacophony of ever-flowing lines connected to focal points that out-numbered the mind's capacity to parse their frequency. A faint, but incessant, din of voices added an ambient hum to the already loud air—from speakers placed on buildings, from the cars honking. It was easy enough to tune out that quiet yelling, but it continuously felt like someone was whispering nearby.

Staring at it, Chuck only then noticed the strange, electrical firmament that seemed to hold back the full-ness of this void. Some of the tendrils—some of the *build-ings*—would reach for it, only to press against the barrier. Sending raindrop-against-water ripples across it.

Chuck only then was aware that he was hyperventi-lating. That he was holding his shoulders so tight that it was hurting him. His knees wobbled, wanting to buckle.

Cassandra made a small sound in the back of her throat. Her hand dropped away.

Chuck let out a faint scream, like the kind made when waking from the worst nightmare. A jolt of panic rushed to his mind.

But nothing happened.

The magic wasn't happening. It didn't claw at perceptions. As much as everything else was already making his mind spin, this was equally confusing.

Until, rather suddenly, grimly, horribly, it made sense. *This part they want us to know. This is almost gloating.*

He looked at Cassandra, and she was crying softly. It dripped down her cheeks as she tried—and failed—to get her shaking under control.

"Our town…" she said roughly. "The whole world's gone."

Tears immediately sprang to Chuck's eyes. He offered his hand for hers—and she took it gently.

Chuck sucked in a breath. "Yeah … this is…"

Cassandra let out something that was both an exhale and a pained gasp. She rubbed her face with her other hand. "I can't… I can't accept… fuck…"

Chuck squeezed her hand. "I know… I know…"

"What are we going to *do*?"

"I… I…" Chuck tried to hold himself together. He gritted his teeth against his own panic. There had to be a way to move forward. "Cassie… Cassie… you can have thirty minutes later, okay? Okay? We can't let this win."

"I'll need years," she said breathlessly.

Chuck stared at her. *Years.* He couldn't even think of that as a metric of time anymore. How could anything exist for years in the wake of *this*?

But there was no one to carry on Chuck's and Cassandra's dreams. And no one to hold Peter and Aoife's for the future.

"Then I guess…" Chuck's mouth was very dry. "…we need to survive."

Cassandra gritted her teeth. "…I want to tear it down."

Her voice was so scratchy it almost wasn't audible. But each word was enunciated with the full force of emotion.

Chuck held her gaze. There was a sensation in his chest he couldn't quite explain. "All of it?"

Cassandra sucked in a long breath, then released it— and she was shaking even harder. But that exhale didn't sound quite the same as sorrow did. It didn't quite have the same energy as a breakdown.

It was more a body failing to contain the fullness of an emotion.

She muttered a few words so quietly now, so quickly now, that Chuck couldn't hear them—but then she looked up at him, and her eyes were shining with tears, and unyielding like stone.

"Chuck?" Cassandra said.

"Yes, Cassie?"

"You understand this ... magic ... more than I do. You get how it works. And if it has a way it works ... then it has a way it can break. I want to take a plank of wood, a shower rod, a flamethrower ... to whatever took the *sky* away. Point *me* at *it*."

Chuck didn't know if what he said next was a lie—but there was nothing else he could possibly say.

"I'll find it."

He was crying again.

"You *promise*?" Cassandra said. "I need you to *promise* it. Please... please promise it. Chuck. I can't stand... I need you to promise it."

She stumbled. Chuck felt like he was going to throw up. Cassandra had held it together for so long. He'd watched her stow away the terror, hide, practically ignore, the trauma of almost-death so many times that he'd almost taken it for granted. On the worst days down in that basement, he'd relied on her being steady.

Cassandra hung her head and let out another breath. Her voice was exhausted; her words deflated. "No. No. No. I can't ask you that. Can't do that. I'm sorry, Chuck. I'm sorry. I can't make you promise that. It's unfair—"

"I promise."

Now it couldn't be a lie. Now it was locked in. There was a part of Chuck that was his conviction, and it was in the chest, and in his head, and it had built him a business, it had built him a community, it had pushed him to survive the hardships of both.

It had gotten them out of one nightmare.

"Cassie, if there is a way, I'll find it," Chuck said. "I don't know how we'll win, but I will find it. I promise."

He looked out again, but not at that sky—at the buildings. Among the skyscrapers were smaller places too. Restaurants, clothing stores; there was even, off on a faraway hill, what seemed to be a news station. And each he knew was a hell. And each he knew was trying to kill the people inside them.

He felt the weight of that, as much as any one person could. He looked back at her.

"I promise you, Cassie."

Cassandra stared at Chuck and set her jaw. Her eyes were red from tears. Terror ripped across her expression—but there are stronger things than terror.

"Then I promise you that I will fight with everything I have."

And a plan. A desperate, risky, dangerous plan started to form in Chuck's head. But it was essentially the same as it had been. The same idea returning—changed, yes, but fundamental. There might not have been a bonfire anymore to find them by, but he needed the citizens of Quill Point.

He needed an army.

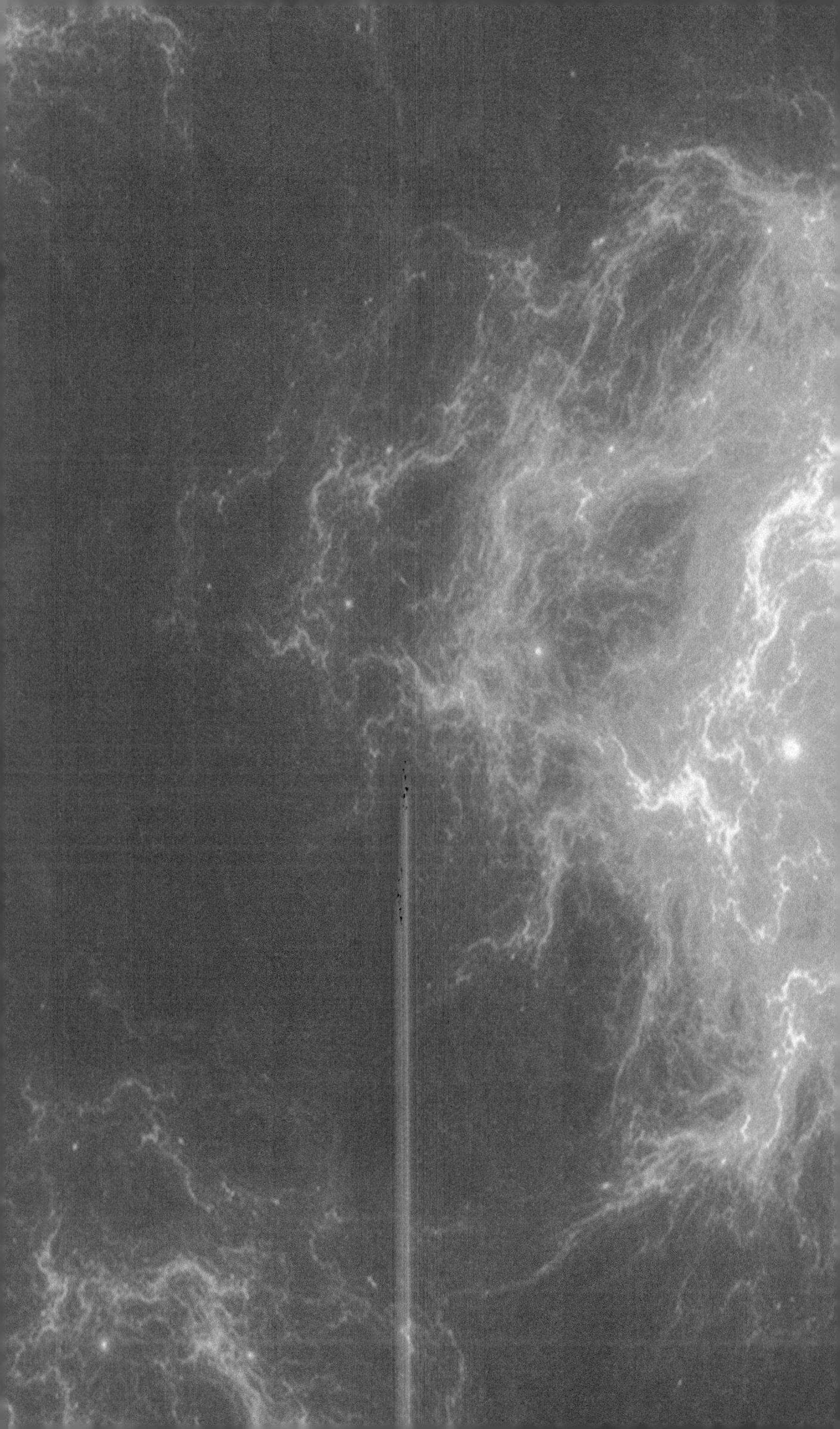

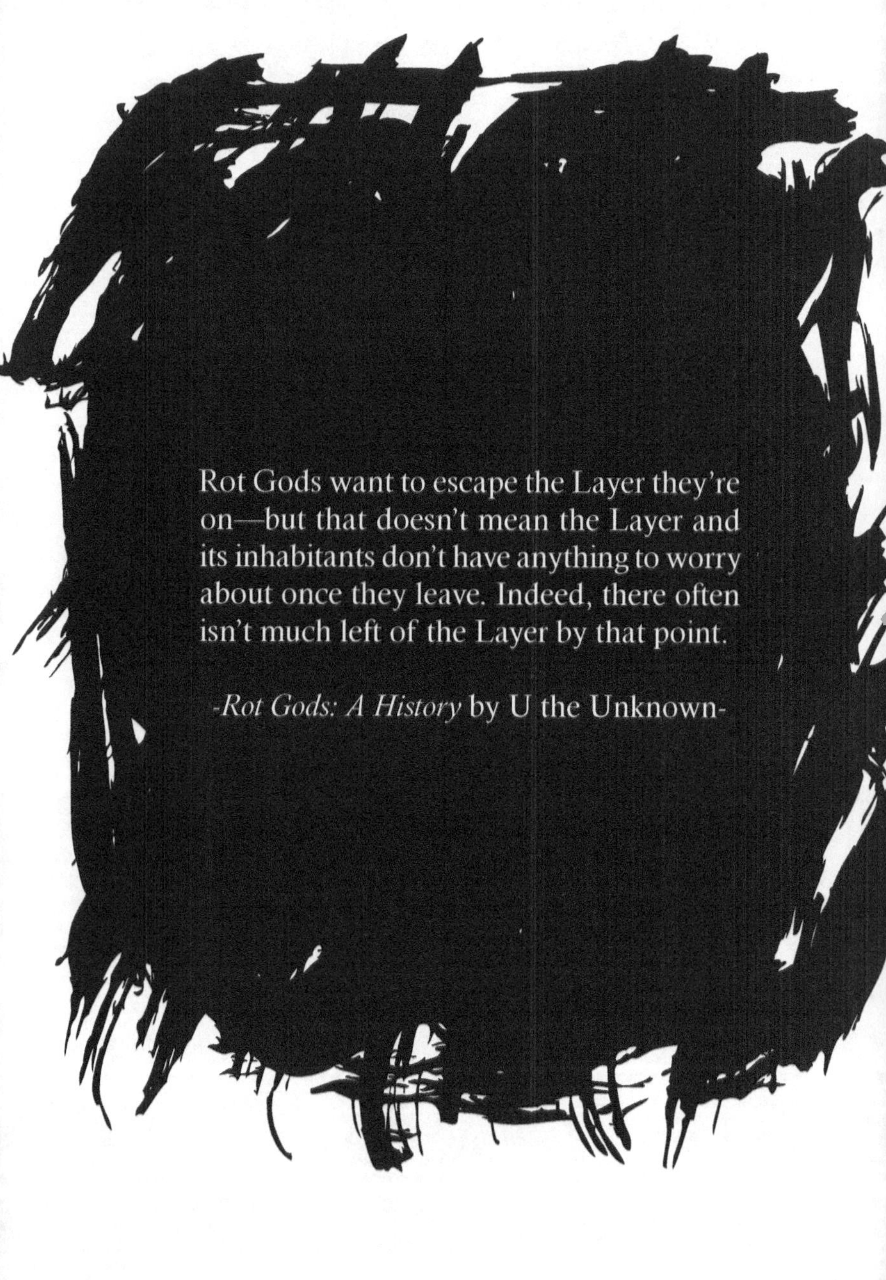

Rot Gods want to escape the Layer they're on—but that doesn't mean the Layer and its inhabitants don't have anything to worry about once they leave. Indeed, there often isn't much left of the Layer by that point.

-*Rot Gods: A History* by U the Unknown-

INTERLUDE ONE

APOCALYPSE BOYFRIENDS

CHARLEY AWOKE IN A DARK MOTEL ROOM. The curtains were thick and dusty, and a fan creaked above them. Still sleepy, he glanced at the door. There hadn't been anyone to buy the room from—the whole motel had been abandoned. They'd broken in and there hadn't been a way to lock the door. A chair was pushed up to the handle. Charley doubted if someone found them and wanted in that a chair would do much to stop them.

Next to him, Dereck made small sounds in his sleep. He did that often. It always sounded like he was talking to someone. But the words were never clear.

Charley turned to look, and then immediately looked away. His face grew red, and he let out a faint, nervous laugh. Surfer abs. How they felt. The residual warmth. Lots of kissing. So much kissing.

Goddamn it, my boyfriend is really hot.

Charley stood up and went to the tiny motel bathroom. He closed the door gently before flicking on the lights. It was too bright. The mirror made him look tired. Then again, with how long they'd been driving—not to mention the conditions while driving—it wasn't surprising.

He thought again about last night.

Last night.

They hadn't had full-on sex of any kind. Not yet. But it had gotten very close. Dereck had kept checking in, getting consent, and eventually, Charley said he wasn't ready for anything further.

Charley turned on the tap, leaned down, and splashed some cold water on his face. He did so several times, then sat on the closed toilet seat. The blood rush of memories took a lot of effort to tamp down.

Maybe it was better to just keep thinking about last night though. Much more pleasant. Without the distraction of his boyfriend, the other thoughts crept in. Every day, the world felt stranger. Emptier. More and more examples of people who'd been affected by whatever had happened. "Emptied People," as Dereck started to call them.

And every day, Charley worried more and more about his sister, Cassandra, and his father. His father was arguably safer than Charley, and when he checked in on him, he sounded okay. But Cassandra was inside the strange formation around Quill Point.

God, that was only a few days ago.

Charley breathed in through his nose, then out his mouth.

One day, you're working a dead-end job in a shitty apartment, he thought. *Then the world turns different. You end up taking a dangerous road trip across the country with your crush.*

You end up kissing your crush. End up finding a motel when you get too tired to drive anymore. End up sharing a bed, even when there were two beds.

Charley looked up at the ceiling. It was cracked and maybe a little moldy. He wouldn't have been surprised if there were roaches hiding in one of those cracks.

He'd forgotten to turn off the water. The sound was almost calming—but reminded him that there might be only so much clean water left on the planet. He couldn't imagine the water filtration plants were still running. Nothing else was.

I can't just sit here. I should go wake up Dereck. And we should … we should leave for the road.

Charley got up and turned off the sink. He didn't actually know what time it was. Ever since the apocalypse, his usual night shift sleep schedule had been tossed around. It was safer to drive during daylight—some Emptied drivers didn't even bother to leave their lights on—but it didn't help him with his internal clock.

Charley quietly exited the bathroom. Some sunlight was peeking through the curtains. It looked a little weird to him. Like it was at a wrong angle. Which meant it was early morning. The time of day neither he, nor Dereck, never would normally see.

Dereck shifted in his sleep, maybe to get away from the light. Even coated in shadows, Charley knew his boyfriend's face perfectly. They'd been friends for so long before. He knew his gray eyes, his short, usually well-kept beard. He knew how strong those arms of his could be—

"Hey, Dereck," Charley said gently. "We should get going."

Dereck let out a faint snore, then flipped to face away from him.

Charley quietly chuckled, then sat down on the side of the bed. He hadn't quite learned his boyfriend's sleep habits yet, if it even matched what it had been before the apocalypse. But he usually woke up if Charley did enough stuff around him.

Charley stood back up and looked around for his jeans. He already knew where his shirt was. He wondered if they could find the remnants of some continental breakfast. The sign outside had promised something like that.

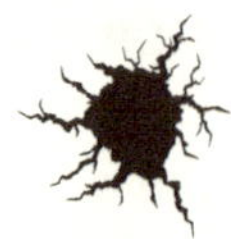

Charley wasn't all that familiar with motels—he couldn't afford to stay in them often—but there was a strange energy to the little nook where people could get breakfast. It was just past the main desk, with a triangular floor plan. The tiles were brown, speckled with white, and there was a single ceiling fan that was just loud enough to continuously draw attention. A line of little puck-like gas stoves sat underneath the metal frame that would've held various breakfast foods.

"Not looking promising," Dereck said.

"No, it does not," Charley replied.

Dereck walked into the room. He looked so tall compared to it. "I don't think we're going to get much out of this."

Charley followed him in. He glanced around. In one corner, covered in dust, there was what looked like someone's wallet, of all things. He debated going to see whose it was, but it was absolutely filthy. A piece of very gray gum was sitting next to it.

Besides, money wasn't of much use in the new world.

"You know what though?" Dereck asked.

"What?"

Dereck pointed out a door painted the same white as the walls. "I have always wondered what they have back there. Do you think it's just piles and piles of unopened cereal boxes and dehydrated egg patties?"

Charley smirked. "I always assumed so…"

Dereck winked. He went over and tried. The handle stuck in his hands and a little light from some mechanism above it blinked red as if to mock him. He tried twice more, before frowning.

"Guess the mystery will always haunt us," he said.

God, he's cute, Charley thought.

Charley gave the room another glance. The odds of him missing something were pretty damn slim. The room had nowhere to hide anything. But there was one other option…

"How okay are you with me stealing more things?" Charley asked.

Dereck seemed to take the question more seriously than Charley had expected. He took a second, face in a half-frown. When he spoke, his voice was a little grave.

"I've been thinking about that, actually. We took all that stuff from the convenience store. Do you ever expect … I don't know … that things might ever go back to how it was?"

"Uh … well…"

Charley didn't have an answer to that one. It hit hard, actually. Life before hadn't been the best, yeah. Besides meeting Dereck, there had only been goals and dreams to look forward to. The job at the convenience store was tedious and a little depressing. The pay had been bad; his rent had eaten up so much of that pay; he'd not eaten a few times because he'd paid too much for other things that kept him alive. It wasn't a system he wanted. It wasn't a system that he could imagine existing forever—but he hadn't wanted the world to end.

I don't want it to go back, and I don't want it to be like this.

"No … no, I don't think we'll ever undo the apocalypse," Charley said. "I think we're living in a new world—if it lasts at all. We can't go back. Infrastructure is going to fall apart with everyone Emptied. Everything was off-balance before. This fucking toppled it."

"Hmm." Dereck nodded his head. "Maybe we can do it better this time."

"Do you really think so?" Charley asked.

He smiled. "I have people I want to spend as much time with as possible."

Charley's face got very warm again.

Dereck stepped right up to him. He leaned down. Charley was only too happy to meet him. When Charley pulled back, he wasn't sure how he was managing to breathe. All the air—all of his mind—wasn't there for a moment.

"Umm … well … umm…"

Charley couldn't help but turn away. The emotions in his chest were too much. It felt like a solar flare was emanating out from him. He took a few more breaths, giggled, then finally stabilized. He turned back.

"I meant… I just meant… uh, huh … wow… I just meant I was going to go see if I could find a keycard behind the desk."

"Oh," Dereck said flatly, then laughed. "I don't even know if that's stealing. The breakfast is complimentary."

"But we didn't pay for a room," Charley said, still a little breathless.

Dereck let out a small snort of laughter. He ran his hand through his hair.

"Yeah, I guess we didn't."

"You still want to see if we can get in there and get toast?" Charley asked.

"Oh god, I could fuck up some toast right now."

Charley let out another giggle, then tried to stop it in its tracks. He nodded a little too much and turned to the desk.

Why are you still so awkward about this? he thought. *You don't need to be awkward with him.*

He shook away the thoughts and pushed away the chair behind the desk. There weren't a lot of drawers to search through, actually. One of them was full of pens. Another had a checkbook in it. The third had a literal pile of keycards. Each one was a simple purple and white, with a black bar to scan.

"Jackpot!" he yelled over his shoulder.

"You found them?" Dereck asked.

Charley scooped up all the cards into his arms, closed the drawer with his hip, and went back into the eating area. A little more dramatic than he needed to be, he dropped the entire armful across the table.

"I fucking found them."

Dereck picked one up and checked both sides.

"Okay, so, this one is for—oh, *our* room, that's funny. We could've just done this."

"At least the door wasn't that hard to break into," Charley said.

"Yeah, for *you*," Dereck said with a smile. He worked his shoulder in a circle. "I'm still a little sore from breaking in."

You didn't seem so last night, Charley thought.

He debated saying the flirt out loud, but the thought of it made his body do things that it was not time for. They had a night of fun. Now was survival again. They weren't too far off from the assisted living facility, from Charley's dad. If it wasn't for the constant concern about the world running out of food, he would've been in more of a hurry to get out of the motel.

Dereck had been fanning through the cards. He held one up and clicked his tongue.

"Okay, I bet this is the one."

"How can you tell?"

"It has the word *storage* on it."

Charley chuckled. "Oh, yeah, that seems like a good sign."

Dereck went over to the door. The device on it wasn't the fastest to register the card swipe, but it did let out a little beep. The light blinked green for a second, then turned off. A faint groan sounded from the hinges, but Dereck pulled open the door. He disappeared into the room.

"How's it looking?" Charley called, wandering over.

"There's not a lot—I think the people who were working here thought of raiding this already. And it's not … uh … the cleanest. Like, this is kind of disgusting. But … wait … is this…?"

Before Charley could look into the mostly dark room, Dereck emerged holding two slightly beaten-up cardboard boxes and four tiny things of milk.

"This is literally it," Dereck said. "Well, except something with peanuts. You can't have those, right?"

A warm feeling spread through Charley's chest. "Right. I shouldn't, anyway. I haven't really tested it much since … when I was a kid. Thanks… thank you for remembering that."

Dereck shrugged his shoulders. "I can't have my boy-friend having an allergic reaction, can I?"

Charley wanted to look away again—he was sure his face was growing redder than ever. But he kept looking at him, smiling.

"I guess we're having cereal for breakfast."

"Guess we're having cereal."

Dereck placed the food down on the table. "You know, it's weird. I haven't had breakfast in a while. I mean, I've pulled all-nighters and then eaten breakfast food, but I wouldn't call that a 'breakfast,' exactly."

"I can't remember the last time I did either," Charley said. "But it actually sounds really good right now.".

"I thought so too."

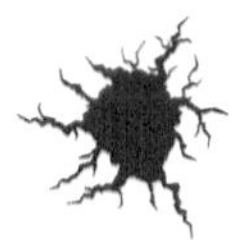

Dereck titled back the glass cup he'd used for his cereal—they hadn't been able to find bowls—and drank the rest of it. He pulled one of the napkins out from the dispenser at the table and wiped away some milk from his beard.

Then he cleared his throat.

There was an intonation to it that made Charley pause the spoon to his mouth and place it back into his half-finished cereal.

"Are you okay?" he asked.

"Well, uh," Dereck started, then ran his hand over the back of his neck. "So, this seems kind of silly to worry about. The world is ending and all. But, well, we're going to make it to the assisted living facility today, right?"

"I hope so," Charley said. "What's up?"

Dereck gave an uncharacteristically awkward chuckle. It almost didn't compute in Charley's mind that he could seem so suddenly awkward. That was always Charley's job.

"So," Dereck began, "I mean … like I said, it's silly. But I've never met your dad in person before. I've never met a significant other's parent before. My relationships never felt … right … for that before."

"Oh," Charley said. "I guess you're right. It's weird. I feel like you two know each other. But I guess I just talked to him about you a lot, so it's felt like—"

"You talk about me a lot?"

Charley sputtered out. "I mean … yes, of course I do."

"That's nice to hear."

Charley failed to keep looking at him that time. He dipped his head and stared at the table for a moment. His mouth felt dry. "Aren't you supposed to be the one who feels awkward right now?"

"I am," Dereck said. "But you being cute makes me feel better."

"Okay … okay … no more flirting for a moment. I can't take it."

"Deal."

Charley let out a long breath, then looked back up at his boyfriend. "Okay, so, yeah, I guess you're meeting him for the first time. He knows you, though. It's going to be fine."

"I just … hmm." Dereck worked his jaw for a moment. "I don't know him all that well."

"Well, what do you want to know?"

"I mean, what's he like?" Dereck asked earnestly.

Charley took another bite of cereal as he thought about how to answer. It had been years since he'd seen his father in person. His father was almost a vague collection of life patterns presumed to have continued. But he also had spent enough time with him to know those life patterns.

"He's … what's the word I'm looking for here? He locks on to something, I guess."

"So, very focused?"

"More like has a lot of dedication," Charley said.

"I think that's a great quality," Dereck said.

"I do too. After mom passed, he helped me and Cassy out so much. I owe him so much—I wish I could do more for him. But that's also just how he is. He picks what he's going to do, and I think he picks very carefully, and fucking hell or high water, it's getting done. It's very 'chin up' kind of mindset. I am almost sure the only reason he's not on his way to me is because I told him I would go to him first."

"So that's why you're like that," Dereck commented.

"What? What do you mean?"

"You're a lot like him then. You and your game."

Charley blinked. "My game?"

"The game you've been designing. I told you before, on our first date, that I know you'll make it unless the world literally blows up or something."

Before we made out for the first time, Charley added in his mind.

"That's different," Charley said.

"Is it?" Dereck replied. "If that's what your dad is like, then I see it in you too."

"You see a lot in me."

"I like looking."

Charley waved out his hands, blocking his face for a moment. "Okay, okay. No flirting rule. No flirting rule, please."

"Sorry," Dereck said.

"Do you have any other questions?"

"I mean, if it's okay to ask, why is he in an assisted living facility in the first place?"

"He's the reason. We told him we wanted him to stay with one of us, either with Cassy in Quill Point or with me. But he could tell. We weren't equipped to handle the medical problem he was having. I still feel bad about it sometimes, really—we could've figured something out—but he wouldn't hear it."

"What was happening?"

"He was having heart issues," Charley explained. "Once he got the diagnosis that they weren't going to fully stop, even with drugs, he just went for his plan, and there was no stopping him."

"Is he paying for it?" Dereck asked.

"My dad was big into saving for retirement. He sold a few investments and Cassy makes enough that she can help out. I did what I could too. I helped drive him there. But yeah, he basically handled it himself."

"Well, okay."

"You nervous now?"

"Oh, I'm nervous as shit, Charley," he replied.

Charley laughed for a moment, then stuck out his hand across the table. Dereck put his fingers in his, and the two just sat like that for a moment. Charley wondered if Dereck could feel his pulse through his hands.

Charley managed to get his voice as level as possible. "Let's get going then. You'll get to meet him today."

"Okay." Dereck nodded to himself. "Okay."

Charley let go of his hand and stood up.

"You're not going to eat that?" Dereck asked.

Charley glanced down. He'd still not finished his breakfast. He knew he'd regret it later, not eating any interesting foods he could. The world will have a lot fewer food options soon. But he was so close to getting to his father.

"You can have it," Charley said.

Dereck pulled the glass to himself and then downed the cereal like it was a shot of vodka. He slammed it down on the table, stretched his fingers above his head, and then stood up.

"Alright. Let's do this."

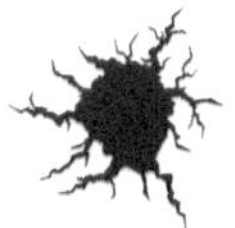

Charley had noticed the subtle changes as he went across the country. Lots of little things added up. The baseline temperature shifted. The grass subtly changed color. It was weird not seeing any palm trees around. Even the air had a different quality than California.

The same style of shift happened in microcosm as they got close to the facility. First, it was all highway— and the hell of avoiding Emptied People parked or aimlessly driving in random places—and then it was roads surrounded by shopping centers. Then fewer and fewer chains until Charley didn't recognize almost any of the businesses he passed. If this had been a different sort of road trip, he would've wanted to stop at one of the cute little coffee places. Maybe try out a restaurant that probably didn't exist anywhere else.

Eventually, though, almost all businesses dropped away. It was tall trees and two-lane roads almost exclusively with gas stations as odd splashes of red and white among the relentless green. At this point, Charley was working off his phone's instructions almost entirely.

"We should probably call him before we get there," Dereck said absentmindedly.

He'd been looking out the window ever since they'd gotten into the denser foliage, but he shifted to sit facing forward.

"Not a bad idea," Charley said. "I think I know the rest of the way. Can you call him?"

"Sure. Is he under 'dad?'"

"Yeah. I never could call him anything else."

"Make sense." Dereck chuckled. "My mom wouldn't let me call her anything else."

Dereck pulled the phone off its stand. "What's your password?"

"Oh," Charley said, his face flushing slightly. "Uh, it's October fifteenth, two-thousand eighteen."

Dereck went quiet for a moment. He hadn't unlocked the phone yet. He turned it over in his hands for a few seconds.

"That's not your birthday," he said.

"No, it's not."

"What is it?"

Charley shrugged. "It's the first day I lived on my own in California. Like, the first night where no one was helping me move, or with me, or anything. I had to get a new phone a few months after that, and I bought it with my own money, and I wanted to remember that."

Dereck didn't say anything.

Charley looked over at his boyfriend. "What?"

"I just, I didn't know that about you." Dereck put in the code. "It's cool to learn new things."

"Yeah, it is…"

Charley looked back at the road.

"Calling now," Dereck said.

"Okay," Charley replied.

A few seconds of the soft ring emanating from Charley's phone. Then the disconnection sound. No voicemail. Charley's hands tightened around the steering wheel.

"Charley…"

"Call again."

"Yeah, okay," Dereck replied.

The ring was the same volume as before—but it didn't feel that way to Charley. It was a blaring klaxon. The machine didn't go to voicemail again. Charley steadied his breathing as best he could. There was a tightness in his chest that seemed like it might just crystalize and stop his heart.

Charley glanced in both directions, then checked his rearview mirror. It had been a lot less populated since they entered this town—and currently there wasn't anyone on the road he could see.

"Dereck…" he began.

"Yeah."

"I'm going to fucking floor it."

Dereck let out a long breath. "Okay."

Charley pulled his foot slightly back, then slammed down with all the force he could. His poor car hadn't been in the best condition before this road trip. The engine shook like it wanted to break out of the car. The wheels screamed with a train whistle's intensity.

Charley's head slammed back into the headrest.

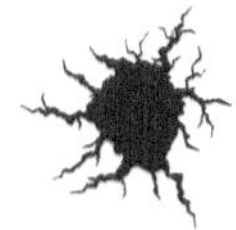

Charley and Derek got out of the car. Charley's legs felt rubbery, and he wasn't sure he was blinking as often as he had been before.

He still started walking, with Derek trailing behind. As they walked, Charley kept noticing something.

There was something off about the scenery.

The actual facility looked like it had when Charley dropped his dad off. The front building was squat, painted a combination of brown, orange, and yellow, with a downward sloping roof. Behind it were more, smaller buildings, a gazebo, some lakes with walking paths, and furthest back were lush Indiana trees that wavered in what wind they could get.

He spotted it.

It was the yard that was off.

Skid marks traced an obvious path to a car quietly burning, half-buried into the dried-up water fountain.

"Shit," Charley said.

"Yeah … that's bad," Derek replied.

And they both sprinted for the entrance.

Dereck was taller than Charley, and it was only through his panic that Charley kept pace. They skirted around the car. It was spewing out enough heat to be worrying. Charley didn't want to know, but still found himself looking. There wasn't a dead body in any of the seats. Not that he could see anyway.

They reached the front door. Dereck pushed open the door—but his luck was the same as in the motel. It shifted enough that it might not have been a lock, but something was preventing him from opening it. He pushed once more, then stepped back.

"Get out of the way," he instructed.

Charley took a second to realize what he was doing. Then he leaped backward.

The bang of Dereck's foot hitting the door made Charley wince. Chunks of wood broke free and scattered across the ground. There was the distinct sound of something metal shifting on the other side.

"I think they blocked it with a chair," Dereck said.

Maybe we were safer in that motel room than I thought, Charley thought.

"Okay, what do we do?"

"Try harder," Dereck said solemnly.

Dereck rammed the door with his shoulder. That did it. Whatever was blocking it clattered across the ground. Dereck stumbled backward, clutching his arm. He let out a faint swear.

"Are you okay?" Charley asked.

"Yeah—that hurt. But I didn't break anything." He pushed on the partially broken door. It swung open without having to turn the doorknob. "And it was worth it."

As soon as it was open, Charley could see that a wheelchair had probably been wedged underneath the handle. It wasn't the only one pushed in the way. There was a mass of them, as well as plastic and metal chairs, and even two or three rolling beds. It was all layered awkwardly, like someone had thought of it in a hurry, but it was enough for it to be a barrier. The metal could easily interlock. They couldn't brute force through it without having to move almost all of it.

Dereck worked that out faster. He started picking his way across, taking careful steps. Charley followed suit, trying not to fall over and bang his head on something.

"What the fuck happened?" Charley said quietly. "Was there a battle here?"

"I don't know." Dereck stepped past a gnarled mass of metal chairs. "But this doesn't seem like a good sign."

"Yeah…" Charley said.

Dad, I hope you're okay. You need to be okay.

"Fuck—there's glass, careful," Dereck whispered.

Charley stopped. He'd almost stepped in it. Some of it looked like white powder, but in the lower light, it was almost impossible to see all of it. There were big clusters, and in some of the piles were the metal parts of lightbulbs.

"Jesus…" Charley muttered.

As odd as it was to think, this moment felt the most apocalyptic yet to Charley. They'd seen roads clogged with cars, some with people in those cars he wasn't sure were alive, and so many abandoned locations. Emptied people, too, unable to care about what was happening to them. But this was something out of a movie. Impromptu traps. Signs of struggle.

Dereck took a calming breath. "We should've gotten the bat."

"Yeah, we should have."

"Do you want to go back and get the bat?"

"What, by myself?"

"No—no, I'd go with you. But I think we need a weapon."

Charley nodded slowly. "Okay, yeah. We know our way across now. We'll go back, and maybe find something else … so we both have a weapon. Yeah, okay…"

Charley turned to go back, trying to recall the best way to pass a triangle of rolling beds. He was considering just crawling overtop them when he heard a new sound. He spun toward its source: a pair of footsteps from around a corner, just beyond the mess.

Every hair on Charley's neck stood up on end. His pulse shot into his temple and jolted down his fingers.

Then an older woman wearing a pastel nighty walked around the corner. Her hair was completely white and very curly. Her eyes were light, almost silvery, blue, and were surrounded by the kind of laugh lines you only get from a life well spent. She had pale white skin and a few flower tattoos on her arms.

She put her hands on her hips.

"I hope you don't think you're sneaking in here."

"Uh…" was all Charley managed to say.

Dereck slightly stepped in front of Charley.

The woman narrowed her eyes, then blinked a few times. A smile grew over her face.

"Oh, are you Bobby's kid?"

"Yes—yes, I am," Charley said quickly.

"Oh, well, look at that. We've been waiting forever for you."

"I… he didn't answer his phone. We didn't know what was happening…?"

The woman clicked her tongue. "Oh, yes, that. We lost a cell tower around here, I bet, or they stopped working on it. I bet infrastructure isn't big on their to-do list right now."

Dereck cleared his throat. "Um, ma'am—"

"Oh please, none of that. My name's Charlotte. You can call me Lotty, that's my favorite name. You can also call me Char, Cherry, Cheery. Any of that, but not 'ma'am.' Swear at me, call me names, yell at me before you call me 'ma'am.'"

"Okay … Lotty," Dereck continued, "why is there an obstacle course here? You put glass on the ground."

"Oh, that was a friend of mine's idea. You just go that way." She pointed out a path. "And you'll avoid all of that. We had to make it so we could get in and out if we needed to."

Charley moved past a cluster of wheelchairs and found that there was indeed a gentle, winding path. He had no idea if he would've noticed it.

"Where is it?" Dereck asked.

"Over here, Dereck," Charley said.

"Just hop over that table, honey, then go around a bit," Lotty said, "and you'll be on the same path."

Dereck swung his legs over the side of a table, slid across, and then landed. After walking around two clusters of chairs, he was on the same path as Charley. Charley gave him an awkward shrug. With the path, it took only a matter of moments to make it to open floor space.

"See, that wasn't so bad," Lotty said.

"Yeah, but why was it even *here*?" Dereck asked.

Lotty sighed. "We've been having some trouble. It was the best we figured out. We didn't have a lot of time—and we were in a lot of danger, honestly."

"What happened?" Charley asked.

"I… it's a lot to explain."

"Please just tell us," Dereck said quieter.

She sighed. "I will explain as we walk. There's a lot going on. But follow me. It's a bit of a walk and your dad has been waiting to see you for a while."

"Um, sorry," Charley said.

"Oh, I'm sure you did your best. I know it's a mess out there. But I don't want to keep him waiting any longer."

"Okay, sure…"

Lotty nodded, then glanced at Dereck. "Oh, but who's your friend? I knew you were on your way, but he didn't mention a second."

"I'm his boyfriend," Dereck said.

Despite the weirdness of the situation, Charley felt a warmth in his chest. It sounded so nice each and every time.

"Yeah, my boyfriend."

"Well, damn, don't you make a cute couple?" Lotty said with a smile. "I'm sure he'd love to meet you too then. Now let's go, let's go, we're wasting time. I'll be honest with you; I don't like standing too close to the doors, either. They almost got a car in here, you know."

She turned, and without waiting, walked around the corner.

"Is this a good idea?" Dereck whispered. "Are we sure we can trust her?"

"I mean … I think I recognize her, actually. Vaguely, anyway. And we need to make sure my dad is okay."

"Okay, good point," Dereck said. "But if we need to run—"

"I will give you a sign."

"What's the sign?" Dereck asked.

"I tell you to run."

Despite everything, Dereck chuckled. "Good plan."

They both followed after Lotty.

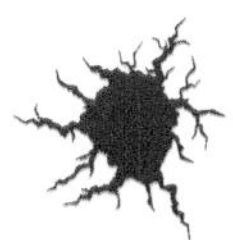

The assisted living facility was in an *interesting* state of affairs. Every outward-facing window had been blocked by a barrier or totally covered, leaving only an enclosed outdoor walking path in the middle of the building as a natural light source.

The inside, though, was still laid out like it had been when Charley dropped his dad off. Comfy old-fashioned chairs with tan coverings. A carpet with a minimalist design of little corn stalks waving in some abstract sun's rays. A fireplace, not currently, or perhaps ever, lit, with a nice brickwork stretching to the ceiling. It was like a hotel met a corporate office met a nineth century writer's study.

It also smelled like someone was baking bread. Charley could feel his mouth watering.

Lotty didn't speak for a few moments but then cleared her throat.

"Sorry if I scared you," she said. "People have been trying to break in."

"Who's trying to get in?" Dereck asked.

"Well, lots of people, actually. I'm not always sure what they want. Sometimes it's money, sometimes it's food. We gave away what we could, but we can't all starve in here—and there's no new food arriving anymore."

Charley nodded along. He and Dereck hadn't encountered anyone violent yet, but he'd been on guard for it from basically the word go.

"It's mostly been easy enough to get them to leave. We outnumber them. But then they did the thing with the car…"

"Yeah … what happened there?" Charley asked.

"We'd set up that barrier, and it was doing well enough to keep people out," Lotty explained, "but I guess someone figured they could just break down the wall. No one saw what exactly they did, but we could hear it. The crash and yelling. When one of us checked, they were already down the road, running away."

"That sucks," Dereck said.

"Yeah, it does," Lotty said. "But we're doing okay."

Charley knew that it was bad everywhere. He really did. But somehow each new thing about the apocalypse that he learned sunk in his chest, weighed down on his heart. It was one thing to see it in movies; it was another to be there for each part of it—

"What the hell!" Dereck said loudly.

Charley broke from his thoughts with a jolt. His eyes went wide as he noticed what had startled his boyfriend.

Where the fuck did they come from?

Lotty glanced back at them. "Oh, sorry, should've warned about that."

There was nothing inherently surprising about a group of around thirty people standing in a cafeteria area, not under normal circumstances. But it was when they were all completely silent. Not even a library or airport could manage this level of quiet.

But there they were. Standing, sitting, or very softly milling about. Almost all of them were assisted living caregivers still wearing uniforms, though a few of them seemed to be from other places. Big box store uniforms covered in branding, restaurant waitstaff with aprons and dress pants, and even a mailperson. A few of them looked at Charley, but there wasn't any care in those eyes.

"Emptied people," Charley said.

"We've been calling them 'tired,'" Lotty commented. "When … whatever happened…"

"We have no idea what it is either," Dereck supplied.

"I figured, but worth a try to ask. Oh well. So, whatever happened, when it happened, a lot—and I do mean a *lot*—of the people working here got affected by it. Basically, all of the caregivers here. It seems more likely to hit people with certain types of jobs. Nurses. Service workers. Delivery people."

"We both worked at a convenience store," Charley said.

"Then I think you got lucky. Tired people can *easily* get hit by cars. It's just unsafe. It's another reason we're trying to deter people. These tired people already need what help we can give."

"That's good of you," Dereck said quietly.

"Thank you," she said. "We're doing what we can."

Charley frowned to himself. He was lucky. Dereck was lucky. They could've been … affected. Unable to care about what was happening. And then, as he thought about it more, a surge of guilt hit his stomach. He'd seen more than a hundred people affected on the road and hadn't done much to help any of them. Not that he knew *how* to help them, or how to undo what was done to them. But it could have just as easily been him in the same situation.

I had no choice, Charley thought. *I need to get to my dad. I need to make sure Cassy is okay.*

"Hey, you okay?" Dereck asked.

"I … god I'm scared."

"I know what you mean. Do you want me to hold your hand?"

"Please…"

"Good … good … I wanted to hold yours."

Dereck took his hand. His fingers were strong.

"Your dad's just a little this way," Lotty said after a moment. "I'm really sure that he's going to be so very happy to see you."

Charley nodded, and despite it feeling like his legs might give out underneath him, he walked. They passed the silent, too-still, emptied people, and went around another corner. Lotty opened a thin door into a hallway. It was full of doors, and gentle music drifted from one of the rooms.

"There are a few independent buildings," Lotty explained, "But this is where a lot of us are staying—it's better if we're all close."

From down the hallway, the music abruptly stopped with a shrill note.

"Dammit," someone said.

"It'll tune eventually," Lotty called out.

"I hope so," replied a thick Chicagoan accent. "But this has not been cared for. Whoever owned it probably used it as a doorstopper."

"Not a very good one," she said.

Lotty gestured for them to follow her. The music continued. They stopped in front of an open doorway. Sitting on a bed was an older man with a white beard, a full head of white hair, brown eyes, and medium brown skin. He was holding a guitar with a ton of damage around its edges and what looked like knife marks underneath the string.

"Hello, Kami," Lotty said. "Look who I found."

"Oh, is this the kid?" he asked.

"Yep," Lotty said.

"About time." He turned to Charley. "You kept him waiting."

"Sorry," Charley said. "There was … a bit of an apocalypse happening out there."

Kami nodded and smiled. "Just teasing you. Glad you made it. It is quite a thing out there, isn't it?"

"Sounds like you've got some shit here," Dereck said.

"Ah, yeah." He ran his fingers along the strings, eliciting a soft note. "It's not been the best week. But we've been doing what we can. Helping who we can—that's really all there is to do."

Charley could hear it in his voice and see it in his eyes: he had *every* idea of what he was talking about.

"Honestly, I'm amazed it took this long for the world to end," Lotty said. "With all the politicians doing what they've been doing, it was bound to happen somehow."

"Yeah, but this is an act of God … or something," Kami said.

"I wonder which one," Lotty replied.

"Not a nice one."

"Amen," Dereck chimed in.

Charley glanced at them all. "I'm sorry—but can I go see my dad now?"

"Oh, sorry, look at me chatting," Lotty said. "When I come back, can you play me a song, Kami?"

Kami teased out a few notes that Charley recognized as a rock song from the 80s. The kind that took seemingly over a minute to build to the part that everyone knew.

"Can do. I think I've almost got this tuned."

"Sounds good to me," Lotty said. "Be back in a minute."

She stepped back into the hallway and pointed at the door at the end. Then quickly walked over. She rapped the back of her knuckles against it twice.

"Hey Bobby boy, you decent?" she said loudly. "Because someone *special* is here to see you?"

"Yeah, yeah, I am Charlotte. But who's here?"

"Give you one guess," she said, and then immediately opened the door.

Charley stepped through the doorway, then stopped. A new, different surge of emotion hit him. Tears sprang to his eyes.

His dad looked like he had before, if a little thinner, a little more tired, than last time. They'd always looked similar. He could see parts of his own reflection. Same brown hair, same brown eyes, same pale while skin. His dad was sitting in a wheelchair, playing solitaire at a little table.

He looked back at Charley. The playing cards gently fell out of his hand.

"Hi Dad," Charley said. "I made it."

"Oh, my god."

Charley rushed forward, leaned down, and gave his dad the best hug he could possibly manage. The returning hug was like he remembered. Like he'd missed for longer than he'd realized.

"I love you, dad."

"I love you too, Charley,"

Charley eventually pulled back, his eyes blurry with tears. He wiped them with the back of his arm and tried to catch his breath.

"You made it," his dad said. "What's it like out there?"

Despite everything, Charley had the sudden impulse to downplay it. To not reveal how bad it was. He didn't want to worry his father. But the situation was well beyond trying to downplay things.

Charley's voice cracked as he spoke.

"I was really fucking scared. It's—man, it's an *apocalypse* out there. Like movies. Like a video game. I can't believe it. The streets are clogged with people who won't move their cars. Everything's being abandoned. We had to break into a motel, and, and…"

His dad pulled Charley back into another hug.

"It's okay. We'll find a way. We'll find a way."

"I'm sorry it took so long. I was so worried about you," Charley said, unable to keep a quiver out of his voice. "When we called … your phone didn't … I was so worried that something had happened."

"I'm okay," he replied. "I don't know why my phone stopped working. It just stopped all of a sudden."

"Did you hear anything about Cassy?" Charley asked.

His dad shook his head. "Nothing. I couldn't get through to her still."

"Okay, well, we're going there next."

Behind Charley, Dereck cleared his throat.

Charley glanced back, and Dereck was awkwardly standing just inside the doorway. Lotty had disappeared at some point—probably for a serenade from Kami.

"Uh, hi," Dereck said with an awkward wave.

Charley took a step back and gestured out his arm. "Dad, um, I would like you to meet my boyfriend."

"It's an honor to meet you, sir," Dereck said.

Bob rolled his wheelchair forward and stuck out his hand. "I've been wanting to meet you for a long time."

The two of them shook hands. Charley couldn't keep the smile off his face. They'd made it to Indiana. Despite everything, they'd made it. One half of his family was okay. It felt just a little less impossible to find Cassy, to save her, to bring his family back together.

He couldn't help but feel like a small weight had been lifted from the middle of his back. Like a sore muscle had quietly gotten better—and was only really noticed now that the pain was already gone.

But a different part of his mind, the part that had dealt with difficulties and failures, was quietly gearing up. The smallest unease grew in the back of his head.

And the sound started just down the hall.

"What more can you take from me!?"

Charley's smile fell.

"What the fuck?" Dereck said.

Charley glanced out the door, then took a step into the hallway. Others were doing the same.

"Oh no … please," Charley muttered.

The unease widened outward.

"What more can you take from me!?"

A different voice that time. Each one sounding distraught, pained, forced out. Then more than one voice chimed in, layering over one another.

"What more can you take from me!? What more can you take from me!? What more can you take from me!?"

Charley's pulse skyrocketed.

It had been too easy.

Lucky about not being emptied. Lucky on the roads. Managing not to get into any care wrecks. Managing not to get attacked. This was an *apocalypse*. Luck only got you so far.

"*What more can you take from me!?*"

Charley rushed back into the room. "We need to go. Something is happening—"

A shrill scream rang out.

He stopped talking. Dread spiraled out.

Too easy. Too easy. Too easy.

From multiple places—almost assuredly the *same* places—there was a hissing sound, like water hitting hot metal. Followed by the smell of burning wood.

"It's starting up again," Bob said, horror spreading across his face. "Something new."

Another scream. Then another. Then another. And then this whoosh.

The fire alarm started blaring, and above them the sprinklers clicked. Charley had a second to close his eyes before foul-smelling buckets of stagnant water poured down on his head.

"Fire!" someone shouted. "They're on fire!"

Charley didn't need clarification. He knew in his gut what was happening. The emptied people, the 'tired' people, they'd been such a strange phenomenon. But it simply hadn't been enough time yet. The formation had appeared, days had passed, and now the windup was done. Hundreds of thousands, maybe millions of people were affected by this.

And now they would burn.

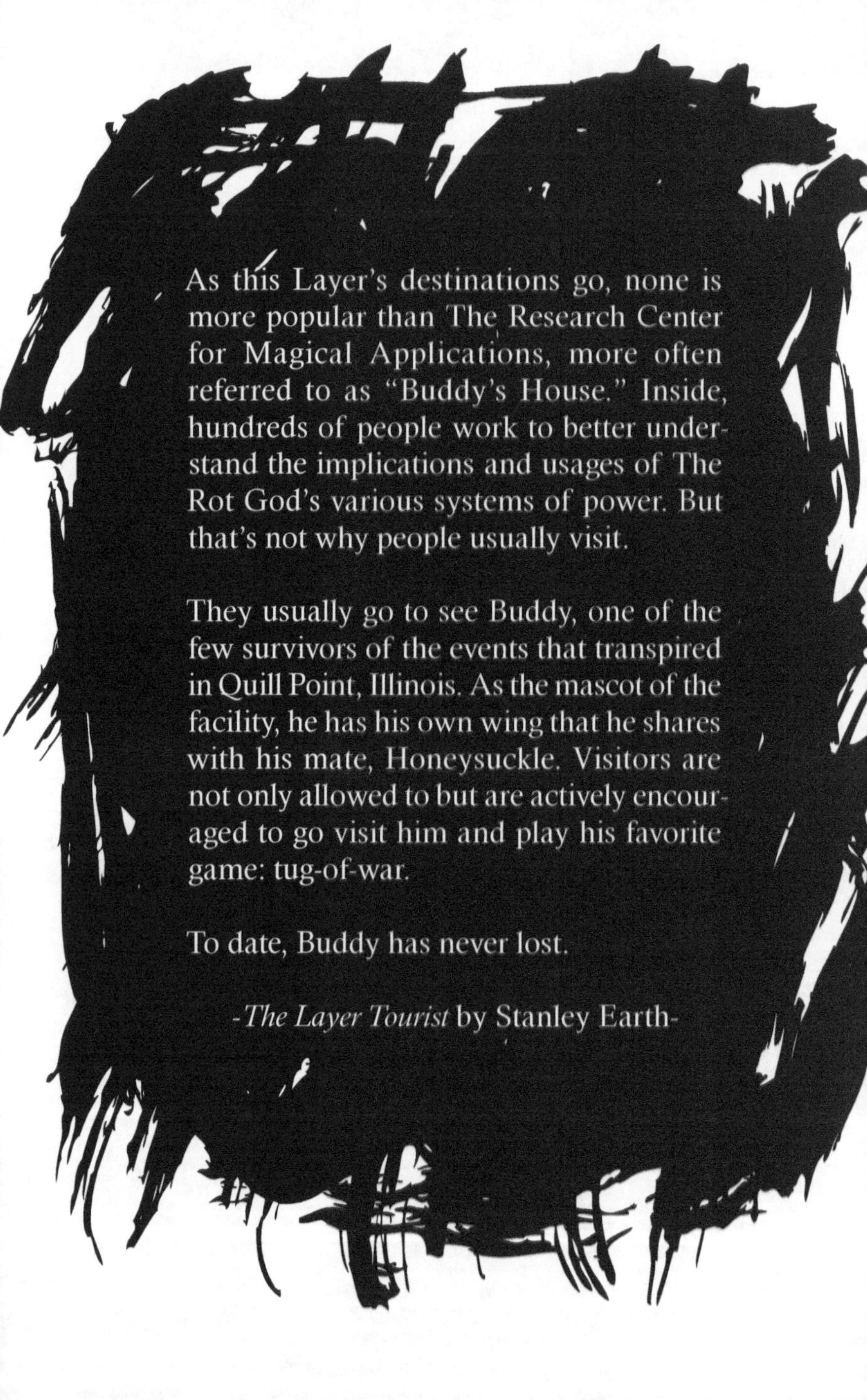

As this Layer's destinations go, none is more popular than The Research Center for Magical Applications, more often referred to as "Buddy's House." Inside, hundreds of people work to better understand the implications and usages of The Rot God's various systems of power. But that's not why people usually visit.

They usually go to see Buddy, one of the few survivors of the events that transpired in Quill Point, Illinois. As the mascot of the facility, he has his own wing that he shares with his mate, Honeysuckle. Visitors are not only allowed to but are actively encouraged to go visit him and play his favorite game: tug-of-war.

To date, Buddy has never lost.

-*The Layer Tourist* by Stanley Earth-

Interlude Two

The Exploits of Buddy the Dog

BUDDY DIDN'T LIKE TO THINK ABOUT THE time before he was adopted by his human, Xander, and his sometimes humans: Saanvi and Henry. Those were bad days. Kennel days. Shoved into too small a place by people who weren't friendly. He would make sounds to tell them, please, let me do anything else, but they didn't listen to him.

And then Xander walked into his life—literally. That scraggly man, with his long brown hair on his head and spotty beard that Buddy licked so many times during their time together, walked past his cage and leaned down, and Buddy looked at him, and beamed all the love he could manage—and he could manage a *lot*—and Xander smiled, and talked to another human who usually ignored him.

And then, a few hours later, Buddy was in the back of a car, in a smaller cage, but he almost didn't mind. He was with someone new, and someone new meant a better life.

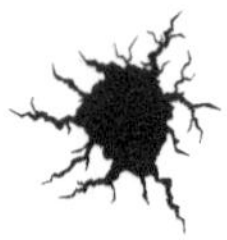

Buddy took a little longer to get used to his new house than he thought he would. Xander had an interesting set of habits. He liked sleeping long after Buddy woke up, and that always confused Buddy. It was light. Light was for fun. Why did Xander like to sleep so long when it was that joyous, sun-bright time?

Sometimes, when Xander slept too long, he would rush up to Xander and lick his face until he also agreed that the sun signaled a good day for doing things. Then Xander would make interesting human sounds, sit up in bed, pull a shirt over his pale white skin, and walk past him into the kitchen.

This, Buddy learned, meant that Xander needed a drink. A little brown drink called coffee, served in a bone white glass, that he made with a coffee machine that whirred. Xander always seemed happier after he had a drink from that machine.

After his wake-up drink, Xander would lean down to scratch between Buddy's ears.

"I love you, Xander," Buddy always said. "Thank you for everything! I love you!"

Then Xander would stretch his arms above his head. His hair would always fall in his face. And then he'd blow them out of the way with his mouth—which was always amusing to Buddy.

When he lowered his arms, Xander would usually say, "It's time to go outside."

Buddy would let out a little bark, happy for the news. "Thank you! That's sounds fun!" he would say.

And then Xander would walk over and get that long leash and clip it to Buddy's collar. Buddy always wondered why he did that. Buddy would never run away from Xander. Not ever. But it was a silly human thing. They sometimes did stuff like that. Maybe, one day, Buddy would figure out a way to tell Xander that he was okay to not attach the leash. That Buddy was a good dog and would walk right alongside him. In the meantime, the leash meant outside.

And wow, did Buddy like outside.

Whatever being made the world, wow, did they do a good job with the whole outside thing.

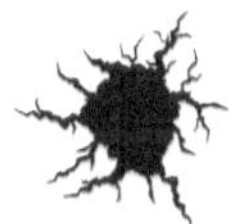

Xander had someone he wanted to be his mate. Buddy could tell. Humans did all these little actions that made it clear when they were attracted to another human.

Her name was Taylor. Taylor had blond hair, brown eyes, and suntanned white skin. She liked to wear hats with little pictures on them.

Taylor had a dog too, named Honeysuckle, and they met both of them often during walks. Honeysuckle was a blond, lanky dog, a little taller than Buddy.

Buddy liked Taylor. He approved of Xander's choice.

"Tell her she's amazing!" Buddy would sometimes instruct Xander when he met Taylor at the dog park. "That'll work! You're both amazing."

But Xander never seemed to say that to Taylor. He would stand and talk to her about other things and move his human arms too much and excitedly, but he would never say, "I love you," or "I appreciate you."

Sometimes, when Buddy really felt like this extended courtship was taking too long, he would look up at Taylor and tell her things.

"Look at his hair!" he might say. "He has such a nice coat! You should be with Xander!"

Honeysuckle would sometimes get in on the project, barking out her own praise for her human, but the two humans would almost always end up stopping talking if they barked too long. It was confusing.

"I've been telling her she should just tell him, but she never listens to me," Honeysuckle told Buddy one time. "She wants to be his mate too, but she's kind of nervous sometimes."

"Xander is too. It's very silly. Can't they tell?"

"They can't," Honeysuckle lamented. "I think they would be much happier if they could do what we do. But, oh well. Humans are still wonderful."

Buddy wagged his tail, happy that another dog agreed with him on this crucial point. "They are! Well, some are. Xander is wonderful."

"If they were mates, we would get to live together," Honeysuckle continued. "What would we play if we lived together?"

"Oh! I don't know … we could…"

And then Buddy would wag his tail even harder as he thought aloud of all the fun things they could do with another dog living in the house. Games like run fast in various directions. Games like bite stuff to see what it felt like to bite something. Maybe they could smell lots of things in quick succession and find whatever smelled the best of the best. The games were endless!

Honeysuckle wagged her tail too, as Buddy talked about it.

Honeysuckle wasn't the only dog Buddy got to talk to. There was Pud, Roller, Fire-Bark, and more dogs that walked and played when Xander took him outside.

Sometimes they didn't go to the park though. They would also go along the sidewalk, by restaurants, and around yards, and Buddy never failed to see things that made him so happy that the world was more than a cage.

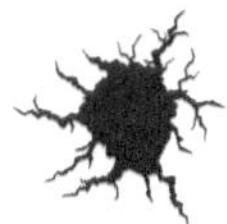

Of all the human oddities, Xander's job was the thing Buddy least understood. Jobs were these long games that humans would play.

Xander's job involved him going to this one chair, in front of this one little computer—a device that, as far as Buddy could discern, was mostly for talking to humans when those humans weren't there. A fact that made it all the odder to Buddy was that Xander hadn't yet gotten Taylor to be his mate yet.

But the computer could do a few other things. Xander's job seemed to be to write human words. Lots and lots of human words. Buddy assumed someone else would then read them. Xander did this by moving his fingers really, really fast across a lot of little human symbols, and then those human symbols would appear on the computer. And then, sometimes, he would make them all paper— and the paper would smell weird for a while, like a very little fire. One time Buddy barked at the paper, in case it *was* fire, but then Xander told him it was okay, and that was enough for Buddy.

Despite not fully understanding what was happening, it was nice to see how happy Xander was because of his job. Because a happy Xander was better than anything else in the world.

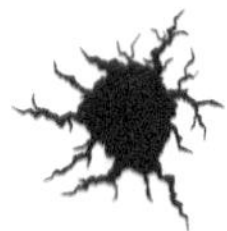

Sometimes, though—Buddy was never quite sure why exactly—Xander would radiate unhappiness. Dogs like Buddy, maybe all dogs—but he couldn't check—were able to sense when their human, when their Xander, was sad. Unhappiness. Sadness. Worry. It radiated in a way that Buddy could sense across the whole house. Xander's nightmares were quieter, the hurried rush of his heart, but when he was sitting on his couch, staring at the television, it was obvious.

And if a dog, if anyone on this Earth, really, could be said to have a purpose, then this was Buddy's: to cheer up his human, and to continue to cheer up his human, and to be a companion that doesn't judge in the slightest.

It was a dark, rainy day when it got to be the worst it had been in a long time. A day where Xander hadn't even taken Buddy for a walk. The smell of sadness saturated the house. It was like the rain, but more staticky, like the house had been covered in an irritating dandelion fluff.

It was so enveloping, in fact, that Buddy crept up to Xander instead of doing his more usual barreling run that made his little pink tongue flap out. He walked slowly with the slight click of his nails against the tile.

Behind Xander, the lightning hit something, some-where, and a crackle of thunder slashed out so loudly that Buddy almost skirted under the nearest object. Thunder was *horrible*—so horrible that it was almost hard for Buddy to parse. He could hear it rip down the world, tear at the universe's wallpaper, and slap at the drum skin of the sky.

But that sadness from Xander was still there, still coag-ulating around his head. Another lightning bolt flashed, and Buddy steadied himself as the thunder arrived. The destroying sounds were a distraction.

There were important things to do.

Xander's face was illuminated by the television, but the television was on so quiet that Buddy wondered if human ears could even hear it. Buddy could hear it, as a man talked slowly and kept pointing at a line that rose up. Buddy wondered what sort of line could be a bad thing.

He walked closer, keeping his ears tight to his head. The thunder could happen again and hurt again, and that was a terrible threat. Buddy wasn't allowed to get on the couch with Xander most of the time, but this was an exception, surely. Xander would understand that. Or would allow it if it meant sadness could stop.

Buddy was a short little dog, and it took him two tries to hook his front paws enough to pull himself up. Xander didn't look at him as he did this, so it was clearly an advanced case of sadness.

The man on the screen kept pointing at the arrows, the red arrows, and his face was both impassive and vaguely haunted. He looked young, as humans go, with brown hair, a strong posture, and a blue suit that fit him well. But his pale white skin, especially around the eyes, that's where the ghosts were. He moved tired; spoke tired, too.

Buddy hoped the man on the television also had a dog that would be there for him when he got home.

Xander finally noticed Buddy.

"Oh, hey Buddy," he said.

"You are sad, and I am here," Buddy said in a soft whimper.

"Hey, Buddy, how are you?"

He reached out and ran his fingers through Buddy's blond fur, but after a second, seemed to get too tired to continue, and his hand went a little loose and unmoving.

"You are *sad,* and I am *here*," Buddy said.

"I'm not really up for playing today," Xander said. "I can't—you got to eat, right?"

"Yes, I ate food. But that's not important right now. You are sad. And I am here."

"Yeah, I filled your bowl, I remember. I need … I need some time, Buddy. I'm sorry."

That had felt a little like a command, and Buddy usually followed those. Buddy stared at Xander for a moment, pondering this, before finding his conclusion. This superseded commands. He wasn't going anywhere. How, on Earth, could Buddy abandon his human like that?

Instead of doing such a silly human thing as letting him sit there, sad, he moved forward and crawled onto his lap. Xander fidgeted a little, looking down at him with a look of confusion and maybe even anger, but it faded from his face fast.

"I am here," Buddy said and then arched up his head for more pats.

But the pats were not for him. He would enjoy them, but that was not their purpose.

Xander made a noise like he didn't want to do that, but it was a losing battle. Buddy looked at him with his dog eyes and pushed on his hand with his cold, wet nose. There was never a chance in any universe that Xander was not going to pet him. It was an unfair trick, but Buddy only used it if he had to.

Xander relented. He ran his fingers through Buddy's fur again. Occasionally, Buddy would lick his fingers or shove his head into his palm.

This was all a simple message in dog language.

It meant *you are not alone.*

And the air took on a different element. The dandelion sadness puffs turned icy and fragile. Some fell and shattered into little pieces of crystals and then faded to nothing at all.

Buddy couldn't get them all, couldn't undo all the sadness, and couldn't save Xander from that underlying cold, but it was enough, in his opinion, to lessen the pain.

And, as those crystals shattered, so then arrived Xander's tears. Better they were on his face than in his heart. Xander kept petting Buddy's head and tears flowed down his cheeks.

Buddy had a theory. It was untested, unorthodox. But those tears were a part of sadness, and Buddy could gladly, absolutely gladly, take some of that sadness from Xander.

Buddy moved forward and leaned his front paws on Xander's chest. He started to lick at the tears. It didn't matter that Xander instantly started to cover his face with his hands and complain—Xander wasn't aware of how important Buddy's work was.

Xander did chuckle though.

He held up his hands and he let out little laughs. Pleasant laughs that were dancing wind chimes in the air. Buddy let out a dog's smile: he let out a little bark and wagged his tail.

"I love you, Xander," Buddy said again.

Xander cried and laughed in equal measure, and eventually picked up Buddy and put him back on his lap.

"I love you, little guy," Xander said.

"I love you, Xander!"

"The storm is so scary, huh?" he asked. "You can probably hear that thunder from miles away."

"It's not as scary as seeing you sad," Buddy said bravely.

Xander let out a long breath. "There's a lot of scary stuff lately, out here in our human world. God, it's so much."

"I know—but I'm here to help."

"It's just these prices, I guess. I have no idea how I am ever going to afford stuff."

Buddy didn't know quite what that meant, but he knew now was the time to let Xander talk.

"I only have so much left before the loans run out—and I don't know how many books I can even sell. It's a hard world out there. Look at this…"

He gestured with his free, non-petting hand to the screen.

"Up fifty percent. *Fifty percent*. That's fucking absurd. My grandmother got her rent for, like, three hundred a month or something, and even my parents could afford a whole house on one salary. *One salary*. I can't conceive of it. And I don't even want all of that. I'm not trying to get a picket fence and two cars here. I just want a space that's mine, that's mine and yours, Buddy. I want to eat food that I like, and I want to not have to be so stressed all the time."

"I am here."

"You don't have to deal with money. I'm jealous of you sometimes, Buddy. A world of sunshine, right? Is that what you see every morning, little guy?"

"I see you. And I love you. That's good enough for me."

Xander leaned back on the couch. If dogs had a secondary special sense, it was how a human was doing physically. And Xander was really tired. Perhaps tired from things that weren't physical, but Buddy understood that the physical body was often at the whims of emotions. Happiness is energy.

"I've got these books in mind. Like fifty, some days. But a few that I think are really good books. Really good stories. At least … I hope that they'll be good stories. But I also hope that they sell well."

He stared at the screen, and anger flashed through the air. Anger was claustrophobic. It was heartbeats without comfort. Buddy knew that the anger would pass though.

"I need them to sell well. I need them to," Xander said. "This horribleness—these housing prices, it's got to go down. Rent needs to be … better. I don't care what economists say, rent control the fuck out of it. I need all of this to be better, or to burn down into fucking ash. I was lucky enough to get the first loan … and it's going to run out before my career even *starts*."

Xander stared at the ceiling for a long moment.

"I *need* to win. If I can't win at this, then why was I given these stories?"

Buddy could hear Xander's heartbeat. It was loud, but it was focused. It was almost what Buddy wanted.

Xander chuckled bitterly, but it was also tinged with an honest chuckle. A sense of relief that was like a cool outdoor breeze brought into a stuffy house.

"I guess there's no choice … I guess…"

Xander moved to stand, and Buddy shifted off of him and then hopped off the couch. He wasn't going to push his luck on getting to sit on the furniture.

"I guess I should stop watching this depressing shit and get to writing, huh?"

Buddy let out a string of barks.

"I am here for all that you need, and I am here when you are sad, and I am here when you are happy, and I love you Xander and I love you Xander and I love you Xander and I am *here*."

"Now that's a pep talk, huh," Xander said and smiled down at Buddy. "For such a little dog, you sure do have a lot of energy."

"I am here."

Xander smiled again and walked over to his laptop and turned it on.

Buddy, with his mission accomplished, moved out of the room. Xander needed time to focus, and now Buddy was a little tired. If the thunder would let him, if it would stop shuddering the world, he would get some sleep while he couldn't go for a walk outside.

One day, to Buddy's absolute surprise, a familiar smell was with Xander by the door. Xander, in between the new pattern of him writing his symbols in little bursts, being sad for long chunks of time, and then being convinced by a hardworking Buddy to write some more, had been disappearing for a few hours around dinner time. Buddy wasn't sure what that was about—Xander didn't have much else to do except walk or play with Buddy—but he finally got his answer.

The smell got even closer to the door and then Buddy could hear keys, and then he fully understood what was happening.

As he had many times before, Buddy sprinted to the door. He set his paws on the wood and gave it a few good scratches. Then it popped open, and Xander's face looked down at him.

"Whoa there, Buddy. I need to move the door."

Buddy jumped backward and gave an excited bark. "Your mate! Your mate! You got her as a mate?"

"Sorry about that. He's always so excited to see me," Xander said.

"Oh, it's alright. Honeysuckle's the same," Taylor said.

"Can't help but love the little guy for always being happy to see me."

The door opened the rest of the way, and Taylor stepped into the room. She was wearing a different outfit than the type he usually saw her wearing. It was black. It was less covering, more skin showing. Her knees, legs, and shoulders exposed. Humans got cold so easily—Buddy hoped that her being cold wouldn't interfere with Xander doing whatever mating ritual was happening.

"Make Xander happy," Buddy instructed, hoping he didn't sound too aggressive. He didn't want to scare her, but he was also very firm about this. "Xander deserves happiness."

"Hey there, Buddy," she said, moving to sit down on the coach. Then she reached out her hand. "It's nice to see you. You have a very nice home."

Buddy agreed with that. He went forward and licked her hand. It was only polite to greet her with one of the more assuring options. If Taylor was *finally* going to be Xander's mate, maybe even live here, he also needed to be on his best behavior.

"You are so cute," she said to Buddy.

"Do you want that coffee?" Xander asked.

Taylor looked over at him and gave him a small smile. "Sure, what do you have?"

"Oh, I have so many interesting coffees."

"Then make me the best one you have."

"That I can do," Xander said and disappeared into the kitchen.

Buddy wasn't sure about the rules for human mating rituals, but he guessed that Xander was doing it correctly. Getting Taylor a drink must be part of it.

"How are you, little guy?" she asked Buddy. "It really is nice to see you."

Buddy wagged his tail. "It's nice to see you too."

She smiled. It seemed aimed both at Buddy, but also at Xander—even if he wasn't in the room. A smile so big, the emotion behind it spilled into the air.

Human happiness was a sunflower's color. It somehow mixed with the light in a room but didn't change it. It fizzed and popped. Like how a dog dances—in leaps and hops and smiles.

"I really like your owner," Taylor confided in Buddy, with a whisper. "I think I really like him a lot."

Buddy nodded and made a small noise that was like a bark, but gentler. "He's Xander. That only makes sense."

"I think we might want some privacy though," she said.

Buddy wondered why. It seemed an odd idea for him to leave the room. He wasn't a human. Humans only seemed to want privacy from other humans. Xander talked about how he didn't want other people to see what he was writing when it wasn't done, but that rule never applied to Buddy.

But he supposed that was just how humans were.

Xander returned. He put down the slightly steaming coffee and sat on the couch.

Buddy waited a moment to see if Xander was going to give the same instruction, but he seemed to be rather focused on his mate. Buddy supposed that made sense—it was good to keep focus on your mate.

Buddy stayed a moment longer, just kind of looking at the couple and waiting for them to do more than just talk at a softer and softer pitch and lean closer and closer to each other. More and more like stars orbiting the world. The bright shiny energy of the room was getting fuzzier. Like the air was getting its own soft fur.

Buddy eventually gave his tail a wag and then walked out of the room. Taylor had asked for privacy, and it did not strike him as a difficult request to fulfill.

He walked into his and Xander's room and went to his tiny horseshoe-shaped bed in the corner. Xander had gotten him, in the first week of their being together, a little stuffed toy. It looked like a different kind of dog than Buddy. Buddy wasn't sure why Xander thought he would want a stuffed version of a dog when he could instead hang out with a real dog—but it was nice to chew. It was fun when he played tug-of-war with it.

Buddy circled the bed three times—no more, no less—and then lay down, tucking his tail against his body as best he could. But then sounds made his ears flick around. They were making sounds in the other room. Mostly odd little sounds. Buddy had no idea what that could mean, but it happened for a while. And the ruffle of fabric, like when Xander made his bed.

A few minutes later, the two of them were in the room with Buddy. Taylor was somehow even less covered than she had been before. So was Xander. Xander was wearing about the same as when he went to sleep, only a pair of leg coverings that barely covered his legs, more just his hip area. And Taylor was wearing an odd pair of clothing. Both of them were black. One covered her chest, and the other was like Xander's covering, but somehow showed even more of her legs.

They were also pressing their mouths together—and that was what was making that weird sound. Well, the sound actually happened whenever their mouths stopped touching. They would pull apart, and then their mouths would touch again.

It was very odd.

Xander, his eyes a little less focused and yet *more* focused at the same time than Buddy could ever remember, happened to glance at Buddy. Buddy had raised his head to watch this strange, jerky series of motions the humans were involved in.

"Oh, sorry—I didn't know he was in here," Xander said.

"It's okay … is there somewhere he can go?" Taylor asked.

"Yeah, uh, he has stuff in the living room he can do."

Xander walked over to Buddy and very gently moved his foot against one of Buddy's paws.

"Hey, Buddy, I need you to not be in here. We're … uh … we need to have some privacy."

That was an easy request. Now both of them had asked for it, so it must've been somewhat important. Buddy started toward the door, unsure of why Xander seemed to need him to go so quickly though. He kept guiding Buddy with his foot as if Buddy didn't know already where he was supposed to go. It was all very silly.

As soon as Buddy was over the threshold, Xander shut the door.

Buddy turned around and looked at the door for a few moments. On the other side, there was more of that mouth-touching sound. And then someone getting into bed. Then a second person.

If Buddy had shoulders like a human, he would've shrugged. Instead, he simply went back to the living room, where he'd been in the first place. He found the chew toy that he'd been working on gnawing through.

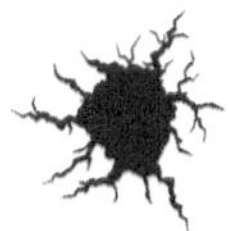

It was occasional, and then more and more, Xander brought Taylor home. Buddy got into his own routine with this, slowly learning the cues for when he needed to give them privacy. He and Honeysuckle got to hang out more and more and play the games they'd planned. They tried not to bark too much, but they weren't very good at that.

It was, admittedly, a little sad sometimes that Xander had less time to spend with Buddy though. But Buddy wanted Xander to be happy—and he seemed extremely happy. The air was often tinged with his smiles and would do that fun thing humans could do, where they could make their own complicated songs. They could produce tones and tunes that Buddy could hear in such wonderful layers.

And Xander would sing all sorts of songs, but the songs themselves always were about her. It was her, and her alone, in a thousand different configurations. Buddy wondered if a human could ever be as happy as a dog—and if this went on, perhaps he would see it firsthand.

One day, Xander went out to get the mail. And when he returned, he was ecstatic.

He had a letter and had already opened it. The inside wasn't some food or treat that Buddy might enjoy, but more human symbols. Buddy assumed those symbols meant good things.

"I got it," Xander said loudly. "They're going to … oh my god … they agreed to publish it!"

He looked around, a smile beaming on his face. His eyes fell on Buddy, and he dropped to his knees and beckoned with his hands.

Buddy ran forward at his command, tongue out and tail wagging.

Xander hugged Buddy. Buddy wagged his tail harder and harder.

"You're happy!" Buddy said. "You've been happy lately! That's so good!"

Xander let out a laugh. "I can't believe it happened. I can't believe it!"

"This is so very good!"

Xander let go of Buddy and walked over to the best cabinet in the whole house. The one where the treats were.

"We're celebrating! We're celebrating today!" Xander proclaimed. "Break out the wine and the confetti and the whole dang band. It's finally the day—it's *finally* the *day*!"

Buddy's vision zoomed in on the box as Xander pulled it out. It was just a simple cardboard box, but it contained all the tasty, delicious, treat food.

Xander pulled out not one, but *two* treats, and dropped back down to his knees. "Here, Buddy. Here's some payment for all the writing help. You're my motivational coach now—and you deserve a big prize!"

Buddy eagerly took the first of the treats and cracked it with his teeth. It was so nice to have a treat.

Xander placed the second one next to him. "You deserve it."

"You deserve to be happy all the time," Buddy barked back.

But Xander didn't seem to hear him. He was getting out his phone from his pocket and dialing someone. Buddy could hear her voice on the other end but didn't bother to listen to the two of them talk. He had a treat.

He had two whole freaking treats.

If Buddy had known that the good news from the letter would have taken Xander away from him sometimes, well … he still would've been very happy for Xander.

But he did miss him.

But he also liked the new people he got to be with whenever Xander was busy doing things with those books he wrote.

Their names were Henry and Saanvi.

Saanvi gave him food she made sometimes, and very often liked to hold him and give him pets on the top of his head. Saanvi radiated a type of happiness that was more mellow than Xander's new bubbly excitement but was also more sustained. It was to happiness that had learned to exist on its own.

Henry, somehow, radiated an even more calming energy. It was a level of satisfaction that bordered on innate. A life well-lived, a life well-spent.

Buddy felt a little nervous for maybe the first five minutes being around the couple without Xander, but it was clear very quickly that he had nothing to worry about.

And soon enough, he learned another thing he liked about them: they loved taking walks. They had hours to let him play with other dogs, to spend time asking Honeysuckle what Xander did when he was at her home and Buddy wasn't. Plenty of time to hear the latest stories of good food and fun smells. Henry and Saanvi, as far as Buddy could tell, were not working at all. They didn't spend long periods of time typing, reading, or making books. Sometimes they had other things to do. Saanvi might be busy cooking or Henry would be deeply engrossed in learning a card game on a video call with his nephew, but they were almost always willing to go out on good days. And even when they couldn't spend time on walks, Henry would often take Buddy for drives. Drives to places that smelled like coffee or food or dust or any combination of the three.

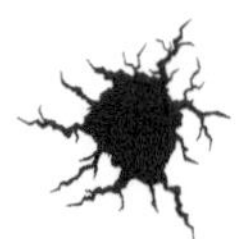

Buddy would never call himself a creature of habit, but days fell into easy patterns. Xander would return, would give Buddy a big scooping hug, and then would spend a lot of time napping and resting and watching television in between more writing. Buddy wasn't sure what Xander did on his many trips, but it did seem to tucker him out.

It was okay though, because even when Xander was too tired to play, he would sometimes call Henry—and Henry would take him on yet more rides and trips. They'd go meet people around the town. Sometimes Buddy even got to go to other people's houses and smell entirely *new* houses! And then, after such an exciting day, he'd still get to spend a few hours with Xander.

The next usual step was, after Xander had a little more energy, Taylor would show up—bringing Honeysuckle with her, and both would stay over for days at a time. This was the best time. All four of them would play together.

But, within a few months of this pattern, the previous would happen again. Honeysuckle and Taylor would go back to their house, and Xander would drop off Buddy with Henry and Saanvi.

Soon enough, Buddy could easily see this being the rest of his life—and he would've been content with that.

Buddy should've sensed that something was about to go wrong. He should've seen how the air was different, how the world sounded different. Dogs are able to sense things more easily than humans. Supernatural things make noises, and dogs can often hear them. But Buddy had never heard a ghost's voice. Never perceived the paper-ripping sound of a Seer entering a Layer. He had no context for that faint background noise.

So he didn't notice the telltale sounds of a Rot God about to Isolate.

He was distracted by other things, more mundane things that happened in the meantime.

He noticed that Xander was sad. Buddy noticed that Taylor looked a little more on edge. They would talk in hushed whispers about someone that Buddy didn't know.

That sadness would float as icy crystals and shatter into cutting edges. Buddy could wag his tail and distract them—but it didn't stop whatever tragedy was creating such sad days and moods.

Buddy never did find out who died.

But it wasn't the last time Buddy would notice death. Though Buddy himself would survive the horrors that had almost arrived, he would still see horrors. More than a dog's heart should ever be subjected to. Not on this or any Layer.

But Murder Sky was almost here.

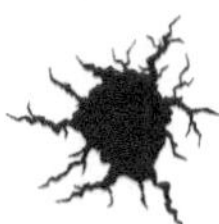

The day it happened, Buddy was out with Henry while Xander was recovering at home from another trip. Henry took him to a coffee shop. Buddy met a new person there.

New people had interesting smells.

They turned into the most interesting people in the world for the first few minutes of smelling them.

This new person's name was Albert Turner.

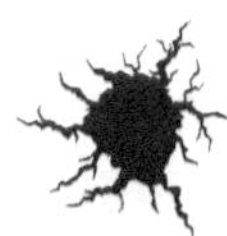

Buddy sat on Albert's lap almost as soon as he got in Henry's car. After smelling him a little more, Buddy licked at Albert's hands, hoping that would help calm him down. It was about all Buddy could do while the sky was making horrible, scary rumbling.

It didn't seem to calm Albert down for long though. He looked at the sky. That was enough to scare anyone.

They started driving. Henry and Albert talked about something that Buddy didn't quite understand. Something about something called a "weather station." But he could hear their panic, regardless.

Suddenly, something far off that Buddy could hear got louder: it forced a low growl out of him. Buddy was sorry that Albert got more stressed from that—but he had to growl now. There was a threat too close.

Everything seemed to speed up after that.

So, soon after starting to drive, Henry stopped the car again. And Albert moved Buddy away and got out of the car.

Buddy briefly worried about him.

But there were other things to worry about too.

Henry started to drive with more ferocity than he'd ever done before. Taking a few turns like he wanted to tip the world on its side. Buddy barked without any direct meaning, barked with overwhelming panic.

"I know, I know, I'm sorry, Buddy," Henry muttered. "I need to get home. I need to get to Saanvi."

The car snapped to a stop. A furious lurch. The world almost tilting. Buddy's whole body felt like it had been stretched out and then put back in its small dog form again.

In the front yard of her house, Saanvi was standing. She was staring at the sky with wide eyes that held nothing but fear.

Then Buddy also looked at the sky.

There might not have been a person in Quill Point, animal, human, who wasn't afraid of that sky.

Buddy's little heart thundered.

But he quickly stopped caring as much about that horrible sky. Because he knew where Saanvi and Henry were now. But he didn't know about—

"…What about Xander?" Buddy barked, a surge of absolute panic overtaking him. "Is my Xander okay?"

Henry was working to get out of the car. Saanvi rushed up to his door. They were asking each other questions—making sure the other was okay. Buddy barely listened. Buddy tried to angle a way to jump past them. He saw his chance and bolted forward. Henry blocked him with his arm.

"Whoa there, Buddy—don't knock me out of the car," Henry said.

"Xander! What about Xander?" Buddy yelled.

"Calm down, Buddy," Henry instructed.

"It's … okay…" Saanvi lied. "It's just a storm, Buddy."

Buddy barked again, trying and failing to push past.

Continuously blocking Buddy as he did, Henry got out of the car. Even when Buddy finally left the car, it didn't help things. The leash around Buddy's neck, for perhaps the first time, agitated him. He strained against it.

"Xander! Xander! I need to make sure Xander is okay!" he barked.

Saanvi moved to pick up Buddy—and Buddy knew that if she did, he wasn't going to get to Xander. Xander, who helped him get out of the kennel.

Buddy pulled against the lease so hard that it snapped out of Henry's hand. Henry let out a yell and barely stopped himself from falling over.

Saanvi called out for Buddy, but it wasn't worth listening to her. Listening was a millisecond that was not getting to Xander.

Henry and Saanvi's place was very close to Xander's. Only a few houses between them.

Buddy had tiny little legs, and they felt like they were barely touching the ground as he shot across the grass. His adrenaline flooded his body with such force that nothing could stop him.

Not even an extremely bright light and an extremely loud thunderclap. Not even so many cars yelling with artificial barking.

Nothing *except* a Rot God Isolating a town named Quill Point.

The sky then shot off continuous, rolling thunder that was worse than any thunder that had ever been. The ground was even less beneath Buddy's paws than before. It dropped away and then slapped back up. Buddy lost his footing instantly and stumbled into the dirt, the kicked-up cloud staining his blond fur. The Rot God's energy turned the air into something that was like an outpouring of human emotion but lacking a core ingredient.

This was rage without an intention of fixing, of solving, of undoing. It was rage for the sake of it, for the joy of allowing it to percolate and explode into violence.

This was greed and the connecting envy but without even the underlying reason of seeking survival.

This was sadism. Sadism because sadism.

The sickness of the world.

Raining down in the form of bursting lighting and exploding sounds and wind so cold even past Buddy's fur.

And the shaking of the earth.

Buddy whined and snarled and shirked away from the ground dealing him blows. Tried to run and slide and roll away. It lasted too long. It lasted too long and too forcefully and too horrendously.

But when it stopped, when the world settled into this new stained formation of itself, with the sky fully as it should never be, and The Rot God known as Greed having successfully Isolated, Buddy leaped to his feet.

Because pain had nothing on a dog's creed.

Protect Xander. Always.

He ran the rest of the way. The door into Xander's house was cracked and slanted, exposing a big enough gap that Buddy could easily get through. As soon as he did, the dust fluttered into his nose and made him sneeze. The air smelled of what had always been behind the walls before. Smelled of the metals that made up the internal pipping. Smelled of the pink insulation for keeping out the chilly Illinois winters.

Xander let out a groan from somewhere in all of it, and Buddy raced to the sound. Past one doorway, carefully over some shattered glass, and then into the living room.

Xander sat on the couch, rubbing the side of his head. Around him was the swirl of dust. And a tree.

Buddy had been around that massive tree many, many times. He'd had fun that time Xander had let him play in the piles and piles of it crinkly leaves.

And now it had cleaved its way through a large patch of the neighborhood. The roots were far, far away, the tree much longer than the house at its narrowest. It was a miracle that Xander hadn't been crushed.

He appeared to be in a state of shock. His eyes were staring at where the television had been, and now that spot was a wall of bark and wood.

Buddy darted forward and bit Xander's pantleg. He tugged. It wasn't safe for Xander to stay there.

"Oh … hey…" Xander said, looking down at Buddy. "That was … really loud. My ears are…"

He touched the side of his head, then dug into one of his ears with his finger.

Xander winced. "Oh, that ringing…"

Buddy let go for a moment and barked, "Come on, Xander!"

Xander shook his head gently. He stood up and almost fell over, his hands briefly braced against his knees. With his still slightly glassy expression, he glanced at where his computer had been before it had been smacked with several hundred pounds of force.

"Glad I backed it up to a flash drive, huh?" Xander said with a strange chuckle.

"Xander, please!" Buddy insisted.

Xander looked down at Buddy, and the expression and the emotion that happened next was like the dust, sweeping out and filling the space—albeit slowly. Confusion. Then worry. Then fear. Then panic.

Proper panic.

"Oh god—what *happened?* Is everyone okay?"

Buddy tugged on his pantleg again, and Xander followed along.

"Fuck … *is* everyone okay? Am I going to be okay? I don't have insurance for any of this," Xander said as they walked. "I don't have enough—the loan … I hope I can … fuck, this is *bad*…"

Finally, they walked out of the house after shoving open the broken door.

And immediately, Xander stopped talking, stopped even breathing.

Buddy looked at him in alarm. Xander looked up at the sky with even more alarm.

"Oh, fuck—oh my fucking god…" Xander said and wobbled a little on his feet. "Oh, my fucking god. What is—what is this—?"

"Xander," Henry called across the grass. "Are you okay?"

"What the fuck is happening?" Xander said, pointing up. "What is going on?"

"We don't know," Saanvi chimed in. "This just started."

"Fuck … was it a … storm? Is this like when tornados make the sky change color? It's going to fade, right? It's not going to be like this…?"

"We don't know," Saanvi said, her voice strained. "We don't know what's happening, either."

Xander glanced at her, and then back at the sky, and let out another chain of swears. He ran his hands through his hair and then let out even more swears.

"We need to … we need to get to the town center," Henry said. "That's the plan, right? That was what we said to do during those meetings?"

Saanvi nodded. "…Yes, I think that's what we're supposed to do."

"No … no…" Xander said. "I need to—I need to go check on Taylor."

"She'll be there too," Saanvi said.

"No, no, she doesn't like going to the meetings. She'll try to… by herself… I need to go check on her."

"Someone will tell her," Saanvi said. "I think it's the safest option if we all stick together."

Xander glanced at her, then shook his head furiously. "I'll just be a little while. An hour or two, promise. Just a couple of hours, okay? Okay. I'll check her house, and then I'll meet you at the town center as soon as I can, okay? I need to make sure she's okay."

"I… well … okay," Saanvi said.

"Be careful," Henry warned, frowning. He looked dazed. Buddy felt a little guilty about that.

Henry glanced back at his own house. The massive tree had barely not hit it.

"Just … be careful," Henry repeated.

"Okay—yeah, yes, yeah, sure," Xander said and turned. "Let's go, Buddy."

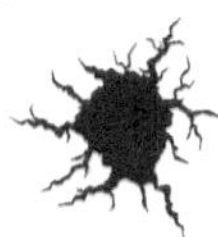

The tree posed another issue. It also cut a line between them and where Xander usually parked his car. They had to take a wide arc to get around it, partially going into the street. Buddy took one last look at Henry and Saanvi before they disappeared behind the tree. The two of them were still talking to each other, not yet going for their car. He hoped they'd be okay.

Xander was focused on trying to use his cell phone over and over as he walked. It kept not working and making an annoying little beep that Buddy didn't like. They went up to the car while he was on his fifth try. It *still* wasn't working. He slammed his other hand down on the top of his car.

Buddy barked in alarm.

"Oh, sorry," Xander said, looking down at him. "I can't get through. I think … maybe the storm is messing with reception. It'll get better, I'm sure. I'm … sure…"

Xander looked off into the distance at a tall metal tower that wasn't a tree. Buddy had noticed a bunch of humans work on that over the course of months. One of Henry's friends had been really mad about it existing. Buddy wasn't sure what it was for.

"Well, at least that wasn't knocked over," Xander commented. "I'm sure it's, like, a loose wire or something."

Buddy didn't know what that meant either. He waited patiently next to Xander.

Xander shook his head one more time, then patted his left pocket—then his right. He took out his keys and looked at them for a moment.

"For once, I guess it's lucky I'm forgetful."

The car made a faint—less annoying for Buddy—beep when Xander pressed a little button on a device that was on the same ring as his keys. He pulled open the door, and Buddy, as was their pattern, jumped into the passenger seat. Only when Taylor was with them did he not get to sit there.

Xander sat down in his seat and closed the door. He tried to start the car. But, like his phone, it didn't work.

"And ... immediately proven wrong," Xander said. "Fuck. I knew I should've gotten gas after that signing. I made it home ... and I thought that was okay…"

Xander pushed the door back open and got back out. Buddy took a confused pause but followed after him.

"I guess… I guess we have to walk the rest of the way," Xander said. "I've never… it can't take that long to get to Taylor's."

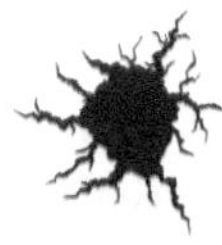

Xander went as quickly as he could—with Buddy barely keeping pace with him. And Buddy's leash trailed behind *him*—Xander hadn't picked it up.

It was annoying to drag along the leash though. Very annoying. So, at one point, while Xander took a second to breathe and pointedly not look at the sky, Buddy managed to push the leash and collar completely off, leaving it lying in the grass.

They got to Taylor's house about ten minutes after that, the whole trip taking about twenty. The house appeared initially empty when they arrived. Neither she nor Honeysuckle, nor Taylor's roommate, Melini, were anywhere to be found. Calling out did nothing, even when Xander did it several times. But Buddy could smell something underneath a burning smell.

He barked a few times at Xander.

"Oh! Do you smell something, Buddy?" Xander asked. "Is she here?"

"I smell something!" Buddy barked. "It might be her."

"Lead the way!"

Buddy did as he was told.

The house was difficult to navigate. Taylor's place was in better shape than Xander's, but only because it didn't have a tree through it. In all other regards, it was a minefield of messes.

The coach sagged into a hole in the floor.

Buddy stayed clear of that.

A collection of glass ornaments was now powder-staining the inside of a cabinet and glittering on the ground.

Buddy had to skirt around that.

And sections of the ceiling sagged downward, leaking in light.

Buddy glanced up through a few of those gaps but mostly avoided them.

"I still can't even get a signal," Xander complained to himself as he followed Buddy. He kept trying his phone over and over. "I can't even call her. How wide-spread *is* this?"

Buddy didn't know. But he imagined it was a lot bigger than Buddy could imagine. Right then, even with the worry of what was now in Quill Point—something supernatural that had arrived to roost—he had to focus on finding Taylor. And on finding Honeysuckle.

When Buddy walked by the oven, going through the kitchen to the other section of the house, Xander stopped. So, Buddy stopped and walked back over. Xander popped open the oven door for a second, and a wave of heat shot out across Buddy's fur. The burned smell was suddenly the *only* smell.

"Oh fuck, it's still on," Xander said.

He turned it off and shut the door again.

"What is happening to the world?" Xander muttered to himself. "Could be some kind of bomb. An EMP maybe?"

Buddy wasn't sure what those words meant. He leaned onto the side of Xander's leg to comfort him. Xander just gently shook his head.

A moment passed. A faint sound.

Buddy turned toward it. That noise was close enough to locate.

Buddy raced toward it. He arrived at a smaller but thicker door. He scrambled his paws against it, digging his nails in. From the other side was another faint groan.

"Taylor?" Xander asked. "Taylor, are you in there?!"

He tugged on the door handle as hard as he could. It rattled, then popped open. The sudden force sent a skittering series of worrying sounds through the rest of the house. Especially through the ceiling. Somewhere, something crashed.

Buddy didn't pay much attention to that though.

The inside of the closet was dark and covered in a fine coating of dust. Taylor sat in the middle of it, clutching her own body. Around her were a series of planks that had all descended as stalactite teeth. She had cuts all over her face and arms, but none of them had stabbed into her. They'd made a cage.

Taylor looked up at Xander, her pupils wide from sitting in the dark for what must have been around a half-hour. Tear stains streaked her face.

"Oh my god," she said weakly, her voice rasping. "Thank god…"

Xander tried to move a wooden board but then had to stop. There was no surface of it that wasn't going to slice open his hand or stab him with splinters.

Xander glanced behind him. "Hold on. I'll get gloves."

"Please hurry…" Taylor said.

"Okay. I will. You're okay … you're okay… stay with her, Buddy."

Xander rushed off, but Buddy could still hear him. He could hear him moving around—and knew where he was. That was very good. It made Buddy nervous to even have Xander slightly away from him so soon after everything that had just happened—but Buddy still stayed by Taylor.

After a moment, Buddy realized the planks were too clustered and sharp for a human to navigate, but it wasn't a problem for a small dog.

Buddy slipped underneath and around and made it to Taylor. Without any ceremony, he laid his body against her side. Taylor looked down at him and started to faintly cry. She coughed hard after a moment—and then spat out a clump of gray spittle.

"Thank you," she managed to say.

"I am here," Buddy said simply.

"I don't know if Honeysuckle's ... okay," she added. "She was with ... Melini."

"Everything is going to be okay," Buddy assured her.

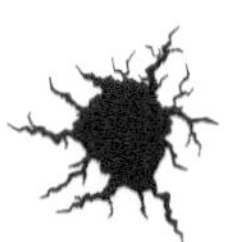

It took a half hour of untangling to get Taylor out of the small space. She spent minutes hacking up phlegm when she finally got a cup of water. She tried to talk a few times before she managed anywhere close to normal volume.

"God... I don't..." Taylor muttered. "That was... what happened? You're supposed to find a sturdy doorframe when there's an earthquake ... but then I got ... trapped... what the fuck happened?"

Xander made a faint sound in the back of his throat. "I ... don't know how to explain."

"What do you mean—"

"The sky changed."

"The sky ... what?

Xander nodded. "There's something weird going on. The sky ... isn't the same color. There's orange and red ... tendrils, I guess you could call them, outside."

Taylor blinked. Then, wordlessly, she started walking to the front door.

"You might not want to ... do that," Xander warned. "It's a lot ... maybe you should sit down before you—"

Taylor threw open her door, then stopped. Her hand went up to her mouth. "Oh ... god..."

"Yeah … I think it might be a weapon of some kind…"

Taylor sagged against the doorframe, slowly lowering herself to the floor. After a moment, Xander joined her on the ground.

Buddy walked up to them and leaned his head against Taylor again. She didn't seem to notice his presence this time.

"This is … too much," Taylor said.

"I know."

"What are we going to do?"

"I don't know," Xander replied.

"Fucking hell," she rasped.

"Yeah. Yeah…"

Taylor put her hand on the top of her head, and let out a long, *long* breath. Her voice got just a *little* louder, more assured. "Okay … okay. I thought something like this could happen. I *had* thought of this. I know what to do … I have an idea of what to do … people have told me what I should do…"

Xander nodded encouragingly. "Do you know what to do?"

Taylor started to say something and then trailed off.

"This isn't what I expected, exactly," she eventually said.

"Oh … well … Henry and Saanvi said they were going to the town center," Xander supplied. "For a meeting or something. We could go meet them. We could…?"

Taylor pursed her lips. "It is with The Mayor?"

"Yeah, probably."

Taylor glanced up at the sky and shivered. "Maybe we should get a weapon. A gun."

"What?" Xander said. "Why that?"

"I don't know … I don't trust The Mayor to … handle this right. And maybe this is a zombie thing? Or a monster thing? Has anyone been acting weird … trying to bite people, eating stuff they shouldn't, anything like that?"

"I … Christ, I didn't think about monsters."

"It's something worse than a monster," Buddy barked. "It's *in* the sky."

The two of them glanced at Buddy but didn't seem to understand what he'd said. Buddy had hoped that his ability to communicate with humans had improved enough lately that they would just accept that explanation, but they went right back to talking.

"I mean … I haven't seen anything like that yet—but maybe. It's only been like an hour. Christ … it's *only* been an *hour*. I keep thinking about it. It makes the most sense if … maybe it's a government thing. An EMP. Maybe they're using a bioweapon or something?"

"Well, uh, I don't feel *poisoned…*" Taylor said.

"Neither do I. Right. Yeah. Let's focus on … I guess we should … um, *do* you know where we can get a gun?"

"Yeah … maybe…"

"Maybe?"

"I don't know if he still has it."

"Oh," Xander said, shifting, so he was leaning better against the doorframe. "Do you have his number?"

"Yeah, I still have it saved."

"Is your phone … in one piece?"

Taylor nodded and pulled it out of her pocket. "I tried to call—but nothing happened. I didn't want to use up the whole battery."

"Mine hasn't been working either," Xander admitted.

"I guess it could really be an EMP," Taylor said.

"Weird kind then," Xander said after a moment spent looking at his phone. "It's … just the cell reception. I can still do this…"

A moment later, a song spilled out from his phone.

Buddy barked. It had a pitch that sounded awful to his ears.

"Sorry," Xander said, stopping the song. "Sorry, Buddy."

Taylor fiddled with her own phone for a moment, then shook her head. "Okay, yeah. It's more like … internet *and* reception. Anything that lets us talk in or out."

"That sounds like a government-based attack to me," Xander said. "They targeted infrastructure."

"Yeah," Taylor said, glancing at the sky. "That does sound like it. I bet cars don't work, either."

"Oh," Xander said.

"What?"

"I just assumed mine ran out of gas."

"It didn't work?" Taylor asked.

"Yeah, it didn't work. I mean, we can try yours," Xander replied. "But I think you're right. I think this is targeting cell phones and vehicles."

"Fuck…" Taylor tilted back her head and let out a faint, worried noise. "Do you think Honeysuckle is alright? She's with Melini. I need to … I needed to do a work-from-home thing. It was a surprise assignment. But we had a vet appointment. Melini took her."

"That explains the burning."

"What…? Oh, shit!"

"Don't worry, I turned it off," Xander said.

"Thanks. Jesus … I was baking bread. I figured it would be done once I was done with the work thing…"

"It was pretty burned."

"Figures," Taylor said absentmindedly.

"What vet?" Xander asked.

"What?"

"Which vet did you use?" Xander asked. "The same one I use for Buddy?"

Buddy remembered the vet that Xander took him to. He was nice enough—but Buddy didn't enjoy the trips. He tried his best not to blame the vet for that. And, at least, Xander gave him treats afterward.

"Uh … yeah," Taylor said. "Same one."

"That's … the next town over," Xander said.

"Yeah … it is."

Xander took a long time to say what he said next. "You know that if the cars aren't working, we can't get there."

Taylor took a shuddering breath, her voice cracking with almost-tears. "I know."

"So … what should we do?"

Taylor held her head for a moment, breathing evenly. Her shoulders bunched up—but slowly lowered. She let out one more breath that seemed to tense her jaw.

"Melini and her *are* alright." She wasn't saying it as a question. "I trust Melini to keep them both safe. And if this is something really bad—I can't help either of them if we're dead."

Fear radiated off both of them, but the word 'dead' really made Xander tense.

So Buddy chimed in: "I won't let that happen."

Taylor glanced over at him, seeming to freshly notice that Buddy was there. She gave the sort of smile it was almost impossible not to give a dog, but it didn't at all reach her eyes. She patted him on the top of the head twice.

"And I don't want anything to happen to him either," she said.

"Okay … okay…" Xander said, partially to himself. "I'll go where you go."

"Thanks. I love you," Taylor said quietly.

Xander nodded. "Love you, too."

Taylor pushed herself to stand. She took a step outside, looking up at the sky. A moment later, Xander did the same.

Buddy moved to follow, trailing behind them.

"If cars really don't work, then we might have a fucking long walk ahead of us," Taylor said grimly. "My friend lives on the other side of the town. I bet he still keeps a few guns. At the very least, he's got food and water tucked away. He's that kind of person."

"A prepper?"

"No, just … cautious."

"Okay," Xander agreed.

Buddy felt very nervous about what the humans were saying. He was afraid for them. Worried and afraid for Honeysuckle too. He wanted everyone in one place, safe. All of them. Melini. Henry. Saanvi. Honeysuckle. Taylor. Xander.

But that wasn't what was happening. That would take bravery to achieve. Buddy considered himself a brave dog—so he would continue to be brave for all of them.

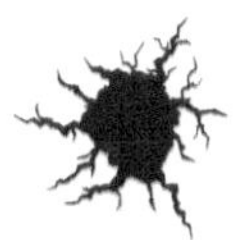

They checked the car. As expected, it wouldn't start. It didn't even groan like Buddy expected from cars.

"Okay," Taylor said. "Guess we're not driving."

"So, walking then?" Xander said.

"Yep. But first, let's get supplies. Back in my house—follow me."

Xander nodded, and the two of them started their way back into the wrecked house. Buddy almost barked at them to stop—they'd just gotten her *out* of that ruined place. They shouldn't go *back*. But food and water did matter. He'd just have to make sure the humans were safe then.

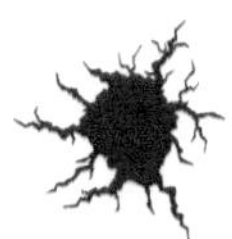

Xander filled empty metallic water bottles with water. The tap, despite the linoleum around it being cracked and flaking, still managed to dispense water. He filled one, and then put it off to the side, immediately filling another.

Taylor was looking into a tall cabinet with lots of shelves. They were stocked with so many objects that Buddy couldn't imagine what they were all used for. When Taylor started calling out names, it didn't help matters.

"Chlorine tablets."

"Good," Xander replied.

"Medical tape."

"Okay."

"Tampons."

"Good call."

"Refrigeration is out," Taylor said. "How do you feel about cashews?"

Xander glanced at her and shrugged. "I'm ambivalent."

"There might be a day where it's the only thing to eat," she replied.

Xander nodded. "I guess I should learn to like cashews."

"Guess so."

Buddy glanced between the two of them. He was starting to get hungry. He wondered if he should ask about that.

"Okay, I'm done with the snacks," Taylor said. "Let me go get some clothes…"

A sudden pulse of stress emanated from Taylor.

"You know what…" Taylor began, "…uh, hey … Xander?"

"Yeah, Taylor?"

"I don't want to go into a room alone again—I … yeah…"

"Oh," Xander said. He gathered up the bottles and put them in one spot. "Okay. Here, let's go pack up some of your clothes—and then we can go by my house and get me some."

Buddy's stomach growled. That decided things for him.

"I need food," Buddy barked.

Xander glanced down at him. "And grab something for you, Buddy."

"Thank you, Xander. It's going to be okay. I'm here," Buddy said.

Xander nodded. "We'll get through this."

"Yeah…" Taylor said. "Yeah—we'll be okay."

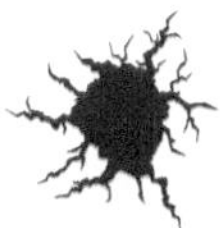

Packed and ready—though Buddy didn't feel very ready—they set off across Quill Point.

And it was eerie how empty it felt. At first, anyway.

As they walked on foot amongst so many stalled, dead cars, each of them sitting like an immovable wall in their path, there was no one around.

Buddy kept sniffing the air, trying to find a cluster of humans, but his efforts never returned more than a faint sign, more a remnant really, of people. The smells he did detect only worried him. Blood, urine, and sweat lingered on cars, and the ground, and in one case there was a coppery stink at the epicenter of a crater that had once been a chunk of road. Buddy stayed by it for a second.

Taylor and Xander also looked—and what little chatting they'd done up to that point abruptly stopped.

For about one hour more, they walked through Quill Point. It grew dark as they did. When night properly approached, nightfall falling, the moon arrived wrong. Round like a ball that Xander might throw but without the grooves. A chicken egg of a moon, surrounded by no happy stars.

"Jesus Christ," Xander said. "That must be—there must be something wrong with the air. It's in the atmosphere, or something, making it look like that."

"Yeah," Taylor said, her voice uncertain. "That's the only way it makes sense."

Buddy didn't need it to make sense. He did know that it was evil, what had happened to the moon. Disquieting, what happened to the moon.

They didn't talk about it anymore. They didn't talk much at all, really. Staring forward. Refusing to acknowledge that a fundamental aspect of the night sky, of living on the planet Earth, was changed.

Buddy felt like he was walking alongside himself. Like his little steps weren't taken by him, and that time was elongated down a long, long path. It was like when Xander left him home alone. But he couldn't even sleep to make it pass faster.

They walked by a large house with its lights still on; it was one of the biggest houses Buddy had ever seen. It had three stories and seemed to stretch in both directions. It had a lot of square places where windows should've been, but they were all broken. Someone had written something in human letters on one of its bigger walls.

Taylor looked over at them and then pointed it out for Xander.

"Jesus, doomsday graffiti already?" he commented. "Don't people have better fucking things to do?"

"At the end of the world?" Taylor replied. "Yes … and sort of, no."

"That's … fair," Xander said. "I wonder if the movies were just correct, or if people are trashing shit *because* they've seen it in the movies."

"I don't know," Taylor said heavily. "I don't really care either. Food sounds good right now. Let's stop and eat."

"Sure."

"Food sounds very good," Buddy barked.

Xander gave what could almost be called a smirk. "Big surprise you like that idea, Buddy."

After pulling her backpack off, Taylor sat down in the middle of the sidewalk. She took out a packet of beef jerky. Buddy took a few steps closer at the smell of it. But Taylor pulled the bag away.

"Sorry, Buddy, I need this right now."

Xander looked around for a moment, anywhere but the moon and sky, then sat down as well. He pulled the backpack over to him and rummaged around. "Here, Buddy, we've got food for you too."

"Thank you," Buddy barked. "I love you both."

Taylor glanced at Buddy. "Sometimes, I swear it seems like you're *almost* saying something we could understand."

"Sometimes I *can* understand him—I think," Xander said. "He'll bark at me, and I feel, I don't know, a little more confident? He used to give me pep talks, I think. Though maybe it's just because his little face cheers me up."

"Honeysuckle is like that too," Taylor said. "Something dogs and cats can do."

If dogs raised their eyebrows to show disagreement, Buddy would've.

A cat? I am way better than a cat.

"I hope she's okay," Xander said.

"I really do too. I hope Melini is too. I have to trust that both of them knew what to do—got to safety. Melini has heard enough of my rants about safety. One of them had to stick."

"You are good at those," Xander said.

"Thanks," Taylor replied.

Xander looked down at the delicious food he was holding, and Buddy eagerly waited for him to open the can it was in.

"Okay, Buddy, let's keep your strength up too. Sorry, I don't have a bowl for you."

"That's okay," Buddy replied.

"Here you go."

Xander finished opening the can and then tilted it upside down. The food slid slowly out, dripping juices, then the congealed mass hit the sidewalk with a plop.

"You are giving me food—that's good enough," Buddy said. "Thank you!"

"See, that one felt especially like he was talking," Xander said.

"I could kind of hear it, yeah," Taylor said, then pulled another piece of beef jerky out before resealing its bag. She shoved the bag back into the backpack. "If we're stuck in a bunker somewhere, maybe I'll try to fully learn dog."

"That sounds difficult."

"There wouldn't be much else to fucking do."

"I guess you're … right."

Taylor looked at Buddy again. She raised an eyebrow. "Oh. When did he stop wearing his leash?"

"What?" Xander said.

"He's been just walking with us this whole time. He could've run away."

"I would never!" Buddy barked, then went back to eating.

Xander blinked in confusion for a moment. "You know what…? I didn't notice. But it's not like we have a leash anyway."

"Nope," Taylor said. "Buddy—you're just part of the traveling group now."

"I am here," Buddy replied.

Xander shook his head. He reached out and patted Buddy on the head. "Good job, Buddy."

"Yep, good job," Taylor said.

Buddy wagged his tail a little more.

"Well, once he's done eating," Xander said, "We should keep going."

Taylor finished her piece of beef jerky. "Yep."

"How far away is this guy?" Xander asked.

"Not much further."

Taylor stood up and brushed off her hands, sending little flakes of jerky spiraling down. If Buddy had a chance, he planned to eat that too. No sense wasting perfectly good scraps.

"Not far at all," Taylor reiterated. "He lives next to that big lake."

"Blotter Lake?" Xander asked.

"Is there another big lake in Quill Point?"

"Good point," Xander replied. "That's still … that's still maybe two miles more of walking."

"Yeah … it is. But that's really not that far."

"I guess," Xander said.

"Not having a car sucks," Taylor said. "Everything seems so far away when you don't have a car. At least this town is tiny."

"I'm sorry, but two miles is actually a *lot* of walking," Xander complained.

Taylor nodded. "Well, you know how I've been saying you should walk more, Mr. Writer? The apocalypse forced your hand there."

Xander let out a little whoomph of air. "Oh god … yeah. Well, true, I guess."

Taylor's expression suddenly changed. "Fuck, I just called it the 'apocalypse'—like it was normal. Have I *been* doing that? Like this is just a thing that's happening. Fuck…"

Taylor shook her head, over and over.

Xander cleared his throat, trying to meet her eyeline. "You okay, there? I mean, within … reason?"

"I mean … *no*."

"Well—"

"How could I be?" Taylor interrupted. "Fucking shit, the world is fucked."

"Well, I was just asking—"

"I'm terrified, Xander. I'm fucking terrified. That's the answer to the question. We're walking through an *apocalypse*. I was trapped in a room, thinking I would die, for a *long* time. I *screamed* for a long time. You couldn't hear me because I could barely talk. There was so much dust."

"That's … horrible," Xander said. "I'm sorry."

"Yeah, it goddamn was horrible," Taylor said. "So, forgive me, but I'm not holding it together well after that, honestly. I'm probably traumatized for the rest of my life—however long my life even is."

"Yeah … I'm not holding it together well either," Xander said quietly.

"It's one thing to expect all of this … and I *did*. That's the worst part. That's honestly almost fucking with me more. I watched the news, I searched for as unbiased news sources as I could, and I kept an eye on stuff, like, I *really* kept my eyes on stuff, Xander. It's easy to expect … and I *did* keep expecting a war—things don't get this bad without things going *bad*—but it's different, fuck is it *different*, when it's really happening … whatever *is* happening."

"I know what you mean," Xander said.

"Do you? I don't know *how* to explain it. You expect a level of, I don't know, calm—I guess—of moving the muscles you … trained. Like you'll just remember what to do, but when the moment happens … I didn't expect to keep wanting to freeze."

Xander looked about ready to cry. "No, I really do know what you mean."

"Okay…?" Taylor said, her breath a little ragged.

"I don't know enough about all of the … world … like you do. And I … I can't imagine what being trapped like that would be like. But I'm scared too," Xander said, looking up at the night sky, and then quickly down at his feet. "I mean … of course I am. Shit. It's … the *world*. I can't begin to explain how fucking scared I am. You know, a lot of artists—"

"Xander…" Taylor said. "This isn't about…"

"No … I mean it. Writers say they want to live on through their art, me included, yes, but I also expected to *live*. To see my art in people's hands is important to me. I expected to see it, at least for a little while. But who knows if there's a tomorrow anymore?"

The two stood almost too still. A gulf between them. Buddy looked from one to the other. Waited. These kinds of moments—they paused reality. But it would flow again soon.

Taylor tensed her hand at her side. "I don't want to be mad at you. That … that won't help."

"Okay … I don't either," Xander said. "I never want to be mad at you."

"Okay." Taylor paused for a moment. "Xander, there … there will be. Okay? There will be a tomorrow. I keep *wanting* to freeze, that's true. But I'm not *going* to freeze. And for there to be a zombie horde, there have to be a bunch of people who fucked up or were in the wrong place or weren't prepared. That's not going to be me. That's not going to be *us*."

"You mean it?"

"Yes, I mean it," Taylor replied.

"Okay," Xander said seriously.

"I'll help all I can," Buddy remarked.

"Good. And … Xander, if the world doesn't die, if we end up the badass zombie killers of the new world, you better write all of this fucking down."

"I can do that," Xander said seriously.

"Okay," Taylor said, her voice full of forced energy. "Okay. We have a plan—we'll get it done. That's what we'll do. That's how we'll do it. Good. Good."

She started walking, but Xander didn't follow right away. He watched her—and Buddy watched Xander, waiting for him to put words to his emotions.

"Hey Taylor," Xander said.

She stopped and turned slightly. "…Yeah?"

"I really am glad I'm here with you."

Taylor took a breath. "I'm glad you're here too."

"I love you both," Buddy added.

"Thank you, Buddy," Taylor said. "That was nice of you—whatever you said."

"I am here," Buddy said, trying to wag his tail—but his heart wasn't totally into it. "I am here for you both."

"At least Buddy's keeping in good spirits," Taylor said, with yet-more forced energy. "That's something."

"Taylor, are you sure you want to keep going?" Xander asked seriously. "I get the plan—and I do agree. But we're also not going to be able to outrun a zombie if we're exhausted. I know that it's a gamble, but we *could* see if we can get into that house for now. Stay overnight."

Taylor shook her head vigorously. "No, no, I want to get a weapon as soon as possible. As soon as we can. It's always nighttime when shit goes wrong. If this is a first attack, whoever's attacking isn't going to wait for it to be sunny."

Xander winced. "Yeah … I didn't think of that. But that does feel right. It's a trope for a reason, I guess."

"Life doesn't follow tropes," Taylor said seriously.

"I know. You're right. You're right. Yeah. Though, I know this is kind of late to ask, but are you *sure* this guy can help?"

"I have to believe that he can," Taylor said. "He also might have a bunker. Which might be useful. I think he's the best bet, especially if shit goes sideways any minute now."

Xander opened his mouth to say something, then stopped. Eventually, he managed to say, "Luck is about all there is now, yeah? That's all we've got."

Taylor either didn't hear or didn't want to respond. And any new conversations failed to happen. By wordless understanding, they started marching into the night that could turn—at any second—into a nightmare.

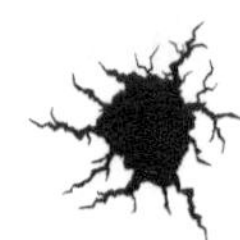

To call where they arrived a house suggested a more home-feeling aspect to the building than it could attain. Sure, the glowing porchlight showed well-painted sidings, and a recently used firepit sat in front of it with the lingering smell of hotdogs semi-burned—but it was a *lifeless* building. Blotter Lake, a ways behind the house at the bottom of a hill, was more lively. The smell of that house. The essence. Wrong and wrong and wrong. It had been abandoned not by people, Buddy could smell the telltale scents of life and activity, but it had all its happiness scooped out. To live there had not been—for so long it gathered its own sort of dust—a real sort of living.

Taylor stopped short, perhaps because she could sense it too. Just to be safe, Buddy barked nice and loud: "I don't like this place."

"This place creeps me out," Xander said.

"It's worse at night," Taylor remarked. "I don't know if he's even home though."

"The lights are on."

"He always leaves the lights on."

Buddy raised his nose, then barked again. Someone *was* here. There, right then, right behind those walls. But Buddy didn't want to meet them. The emotions they gave off and gave their walls were that of reserved anger and regular anger and a calm with an edge of anger. The house wasn't just made sad; it was rendered *sharp.*

A moment later, the door swung open, blaring out light, and a combat knife led the way of an incredibly tall man with incredibly broad shoulders and a sour sort of expression.

He had light blond hair on both the top of his head and framing his mouth; a massive collection of hair stretching above his lips as a mustache and hanging to mid-throat as a beard. Above that, a set of sleep-deprived brown eyes made it clear Buddy was not to bark anymore. The man wore an open flannel shirt with a hairy chest underneath, and his white skin showed signs of a thousand sunburns.

He flicked off the light and looked down at the three of them.

Taylor didn't say anything for a second, only managing a tiny wave of her hand. Then she cleared her throat.

"Uh, hi … Zeke."

Zeke looked them over, and then up at the sky, and then back down at them, and he seemed to deflate slightly. "I take it you're calling in that favor?"

"I mean … when else can I?" Taylor said. "Best time for it. The world's ending."

Zeke shoved the knife into a hip-sheath with a little clack and then reached up and ran his hand through his beard.

"Dammit," he said simply, then spun back into the house.

He didn't close the door behind him.

"That's about as good as we're going to get," Taylor said and took a step toward the porch.

"Uh … that's the *best* we're going to get?" Xander asked.

"He really doesn't like people anymore," Taylor said.

Xander glanced down at Buddy. "…Stay close to me, okay, Buddy?"

Buddy looked up at his human and hoped that Xander knew he had every intention of listening to that order.

Taylor walked up the porch steps. Xander then did the same. Buddy was trying to stay to the side of Xander, so he scrambled up as well. A shockingly loud *creak* echoed through the porch's steps. Buddy barked at it in alarm before realizing it wasn't dangerous.

Taylor winced. "Sorry, Zeke."

Zeke didn't answer from within the house—but Buddy felt even more nervous.

The inside had all the same smells but had been allowed to really stagnate. It was in the walls, curling through it like it had veins. When Taylor closed the front door, it was even more obvious.

Zeke stood in a doorway to the rest of the house, leaning against the doorjamb. He stared, his brown eyes stoney, before sighing, deflating.

"Taylor, when I offered to help you out, I was expecting you would need me to, like, move something for you. Or fix your roof, or your car. This feels a little more invasive."

"I mean, I haven't asked you for what I want yet," Taylor replied.

"I assume you want a rifle?"

Taylor shrugged her shoulders. "I'm expecting zombies. Do you think a handgun would be the better choice?"

"I have no fucking clue what's going on," Zeke said, shifting to lean against the other side of the doorjamb. "It could be government. Ours or somebody else's. Maybe they're testing shit. I've seen fields of corn that shouldn't have died like they did. Maybe we're the next batch of corn."

"I mean, that was probably climate change," Xander offered.

Zeke glared at Xander, and the air got sharp.

No one was allowed to look at Xander like that. Buddy walked forward, puffing up his chest and giving a small rumble in the back of his throat.

Zeke looked at Buddy for a moment, and the sharp energy stopped. Zeke smirked.

"Cute dog you got there," Zeke said.

Xander crossed his arms. "His name's Buddy."

"Good name too." Zeke clicked his tongue. "What happened to yours, Taylor?"

"We don't know."

"Oh." He looked away for a moment. "Sorry about that."

"She's a strong dog—she'll find her way back."

"Good thought," Zeke said, shifting his jaw and sighing. After a long pause, he looked back with intensity. "Well, alright, and I take it this is the writer you're dating, Taylor?"

"Yes," Taylor said.

"Hmm," Zeke said, then shifted to stand straight. "I'm not sure I get the appeal."

"I am *in* the room," Xander complained.

"Yeah, fucking can it, Zeke," Taylor snapped. "That was fucking rude."

"Xander is a great mate for Taylor," Buddy added. "He's just great in all cases!"

Zeke nodded his head like he understood Buddy, then looked at Xander again, this time without so much judgment.

"Okay, yeah … Xander … it *was* probably climate change," Zeke said. "But, even if it is, that's also their fault anyhow. Nothing good comes from corporations playing against us like this is poker."

Taylor clicked her tongue. "Are you going to let us have a gun then?"

"Do you really think that a gun, or my bunker, or anything I have here, is going to help much?"

Taylor sputtered. "*What*? Isn't that, like, the whole point of this?"

Zeke glanced down, sighed, then slowly glanced back up. "It's more for peace of mind, I guess. I knew things were going to go bad. With how the world has been going, it's ridiculous not to expect something really bad to happen. But … the moon fucking changed, Taylor."

Taylor slightly tilted her head. "Have you been drinking, Zeke?"

"I think I'm entitled to it," Zeke said. "The world's about to end."

"Then you should be thinking clearly! What was all of this for if you're just giving up the second it gets real?"

Zeke shrugged.

"No, don't you dare just shrug at me!"

Buddy barked. Fighting like this—yelling like this— wasn't going to help matters.

Xander stepped between them.

"Look. Stop. I don't know your two's history. But I do know, Zeke, that you do have some survival tools that we can use? We don't have to go into a bunker—and we don't have to worry about the whole world ending yet. People in, like, hurricanes and stuff survive because they have water and food. And there's always someone alive in zombie books. So, before anything else gets fucking messed up, maybe we at least look at what you've got? Please?"

Zeke let out an exasperated sigh. He scrubbed his face with his hands. He pointed at Taylor.

"Okay, you, you're certified, so you can have a *single* one of my rifles. But you—" He swung his hand toward Xander, then let it drop at his side. "—are not getting even an inch close to holding anything resembling a gun, you hear me?"

Xander frowned.

"Is that *clear*?" Zeke said.

"That's clear," Xander said roughly. "I *get* it. Thanks."

"Fine," Zeke said. "I'll go unlock the cabinet."

Zeke turned and walked through the doorway he'd been leaning against. He disappeared into the house.

"What is his deal?" Xander asked quietly. "How exactly do you know him? You've never mentioned."

Taylor pursed her lips. "Do you remember that I had a brother?"

"…Yeah. Thomas, right?"

"Yeah."

Xander cleared his throat slightly. "He … um … passed away, right?"

"He died, yes. But before that, well, he and Zeke were friends all through high school, and even before then. We've always been an outdoorsy family. My family liked to go out hunting sometimes. My grandfather and grandmother especially. And Zeke and Thomas would go together, with them, sometimes with me."

"Did he … did Thomas … while hunting?"

"No." Taylor cast her gaze up to the ceiling. "Thomas was … I don't know how to describe it. I don't think he liked civilization much. He didn't like to be in the same place for more than a few hours at a time. I don't think he slept very well either."

"Okay…?" Xander asked.

Buddy could see sadness radiate off Taylor. It was a different type of sadness though. Older sadness. Ambient hum sadness.

Taylor spoke quietly. "One night, Thomas went for a walk. He did that a lot, so no one was surprised. The woods around here aren't that bad. But then he didn't come home. And then we didn't find him for … for a long time."

"Oh," Xander said. "Why have you never told me?"

"It's an old story," Taylor said. "It's hard to make peace with something you think about all the time."

Buddy walked up to Taylor's leg and leaned into it. He hoped he could help with this.

Xander ran his hand through his hair. "When you say, 'we' found him…"

"Yeah … Zeke found him," Taylor said. "I don't think he's been the same since."

"Oh god," Xander whispered.

Taylor glanced at where Zeke had gone. Buddy tried to comfort her even more.

"We were never much of friends, but—we never lost touch. I always know where to find him, at least. I think Thomas would've wanted someone to check up on him. I wish I'd been here more."

Xander nodded his head. He didn't say anything.

Taylor leaned down and petted Buddy on the head, but it was a perfunctory motion. A whisper of sadness was even in her fingers.

The two didn't talk further, and Buddy didn't break the silence either. The clatter of Zeke opening, then closing, something large and wooden ran through that house.

A moment later, Zeke walked back through the doorway. He had two hunting rifles held over one shoulder. Buddy glanced at the guns. He didn't know a lot about guns—just that they made loud noises on television.

Zeke offered one of the rifles to Taylor.

"Thank you," Taylor said, taking it. "Even if we're not using the bunker, we can stay here for a while, if you want."

"I mean … I guess. If you want to stay for a bit, you can, I suppose. I can get you a drink if you want." He paused for a moment. "You too, if you want."

Xander shrugged awkwardly. "I tend to only drink wine, actually—"

Zeke gazed at him with such a withering look that it made the air seem to change. Xander wilted like gravity had turned against him. Buddy was about to bark, but—

"I'll … I will take whatever you offer," Xander said.

"Good," Zeke said. "We've got whiskey—"

"*Thirteen!*"

The voice was from the sky.

Buddy's heart jolted. His ears went flat against his head. Something running much deeper than thought overtook his entire body. He barked loudly. His bark was a warning system, a klaxon, turned on, and not allowed to stop until the danger was known.

"*Thirteen!*"

Zeke looked at Buddy and had his own emotional change. It also seemed to overtake him in an instant. His face; his demeanor. He didn't bother to go around anyone during his path to the door—and Taylor had to move out of the way. Zeke flung it open, shifted the gun in his hands, and aimed out into the night, sweeping it back and forth for what felt like the longest moment in existence.

"*Thirteen!*"

Buddy kept barking, even if it was hurting his throat. That monster voice that had just called out was barely a voice. It was the horribleness that had invaded Quill Point, and it was cackling, taunting, outpouring delighted hate.

"Shut the dog up," Zeke spat.

Xander dropped down and clamped Buddy's mouth shut.

Buddy's little heart thrashed.

"*Thirteen!*"

"What the fuck is it?" Taylor whispered, glancing about.

"You shut up," Zeke whispered back. He quickly swept the night with his rifle one more time, then shut the door. "We're going into the bunker. It's downstairs—the door to the basement is at the end of the hall. Now be fucking quiet."

Buddy kept struggling to bark. Humans were so strong—Xander kept his jaws stuck together. But Buddy needed to tell them. His entire body was shaking. They needed to know. They needed to know. *They needed to know.* His humans were in danger. Monsters were on their way. Monsters and demons and deadly predators.

Zeke padded gently across the room, gesturing for them to go somewhere. Buddy could barely think about that, though. A rumble was building.

"THIRTEEN!"

Everyone froze in alarm. Xander let out a small scream. That one had been so loud.

"*Twelve!*"

"Shit, shit, shit, shit..." Xander cried. "It's counting *down*!"

"Don't *fucking* talk," Zeke said.

"But what is it counting down to?"

"Doesn't matter," Zeke said. "Shut up. Get your ass downstairs, now. Come on, Taylor."

Zeke started down the hallway.

"Come on, Xander—we've got to go," Taylor said.

"I'm trying. Buddy, you need to calm down. I *need* you to stop."

Buddy growled into Xander's hand—but not at Xander. Never at Xander. But he would growl at the supernatural. That thing that was sitting above the world. That was going to hurt his humans if he didn't do something about it. Buddy pushed with all the force his jaw could muster.

"Fuck—sorry, Buddy," Xander whispered, then pulled him off the ground.

Usually, when Xander picked him up, it was slow—it was gentle. This one made Buddy's head spin. Xander hand was still clamped around Buddy's mouth, and no matter how hard Buddy whipped his body back and forth, Xander wouldn't let him go. Then Taylor also grabbed onto him—and there was no way for him to move.

A sudden surge of sadness hit Buddy—why were they not listening to him? Didn't they understand?

Taylor glanced up at the ceiling for a moment, fear radiating off her. She almost released Buddy, her grip lessening. But not enough for Buddy to get to the ground. Xander's hands were weakening, sweating too, but Buddy still couldn't crank his jaw open enough to yell out to them.

The two humans walked Buddy down a hallway, then to a set of stairs beyond an open door. Down below, Buddy could hear Zeke swearing underneath his breath.

Outside, Buddy could hear different animals rushing around. A pack of birds flying with all their energy across the sky—trying to get away from the same thing everyone in Quill Point should be running from.

Buddy almost broke free again as Xander took steps down the stairs. Each motion a sudden, jarring jolt through Buddy's frame.

The basement below was so dark that Buddy could barely see it as they descended. But there wasn't a lot to see. It was mostly a flat expanse of concrete, with a sparse wooden chair and a round table placed seemingly randomly in the room. The main feature was at the back of the basement. Build into the wall, there was a big metal door, with metal walls off to either side of it.

Zeke was punching in numbers on a small keypad built into the metallic wall. The door gave a small hiss, then popped open slightly. Zeke grabbed the imposing door handle and yanked it open.

"Come on," he whispered.

Taylor and Xander hurried to the metal door and into the room. Buddy was getting too tired to fight back anymore and started to sag against Xander's chest. He wanted to tell them. He would tell them … as soon as they let him.

Zeke shut the heavy door and slapped a button. There was a series of strange clicks, and then he let out a faint breath. He put the rifle down against the wall and stared at it for a moment longer than seemed necessary.

"Okay … we should be fine to talk now," he said heavily.

Xander let Buddy's mouth move.

"Monsters!" Buddy barked immediately, though he felt a little out of breath. "Monsters! Monsters! Monsters!"

"It's okay, Buddy, it's okay. I'm so sorry," Xander said, putting him on the ground. "I'm *so* sorry."

"There are monsters, Xander!" Buddy barked. "The monsters are coming!"

Taylor leaned down and started to pet Buddy on the head. "Hey now … hey there … it's okay, Buddy. It's okay. We should be safe in here."

"*Are* we safe in here?" Xander asked.

Zeke let out a long breath, and he even sounded a little scared. "I mean, I guess that's why I spent so much fucking money on it, right? It's a nuke bunker. It's made to get hit by nukes. That's why they're counting down, right? They're going to drop a nuke on us…"

"I mean, maybe…" Xander said.

"It's not a bad guess," Taylor said, stopping petting Buddy. "But maybe not…"

Zeke took a second to process his thoughts. He clutched the back of his head, his eyes staring intently at nothing. "Oh, my god … it's going to happen … they're going to drop a nuke on us."

"Maybe not, though," Taylor reiterated.

"The monsters are here," Buddy barked.

"Please, be quiet, Buddy," Xander said. "I won't grab your face again, but I need you to be quiet for me."

Buddy let out two more warnings in quick succession, but he was out of breath, and Xander had told him to be quiet so many times, and he hated not listening, and he couldn't hear what was happening outside anymore, and he was tired now. So, he stopped. But, by stopping, he let the terror inside, the one that sat behind his panic.

And a faint whine escaped his mouth as his pulse continued to thrum.

Zeke's breathing had gotten faster and faster. Buddy did not like the emotions rolling off him.

"Oh, Jesus Christ. Oh, fuck—I don't feel so good." Zeke clutched at the sides of his head. "God, it's really happening."

Taylor stepped toward him. "Zeke, calm down."

Zeke straightened slightly. "Fuck, Taylor, how the fuck would I do *that*? What sort of fucking statement is *that*?"

"Okay, that's enough," Xander chimed in. "Calm down."

"Fuck off," Zeke said. "I don't want to be stuck down here with you."

"Well, neither do fucking I," Xander shot back.

Taylor glanced between the two of them, anger building on her face. After a second, she clapped her hands together hard. Buddy's ears went flat against his head—that had been *loud.*

"Hey! Will you both calm down? We need to think about what we're going to do here. If we're stuck in this, we need to think about resources. We need to think about what we're going to do."

Zeke shook his head hard. "I'm not fucking stocked for three people, Taylor. Let alone three people and a *dog.* There's no thinking about this now. Fuck, we're going to die down here."

If Buddy knew how, if Zeke would let him, he would comfort him as best he could. But Buddy had a feeling if he even tried, it would result in him getting yelled at.

"We're not going to—" Taylor stopped suddenly. "Okay. We just need to not talk for a bit. How about that? Find a fucking corner, and everyone have a fucking breather?"

Xander slowly loosened his hand from the fist he'd made. He nodded.

"Yeah, okay."

Zeke glanced between them. "Fine. But he doesn't get to be by any of the guns."

"Why would I—?" Xander held up both his hands. "Yep. Okay. That's fine. That is truly fine."

"Okay," Taylor said, then let out a long breath. "Okay, everyone? We all agree that we're going to a fucking corner now?"

"Okay."

"Okay."

Buddy looked at the humans, not fully understanding the cocktail of emotions that was now flaring through the air. But he agreed that none of them hitting one another— which felt eerily possible—would be a good plan.

Xander slunk off to the furthest corner from the door, and, naturally, Buddy followed him.

It was not a lot of steps to do so. The room wasn't as small as a kennel—but proportioned to humans, it wasn't that far off. The floor was a very hard material, and the rug between Buddy and it was so thin that his nails still clacked against it. Most of the wall space was taken up by white plastic shelves, each of them stocked with the kind of food that Buddy associated with a pantry. Cans and bottles and plastic containers. There was also a faint chemical smell to the whole thing. It didn't smell like a place people had been in. Not yet anyway. It probably would quickly smell differently with three humans shoved inside.

Xander sat down against the wall, legs spread out, arms laid loosely on the ground, with his palms pointed upward. He stared out at nothing. His eyes were the same as when he watched the news. The sadness and stress radiating off him like it was leaking from his pores.

A quick glance around showed the other two were in similar states.

Taylor had tucked herself into a ball. Knees pressed up to her chin. Arms wrapped around herself against the world. They'd freed Taylor from being trapped before—but now she was the same again. Without the planks of wood, she'd still found herself stuck.

And Zeke held one of the two guns against his body, the other at his side. His fingers were closed so tight around one of the barrels that it made his knuckles stand out. He was muttering something, but Buddy couldn't quite tell what he was saying.

The sadness choked that little room.

And Buddy was just a little dog within it.

Dogs can accept a lot—but the speed at which the world changed was also a lot. There had been a pattern. Walks and naps and love. The pattern was gone. Buddy didn't know if he wanted to understand enough of the world to know all that was happening to it.

The door to the bunker groaned.

That woke the humans up.

Zeke scrambled away from it. His hand shook as he shoved the extra gun for Taylor to take.

Taylor bolted to her feet and scooped it up.

They both aimed it at the door, both of their breaths ragged.

Xander started swearing, shaking slightly, and then covered both ears with his hands. He cowered, pressing himself into the metal wall.

The door groaned again. The metal at its edges started to warp and bend. Several small pops sounded as the air-tight seal broke. It took only another second for the door to snap right off and fly away into darkness.

Taylor and Zeke both fired their rifles.

The *noise*. The *brightness*. Guns weren't just loud. They were the loudest noise in the universe. A big bang that could form another dimension. The sound didn't so much echo as fling itself about with a horrific abandon. Buddy's whole world disappeared into ringing.

But Buddy could still see *something* beyond that doorway. Something that wasn't shaped like a human. Or any animal he knew. It wavered for a moment. Then, with a sudden motion, it disappeared up the stairs, into the house. It was so fast.

It looked a little like a hand.

Then someone spoke. Buddy couldn't see who, but it was a little kid's voice. The sound of it … cut through the ringing in his ears. That was the only way that Buddy could think of it. The voice just bypassed all.

"Oh, hello there. I didn't think hide-and-seek was one of the games I'd play with you all."

"What?" Zeke said.

"Hello?" Taylor asked. "Is … what the fuck…?"

"Show yourself!" Zeke yelled.

Buddy's nose twitched. An instinct flared. A bark forced itself out of him. Then, almost as quick, his hackles went up, and he started to growl.

Monster.

"Oh … I knew that it would be fun to take over a Layer," the little boy's voice said. "But I didn't think it would be *this* much fun. You're like … oh, what word do you have for tiny things that are so easily killed? What's your lowest still-visible lifeforms?"

Taylor and Zeke looked at each other. Buddy barked. Xander was still covering his ears.

Zeke took a cautious step forward. "I said, step out in the open."

"No?" The voice giggled. "How about no?"

Zeke took another step—then it happened. The thing that had been in the doorway briefly appeared again. It was so fast that Buddy only perceived it as a blur.

It hit Zeke.

Zeke flew off his feet into the back of the bunker so hard that he popped. Blood expelled outward, coating the walls and the ground and then several mangled, snapped, pieces of a person fell with a thunk.

"No, no, I got it now! A 'bug!' That's what you're like! Oh, that's a good word. Finally, a human word for something that isn't like trying to talk about astrophysics through pinafore. A little 'insect.' Bug. Full of liquids. You even pop like a cockroach. You're all so small from the sky. I stomp. I stomp and laugh and crush."

Xander was whimpering, almost hyperventilating. Taylor was almost in the same state but still held up the gun.

Buddy wanted to attack—but what could he attack? And, even if he could … there was a feeling. Something deep and primal was telling him that he was not the predator anymore. He was the scared hare. The ancient elk running from the wolves that once were his ancestors.

Buddy may as well have been trying to take down a storm.

The little boy's voice didn't seem to notice any of this.

"Oh, that was fun. But unfortunately, I still need thirteen of you. Twelve more. We need to stabilize this Isolation. I really shouldn't waste any more time."

Buddy could hear it: the scream through the air. He could hear it a second before it happened.

The house's roof broke, then the floor above broke, then the ceiling of the bunker shredded—metal screaming. All of it was torn aside by a quick moving shadow, to reveal a massive something, up in the sky. Something so big that it defied any understanding of organic life. A whale was a guppy. A dog was a speck.

"Thanks for the fun," the little boy yelled out.

Xander screamed.

Taylor, shaking arms barely managing to hold the rifle properly, fired up into the sky over and over. The flash of the gun illuminated the layers of the building.

Whatever was up there didn't care about it.

Buddy raced to Xander's side and tugged on his leg—there wasn't any other plan but to run now. There was never a chance of fighting this. Never.

Xander ignored Buddy's screaming barks, and instead he pulled the second rifle from the slurry that was Zeke. Xander fumbled with it, blood sticking to his hands. Then, awkwardly, his face pale, Xander aimed it up to the sky.

When he fired, the kickback slapped him down to the ground. He took a second to recover, propping himself up, and then continued firing. The recoil driving him down, but never making him stop. The barrages had already made Buddy's ears ring even worse. He could barely hear anything else at this point than that concordant, shrieking ring.

Buddy got out a single bark more before a hand struck Xander.

The concave of the palm happened to hit Xander's arm first, and it folded it, and the gun curved into his chest.

191

The sudden rip of bone and muscle let out machine-gun pops, and Xander hit the ground with a loud slap.

The hand, as quick as it had arrived, shot back up into the dark.

And then Xander let out a scream that threatened to break every form of reality that Buddy had ever known. A dog is not meant to hear the dying screams of his human. A dog is not meant to *outlive* his human.

Buddy rushed forward to Xander's side, licking his face. That was the only possibility. In the panic of it all, Buddy held onto the strange belief that licking Xander's face could, in some way, help.

Xander looked at Buddy for a second—perhaps just drawn to the noise.

Xander's eyes were red *and* filling with blood. It was almost like Xander was a pot unable to hold water anymore. A series of cuts cracked his face, pouring down in lines and layers. His lips were split, his chin split, his tongue sliced down by his own teeth.

"Xander!" Buddy cried out. "Xander! My human! I'll protect you. You're okay!"

Xander tried to talk, only for oil splats of blood to erupt through his throat. He coughed up a larger burst of blood before managing to say his last water-logged words.

"Buddy…"

The hand returned. It crashed down so hard it made Buddy skid across the floor.

It didn't get him far enough away to avoid being coated by a pop of blood. Buddy couldn't smell anything else but copper.

His mind reeled. The world wasn't for just a moment. This sort of shock does not electrify—it turns all the nerves to nothing in the wake of it.

Dogs cry in their own ways.

Small dogs tend to bark the loudest.

"Xander. Xander. Xander. No. Xander? Why. No. Not this. Xander!? Why are you—this isn't … Xander. Xander? Xander? Xander? Why aren't you moving, Xander? No. No. No. Not now. *Xander*!?"

The hand picked up the bone-jutting, deflated flesh tarp that had been Xander with pinched fingers. It shifted to hold him in its palm and used its massive thumb to examine his head. What was left of it, anyway. A good chunk of it was broken—and the insides had mostly flowed away.

Buddy barked so hard, but the hand didn't seem to care about it.

It did react to Taylor shooting it. Just a little.

The bullets made little ripples as they impacted, and even made the hand sway slightly. But it still continued examining Xander's body for another moment.

Then it flung Xander's body straight up, out of the roof. Formed a finger gun at Taylor, pretended to shoot back at her, then zipped away into the sky again.

Buddy couldn't quite keep himself upright. His paws failed him, and he crashed to the floor. The world was drifting back in from his shocked state, but it was a flat place, without dew or wind or sunshine.

Taylor yelled, screamed, panicky said something—Buddy couldn't quite hear her. But he could feel the rumble of her moving out of the room. Going for the doorway at the top of the stairs. Buddy had a vague thought that he could, should, was obligated to follow her—that without Xander, Taylor was the next person he was required to help. But he couldn't get his little body to do anything.

"*Twelve!*"

The ceiling broke again somewhere else in the house. "*Eleven!*"

And Buddy cried. He lay down there in the broken, useless bunker, on the night of Murder Sky, next to where Xander had been, had been hurt, had been failed to be protected, had been … killed … and Buddy cried.

What else was there to do?

The hand didn't return for him. Nothing did. Xander didn't call for him. Honeysuckle didn't bark. Henry and Saanvi didn't offer him a calming word. Buddy cowered and curled in on himself when he was capable of doing anything at all. The counting continued outside, several other horrible sounds accompanying it.

Until it yelled out, "*None.*"

The world turned more and more quiet in the wake of that word. Perhaps it had been secretly declaring the number of things to be hopeful about. Perhaps it had been counting down the remaining joyful things in the world. Buddy didn't think—thinking took energy he didn't have. Time passed, maybe slowly, maybe fast. But it did pass. Emotional pain, after all, needs time to be able to percolate, unspool, and fester.

I am here, Xander. I love you, and I am here.

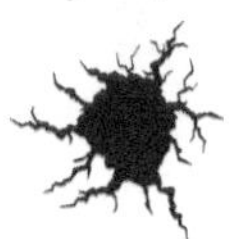

Even with it having a ruined roof, the remains of Zeke's house worked as shelter. It didn't rain. It hadn't rained yet. The sun returned for the morning. The still-colder breeze made Xander's blood sticky and coating on Buddy's blond fur, but he didn't try to lick it away. He didn't want to taste his dead human's blood. So, it sat, making it impossible for Buddy to smell much of anything else. The ringing in his ears slowed and then stopped—but everything always sounded muffled after that.

Eventually, he managed to get himself to the edge of the lake and wade in it. The blood spiraled away from him in faint streaks. His fur, matted down, hung as a weight.

The smell of blood faded, but not the smell of Xander. Buddy's head lifted, and he looked around Blotter Lake. Xander was dead—he knew that—but why could he still smell his owner out there—

His little legs flung him forward. He pushed himself out of the water and ran along the lake's coast. The smell was *there*. Past the bushes. Near that tree. The spot where a few things had washed up. Tires. Logs. Bottles.

One other, new addition.

Buddy stopped with a half-skid.

Buddy let out a faint whine.

Dead. Xander is dead.

But Xander was still there. How could he not walk over to Xander? Each step was heavy, and the sight horrifying, but Buddy still got close, and then laid down next to Xander's body.

If dogs held funerals, the howl he sang would've been it.

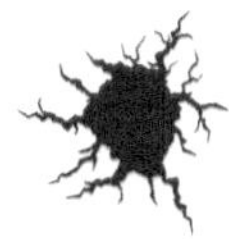

Buddy felt like he didn't exist, full of only memories. Propelled by instincts that chattered in his head. To follow the sounds of squirrels as they ran past. Investigate the possums. Maybe find out about those crickets making their songs. Maybe this, maybe that.

Many days passed. Zeke's food rotted in the fridge, in the cabinets, but enough was so far edible. Buddy had found his new routine, and it was called misery.

He knew, vaguely, that the rest of the world was still out there. That he could go explore it. Maybe find Henry or Saanvi if they were still alive. But he couldn't muster that will for long. He didn't detect their smells. Had no way to start looking. When he sniffed the air, the only smell that mattered most of the time was the faint stink of his owner rotting by the lake.

But then the smell of fire.

Buddy perked up at the faint smell of smoke wafting on the breeze. It was far off—but so strong.

Buddy had a choice, then. He could stay in Zeke's house forever. He could lie there and eventually melt into the grass. Or he could go. Find the source of the smell. Try to find Henry and Saanvi.

Buddy went off in search of them.

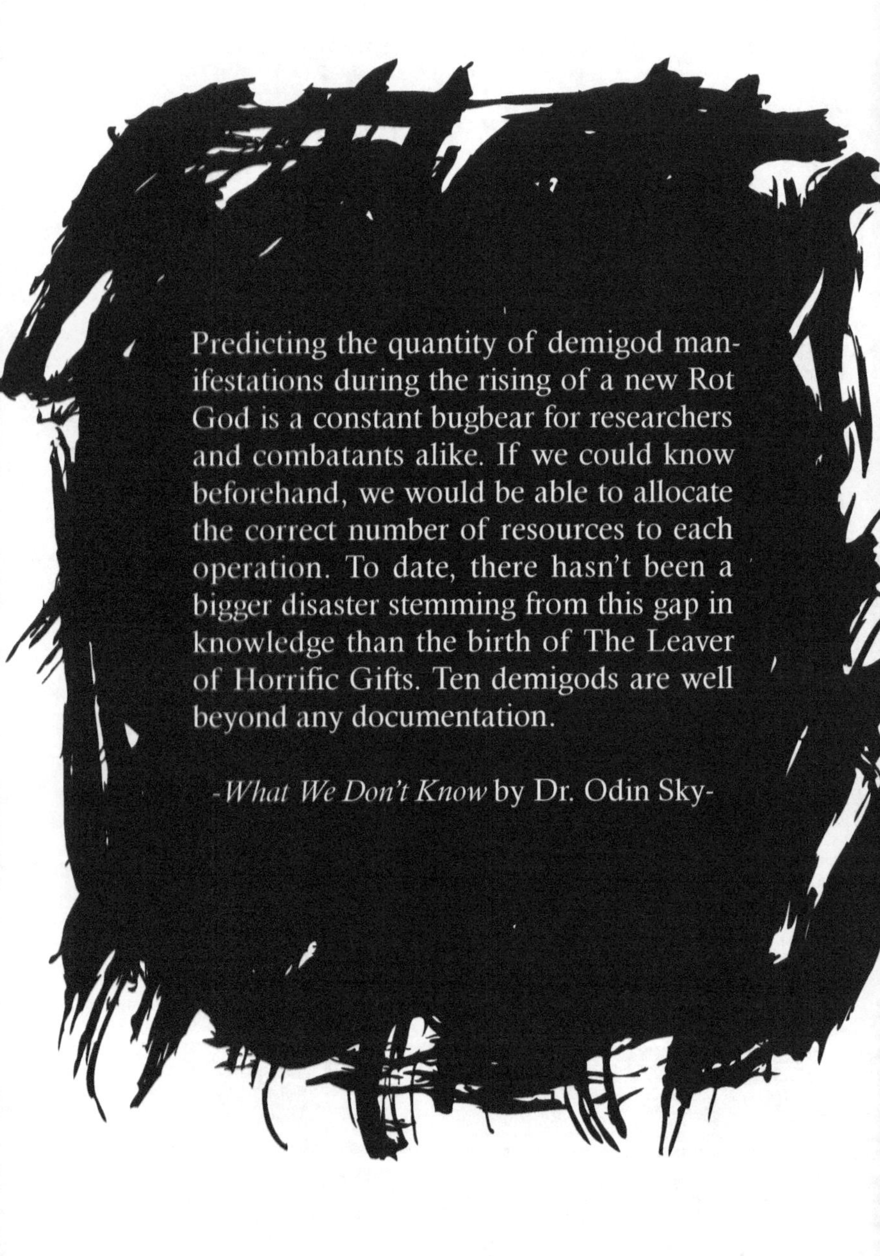

Predicting the quantity of demigod man-
ifestations during the rising of a new Rot
God is a constant bugbear for researchers
and combatants alike. If we could know
beforehand, we would be able to allocate
the correct number of resources to each
operation. To date, there hasn't been a
bigger disaster stemming from this gap in
knowledge than the birth of The Leaver
of Horrific Gifts. Ten demigods are well
beyond any documentation.

-What We Don't Know by Dr. Odin Sky-

Interlude Three

The New Seer

Thea stared down the Lord of Greed as all of reality shifted around her. The Emergence had started, and she could feel the off-ness of everything.

But she ignored all of that for the monster that stared her down.

The Lord of Greed had once been a child, a teenager. One of The Mayor of Quill Point's many soldiers. But now he was—in a certain way—more like Thea. The Painting that Knows He is a Painting may have been *her* origin, but they both were changed into something else by gods.

Thea didn't imagine this would make them have any common ground.

The Lord of Greed walked over. Since Thea had changed, all other people around her had been so slow-moving, so languid—like they were going through thick air. But not this Lord of Greed, not Hunter. His movements were as smooth and as fast as hers.

He gently tapped on the window in front of him and shattered it. To Thea, the glass fell in slow motion.

"Can you hear The God of Greed singing?" Hunter asked, cocking his head. "You smell like my god, but wrong. You smell like something I should rip apart."

Thea had never been one for fighting. Had never really been in a fight either. She ran a bookstore in a quaint little town. The worst she dealt with was passive-aggressive patrons from neighboring towns and escorting out the occasional intoxicated person who didn't know where they were but did like the smell from all the books.

But she still stood her ground. If she turned her back … he was so fast. She watched carefully as Hunter stepped into the building with her.

Hunter picked up a book from the nearest shelf without looking. He held *The Big, Damn Drop: A Novel* roughly, then squeezed. The binding and the paper inside both ripped.

"I hear so many things now from The God of Greed," Hunter said. "I hear that I should kill anyone … who is…"

He lightly snapped his teeth columns together.

"A 'Seer.' We can't have a *Seer* during Emergence."

He stalked forward, swinging his arms gently from side to side. Patches of white mold were growing out of wounds in his arms; its anemone-like lengths waved in a breeze that wasn't there.

The portal Thea had only just learned how to open up effectively had now shut, and she was already exhausted. She found herself taking a step, then another, backward, adrenaline ratcheting up her pulse. But she was different now. She was extremely dangerous, wasn't she? Her arms didn't have any new muscles; her legs were still the same legs that sat behind a desk. But she was also a being with a Sub-Layer, only partially connected to any Layer.

She wasn't quite real, and thus not quite bound by the rules of physics.

So when Hunter sprang forward, swinging for her head, it was different than it would've been. Instead of freezing, flinching away, or straight-up dying—she did something with all that power. She managed to duck underneath and shove him upward in the chest as hard as she could. It didn't have the usual reaction.

To Thea, it was a little like smacking her hand against a brick wall—and *then having the brick wall fly backward.*

Hunter was shot airborne. He crashed into the ceiling of Stylus Books and belly-flopped down on an entire bookshelf. Paperbacks and hardcovers spilled out where they weren't simply snapped in two.

Thea winced. She'd spent all of her life cherishing books, giving them a home, and then finding them new homes with readers. To see so much destroyed already…

Thea flexed her hand. It wasn't even sore.

"Get out of my shop."

The Lord of Greed didn't so much stand back up as leap back to standing. Some part of Thea's mind understood that to anyone else, at least anyone without her new abilities, that would've looked like he'd snapped between poses.

Hunter shook his head. "So … you *are* dangerous then."

Behind him, reality outside was wobbling even more. The orange tendrils of the sky were building up more and more into structures, overlaying the town. Thea had no idea how much longer Stylus Books would exist as it had.

I'm so sorry, grandma. I can't run your store anymore.

"I don't want to hurt you," Thea said, holding up her hands. "You're just … being affected by something. You could still be in there, somewhere."

Hunter chuckled, and it sounded like crackling flames.

"You think I'm blighted? You think this is a curse?"

Hunter ran forward.

"This is what I *deserve!*"

Thea flinched but managed to steady her nerves. The way Hunter was running was, despite being ultra-fast, extremely sloppy. Gangly like—well—like a teenager.

And, probably like a teenager, completely overestimating their abilities and their invulnerability.

Hunter dropped a hammer-blow aimed for her head.

Thea blocked with her forearm, and the air snapped. A shockwave swept all of her hair back. But it hadn't hurt more than lifting a heavy object.

Hunter pushed down, leaning his whole body into the blow. Thea had to tense her legs a little.

"Am I … *stronger?*" Thea asked.

Thea pushed back. Hunter stumbled, drawing away from her. He snarled and dove at her with his massive teeth. He went right for the neck.

No one would've given Thea points for her uppercut's form, but she still curved her fist underneath his jaw.

It didn't just snap his mouth shut; it made him go slightly upward again. Like he'd taken a small leap of joy, while trying to break his teeth. He stumbled backward, confusion spreading across his face.

"Oh yeah, I *am* stronger than you," Thea said.

She stepped forward and Hunter stepped back.

"I've been … magic … longer than you," Thea said. "And your god is just trying to Emerge. *Trying.*"

"I'm supposed to kill you!" Hunter yelled.

He took another swipe at her.

Thea stepped back easily. That motion had been slower.

"I don't want to ask a second time," Thea said. "Get out of *my grandmother's store*!"

She did a simple kick into the center of his chest. There was another explosion of air. And this hit drew blood. Hunter went through the other window, exploding out glass, and crashed into the ground. A loud, angry grunt erupted out of him, but he didn't get up.

Thea blitzed outside and stood over Hunter.

She hadn't killed him—but she'd hurt him a lot more than she'd intended. The spot where she'd kicked him was bleeding so much. A massive red stain was flowing out. She'd managed to shatter a few of his column teeth.

Hunter opened his mouth. A spatter of blood preceded his words.

"Fucking ... Seer..."

Thea winced. There wasn't a lot she could do for him, but at least he wasn't going to attack her any time soon. She glanced back at her store and almost teared up. Broken windows, a destroyed bookshelf, and it looked so small on top of that. The new rot buildings were rising around it like skyscrapers. She knew Stylus Books wouldn't last long. It was an independent business in the middle of greed taking over. Most small businesses barely survived in scenarios where the supernatural *wasn't* involved.

She needed off this Layer. She needed to get back to Cynthia. The look on her face right before she'd shoved her through the portal flashed through her mind, but Thea did her best to shake it away. She would make it up to her, somehow, and apologize. She would hold her wife and give her the biggest kiss she possibly could and apologize over and over. Once she figured out how to leave.

Since Irena had never made it off the Layer, as far as she knew anyway, Thea didn't have any instructions for how to portal herself out.

Behind her, reality cracked slightly.

Thea's shoulders bunched up, and she spun around.

As she'd predicted, Stylus Books didn't last long.

It still hurt even more to see it happen. Of course it did. Her books. Her memories. A thousand of them were in that building. In the walls and the floors of that structure. She'd learned so much about what it took to run a business, what it meant to foster a community, and had learned a lot about herself the whole way through. Stylus Books *was* hers. But now that she was a Seer, she already had been changed into someone new.

Stylus Books didn't so much crack or implode as was swallowed. The red tendrils moved around it, flowed through it, making wood twist, and the bookshelves fade down into the ground like dropping elevators. Thea stepped back further. The changing virus wasn't just limited to the buildings. The ground beneath her feet was turning to asphalt—cracked, badly maintained asphalt. Little patches of plant life were dying, fading, crinkling away into nothing.

Even the air was being affected. Smog was being summoned wholesale to stain the air.

It was all happening so damn fast. Once the Emergence began, the Isolated area was barely holding onto its original shapes.

Thea glanced around nervously. Still, only Hunter was nearby. No other monsters or demigods had seemed to detect her—but that was increasingly less likely to be the case. She knew, at least for the time being, she should be seeking some kind of unmodified shelter. Some patch where she could hide until she could figure out what to do next, but she stayed a moment longer. One moment more. One last look as Stylus Books faded into something else.

Its final moments looked like it was being bullied by bigger buildings. They loomed on either side, pushing inward, even going so far as to bend into the side of Stylus Books—and then crashed into it. There was a faint pop. Then there were three of those massive, twisting, skyscrapers and there was no remnant of her beloved shop.

Thea turned to go. Only to find another set of similar buildings facing her. Thea's pulse skyrocketed. The ground beneath her was shifting again. The dark, cracked surface was starting to develop into tiles. It enveloped Hunter, coating him in squares, and then his figure slunk down into the ground.

"Oh … shit…" she said.

She knew that if she jumped, it might get her out of whatever was happening. She was pretty sure she'd travel at least half a mile from a leap. But, at the same time, she had no idea where she'd end up if she did. The whole of the town was morphing. It would be like sending up a rocket without any knowledge of where it might land.

The whole world wobbled again. Reality let out a faint whining rumble. Thea clutched her head to stave off the sudden surge of awful nausea.

When she glanced up again, she'd lost her chance to leap out. A white, too-high ceiling was above her, with piping coiling about its surface. The tiles were surging along their path. Walls rose around her and ripped into shop fronts like pulling open a chest cavity. Advertisements, without words, squirmed onto walls. So far away, a set of sliding glass doors opened and closed like it was testing its jaws.

Thea took off running.

To the outside observer, she was basically a gliding blur. A rush of air with the vague colors of her clothing and skin. But to her, she was running on a treadmill that was increasing its belt length with each stride.

This new mall didn't want to let her go.

Each time she put her foot on the tile, it expanded to add twenty more tiles between her and the exit. Then, cruelly—Thea was almost sure the building was fully aware it was doing this—it curved the escape away, expanding the space even further.

Thea stopped running. She took a long breath. She didn't need to. Compared to opening a portal, running was *nothing*. But it still felt nice. Centering.

It wasn't calming enough. She stamped her foot down in annoyance. Tiles exploded underneath her shoe, sending shrapnel out in several directions. But then, with a slight clicking noise, the pieces slowly pulled themselves back into their squares.

Thea watched with some level of awe as the pieces arranged themselves back into place. They interlocked perfectly, like a jigsaw puzzle, even moving some dust back into place. Then, in what was slow to her, but probably quite fast, they fused back into one mass. It was completely fixed.

"I thought malls were dying out," Thea muttered.

She *was* still going to figure out how to travel the Layers. She *was* still going to find her wife and her friends, and, if necessary, leave all of this horribleness behind her. She *was*. But first, it seemed like she might need to find her way out of this fucking massive mall.

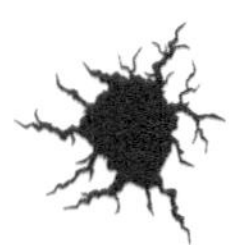

Thea suspected that people would end up pulled into the mall with her, but she hadn't expected it to be so *gradual*. She walked for what seemed like an hour before she noticed the first person. Naturally, the person was inside one of the stores. She wasn't looking at her.

The store itself wasn't one that Thea knew. It was very punk. Very rock and roll. It reminded Thea of something Cynthia might wear when she wasn't working.

The storefront mostly consisted of a black and purple arch with two black curtains draped behind the windows. Just inside, sitting on a satin pillow, was a skull. And considering what had created the mall, there was no reason to assume that it wasn't a real skull cleaned of blood.

The girl was folding clothes, one after the other. She placed them in a series of piles, moving on as soon as one got too high.

Thea walked closer, moving at human speed as best she could. It was hard, like moving across ice without slipping.

From a distance, it had seemed like the shirts were covered in logos and art for bands. But as she got closer, she could see them better. They were blurry. The logos and pictures of band members dissolved into basic shapes and colors.

The girl kept folding them. She was making some kind of noise. Vague, unfocused noise. The sort of thing hummed without thinking. It was very discordant. Thea took a step closer, then caught herself. She'd read enough horror stories. It was a terrible idea to touch this girl's shoulder or say anything to her. It was probably a sure-fire way to get attacked. This scenario had played out a thousand times in a thousand books, and Thea had read many of them.

So, with a blitz of movement—skating across the ice—she was back in the middle of the hallway.

The girl kept folding the shirts for another moment, then, having none left, let her arms drop to the sides. Her shoulders twitched slightly, then she went into the store. She passed the skull. Went past a few stands of shirts. Then walked alongside some jewelry and some hoodies. And was gone. Not into the shadows. Not behind a door. It was like she'd dropped away.

And she hadn't actually moved her feet the entire time.

A second later, a voice that was probably the girl's screamed out.

"Stop it! Let me out! What are you doing to me?!"

And then it stopped again.

Thea shivered and backed away further. Her hands were up, but there wasn't anything to hit yet. There wasn't anything charging at her. But she was sure she didn't want to be by this shop. She blitzed away.

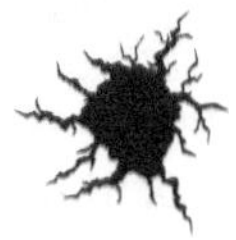

The mall had seemingly stopped forming in real-time around her, but it still had some tricks. Kiosks snuck in when she wasn't looking. Rings of countertops with dispensers for ice cream or other sweets would suddenly be around. A soft pretzel stand with a little cloth rope was off in the distance where there had been nothing but open tiles.

New noises were also creeping into the strange mall. The pretzel machine let out a faint whine and hum. Ice cream machines turned their little engines over, keeping their contents cold.

She knew all of it was rot. Was god magic. An imitation. But it felt so much like when she'd been to malls, especially during her younger years. Places that used to be so full of life before online shopping replaced most of them. It was dreamlike. It was strange. But it had enough details rights to ping the nostalgic part of her.

There still wasn't an exit in sight though.

No going home after a day spent hanging with friends.

She thought about trying to go through a wall directly. Thought about sprinting as fast as she could in one direction, and seeing if the mall would now let her out. But she didn't want to be too exhausted. Whatever was outside the mall would probably be even worse.

She moved at a Seer's general walking pace.

She went past a kiosk that seemed to be selling a bunch of different kinds of jewelry, but all of them glimmered in a weird way. Thea paused to look at it, and faintly, in the glass's reflection, was a screaming face. She jerked back and looked away. Her pulse felt like it was going to push her heart out of her chest.

It took her a moment to shake that visual. Thea didn't think she could do anything to save the person—like the person at the other store. They were possibly already dead.

She tried to steady her nerves as she kept exploring.

More people appeared soon after.

The mall was slowly populating now. Like the kiosks and the stands, it was only when she didn't happen to be looking. She would glance one way, and then back, and there would be a person behind the counter. Another lingering by a shopfront.

There was never any comfort to be had from this. No one seemed like they'd just wandered in. All of them, without fault, would be looking away from her. They would always shift in just the right way so that she could never see their faces.

And they were making that sound. The one the girl folding clothes had made. A faint hum, or a song. It gently flowed through the echoey mall.

Thea nearly jumped to the ceiling when she heard it behind her. She spun around and found that it was a kiosk that seemed to be selling soda of some kind. Maybe. The branding wasn't clear. There was a faded poster stuck to the front of the kiosk. Five different drink colors, none of them matched aesthetically. Not in design, or even the bottle shapes.

The person behind the counter had blond hair, pale white skin, and a faint birthmark on the back of his neck. He was facing perfectly away from her.

Thea was about to run again when she caught enough of the faint singing to make out a few words.

"…It hurts … I don't want to … this isn't what it was supposed to be … it hurts … it hurts…"

Now that she heard one example, all the others dialed in. The whole mall, from every direction, was softly screaming out for help. Thea was increasingly tired, hungry, *trapped*, and surrounded by the damned.

After a long time wandering, and avoiding the increasing population of this rotting mall, Thea tried to think of something else that might work. Without much else to go on, she started thinking of the general formula of a mall. Maybe there were some rules maintained.

Rules like how the large clothing stores often had multiple floors and often led to outdoor exits.

So, when Thea found one, the entrance a wide, wide rectangle, she walked inside it, not away from it.

The second she stepped over the edge, it got a lot colder. The air conditioning kicked up with a roar. And then there was a faint echo. The muttering was closer here. Wandering from around various corners were the employees. Their name tags were blurry somehow and had pictures of their faces locked in screams on them.

But the people were always looking away from her, as usual. Some of them had to be uncomfortable straining their necks that much just to avoid her seeing their faces.

Thea went straight for the back wall at high speeds, but immediately found she'd been rerouted somehow. She'd gone sideways, arriving in the middle of things instead. The clothing racks were rings of metal covered in mostly shirts—and they were spinning slowly.

A faint smell started up.

Oil. Ozone. Ash. Then sharper. Rot—not magic rot—but garbage rot. The stink left on a garbage bin after it has been taken out. The smell of an overflowing garbage can at a park that the city didn't allocate a budget to have someone handle.

Thea held her hand over her nose.

She zipped in one direction, then another. But she was still in this weird dance. Still unable to get an obvious escape route, either back into the mall or out of it. The entrance that she'd come in through was occasionally visible among the swish of clothing, but it seemed like it kept moving.

Then Thea let out a faint shriek.

Someone was moving through the clothing. Walking with purpose. The clothing racks didn't spin them around or divert their path.

He was a man with snow-white skin in a nice button-up shirt, a shiny black hat, and stylish brown dress pants. His head was pointed down, but Thea couldn't hear any muttering coming from him. Only the sharp click of his shoes.

The smell was getting worse.

Thea took a step back and bumped into a clothing rack. The clothes she touched didn't like that. They exploded into little particles of fabric.

"Sorry—they don't last long."

It was clearly the man talking. His voice was calm, slow, quiet. Thea didn't believe the apology for a second, but he did still sound genuinely apologetic—like it was just as bad for him as it was for her.

"We can't sustain profits if we don't rely on repeat customers."

One of the rotating clothing racks slammed into Thea's side.

It *hurt*.

She zipped away from it. And another darted at her. She kept trying to find a way to navigate—but the clothing racks had to have been moving incredibly fast. They buffeted her about.

"Short shelf life … a necessary evil for this whole thing. Nothing I can do. It's all market *forces*."

The man's hand shot up, and so many of the clothing racks coordinated an attack, descending on Thea. She immediately tried to shield herself with her arms, but it was like getting hit by a crowd of people. Hands and feet and shins slamming into her.

She pushed them back as best she could, metal screeching and screaming. It was like forcing back an engine, all gears whining. Thea couldn't imagine how much force she was outputting—and how powerful the simply looking clothing racks were in this new version of reality.

The grinding sound turned into a roar, but she still kept holding them back.

"Stop!" she screamed out.

She gave one last push, as hard as her Seer powers would let her. It felt like she'd produced a shockwave. The clothing racks skidded away from her; the clothing exploded out into dust, leaving tornadoes of bare clothing racks dancing away from her.

The man still was not looking at her. His head was still down, his large hat leaning forward.

"Sorry … so sorry…" the man whispered.

Thea took a step toward him and then winced. A sharp pain went through her side. She looked down. A blooming red was slowly growing. A drip ran down her pant leg in a thin line.

"I am so sorry about all of this," the man said. "I mean, you have to understand how it all works. I didn't make the system—I was born into this whole thing, same as you."

"You were born *of* the system, asshole," Thea shot back, raising both fists. "You're made of it."

The man gently lifted his hand to the brim of his hat and ran his finger gently across it.

"And how does someone like you know so much about things like us?"

"I'm a Seer," Thea said.

"Yes … but that doesn't mean you know the way that we are. Can someone really know a divine if they do not know the nature of them? Are you sure this isn't the way it should be?"

"I thought you were sorry about the way things are."

The man took his hand off the brim of his hat and placed his thumb and middle finger together. The air got a lot colder.

"Business is business," he said cheerfully.

At the same moment he clicked his fingers, and every single clothing rack rushed forward, Thea reacted, mainly on instinct. Rather than jump upward or run, she pushed her own head backward, rolled her weight onto the back of her heels, and pushed off.

She didn't know how much was her new strength and how much was her being slightly out of sync with the Layer she was on, but she propelled herself a distance that shouldn't have been possible. There wasn't any noticeable drag, no wind shear. It wasn't flying—but it wasn't quite a normal hop, either.

She was fairly sure she'd just traveled well over forty miles an hour.

Her body even knew how to land without looking. She landed elegantly, except for the tiles exploding underneath her feet. The man quickly snapped his fingers again and the clothing racks stopped.

"Darn," he said simply. "Guess we're done."

Thea was confused for only a moment before she realized she wasn't inside the clothing store anymore.

The man finally looked at her, tilting back the hat for a moment. His eyes were a piercing, icy blue, but the skin around it, and the lashes, looked infected somehow. There was a growth pushing its way out of the edges. Something slightly runny. Something purple and green.

"Oh … that was … well, I am so sorry that things had to be this way. All we want to do is make nice clothing, you know. It really is just what I do," he said.

He titled the hat back down.

"I'll be on my way now. There was nothing personal, I assure you."

Thea didn't respond to that. It didn't sound like something that was intended to be responded to either.

The man spun around and walked through the rows of clothing. As soon as Thea lost sight of him behind a rack, he didn't reappear.

The people that were working in the shop started to meander around again, having inconspicuously gone away before. They didn't look at Thea, just muttering those words over and over again.

Thea stared—waiting to see if this was a trick—but nothing else happened. The shop, for the most part, looked like a normal shop again. The few racks that she'd fought with didn't magically heal like she expected though. They were still lacking their original wares. Some of them were still bent.

How isolated are monsters in this new world? Can they leave their spaces?

Thea suddenly winced. Her side really hurt. Lifting her hemline, she examined the wound. Or what should've been a wound, given the amount of blood that had been leaking from it.

Now there was just a rough patch of skin and some sealing cuts. A few scabs were already fading. But the whole thing looked weird. Blurry, almost.

Injuries to you aren't quite real.

Thea stiffened slightly. Over the past while, she'd been exposed to so many strange ideas and sensations. Her reality was one of many. Gods were real. Monsters were real. She had superpowers. But the one that was the hardest to grapple with was that she'd transcended her own dimension and was only somehow connected to it now. It was such a metaphysical concept, so alien, that she filed it away in the same drawer that held other brain breaking concepts. Stuff like wondering about the actual size of the moon, a star, the distance between her and the sun. Stuff like thinking about if Heaven or Hell existed, and if eternity was a thing, what *forever* felt like.

The wound turned less and less real. It faded into a dream idea—a trick seen when turning one's head too quick in a shadowy space. She didn't have an injury. Of course not.

She also noted that her blood seemed to be following similar rules. It wasn't quite there. And then it glimmered, shimmered, and wasn't anymore.

And that opened the box of thoughts she didn't want to deal with one more time. Because, taken logically…

If I die here, they won't even find a body, Thea thought. *I won't even get a grave.*

Thea couldn't explain why that concept bothered her so much.

I guess I always assumed I would get buried next to Cynthia, or cremated, so she could keep me in an urn. We hadn't talked about it much.

She tugged down the shirt hem again and looked one more time at the clothing store. The man still wasn't there. But it didn't really change the end result: her plan for a possible escape option had been thoroughly dashed.

Thea wracked her mind for anywhere else in a normal mall that might have an exit. Malls were mostly cookie cutter things.

The next best thing she could think of was through some kind of restaurant. Usually, they sat on the outskirts of malls as almost independent structures, but with doors inside the mall.

The fact she was slowly growing more exhausted—and hungry—made the decision feel even more appealing.

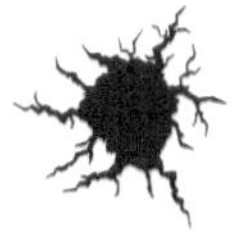

Thea did eventually find a place modeled after selling food—but it wasn't one restaurant. She was rounding a corner, vigilant, a little nervous, a little riding the adrenaline high of launching herself airborne by her own power, when the space opened up.

The corridors of the mall hadn't been exactly narrow, set to allow hundreds of people to walk them—but this was basically an auditorium crossed with a greenhouse dropped in the middle of the mall. To call it a food court was to diminish the absurd size of it.

It could easily fit a whole other box store inside. The ceiling stretched several stories up into glass. The sun wasn't visible though. Rather, it was a dome of red and orange tendrils, heavily latticed, and making the light come down as red streams. It had an almost radioactive glow that made Thea nervous.

The actual floor plan consisted of rows and rows of bolted-to-the-floor tables, each of them shiny chrome. They were interrupted in their uniformity by little patches of what seemed like faux grass, cutting a grid of sorts through the whole food court. A little way back, there was a singular kiosk with a large sign above it flashing like it was announcing road work ahead.

It read, in slowly crawling letters:

Do not question the price.

Then, every so often—with a long enough pause that Thea had almost looked away, it flashed to a different set of words three times.

We choose not to make things cheaper.

Thea winced. This already felt like a bad idea. It was empty—no one was even muttering. It had a vague chlorine smell, like a public pool.

She was almost sure it was a trap.

But in the back of it, way, *way* back, was a large glass window overlooking Quill Point. Or what had been Quill Point. A skyline of strange, bending buildings reaching for a skyline of...

Thea blinked in surprise. She had certainly seen—in so many dreams—the connection of lines and focal points that was The Cacophonous Layers. But it was weird seeing it take over Quill Point's sky.

The main question she had, though, was if her fists could break that glass.

Thea walked right up to the line; the almost too-austere division between the mall and food court. The food court tiles were a light blue.

She braced herself and placed only one foot over the line.

Nothing happened. Except she could suddenly smell food. Her stomach—against all of her wishes—growled. A sweet smell wrapped through the place. The rolling and pleasant aroma of vanilla ice cream.

She glanced at the rows of restaurants on either side. They were all empty. Each overhead light was on; the slate gray, pebbled tile countertops were shiny. The words above the restaurants—displayed through the medium of individual plastic letters—were all shifting.

But when she looked at one of them for more than a few seconds, they finally settled on what they were trying to say.

Closed Because of Chain

With a ripple, all the signs turned to say the same thing.

Well, most of them. Every tenth or so didn't change—displaying squiggles that made Thea's head hurt to look at too long. She looked away from it all.

Is this a good idea? Thea thought. *I could keep observing for dangers, but it might not help. It might just be more of this. I think I need to take a chance.*

After taking a breath, Thea sprinted forward. She avoided the small patches of grass. Some part of her told her not to touch them.

The floor didn't change this time to make her take longer, but the place was *so* massive that it still took her a few moments to travel a quarter of it.

You could've had a car race in this mall, Thea thought to herself.

"Hey there, want to try a sample?" shouted out a voice.

Thea stopped with a skid, her hands coming up into fists again.

"Oh, sorry!" the voice continued. "I'm sorry to interrupt you. I just have these free samples."

Thea didn't break from her stance. Didn't break eye contact with the new person once she found him. She could run, but that would mean exposing her back to whatever fresh hell this was.

Though it wasn't clear what exact form of hell it actually was. There was no reason to think the person who'd spoken wasn't a monster, even if he looked like a regular teenager. His hair was a light blond, and he had sun-tanned white skin. A small mole was on his left cheek, by his brown eyes. He was wearing a light blue uniform and a snapback with a logo on it. The logo was a large stack of gold.

With her fists still up, Thea said, "No … no thank you. I don't want any."

"Oh?" the teenager said. "That's weird. It's free. Like, you don't have to spend any money on it. Why wouldn't you want it? There's not a lot of options around here…"

He waved out his arm at the other shops.

"And I can tell that you're getting a little hungry."

Thea's eyes narrowed. "I told you, no."

"Hmm…"

The teenager scratched his head, then shrugged.

"I mean, okay. Your loss. We have a chain for a reason. I'm sure you'll come around eventually to it. People have no choice but to eat. And we here at the Greed Chain are here to help you—"

Thea almost didn't react in time. She only just heard the crackle of force behind her.

She ducked, dropping to the ground with her hands over her head. The rush of wind was immense. She looked up as it passed. It was a long silver chain, each link the size of a human arm, flowing through the air like it had been shot from a cannon.

A second later, it crashed into the restaurant the teen-ager had been at a moment ago with a *bang*. The wall at the back crunched, powder flying outward, and then the chain pulled taut. It hung above her, heavily vibrating and emanating a cold aura that made Thea's skin crawl.

Thea shimmied to the side and stood back up.

A quick look around showed the chain had shot out from a restaurant behind her. Specifically, from a porthole in the back wall that hadn't been there before. But was now in the back wall of *all* the restaurants she could see.

"Oh, I thought that would work," the teenager said. "Damn, you Seers are *fast*, huh?"

Thea spotted him instantly. He was now standing behind a different counter. He leaned on the counter with one arm and waved to her with the other. After a second, he let his wave drop and he blew out a raspberry.

"Which sucks. I'm not really supposed to deviate from the manual, you know."

Thea hoped the metal chairs weren't supernaturally heavy.

They weren't.

She chucked it at around seventy miles per hour.

The teenager ceased to exist, and a chain flew out from the porthole. It hit the chair—the chair exploding into massive metal fragments—and kept on going.

This time, Thea had plenty of time to dodge out of the way. It soared past her.

"Are all Seers this annoying, or just you?"

Thea spun around. Another restaurant counter. The same teenager looked profoundly bored.

Should I go for the glass still? Thea debated in her head. *Or should I just get out of here?*

"What are you?" she asked aloud.

"You mean besides a 'monster;' as I'm sure you've so colorfully described in your head? Like, what manifestation of the concept of Greed do I represent specifically?"

"Yeah…" Thea said, still thinking. "That's my question."

He blew out a raspberry. "I'm not explaining that."

Thea made her decision. The glass wasn't worth it. It might not even break. Another dead end. Another trap for her to deal with. She wasn't going to risk getting hurt more than she already had risked. Even if she had healing powers, she didn't yet know how they worked.

"The last guy was a lot more willing to," Thea commented.

"Yeah, well, don't care enough."

"Hmm … well…" Thea tensed her legs. "Bye—"

Thea sprinted as fast as she could.

And yet, the teenager's voice arrived with exactly the same tone and speed and distance as before.

"Do you really think outrunning us works that well?"

Every restaurant's lights flashed with the sound of a lightbulb bursting. The rattle of several chains filled that enormous space.

Thea spun her body, narrowly avoiding one of the chains as it zipped alongside her. She had to use a swing of her arm to change her momentum enough to avoid the second one. A third didn't aim for her, but instead shot across her exit path. She almost kicked it, but there was something around the edge of the metal. More than just a vibration—a humming. A warning.

"You'll like being part of a chain," the teenager said. "Every business will be, eventually."

The chain wobbled in the air even faster. Even to Thea's eyes, it didn't look like it was quite real anymore.

Like a picture taken of a moving object, all smeared and blurred.

It split suddenly. The links unfolded themselves, stretching down and up. They swiftly formed bars, too dense for any person to fit through.

More and more chains fired across the court and then did the same, forming in front of her. Walls and walls between Thea and the exit.

The teenager let out a derisive chuckle. "It's so nice to have a unified brand, huh?"

Thea gritted her teeth and thought fast. She wondered how strong the bolts holding down the tables were. Seers were strong, but were they strong enough to rip metal, possibly supernatural metal, out of the floor?

Now's the time for testing, Thea thought.

She kicked the underside of the table, and the metal ripping sound was horrible, but it did work. The chrome table shot up into the air, flipping unevenly. With a level of timing only super-speed offered, she kicked it again at the perfect time. The front of the table slammed into the chains.

It didn't break the chains, but it did make an explosion of sparks. A sudden sharp smell of ozone filled Thea's nose.

The table was still intact.

Rather than let it fall, Thea raced forward. She grabbed the table's base, braced her shoulder on the underside, and pushed it into the chains.

She couldn't help but think of a battering ram smashing through a castle door.

Links snapped, chains crashed around her, and it sounded like bones snapping in some accident. Thea pushed forward. In only another second, she hit the next wall. And then the next. Metal screamed. Massive lacerations cut through the metal table; the connection between the base and the top started to rip.

Thea kept pushing, yelling obscenities the entire time.

With a final surge of noise, she stumbled onto the regular mall tiles. She let the table fall. The lack of sleep, food, and now a truly massive amount of physical effort left Thea gasping.

The teenager sighed, but he sounded further away this time.

"Oh. Break time, I guess."

Thea scooped back up the table and held it, just in case. But the chains, both broken and not, were dissipating into a blue mist. Slowly, corrugated metal shudders dropped across each restaurant front. The one kiosk in the middle's sign went out.

Thea stayed vigilant for another moment, but she got the rules now. Each monster had a section of the mall—and it didn't leave it.

She glanced down at the table and took a long breath, then dropped it again. The last few moments were catching up to her—what she'd just done. What had happened fighting against Hunter.

How did my body know how to do that?

Things had happened so fast; she hadn't considered that part of it. She waved her arms through the air and knew that it was a blur. She took a blitzing step from one side to the other. As weird as it was, she'd accepted that part of it enough. She was hyperreal. Existing in her Sub-Layer and on a Layer simultaneously. Her movements were heightened, her senses sped up to keep pace, and a lot of knowledge of the Layers had been dropped into her head. But that didn't explain the thing with the table. That went *beyond* normal actions sped up and bolstered.

Still looking out at the food court, she thought about using a knife as a weapon. Envisioned stabbing a big monster. And instinctually, her body shifted into a stance that kept her frame small, her reach as long as possible, and her muscles loose enough to adjust.

"Holy…"

Trying to somehow surprise herself, Thea quickly thought of a boxer. And just as fast, she curled her fists and shifted her stance. She didn't need to check—she knew it was perfect. A stance only someone who'd been in countless white-knuckle boxing matches would find so effortless.

She relaxed and stood normally again.

But her mind raced.

Seers know how to fight automatically. The Painting That Knows He's a Painting gave us the ability to fight. No. He gave us the ability to kill. I almost killed Hunter … without trying. Why would he do that?

In all other situations, with all other questions, Thea would reach for a book. Books always had an answer somewhere. It could tell you how to run a business. It could tell you how to help your wife sell her coffee. A book was sanctuary. But this wasn't something anyone on her Layer would've written about—except for maybe Irena Ink, and Thea hadn't found anything about this.

This is something only another Seer can tell me.

"All the more reason to escape," she said aloud.

As if to contradict her, a surge or hunger flooded her stomach. Her eyes felt rather heavy. The exhaustion already pressing on her grew in pressure.

There was no way she would let herself *sleep* in this place, so there was only one other option.

"Okay … first I get food, then I escape."

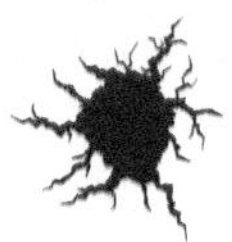

Thea wandered more. There weren't even any other possible exterior shops nearby the food court. It was right back into the mess of things. More people turned away, whispering. She passed a tea shop, a lingerie shop, and six different places that seemed to sell very similar clothing options.

She stopped briefly in front of a place that sold furniture. A few chairs had things squirming underneath the upholstery. Thea shivered at the thought of what might attack her if she were to go in. She kept picturing some sort of sentient waterbed that would try to drown her.

None of it was food, anyhow. Food was becoming a pressing need. Thea was getting lightheaded.

But it was still another half hour before she found an option. It was another kiosk. This one had a person standing off to the side, gently rocking on their feet. They were wearing a red shirt covered by an apron with a cartoon pretzel on it, a small snapback hat, and jeans. They had dark blue hair, medium brown skin, and a set of rhinestone glasses covering their brown eyes.

The kiosk by them was full of salted pretzels. The pretzels looked almost glossy, sitting underneath those lights. At least ten of them filled the air with the smell of baking bread.

Thea's mouth watered. She'd never really been one for pretzels, but right then they were the most appealing food in the whole world.

Thea walked as slowly as she could make herself. The person by the kiosk hadn't reacted yet, if they even would.

"It's going to be okay … someday," they said. "It's going to be okay … someday…"

I hope that it will be, Thea thought.

The display case didn't seem to have any kind of lock, but it also didn't have a handle. Examining over the counter, Thea found that it hadn't been manifested with any intent for it to actually be usable. There wasn't even a register.

It's a prop. But they put—probably—real food in it.

Thea glanced at the person again. They'd stopped talking and were now making a little pained sound in the back of their throat. Occasionally, they would wince. But they still hadn't noticed what Thea was doing.

Thea placed her hand on the glass. A seed of doubt was growing. Would the food inside be real food? Was it poisoned or a trick of some kind?

The Rot God could've probably instantly killed all of these people—but didn't. Rot Gods need to kill people symbolically, at least a lot of them, to escape a Layer. Could've done that with starvation, that's a byproduct of greed, but then they wouldn't bother making food.

It was tentative logic, and Thea knew it.

But her stomach rumbled again.

Her body felt weak.

Thea closed her eyes hard. Could she keep going without eating? She hadn't eaten in so long. She'd been so preoccupied with the portal—and that had been exhausting. Was this a risk that she had to take *now*?

If I get attacked again, I'll lose.

A twitch of her fingers, and they punctured holes. If it had been glass, she would've shattered it instantly. Thea grabbed the edges of those holes and ribbed the entire panel away with a slight pop. The smell of pretzels slammed into her nose.

The person didn't seem to even notice.

Thea reached out for the pretzel, then stopped. She stared at the food.

It's too convenient, she thought. *I didn't have to fight anything. There wasn't even an alarm. Even a normal mall would have something to protect their products, right?*

Thea shook her head sadly and stepped back, then kept stepping back. A shot of hunger stabbed her. She could try to go down to a slower pace—maybe not moving super-fast would help her keep whatever calories she had left.

As before, it took more effort to move slowly.

Thea let out a soft cry. Of hunger, of frustration, and of all that had happened so far. Really, she was surprised that she hadn't broken down yet. Maybe the dreams had desensitized her. She *had* seen worlds end. Seen gods rip apart Layers, killing everyone in them. But, at the same time—

I may never see my wife again.

This whole Layer might die.

My bookstore was obliterated.

I'll never be quite myself again.

She found herself curling inward. Her thoughts, yes, but also her body. Her hand was on her stomach, and then she had her hands wrapped around her middle—and then sorrow shook her bones, spasmed her muscles.

I may never even make it out of this mall.

Behind her, the faint pounding of shoes against tile.

Adrenaline can overcome even some of the worst hunger pains. Thea whipped around, her hands up. The force in her hands could—and had—shattered steel.

But this wasn't a threat. Not exactly.

A boy, about college age, was running through the hallway, making a serpentine pattern, though nothing appeared to be chasing him. He was moving at normal human speeds.

Thea vaguely recognized him. As Thea watched him move in slow motion, she kept trying to remember where she knew him from.

A second. A moment. Thea's eyes widened slightly. She didn't remember him directly. Piper's voice echoed in her head. That girl that she'd seen at the grocery store a ton of times. She'd introduced Thea to her brother one time—and you don't run a small business in a small town and not get a handle on remembering faces.

But what was his *name*?

The boy skidded to a stop—which looked really weird in slow motion—and plunged his hand into the case. He scooped up two pretzels.

The person ostensibly guarding the case reacted this time.

They wobbled a bit like they'd just gotten dizzy, and half-turned toward him. They didn't lash out and attack though.

"Please don't … they might do worse things to me…"

Thea could finally see what their faces looked like. Their eyes were incredibly wide, about as wide as they could be without breaking something. Each and every vein was flared red and agitated. A collection of what looked like paint coalesced around the bottom of their eyes like unshed tears. The rest of their face sheened with sweat, looking like they were trying to break a fever.

Thea winced.

The boy shook his head sadly and kept backing away. He stuffed one of the pretzels into his mouth. Crumbs flaked down his chin.

Thea remembered his name.

"Sean!?" she called out.

Sean glanced her way, then ran. The other person took a few steps, calling out weakly for him to "please, please, come back," but didn't seem to have the energy to do much else.

Thea debated what to do for a moment—then blitzed.

She flew past him, then stopped in front of him. She gently put out her hand, trying to put not a single iota of muscle force into it. If a Lord of Greed bled from her hitting him, Thea had no idea what she would do to a non-Seer.

Sean couldn't react fast enough. He crashed into her hand and fell on his back. Both pretzels flew. Thea caught the dry one like it was simply levitating. She held it out to him. The other, sadly, fell to the floor.

"You're a braver person than me," Thea said. "I was worried those would be … bad for me."

Sean scrambled backward. "Fast. Holy shit, *so fast*. Fuck—*fuck* … leave me alone!"

Thea smiled as warmly as she could. "I'm not going to hurt you—I'm on your side. I know your sister. We've met actually."

Sean continued to scramble away. The muscles in his neck were tensed up. His eyes were ablaze with fear, but it wasn't exactly panic. It was like his sister, like when Thea had interacted with her. That look was tearing apart everything it could. Even though she knew better, Thea could swear he was trying to read her mind.

"I don't know if you ever went by Stylus Books, but we met that one time at the grocery store, remember?" Thea continued. "Your sister helped me with my groceries?"

Sean finally stopped; his eyes narrowed.

"Thea?" he asked.

Thea gave an awkward wave. "Hi there, Sean."

"How did you do that … humans can't do *that*."

"Yeah, I'm not sure what I am," Thea said, waving out her arm at normal speed, then going super-fast for a moment. "Well, okay—I *do*. It's called being a Seer. But it's really hard to explain."

"This is a trick," Sean said. "Go away."

"I could … if you really want me to. I won't follow you. But I don't know how you'll survive in all of this. I've barely survived, and I'm well—more durable than you. A lot more durable, actually."

Sean gritted his teeth. He didn't say anything.

"Here, uh, do you want the other pretzel?" Thea said, offering it again.

Sean stared at that too. He looked like he wanted to say no. But his stomach answered for him. Hesitantly, he stood up and took the pretzel from her.

"My sister," Sean said. "Seen her?"

Thea shook her head at human speeds. "You're the first person I've seen that isn't acting … possessed."

Sean nodded. "I've seen people I know. They don't respond, or they start crying. They aren't themselves."

"That sounds about right," Thea said.

"Why aren't you?" Sean asked pointedly.

"I don't know, exactly. But it's probably for the same reasons that I can do all of the stuff that I can do now. I was in the middle of fighting, and then this place formed around me…"

Thea stopped. It hadn't occurred to her until now. She'd been somewhat assured by how easily she'd surprised Sean, but she had no reason to trust him. Monsters could look like teenagers—why couldn't they look like someone she knew?

Thea tensed, just a little.

"Why aren't *you* affected?" Thea asked.

Sean blinked in surprised. He shivered. "I was … trying to get to my sister. There was this crowd of people. And … monsters. Monsters killing people. The Mayor's Men. There was a lot of … screaming. The air went weird. I don't know what it was, but the air went weird…"

"I'll explain that later," Thea said.

Sean raised an eyebrow.

"Did you have something to do with this?" he asked.

"No, just some knowledge that you don't have."

Sean frowned. "Okay. Good. Fine. Well, the air changed a lot, and I was…"

Sean shivered.

"My memory is … wrong. Not missing. *Wrong.* I was in a weird state. My mind wasn't quite working right. I couldn't think past the next moment, couldn't daydream. Couldn't calculate. But I was also so stressed about something. It was hard to focus on what it was. I was scared though. Freaking out. But my body kept moving. I kept saying something."

"How'd you get out?" Thea asked, a little softer this time.

If this is a trick, she thought, *it's one hell of a trick.*

"The clothing rack I was working on … went away from me. Then it came back broken. I kept trying to put clothes on it, but I couldn't. Then I woke up."

Thea blinked. "Oh. I did that."

"What?"

"I had a fight … with those things. The clothing racks. I don't know all of the rules yet, but there are monsters here—and they attack usually with metaphors. Or with objects associated with those metaphors."

"That doesn't…" Sean's eyes went a little misty. "Oh … like the god. That makes sense."

"You know about the god?" Thea asked. "How?"

Sean looked at her, then at his pretzel, then around. His shoulders dipped.

"You're not a monster, are you?"

Thea let out a little awkward chuckle. "You're not either, yeah?"

"I'll trust you for now," Sean said. "But if you attack me…"

"Understood," Thea replied.

She glanced around. There was a small collection of chairs that didn't seem to be squirming with untold horrors, was secretly some kind of monster, or able to override human minds. Seemed to be.

"Well, you don't seem to have been poisoned, so I'm going to go super speed and get myself a pretzel or five. And then we can sit down for a moment. I think you and I need to swap stories."

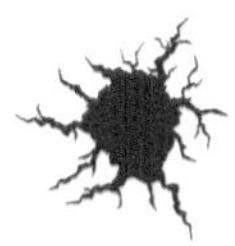

There was a lot to talk about.

So much.

Thea demolished the pretzels as they both tried to put the impossible into frameworks the other could understand.

Sean told her of hearing Grace's voice. Of the chase to find her. How Piper had pushed into danger. He almost couldn't manage to describe a room he'd found full of dead people. Then, his voice quavering, he talked about how they'd tried to run from the sight of that room— and how they'd instead found a different, horrible place hidden beneath the courthouse.

A place with a massive golden orb. The Mayor of Quill Point gathered around it with his Mayor's Men, now called Lords of Greed. Sean talked about racing out of the underground place, chased by them. About the massacre when people arrived to help Grace.

Then Sean told Thea more about the moments before the world shifted—when he lost track of his sister in all those screams. And it was obvious, even as he spoke, that those sounds were still deep in his head.

Thea listened to all of this. She wanted to give him a hug—but Sean didn't strike her as someone who would appreciate that.

When he was done, Thea told Sean what had happened to her.

Thea talked about the Painting that was another god. She talked about what she'd become. She told him some of what she knew. Some. To explain the scope of the Layers, the death of so many—she didn't know if he would believe her or be able to handle it. She didn't even say she couldn't herself travel to other Layers. But she explained it enough.

"…I sent my wife and my friends into a different place. I can do that now. I can still do that, I think."

Sean was handling it better than she expected. He only looked slightly faint. Slightly like he was about to fall into an existential crisis that would take days to overcome.

"So, yeah, I can do that," Thea reiterated.

"Jesus … okay?"

"So, Sean, would you like me to portal you out too?"

Sean blinked a few times. He kept touching his own face like he expected it not to be real anymore. But, after a second, he shook his head and focused his gaze on Thea.

"What would that mean?"

"It means I would send you to a world, a place, where this isn't happening. You would be safe there. But I don't know if I could bring you back. I don't know if you would ever be able to come back here."

"I can't," Sean said instantly.

Thea frowned. "What?"

"My sister is still here. I can't."

Thea didn't respond for a moment. Her stomach felt sick for a new reason. She tried to work out how to say it. How to present this information. It felt even heavier than all she'd said before. But she *had* to say it. It was the dire reality they now inhabited.

"…She might not even be alive, Sean."

Sean flinched. His hands tightened. But after a moment, he looked even more determined.

"I know that. It doesn't matter. I can't ever leave her. I would never let something happen to her if I could do something about it. I'm her big brother. I *protect* her."

Those words were iron. Unyielding. Thea found herself nodding. She understood completely.

"Okay. Then we need to get out of *this* place and find her. She could be anywhere in this mess—maybe one of the other buildings or locations. We might have to…"

Thea trailed off and looked at her hands. What might she have to do? Fight things. Maybe kill things. There was a monstrous world out there that wanted her dead, and what would she be willing to do to survive in it?

Why did The Painting God give us the ability to fight? Was it to inconvenience other gods? Was it simply for amusement?

Does it really matter why?

I can't leave this Layer. I don't know how.

But even if I could, am I really willing to abandon my home, these people, to all this?

"Thea, are you okay?" Sean asked.

She looked back up and nodded her head. "I think we need to do more than save people."

Sean flinched backward. "What can we do *except* save people? This is … so much. This is gods. What are we supposed to do?"

Thea let the words tumble out.

"I think we all need to save each other. I don't think we're the only people trying to fight. I know the people of this town, and you do too, and I bet there are little wars happening all across it."

"Little wars," Sean repeated.

Thea stood up and looked across that massive mall.

"Sean, you told me that when I interrupted you, that you woke up. That you could leave the store where you were."

"Yeah. I could think again."

Thea smiled. "I'd been so focused on trying to escape that I missed it. I didn't think much about what we *already* have here. This mall … it's *full* of trapped people."

"Wait…? Are you thinking?"

"Small wars—small armies. These fucking gods think they can stow us away in little hells and nightmares. The Mayor's manipulated us for so long, I bet he doesn't think of us as a threat. But Quill Point is full of good people. That's what a town is: people. I don't think they expect us to fight back."

A grin grew on Sean's face. "They put so many of us in one place. They fucked up."

"Oh yeah, they really fucked up."

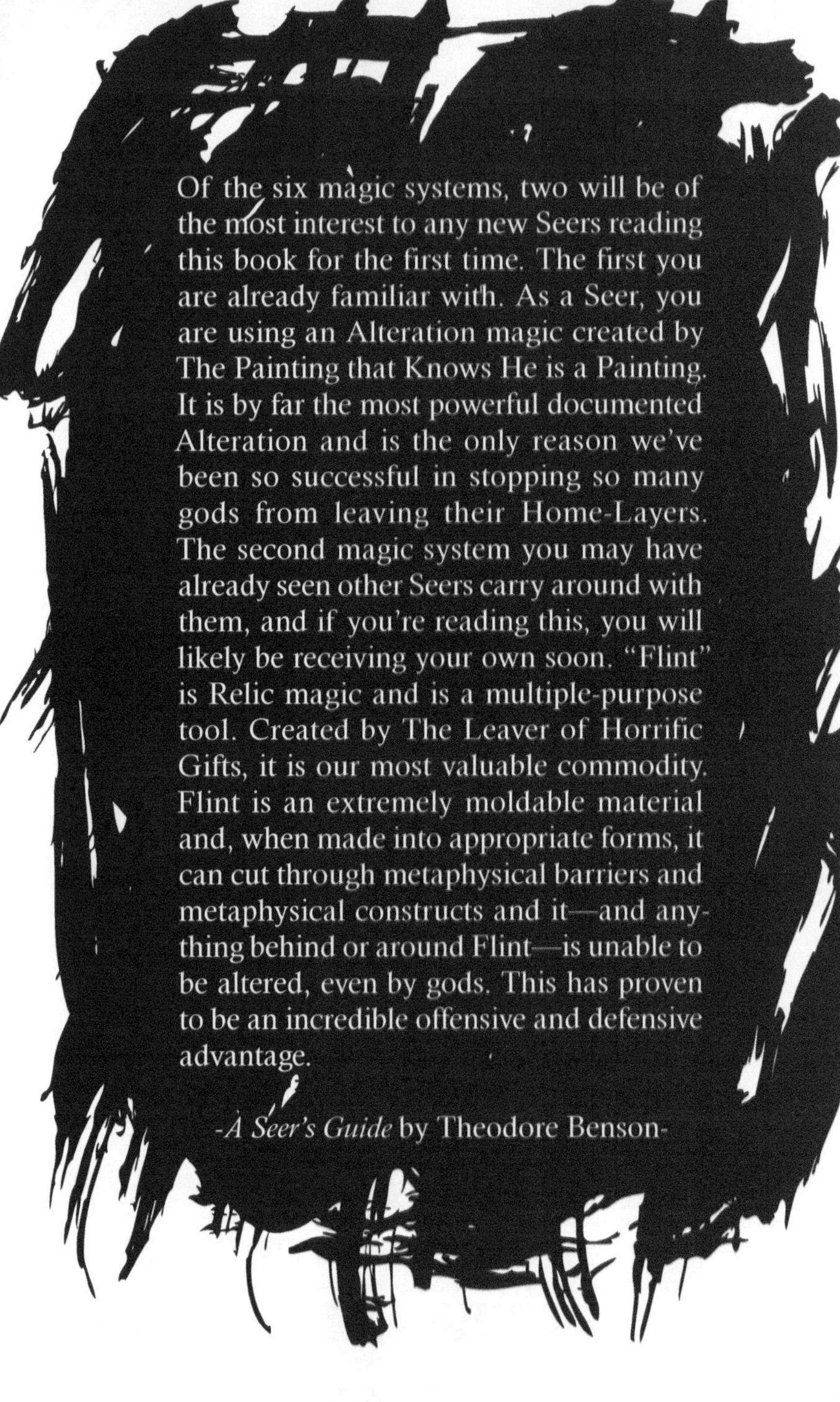

Of the six magic systems, two will be of the most interest to any new Seers reading this book for the first time. The first you are already familiar with. As a Seer, you are using an Alteration magic created by The Painting that Knows He is a Painting. It is by far the most powerful documented Alteration and is the only reason we've been so successful in stopping so many gods from leaving their Home-Layers. The second magic system you may have already seen other Seers carry around with them, and if you're reading this, you will likely be receiving your own soon. "Flint" is Relic magic and is a multiple-purpose tool. Created by The Leaver of Horrific Gifts, it is our most valuable commodity. Flint is an extremely moldable material and, when made into appropriate forms, it can cut through metaphysical barriers and metaphysical constructs and it—and anything behind or around Flint—is unable to be altered, even by gods. This has proven to be an incredible offensive and defensive advantage.

-*A Seer's Guide* by Theodore Benson-

Part 2
The Infinite Diner

Chapter 20

GRACE WAS TIRED. SHE KNEW TIREDNESS well. But there wasn't time for rest. There was only the time before the next ding of that bell.

That bell that haunted her nightmares.

Declan rang the bell and slapped the paper down on the tiny window that had not been part of the Ink Well Diner before. He ran off again, sprinting into the lunchtime fray.

The paper itself was a little white sheet. The worst paper The Manager could find, she was sure. At least the paper was dry—this time. And the order was easy—this time. Of the various orders she'd seen, this was one of the more normal ones, actually.

It read:

> *An omelet with a side of roasted*
> *potatoes. Two fried eggs over easy.*
> *Orange juice without pulp. Coffee with*
> *the pulp. A secret that you didn't*

want to tell someone whispered into the second potato you cook.

She read it once and got to fucking work.

Grace had worked at the diner for a long time. So long almost everyone in Quill Point knew her name. She'd worked it overstaffed, and she'd certainly worked it understaffed.

Before Caleb was … gone, they spent many, many days basically running the entire place by themselves.

She had fought through the hell that was the lunch rush at its chaotic peak in a small town with enough frequent customers to fill the booths, tables, corners, and lingering space next to the counter to capacity.

To call it muscle memory would be an insult. She'd held or overseen every position at one point or another. Cleaned the bathroom until she'd grown numb to the disgust. Biked orders around Quill Point when they'd briefly offered that. She could cook the meals, run the tables, clean the whole damn place. Grace knew the flow, and she knew the rhythm. It was a dance. It was a whirlwind.

Before, that was.

Before things changed.

The flattop grill heated so hot it made sweat threaten to drip down her nose. She cracked the eggs efficiently. She whisked like she'd won an award for it.

Grace's vision blurred a little from tiredness—but that was okay. She could do this with tiredness, no problem.

Next came the orange juice. She took out a strainer, poured the pulp-filled stuff through, caught all the pulp. *All of it.* And then dumped the messy orange strands into a mug. She filled that with *strong* black coffee.

Declan slammed down another piece of paper. He rang the bell. A surge of fear passed through her—but she shoved it *way* down. Her focus was not allowed to slip. She was not allowed to feel sad or stressed, not when someone was counting on her.

She flipped the two eggs and the omelet.

Next up, she pulled out a knife. Laid the potatoes down. Split the first one in half like she was cleaving open someone's head. The visual *almost* made her wince.

Grace was fairly certain she hated breakfast food now.

Potatoes went to the heat. The eggs went off onto a plate. She flipped the omelet.

She cut another potato open and leaned level with it. For a single second, she hesitated—but there was no hesitating here. Not in The Infinite Ink Well Diner. Not with what was at stake.

"I didn't like Katrina's favorite movie when she showed it to me in college," Grace said.

The omelet went off the grill. The potato went on the grill.

Almost there.

Declan ran by, slapping down another order paper. The bell rang. Grace's pulse soared. Her heart rate thumped through her body.

She *needed* to handle those other orders.

This order was cooked enough. On the plate it went. She *glided* across the kitchen like she was on skates, placed the food, ready to be delivered, on the delivery window's ledge. She snatched up the other two orders.

The first one read:

Give me the blood of a pig, drained
from a pile of pork chops. Coat it in a

mixture of every spice you hate the smell of. And a chicken-salad sandwich made with the intent to be for your next meal break, but instead give it to me. Skip your meal.

Grace fought back a sob.
She had to keep the customers happy.
She *had* to keep The Customers happy.

Chapter 21

THEY HAD A FEW PLANS IN PLACE. EVERY two hours, Declan and Grace switched places. It helped keep them both from getting too worn out.

It had been two hours now.

The timer went off. She opened the door. And Declan stood there.

It was still a little weird to see him, even now. Declan wasn't someone she'd interacted with that often, all told. She'd considered him a friend, sure, like anyone else in Quill Point. He showed up occasionally, getting vegan things on the menu. Sometimes he needed kindness and good customer service. She'd been happy to provide it.

But then the hospital burned down. Then they ran into the forest. Then they faced horrors beyond their imagination. Fought them even. Grace had saved his life. Declan had saved her life. It's impossible not to be connected after that.

And now they were here, in a new horror, in a night-mare that was somehow even worse than that opulent house with so many monsters in it.

Like Grace was sure she also did, Declan looked more worn out every day. His brown hair had grown long, falling around his face, and obscuring his green eyes—and the massive bags beneath them.

He shifted a strand of hair away from his injury. The Monopolist, one of the monsters they'd faced in that house, had partially ripped skin off his face—and it was still healing. They'd killed The Monopolist, and The Oil Baron, and The Lobbyist that day, but all the wounds were still healing. Grace had plenty of her own. Hunter had slashed a baton across her face, for one.

When Grace did manage, so rarely, to sleep, those memories would return in dreams. The sharpness of pain. The sight of monsters. Remnants of graphs and charts declaring the end of the world.

"They're being a little … p-picky today," Declan said, leaning against the doorframe. "I don't know if I can…"

A new surge of fear bubbled up in Grace, dispelling any other thoughts. Without Declan to help, she would have to have Greg do it—and Greg had two marks to his name already.

But, before she could even think of what to say, Declan shook his head slowly.

"No, no, I'm sorry. I can do it. I'll do the cooking now. But can you handle The Customers for the rest of the day?"

Grace's pulse lowered just a little. "Yeah, that's fine."

"Thanks so much," Declan said.

"You're welcome."

Declan held up an order paper. "I've got this one already. It needs me to tell the bagel how much I hate the world—and then slather it with cream cheese. Honestly, not the hardest order I've had to deal with in a while."

"You sure you'll be…?" Grace started to say, then stopped herself.

They'd made a rule, after a day or two of being trapped in the diner. Questions like that were pointless. Not even worth asking. Quill Point was in the middle of a god's ascension. If they were going to find a way out—if any plan was going to work—they didn't have time yet to process all of this.

I am going to have a lot of emotional issues later in life, Grace thought. *If I survive, that is.*

"You ready to go?" Declan asked, moving right past the faux pa.

"Yeah, yeah. I'll go find out what else they want."

Declan nodded and stepped past her, muttering underneath his breath. Mostly swears. He'd taken to doing that a lot lately. It was—in an odd way—nice to see Declan have that outlet. It was a spark of fighting.

If they made it out of this, if they survived, Grace would make sure he never felt like that again. That no matter what, if they made it out of this, she and Declan were going to make sure the other was okay. That they weren't clouded with negative thoughts. That either of them could answer the question of how they were truthfully, without judgment, and if the answer was bad, that they had each other's backs. That they were not alone.

She loved Declan. And she would do the same for anyone she loved.

You need to get going, Grace thought. *You can't get a strike.*

Grace took a calming breath.

It failed to calm her.

She stepped out into The Infinite Diner, facing, once again, what The God of Greed had done to it.

It had once been mostly a big, chaotic room. A labyrinth of seats and elevated areas. It wasn't easy to navigate—but Grace had learned it like the back of her hand.

It had changed *slightly* in the interim.

The main, center section was the most like a traditional restaurant. A large wooden table, austere to the point it wouldn't look out of place in a castle, sat surrounded by smaller, plastic tables intended for parties of four. And all of that was ringed by comfy, circular booths with mostly intact linoleum.

But that was only the center—the rest of The Infinite Ink Well Diner sprawled out against the whims of gravity. Two tunnels broke off in different directions, each of them in a suspended loop. It looked like someone had taken the once-flat floor of an aisle of booths, and then twisted that paper so its end corners touched. But the things inside had not fallen—and when Grace had to walk down either tunnel, her feet were always on the floor. Even when looking back showed the rest of the restaurant upside down, or even at a perfectly sideways angle, she was always on the ground. She just wished her inner ear would get the memo.

Fortunately for her, the person with their hand up next was in the normal section. Unfortunately for her, though it never prevented her from breathing, a new peculiarity had been added to even the regular part of the diner. It had been subtle at first, but grown over time: food smells never seemed to dissipate.

As soon as Grace stepped in, she was buried in the overwhelming fragrance of coffee, cream cheese, garlic powder, pepper, burned toast, bacon, sausage, sourdough bread, chocolate, honeydew melon, pig blood, cow blood, chicken blood, fried potatoes, rosemary, pineapple, and even more.

So much more.

It made her eyes water, and each time she opened her mouth it was like she'd inhaled the collective contents of a grocery store.

But she had to have a nice, friendly face—no matter how she felt. That was the job.

She didn't want a strike for not doing her job.

She approached The Customer raising his hand.

CHAPTER 22

THE CUSTOMERS MADE THE ENTIRE broken reality of the place seem tame in comparison. Grace had killed monsters and felt their blood splash on her as she attacked them. But it was another matter to talk to a monster, serve it food, and try to keep her face as natural as possible.

It had been only a few hours since she'd had to talk to a Customer, but she still felt her blood run slightly cold. It was only through a lot of training, a lot of exposure, that she didn't react like she had on her first day.

The Customers were patchwork people. Their heads looked like a series of blocks; each feature only consistent in their anger and disdain. The seams between didn't leak blood or anything, but she could see the cross-sections as they swiveled about. This one was male, and in that moment—Customer's face change every five minutes or so—he had a large red beard, black hair, blue eyes, and a mouth with two layers of teeth.

"Can you get to my order now, huh?" The Customer said. "I've been waiting for a whole thirty seconds."

"Yes, I'm so sorry," Grace said automatically.

"You should be—I'm tempted to report this to The Manager. What sort of establishment are you fucking running? I swear to Greed, is it so much to ask for instantaneous orders? Why do I even need to say my orders, anyway, huh? I tip way too well to not have psychic orders received on the spot."

Grace's smile somehow didn't falter.

"I'm so sorry about that, sir. I'll check if I can ask my manager about ... uh, having us able to hear more thoughts."

"Fine," he said. "But I won't leave a tip or anything for this one. I expect better service."

"Of course, sir," Grace said. "In fact ... the whole meal is ... on the house. To make up for any inconvenience caused by this."

The Customer blinked, and then his face altered. His mouth drifted to the left slowly, with a series of clicks, then fully swiveled away. Replaced with a mouth with nothing but incisors. Fronds of something that looked like white mold pushed through the narrow gaps in his teeth, then slunk back away.

Grace tensed slightly.

"That's more like it," The Customer said in a much deeper voice. "That's much more like it."

He leaned forward and dragged the menu toward himself.

"Now, I shall figure out what I want."

Grace waited for it. Some part of her, even after all this time, hoped that it could be a normal order for once.

That it wouldn't have an odd request attached, almost assuredly added for the sake of making them scramble.

"Now, now, now, Grace, what I have decided I very much want is—"

The Customer looked up at her.

"—A small soup. You get that? I want it *small*, not whatever size you have. I want it the way that I would want it small."

The Customer held up his hands to show her the exact dimensions.

"Okay, sir," Grace said.

She drew on the pad of paper, lengthwise, the exact dimensions of the bowl he wanted.

"Got it, sir," Grace added.

"Excellent," The Customer said. "Now, I want that with shredded cheese—you get that? I can see you're not very attentive, so, do you *get* that?"

Grace smiled back. "I'm writing it down as we speak."

"Yeah, yeah, that's great," The Customer replied, waving out his hand. "That's fine of you. So then, next up—are you ready though? Can you handle it?"

"Yes, sir."

"Why do you keep calling me, sir?"

"Sorry," Grace replied quickly.

"No, no, go back to it. End every sentence with it, actually. I don't make the kind of money I do to have someone like you not treat me with respect."

Grace nodded. "Got it, sir."

"Okay. Well, then. I'd like a steak. Cooked rare. No medium rare bullshit, not anything else. Get it right or do it again. And do it fast."

Grace noted that down.

"Okay, sir," she said. "What type of steak would you like, sir?"

"What?" The Customer asked. His eyes swiveled away, replaced by silver ones. "Why are you asking me questions still? I ordered."

"I'm so sorry, sir. I need to know what kind of steak you want, sir."

"What do you mean what *kind* of steak?"

"I ... uh, sir, well, sir, there's porterhouse, T-bone, sirloin ... sir..."

The Customer rolled his eyes. "God, you really need to get on that mind-reading thing. Honestly, it's just bad service not having you understand what I mean. This menu is for me to order, not for you to impose."

"So sorry, sir. So, so very sorry ... sir."

He let out an annoyed huff. "Porterhouse, then. And before you fucking ask, yes, add a baked potato."

Grace wrote that all down and nodded. "Got all that, sir. Anything else, sir?"

"No, I think ... I think that's all."

Grace almost breathed a sigh of relief. At least, at the very least, it wasn't that hard of an order for Declan to prepare. But any outward emotion like that wouldn't have been appreciated by a Customer.

"Okay, sir," Grace said. "I can get right on that for you, sir—"

"Oh, no, wait—I would like to make a substitution, actually. I changed my mind about a few things."

That, despite everything, almost got Grace to snap. She didn't mind fixing someone's order in any normal context. But she knew The Customers. She knew what it meant when *they* said that.

"Yes, okay, sir," Grace replied. "What would you like to substitute, sir?"

"Ah, yes, so…"

And sure enough—it was a slight tweak on everything he'd just ordered. *All* of it. The new order consisted of mushroom soup with croutons, medium-well sirloin, and a side of broccoli with freshly ground pepper flakes.

"Did you get all of that?" he asked.

"Uh … yes, sir. Thanks so much, sir." Grace nodded to him. "I'll get to that as soon as I can, sir."

"Excellent," The Customer said.

Grace turned away. She took a small, calming breath. Her blood was boiling, her head hurt already. She was only allowed to carry one notepad at a time—and they only had ten pages in them. One order, from one Customer, had burned through two.

And if any of them complained…

She repressed a shiver. The punishment for that…

It was just like Cassandra had said.

"Symbolic, but can kill us."

And, if she could, if she was with Chuck and Cassandra and Peter, if she knew what had happened to them, Grace would've told them what she'd added to the theory. Because it wasn't just could and would kill them.

No.

Symbolic, but can kill us—and wants to kill us so very badly. Delighted, in fact, at the idea of killing us.

"Oh, waitress? One more thing, sweetie."

A shiver passed up Grace's spine. She looked back at The Customer. He had his hand laid out toward her.

"I'd like to seal my order."

Grace spun back around and nodded. "Um, yes, of course, sir."

"Give it here," he said.

Grace took back out the notepad from her apron pocket and ripped out the second page. She glanced it over quickly. Grace had a second, at most, to do this before The Customer would complain. She'd gotten very good at memorizing orders, in case it became unreadable for Declan. It was a skill she basically couldn't help but pick up over time back in the normal version of this job. But still, a shot of nervousness spun through her as the words of the order cascaded through her brain.

"Yes, sir. Here you go, sir."

The Customer took the paper from her, looked it over, and opened his mouth. A tongue didn't emerge. Instead, something white, spongey, porous, with long white stalks lively curling emerged from his mouth. It lifted itself awkwardly, like it was being suspended by wires.

The Customer licked the piece of paper, leaving a pinkish slime over it.

"Oh, this'll be such a tasty meal. I can tell."

He handed it back to her. Grace barely didn't retch from the slightly sticky sensation.

"I'll get it to you as fast as I can, sir," Grace said.

"Yes, yes," The Customer said, turning his head away from her.

Grace waited a moment—making sure there wouldn't be any more substitutions or anything else. Then she dealt with the piece of paper. It was always a slow process of working through to the inevitable conclusion. A desperate calculation to not do what she always ended up having to do.

She couldn't stick it in her pocket. It would be impossible to get it back out. Couldn't hold it, either. She had other orders to take.

So, she stuck it to her shoulder—even if it was mildly caustic through the clothing.

There was no time.

Other Customers waved their hands at her, impatient. Wanting for her to take their orders.

Chapter 23

THE END OF A SIXTEEN-HOUR WORKDAY finally arrived. Even in this place, she got a break. The Manager never seemed happy about it, but even he had to give them time to sleep. Despite everything, the strange new world of The God of Greed did not seem to want to kill them outright. Grace took no comfort in that. The Customers and The Manager disappeared, and everything grew quiet, but the dread lingered.

They couldn't leave the diner either. None of them could. The door wasn't locked or anything, but they all followed the rule. Escape attempts would constitute instantly three whole strikes, and Grace had every confidence that The Manager would be able to track them down. The world outside wasn't a place she was ready to navigate—what she'd seen had been nightmarish and strange. She'd be an easy target.

She stopped by the register alcove to check on Declan. He'd managed to survive another day.

Now there was the night to deal with.

She found him leaning against the counter, right next to the register. He tried to look nonchalant. After a day of faking smiles for monsters, he wasn't doing a good job of hiding emotions.

"How'd we do?" Grace asked simply.

"We made a lot," Declan replied.

Grace nodded. She didn't know if anyone could hear them—if The Manager was still around, somewhere. But they'd proven well enough, through multiple tests, that no one was watching after the monsters disappeared. They would've been killed by now if someone had been keeping tabs on them.

"Want me to help you count them?" Grace asked.

Declan shrugged. "Don't you need to wake up Greg?"

"I can help for a moment."

"That'd be nice."

Declan opened the register; it popped open with a faint *ding*. As gently as he could, he scooped out a few coins. Declan then handed her one. Grace was somehow always surprised by how heavy it was.

"Why do you think they pay us at all?" Grace asked, mostly out of habit. They'd already had this conversation—but there were only so many safe topics of discussion. "I don't even know where they get the money?"

"I guess it's just the metaphor," Declan said. "Greed is a lot more abstract if there's nothing physical about it, I guess."

"Hmm, guess so," Grace said.

"Are you excited about the big dinner?" Declan asked.

"Well, I think we have everything we need for it," Grace replied. "I want to make a good impression on them."

"Me too," Declan said. "I've been studying the recipes for it when I have free time."

"That's a good idea."

A silent moment passed, as it always did.

"Want to play the radio while we count?" Declan eventually asked.

"Is there music on right now?"

"Just the usual stuff," Declan said.

"Better than nothing," Grace said.

Declan walked over to the large red radio suckered to the countertop. It was likely quite heavy—being seemingly made of solid metal—but there was no way to pick it up. The front of the radio had three dials. One turned it on. The second raised the volume. The final was for show: it only ever got a single station.

Declan clicked it on, and a soft, corporate instrumental wafted out of it. Grace hated it. It sounded like stuffy offices. It sounded like slowly bucking under the weight of days that consisted of a hypnotic repetition.

"Turn that up," Grace said enthusiastically.

"Can do!" Declan said.

The sound enveloped the area. Declan rushed back over. They only risked doing this for a few minutes at a time.

Trial and error confirmed that the register itself worked the best. The shavings needed to have a specific quality.

Grace sawed the side of the coin against a corner of the register. It was also suckered to its spot. Grace caught the little flecks of metal in her palm as the coin's edges were sawed down. She waited until Declan finished doing the same for his coin. They only got a little from each. The Manager might've noticed otherwise.

They both went through two more coins before Declan gave Grace a firm nod.

"Well, looks like everything is accounted for," Grace said. "We made a lot of profit today."

Declan flinched slightly. He was very not fond of the word *profit*. Grace couldn't blame him. She'd been busy fighting The Monopolist, but Declan had told her more about what happened with The Lobbyist. With Aoife.

"Yeah … yeah, we did make a lot," Declan said.

Grace got up and turned off the radio. She returned and took a second to lean against the counter. The exhaustion always hit in waves for her. She took a long breath, stabilizing the uneven sensation in her head.

She turned to look at Declan.

"Are you going to stay up?" she asked.

"I think I need to learn a little more about the recipes. We only have a little more time. There's still five pages to learn. I'm still not sure I've got the wine sauce right, and I don't have that much extra to test with."

"Fuck, okay."

"It'll be fine. I'm a fast study."

"You're sure?" Grace asked, a little nervousness creeping into her voice. "Didn't you pull an all-night yesterday?"

"It was two days ago. And I think that it'll be fine," Declan said. "I think I can get it done in the next hour or two."

"Okay. Well, I'm going to try and sleep."

Declan looked at her for a long moment.

"Sounds good," he said.

Grace couldn't help but smile then, despite all the other emotions in her head. Declan was one of the few people in the world who understood her, it felt like. She was acquaintances with everyone, had served everyone, but not many of them were actually friends. But Declan understood the hell that sleeping was for her. Understood her insomnia. Understood that she didn't like to talk about it.

And, so, he didn't ask about it.

It was so nice not to be asked about it.

"Well, good night, Declan."

Declan looked up at her, and he gave what little of a smile he could muster. Sometimes, Grace wondered how much of a fog of sadness he had to press past for gestures like that.

"Good night, Grace," he said.

"I love you, Declan."

Declan gave out a little sound like he might cry, but his smile held. "Love you too."

Grace looked at him for a second more, then walked off. She had one more thing to do in her new nightly routine.

Chapter 24

BEFORE SHE WENT TO HER ROOM, SHE stopped in front of the occupied broom closet.

She hesitated a moment, then knocked.

From the inside came a low groan. Then someone moving around and at least once banging into something.

"Fuck … fuck that hurt," Greg said. "Goddamn it."

"Sorry," Grace said quietly.

A moment later, the handle spun, and Grace stepped back on instinct. The door swung open too quick, followed by Greg slinking his way out of the cramped closet. He blinked a few times, and then let out a massive yawn.

Greg somehow looked put together despite just waking up. He'd never call himself the term *influencer*, but back when social media was accessible, he'd had a *substantial* following. He was tall, with chestnut brown hair, white skin with a perfect tan, and striking green eyes. If the world hadn't ended, it wouldn't have been a surprise if he'd somehow landed an acting or modeling role.

He yawned one more time as he looked at her.

"Oh, hi … Grace…" He deeply frowned. "If you're here … that means that it … it wasn't a dream. Fuck. We're still in Hell."

Grace almost sobbed. She couldn't help the sudden emotion. After keeping it together for Declan, for The Customers, for her own survival, something that casual stabbed her gut.

It was that one word: *Hell.*

Even on her worst days, she'd never imagined that word might be close to describing her existence.

Grace quickly wiped away the tears that had escaped. "No, I'm sorry—it wasn't a dream. I'm so sorry."

Greg seemed to wake up a bit. He put his head in his hands. "Oh fucking god, okay. Okay … okay … okay…"

"I'm so sorry," Grace repeated.

"Is it that time again?" Greg asked.

"Yeah … it is…"

"Fuck," Greg said loudly.

"Yeah…"

Greg spun around and fished around in a pile of clothes. Of the three of them, he had the most still clean clothing. They used the sink when they could, but there wasn't time. And the soap was limited, its container bolted to the sink, and was quite caustic.

The one he fished out had the logo for Izzy's short-lived band that had broken up years ago.

"Let me change quick," Greg said.

Grace nodded and pushed the door closed. She leaned against the adjoining wall. A moment later, Greg emerged wearing the tee-shirt and a pair of black jeans.

"Same plan as before?" Greg asked.

Grace nodded. "Yep. You know what to do?"

"I do," Greg said, "but I do feel like you should give me more to do than prep work."

If you fuck up anything else, Greg, they'll kill you.

"It really helps a lot, actually. And it does take you all night, doesn't it?"

"I mean, yeah."

"Then this works."

Greg wilted a little and Grace felt a little guilty. She did wish she could have him do more, but he had no cooking experience, and, though rather marketing and media savvy, she didn't trust him in the kitchen. They were in enough danger without someone who hadn't worked in the service industry before.

"Fine," Greg said. "I'll wake you up in six hours?"

"Make it five. We have so little time."

"Grace, you got to sleep more. You have to sleep sometime."

Grace rolled her eyes. "I got this. Don't worry. Once we handle this big thing, I promise I'll get a lot more rest. Now, go do prep work, dude."

"You promise?" Greg asked.

"Yes, I promise."

"Okay," Greg said.

He shrugged his shoulders and walked slowly toward the kitchen. Declan was likely waiting to give him a little overview of what to do. And then they'd leave him to his own devices.

Grace waited one more moment, then went the few steps to her own broom closet. Somehow, she missed sleeping on the air mattress in the old version of the diner.

CHAPTER 25

S OMEONE KNOCKED ON GRACE'S DOOR, but it wasn't Greg. When she opened it, Declan stood on the other side, his eyes bloodshot. He was standing up straight for the first moment, but then he slumped hard against the doorframe. It looked like, for a second, that he was going to slink down to the floor.

But he didn't. He just let out a faint chuckle that sounded more like air leaking out of him. Then he nodded at her.

"Hey, Grace … time to wake up."

"What happened?" Grace asked.

She was pretty sure she knew, though. She knew that look on someone's face. Her pulse spun, twirled, sprinted faster and faster in her chest.

"It was a lot… There was a thing on the fourth page…" Declan took a steadying breath. "I didn't know we'd needed to make it by hand. I didn't know how to bake…"

Now that he mentioned it, Grace could smell the faint scent of smoke on him. The skin on his nose looked a little sunburned.

"Was there a fire?" she asked.

"There *was* a fire," Declan responded. "I … well, Greg and I, cleaned it up … as best we could. But I can't … I'm so sorry. I didn't sleep at all."

"Shit."

Grace's mind started going as fast as her pulse. This wasn't the first time she'd dealt with everything going wrong. Hell, she'd seen her fair share of lunch rushes descend into nigh-anarchy. All it took was one person spilling a tray of silverware to swing the vibe of a restaurant.

I need Declan to cook. We can't risk anyone else handling the serving but me. Not with what's happening in two days—

No, one day.

Tomorrow.

Fucking shit, this is bad.

Greg will need to handle customers. I can't trust him to cook. Hopefully, he can handle that.

"Okay…" Grace said aloud. "Okay then. How short of a nap can you get away with?"

Declan nodded his head, then shook his head. He rubbed his forehead.

"Sorry, what?"

Grace's jaw tensed. "How long of a nap can you get away with before you'll be okay to work with The Customers?"

Declan's eyes didn't seem totally focused. "An … hour? I guess?"

He needs at least three, Grace thought. *A whole night, actually, but we don't have time for that.*

"Okay," Grace said aloud. "I'll wake you up when it's time. Go lay down now."

Declan nodded. He shifted to stand, but almost instantly fell back against the doorframe. He closed his eyes like he was about to fall asleep right there and then.

"Declan, go to your bed, now," Grace said firmly.

His eyes opened, and he nodded slowly. This time, he successfully pushed himself off and wandered to his room. Grace didn't stop watching him until the door closed.

Then she sprinted for the kitchen.

They had so little time before The Customers returned from wherever they went at night.

CHAPTER 26

THE ORDERS ARRIVED AS STRANGE AND difficult as always. There was no reprieve from the odd requests. Each and every one, without fail, had some additional issue to it. Some tiny detail that seemed tailor-made to be unpleasant for her.

In a very real way, they threw Grace off her game more than the monsters making the orders. More than the constant and lingering threat of horrible death. Even for the most difficult of the pure cooking challenges, she could rely on her training to get her through it.

But these were truly random.

*Admit to the vegetable soup what
you're most afraid of right now.*

"I'm afraid of dying," Grace told the soup as it boiled.

Once it was done, she poured a large ladle of it into a bowl. Then got out the pepper grinder and kept going until her eyes watered and it took all her effort not to sneeze directly into the soup. She wasn't going to give them a single thing to complain about from her.

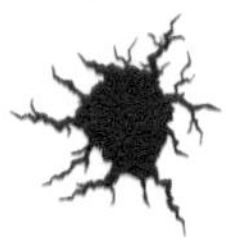

Salt this steak with your literal tears.

The problem wasn't so much that she couldn't get herself to cry. That much took only the smallest weakening of her emotional walls. The issue was *stopping* crying.

The issue was not letting in all the fear that sparked in her brain and slid along her nerves.

Even before The Infinite Diner, she'd seen things when she'd looked too long at that screen in the house surrounded by slaughtered bodies. The graphs and charts that had shown her the future of the world if the environment wasn't fixed. She'd witnessed mass extinctions, mass suffering. And then, toward the end, her own hope for the future had started to melt out of her.

It was still with her. In the back of her mind.

Even before this current hell, she'd been dealing with all that.

At the very least, she got her face over the steak, and the first few tears splashed down on the meat, mixing with the butter sauce she'd just made.

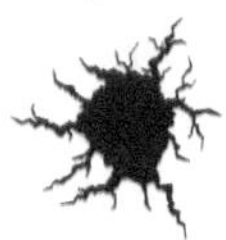

Stand as close to the fryer as you can while frying the tater tots.

Grace took a little longer than normal to start on that one. She stood by the massive silver oil fryer, with a bag of frozen tater tots next to her.

She took a calming breath, then placed the tots into the rack and lowered them in. She stayed right over it, even when it felt to her like the grease might leap at her. The warmth made her back slick with sweat.

Grace kept looking down into it. The churning mass of golden yellow liquid. She couldn't see her reflection in it, but she couldn't help but imagine it.

"One more day until it happens," she muttered. "One more day."

The timer went off. She pulled out the tater tots and laid them out on a plate. She frowned. One by one, all of her comfort foods had been ruined by this place. There had been a day where she would've loved some tater tots.

There once were also days were she seriously considered she would live to see old age.

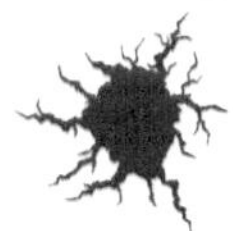

Heavily smear my burger with the
blood directly from your left hand.

As Grace read it, her heart sank. She'd always suspected that she'd get an order like this. But she'd been lucky so far. Nothing but tears and sweat and spit.

Her stomach churned. The idea of wanting to eat a burger like that made her feel ill. The Customers were monsters, yes, but this wasn't just wanting to eat flesh. This was so precise.

She had no choice, of course.

The alternative was so much worse.

She went to the storage space. It was always full to bursting; refilling when no one was looking. Over time, she'd gotten a handle on it though. It sometimes limited items—like the wine Declan was working with. But mostly it replenished everything, just in different places.

But there was a *slight* logic to where things went, at least. The variations in container sizes ensured—unless the Diner's dimensions warped even further—that they couldn't put things in places that were too crowded for them. And, better yet, the actual containers never changed.

She found the hamburger meat quickly. It was in a massive box toward the back.

The order had called for a single patty. No cheese. No onions. Not even salt or pepper.

Blood is salty.

Grace shivered. She placed the meat patty down on the heat. It hissed as the residual ice almost instantly melted into steam. The faint smell wafted alongside the steam.

Grace felt like she was getting closer to joining Declan in being a vegetarian.

She grabbed the spatula and waited another moment. Then she flipped the patty. A little squirt of meat juice popped out the side, hissing across the stovetop.

Grace gagged, almost puking, before swallowing down the sensation. She turned to get the buns for it. She gagged again as she walked.

The buns stuck together, so she pulled them apart. A rumble passed through her stomach. She took a deep breath. She grabbed the steak knife as she walked back. It clattered slightly when she laid it down.

Keep it together. You can do this. You have to do this.

When she returned, the burger was done. Expertly, she moved it to the bun. Steam continued to waft off it, spiraling up in little white plumes.

Grace debated how she was going to do this. And then felt a surge of sickness at having to consider how to go about this.

Another order slapped down. The bell dinged again. *You don't have time.*

Grace sucked in a massive breath. She held that small amount of oxygen inside. Let it bolster her.

She held up her left hand and slashed across it with the knife.

There was a singular moment, almost too quick for her mind to catch, where the skin had a simple line through it. Before even the pain made the trip down her nerve endings.

Then red pooled out, dripped like raindrops, then flowed as a sheet of blood.

A swear tried to escape her mouth, but she gritted her teeth. Her entire face tightened up. She looked down at the burger. The grease on it gave the meat a slight sheen.

She slapped her hand down on the burger.

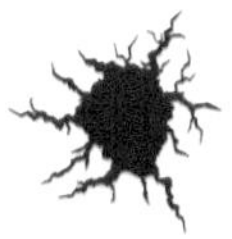

Garnish the top of my meatloaf with EXACTLY three drops of blood from your left index finger.

Grace had only just finished wrapping her injured hand when that instruction arrived. She'd made a rough covering out of napkins and bound it with the rope she'd pulled off the beef in the back.

At least with this order, she had a little time to let the first injury heal. The meatloaf cooked away in the oven—handmade, as instructed—as she worked on other things. She kept having to replace the napkin. The blood seeped through quickly. It was mostly adrenaline keeping her going.

When the ding sounded off, she cringed.

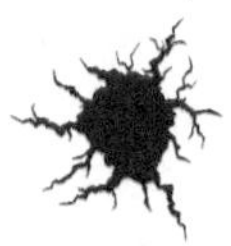

A fresh cup of lemonade bloodied by your left hand.

The note was the slimiest she'd ever seen it. The weird spittle nearly reduced the paper to a pile of slush, the words barely readable.

This, of all things, was what made Grace realize.

Not only had they upped the cruelty in their orders, but they'd also been coordinated. She could so easily imagine the little laugh passing from booth to booth as The Customers plotted.

But what could she do?

Grace forced back tears as she walked over to the supply closest. The layout of the food in there had changed again. A large container of relish sat so close to falling off the edge of its shelf.

And the container of lemons, easily over fifty stacked high in a wooden crate, sat right at eye level. When she took one out, they were spotless ... clean. When she took one out, another perfectly fell into place.

She grabbed ten of them. That seemed like enough. It seemed like way too much.

The quickest knife to get was the one she'd used to slice her hand open. It went through the lemons, halving them, leaving a little trail of juice on the wooden cutting board. She didn't have time to dawdle, but Grace wished that this part took longer. For once, she wished that she wasn't so damn effective.

A mantra flitted through her head.

The Customers won't win. The Customers won't win. The Customers won't win.

Grace really wished Declan was awake. She wouldn't have been so scared if he was nearby.

She juiced the ten lemons. Helpfully, her left index finger was bleeding again. She was pretty sure she hadn't blinked for the past minute.

She turned away to get the sugar, but it was already near her. The bag sat on the counter. She hadn't moved it there. It was a massive white bag, more like what was usually used for flour. But there was the label for sugar…

And beneath it, written out, were the words:

Having fun, sugar?

Grace nearly snarled at it. A simmering anger was in her fucking bones.

She picked up the bag and slapped it down next to the cup. The back of the bag had a smiley face drawn on it. She ignored that as best she could and scooped out the required amount of sugar. It mostly dissolved into the lemon juice.

But it wouldn't fully—not without someone stirring it.

Grace's hand shook as she held her hand over the cup. She couldn't imagine how badly this was going to hurt. She closed her eyes. Maybe that would help.

It didn't.

She plunged her finger into the cup, and the lemon juice found her finger's cut immediately, and then the slash in her palm. The sugar found them a moment later.

Her jaw tensed, her shoulders tensed, her eyes were closed so tight, but the swear broke free all the same. Grace nearly fell over, her legs wanting to buckle.

She pulled her hand out, knocking over the cup. She covered her mouth, the lemon juice and blood dripping down on her shirt. Tears and whimpers spilled out of her, but mostly her mind fixed on one thing.

Strike two.

CHAPTER 27

"**W**HAT FUCKING LANGUAGE! WHAT IS happening in that kitchen? How dare you say something like that! You've completely ruined my dining experience! I demand to see *The Manager*!"

Those words. That phrasing and intonation. It warped the air. Twisted and slid like a ripple on the surface of the walls. It kept echoing, kept sharply repeating itself.

At least until—

Grace's gaze fell on the door.

It opened, and The Manager stood there.

Stood is the wrong word for it. Existed was closer. Overwhelmed was the most accurate. The air, the temperature, it fell back in fear from the radioactive glow of The Manager.

Grace had only met him a few times. Once was when she'd started her Endless Diner nightmare, and another was when she'd gotten a strike. He was, at a glance, similar to The Lobbyist. A human-shaped monster with white skin and brown hair who talked like a person—for the most part. He wore a white button-up shirt with a blue blazer over it, creased black dress pants, and solid blue shoes. The veins around his eyes glowed blue.

He took a step toward her, and the air shifted. The Manager's edges, his frame, were a doorway to a wide-open room always barely visible behind him. Figures stood in that place, listless and strange.

When he spoke, a thick smog, like car exhaust on a snowy day, leaked from his mouth.

"Grace," The Manager snarled, "What do we say about The Customers? What do we *always* say about them?"

Grace took a step backward; her heart was hammering so loud. She couldn't think—couldn't form the words in her head, let alone say them out loud.

The Manager marched at her. It felt like being run down by a car. He was so much taller than her.

He opened his mouth and frigid air spilled over Grace's face.

"Well, Grace, I'm waiting?"

Grace swallowed hard. "We need to … we need to keep them happy, sir."

"That's right," The Manager said. "That's right Grace. That's what you're here for. That's what The God of Greed demands of all of us. Endless toil."

Grace nodded.

The Manager nodded back slowly. The blue veins were spreading further through his face.

"I'm glad you agree," The Manager continued. "Because I don't want to have to do what I need to do, Grace. I don't want to inflict any disciplinary actions on you. Not before tomorrow. We need you around for that. But I will reschedule things, find new servers, if I have to. Greg is at two, Declan is at one. And now you're at two.

I don't need all of you. If it comes to that, I *will* have to, now, won't I?"

Grace nodded again, but The Manager fixed her with a look.

"Yes, sir … you would have to, sir," Grace said.

"I would! And they are eager, you understand?"

From around The Manager's edges, things peeked in. Things wearing suits. Things with thirteen eyes each, placed on their head randomly.

"They will dish out the punishment," The Manager said. "They will make sure that all of you … eventually … die."

"Okay, sir."

The Manager smirked. "You'd be honored by them killing you?"

"It … it would be an honor, sir."

The Manager chuckled. "Good."

Then he turned away, walking toward the door. But right before he got through the door, he stopped. A cloud of that cold smoke drifted up, filling the doorway.

"I am aware of what you and Declan did, you know."

A shiver went up Grace's spine. "What's that, sir?"

"We are not made without knowledge of things. You and Declan killed The Monopolist and The Lobbyist. And your little friends Chuck and Cassandra killed The Oil Baron. A human killed us. That's an insult I cannot ever forget. That none of us will ever forgive. So, when each of you dies, when I make your death horrible, remember that. Remember that you only brought this on yourself. You could've let yourself die in that forest. It would've been less painful, I assure you. A little cut on your hand will feel like it's nothing. That moment, when you fail, when I get to sacrifice you to my god, will be the most painful thing you've ever experienced."

The Manager looked over his shoulder.

"Now, finish up that lemonade. I think it could use one more good stir of a bloody finger. And then go wake up your friend. You upset a customer, and I think all of them are entitled to a free slice of pie. I do so wonder how many *different* flavors they will ask for you to make?"

Chapter 28

Garnish my slice of cherry pie with a pile of hair pulled out by hand.

Declan held his hand over his mouth as Grace stood behind him. Grace then tugged out twenty individual hairs. One at a time. As quickly as she could. Declan's back was so damn tight. When he turned around, tears were streaming down his face, but he nodded to her.

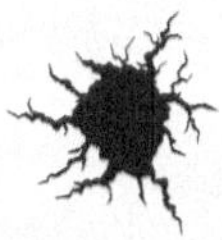

Tell my apple pie slice what you had nightmares about as a child.

"When I was a kid, maybe twelve," Grace began, "I had a reoccurring dream. I have no idea what started it. In my room, there was this one window that was broken a little.

The curtain rod would always dip to the side slightly. It would let in the light at sunup. I hated waking up that early. But for that week … I don't know what made it reflect like that…"

Grace shivered. She still didn't like thinking about those nightmares.

"But it looked like a pair of really bright eyes. I had dreams about a face that I could only kind of see. Those eyes would get closer and closer. I'd be trapped in my parent's car, trying to hide underneath the seat … and it would be there, staring at me. I never saw it, but I always knew…"

Grace took a long breath.

"I always knew that if he got into the car, he had metallic fingers. And I would…"

Something in her chest twinged, and Grace had to suppress tears.

"I knew, if The Spotlight Man caught me, I would die."

CHAPTER 29

GRACE KNEW THAT THIS COULDN'T CON-tinue. The whole thing had to fall apart sooner or later.

Greg couldn't be trusted to cook, so he'd been dealing with the verbal abuse of The Customers for so long. For the brief moments she could see him when he dropped off orders, he either looked at the edge of yelling with anger, crying, or going completely catatonic.

She couldn't do anything to help him.

They'd only just gotten through the pie orders, finally getting the last out the door. Flour was everywhere; it was in Grace's hair, on her clothes, coating countertops.

But that didn't mean they were done.

Regular orders spilled in, just as they had before. Not all of them called for blood, skin, sweat, tears, or hair, but they would occasionally happen. Grace had eventually found masking tape, so they'd at least been able to keep the napkin bandages stuck to their bodies.

She couldn't help but imagine each and every one of those wounds festering, getting infected. If she didn't die to … the thing The Manager would do to them if they failed, a fever might manage it.

Grace barely paid attention to it though.

She was more worried about Declan than herself. All told, he had only gotten around two hours of sleep. More and more, he would stare into space, forget things, or simply move slower than he had before.

Grace was also at her limits. Her limbs ached. Her heartbeat would get faster and faster until she was sure she was about to pass out.

The orders didn't stop.

The orders didn't fucking stop.

CHAPTER 30

GRACE BLAMED HERSELF. SHE SHOULDN'T have—but she did. It started with her. The chain reaction.

She was doing dishes. Sometimes they had to do them in the middle of the restaurant order warzone. Greg had done his best to clean as many as possible, but with the extra pies, it had piled them high. The one that started things wasn't a pie tin though. It was eggs that had missed Greg's morning sweep.

Grace hated cleaning up eggs. It wasn't any more gross than anything else, but something about the thin membrane of eggs stuck on a plate struck a nerve.

Maybe it was because of how much work it often took to scrap off. The wire brush would take off chunks of it—but only chunks—and then the egg would stick in the brush.

Maybe it was because of the smell. Grace had worked many, many breakfast shifts and certain smells could turn unpleasant from that familiarity. At least from time to time. Coffee, especially burnt coffee. Ketchup. Fuck, sometimes she *hated* that sugary smell of ketchup. And, of course, eggs. Pungent, slimy, over-salted, ketchup smeared, burned, so it caked to the pan, eggs.

She was lost in thought when it happened. The kind of thoughts that sleepiness delivers.

Water hadn't fully drained off a plate when she tipped the plate toward herself. A huge splash of cold, filthy water splashed down on her.

And, normally, she wouldn't be fazed. Grace worked in the service industry—there's no way to avoid gross stuff getting on her from time to time. But it was more water than she expected.

It made a puddle.

The Manager hadn't considered safety in that kitchen, obviously.

There wasn't even a non-stick rug beneath her feet.

Grace slid left, instantly off balance. A shot of pure vertigo hit her as she toppled. She almost didn't have the reaction time, the presence of mind, to catch herself on the countertop.

Her shoulder bumped into Declan. And if she was merely wobbly, he was practically thrown off his feet. He stumbled backward, feet barely managing to keep him from falling on his back.

For the rest of Grace's life, she would remember these moments. The sounds. The looks on people's faces, both alive and dead. She turned in alarm, standing there, in that kitchen, too far away to do anything. Too far away to stop this.

The door to the kitchen inched open.

"We've got more pie tins to deal with—"

Declan slammed into the door, and it snapped shut. Then there was a crash. Greg swore, loudly, as a crescendo of pie tins hit the ground. The clatter of them echoed for much longer than Grace thought they should.

No Customer even yelled out a complaint. It was like this had been expected.

The door inched open again. Declan scrambled backward. Grace's heart felt like it had stopped. The air in that place was so fucking cold.

The Manager stood on the other side. He looked *happy.* He had one hand on Greg's shoulder, but that seemed to be enough. Grace, Declan, Greg, they all had been warned what would happen if they got three strikes. They all knew.

CHAPTER 31

"**I** WONDERED WHO IT WOULD BE," THE Manager mused. "One had to be the first—and a threat hangs until it is taken."

Grace glanced around. Her eyes fell on that same damn knife one more time. Objects made by these monsters could hurt them—but it had never been feasible to fight before. Too many Customers, too much danger.

But … but … but…

She picked up the knife, her hands shaking.

"Let him go," Grace said, her words stronger than she felt. "Fucking … don't touch him."

The Manager glanced over at her.

"That's cute, Grace," The Manager said, looking over the knife. "You expect that to do anything at all?"

"It's … a knife…" Grace managed.

The Manager rolled his eyes, and then the space around him expanded. Those many-eyed things stepped out from a room that couldn't exist.

Grace stifled a scream and almost dropped the knife. Even after everything, the sight of monsters would never be blasé. Would never be something she could just witness.

They were very thin, pale white creatures with seemingly no room for human-like organs. In a circle, by what Grace couldn't help but think of as the neck, was a ring of lamprey-like mouths. Those mouths opened and closed like gasping fish, but produced a chittering sound, like grasshoppers in a chorus.

"Pin them," The Manager instructed. "And punish Greg. He has three strikes."

At least ten of those monsters stepped forward, and more followed from the other place. They instantly filled up the kitchen.

Declan barely had time to react before three of them slammed him into the wall and pressed him there. He struggled—but had no leverage and no weapons.

"Let me go," he yelled. "You fucking—"

One of the monsters slapped Declan's head against the wall. When Declan tried to talk again, tried to express a single syllable, they did it again. A little pink spittle leaked from his mouth.

Grace's heart sank, but she couldn't do anything to help. The other monsters focused on her. They approached Grace a little more warily though. Five of them fanned out, chittering. Grace scanned her gaze back and forth, trying to not let any of them out of her sight. She backed up slowly, trying to get something solid behind her.

She bumped into something—but it wasn't what she'd hoped.

An arm wrapped around her throat from behind. The skin of the monster was dry, almost coarse. She slashed wildly with the knife. She felt it cut into something.

The monster chittered in pain and let her go. Grace scrambled forward. She gripped the knife tighter.

The other monsters closed in. One punched her in the side. It hurt about as much as a human punch—but that was plenty enough. Grace gasped, but still slashed at that one.

It turned out the monster didn't have blood, just something that looked like the mold that grew on a sandwich left out too long. It oozed out quickly.

Grace took a step forward, slamming her foot down. It was enough to drive the monster back. It wasn't enough for the other ones.

A different monster punched her in the gut so hard her legs buckled, and another grabbed her arm. It twisted her wrist until she dropped the knife. Its gentle clatter as it hit the kitchen floor was so quiet compared to Greg dropping the pie tins.

Disarmed and gasping, Grace couldn't do much to stop the rest of the monster from pinning her. One even picked up the knife and held it up close to her throat.

"I suppose I shouldn't be surprised," The Manager commented. "You're not much of a fan of industry."

Grace wanted to snarl at him—but Greg's panicked screams caught her attention. Her gaze snapped to him. And even though she knew what she'd see, she still gasped.

The punishment.

They always kept the fryer going. All night, every night, and each day, for the whole time they'd been there. The oil always hissing and sputtering.

The monsters, two of them, were holding back Greg's arms. A third was standing directly behind him.

"Please—please—please—" Greg kept screaming, his words blending together into a cry.

"Let him go!" Grace yelled.

Then a soft bit of pain. She couldn't look down, but she could feel the gently running blood where the knife had lightly cut her.

The monster chittered softly.

"Gregory, Gregory," The Manager began, "you have gotten three strikes. You have been nothing but terrible for this business, for this kitchen, and it is with great pleasure that we let you go. You're fired, Gregory."

Greg let out a wail, a cry without words.

Greg couldn't even brace his hands on either side of the fryer. They pushed his entire head into the oil with a mighty splash.

Greg's shoulders shook back and forth. He thrashed down in that oil. Some of it spilled on the monsters, but they didn't seem to mind.

It took so little time for Greg's legs to go slack. But he didn't get a chance to fall. The monsters caught his dipping body and then pushed more of him into the oil. Past the shoulders, almost to his chest.

It took too long. It was so quick.

Greg didn't move, resist, or do anything anymore.

The monsters yanked him back out, turned him around, and laid his corpse against the side of the fryer.

Grace didn't look away in time.

There wasn't much left of his face except for the skull and teeth.

Chapter 32

"Get Gregory outside," The Manager said. "The tendril shoots need to take him to The Spire."

A monster nodded, and another went to open the doorway out into the main area. Grace briefly saw the pie tins, still lying in a pile. As sickening as it was, she'd probably have to pick those up.

A third dragged Greg's still-smoking body out. The Customers started clapping like it was the end of a theater play. A chill shot up Grace's spine.

"Now, I hope that taught you something," The Manager said. "We have a big plan tomorrow—some very important people will be here—and you need to be as motivated as possible."

Grace couldn't help it. She glared at him.

The Manager chuckled, a little cold smoke leaking from his mouth.

"Grace, there will be a day when I also get to order your lungs filled with oil. When third-degree burns will shred your intestinal wall. And when that happens, I won't miss you a single bit. You should be grateful for all of this. We sacrifice you humans in ways that fit our nature—but we only *have* to do that for a certain percentage. There's nothing stopping me from ordering your death right now."

The Manager waited a moment, perhaps for that to sink in. But all Grace felt was grief occasionally overshadowed and hidden away by a cold, frigid, frostbitten rage.

One more day, then. I'm so sorry Greg … that I wasn't able to help you soon enough. I will … I don't know. But Declan is getting out of this. I won't let this place take … I won't.

The monsters released Declan and Grace. They wandered toward The Manager and seemed to dissolve into light. A moment later, their eyes peeked out from that strange place always behind The Manager.

"Well, now, I suppose Greg's entrails have gone to their purpose. As for you two, the shift is not over. I expect the best work from you today—and then even better work tomorrow. Our guests desire that feast. Just because you saw something horrible, doesn't mean Greed doesn't keep on ticking."

The Manager walked out of the kitchen.

Grace stared at that door. The rage still bubbled in her. She stirred it, let it simmer. Back in the climate change house, rage had been her weapon. Rage culled fear. It was the closest thing to hope that was readily available.

She didn't think of it as a call to arms, but a thought formed crystal clear in her mind. It had been there for a while. An impetus, perhaps, for the plan they'd been hatching—the plan that hadn't been used in time to save everyone. But it would be used.

The single sentence. Oh, that singular sentence. It was as sharp as the knife.

Don't fucking mess with the person who makes your food.

CHAPTER 33

DECLAN AND GRACE WORDLESSLY FELL into prepping. Cleaning the dishes. Putting out the ingredients that didn't need refrigeration. Without Greg, it would take them almost all night. Grace was aware that only nightmares would find her in what rest she could claim.

They didn't go back to their little rooms. Declan slept on the floor while Grace continued working. Grace felt herself almost disentangling from her body from sheer exhaustion. More and more manipulating a self-puppet than being in her body. Her fingers felt numb. Her heartbeat didn't seem like it was there at all. She would've suspected she was dead, if not for the hiss of the always-on oil fryer.

Declan awoke sometime while she was cleaning pans. He groaned slightly as he got off the hard floor. Then went over to the radio.

Grace glanced back at him.

"Going to listen to some music?" she asked.

"I feel like I need a little more before the big day," he replied.

"Sounds good," Grace said.

She went back to cleaning, but, even underneath the cranked-up, banal music, she could hear the faint sound of coins chipping away.

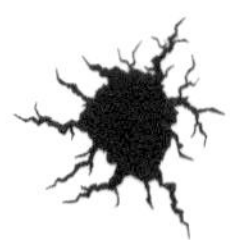

The morning arrived without The Customers. They weren't scheduled for the day. The Manager wanted the place only for the esteemed guests. In terms of workload, with all the prep they'd done, it was actually set out to be one of the lighter days.

That didn't make it any less stressful when the bell for the front door rang.

"Come out you two," The Manager called. "*Now.*"

"Oh, you don't have to make such a bother," said a voice.

And Grace, halfway to the kitchen door, nearly froze. She'd known he would be here. But it didn't make hearing his voice any better. Her joints almost locked, and her breath sped up slightly.

On the inside was rage.

Hatred.

Grace had spent her life not hating anyone as much as possible. She didn't want to have hate in her heart. But *him*...

The calculation of his voice—a certainty in his words that once were formed of manipulation but had stopped hiding that knife. Now, it didn't obscure malice and vile intent—it dressed them up for the dance.

She hadn't seen him that many times before the end of the world. Too bougie for the Ink Well most days. Only eating there with those he oversaw—and only when it was presumably advantageous.

The Mayor of Quill Point.

No, *The Ascended Mayor.*

Grace's polite, customer-friendly face nearly cracked when she saw him. She had seen the new him, down in that strange underground place, but it was still unearthly. Still another thing beyond what the world had been. The Ascended Mayor's skin was coated in a golden aura, his eyes and veins and behind his teeth all glowed with a sharp light.

He looked more like the monsters she'd fought and served.

That change didn't surprise her.

"Of course we need to roll out the welcome wagon for you," The Manager said.

The Mayor of Quill Point smiled. "Well, The God of Greed, praise to him, did set aside special kitchen staff just for us. I'm so glad to use them. Torture is more fun when you can see it in their eyes."

He looked right into Grace's eyes—and she held his gaze. She couldn't show her thoughts on her face, but the smallest resistance kept her from crying.

The Ascended Mayor eventually looked away.

"What happened to the third one?" he asked. "I grabbed a third just to see what would happen."

"I'm afraid he wasn't up to snuff," The Manager said.

"Oh, well, that's unfortunate," The Ascended Mayor said. "But not surprising. I did suspect he would fail. Every establishment needs to have some sacrifices emanating from them; we can't have everyone here survive for too long."

Grace kept picturing punching The Ascended Mayor in the face.

"Do tell," The Mayor of Quill Point continued, "how did you decide to murder him?"

"As you suggested, he was fried until dead," The Manager said.

"Ah, that was an inspired choice, wasn't it? I'm glad you took it as a suggestion."

The Manager nodded. "Your advice has been sublime."

"I do feel as though I am getting much better at this, thank you. It's a new paradigm; a new world. I've been learning as much as I can about the greater scope of your designs."

"Truly, there's so much to it," The Manager said.

The Mayor of Quill Point adjusted his collar. "And how! The God of Greed has been asking me such interesting questions lately. He's letting me pick the death sentences of a few of my constituency, sometimes, when the others aren't in charge—and what inspired decisions they have made! I have to say, this has been a wonderful experience. It's been so relaxing. Much easier than in my old career. There's no worrying about pleasing the voters or reelection."

Grace was now thinking about seeing how many punches it would take to break every bone in The Mayor of Quill Point's face.

"I'm sure, I am sure," The Manager commented.

"But enough about that for now. There'll be plenty of talk to be had when the others arrive. I figured it was about time to have a wonderful meeting at this hallowed establishment."

Grace glanced at Declan. He was having a much harder time keeping the disdain off his face. But no one had said anything about that yet. Grace suspected both The Manager and *especially* The Ascended Mayor enjoyed talking.

"That's great to hear," The Manager said. "We have a seat all prepared for you and the others."

The Manager spun around, gave a cold glance at Grace, and then snapped his fingers. The Infinite Diner lost some of its space. The long, reality breaking tunnels collapsed into nothing, and the walls zoomed close. A gold chandelier dropped from the ceiling, jangling and swinging for a moment. Then, as if gripped by a massive hand, it stopped swinging. Several yellow lights glowed from strange bulbs.

The massive wooden table shifted. Grace couldn't quite grasp what she was looking at. But then it was set. A blue tablecloth covered it. Sets of utensils were wrapped with blood-red cloth. A series of candles burned away; their flames larger than should've been possible.

"Incredible," The Mayor complimented. "Truly, you've thought of our needs to the utmost."

"I've done my best," The Manager said. "Grace here— our veteran of the industry—will be taking the coats, or whatever else our guests wish to shed, at the door, while Declan will be finishing preparations."

"Excellent," The Mayor said. "Just excellent."

Chapter 34

GRACE STOOD BY THE DOOR, WAITING for the first of three guests to arrive. As she stood there, the intense every-food smell gone, she thought about the last thing she ate—and if it would be her last meal. By the end of this, either her plan would work, or she would surely die. Even if the plan worked, there was every chance she would die anyway.

Like Aoife.

Like Greg.

She hoped that, at the very least, Declan would survive. If not her, then at least him. Let her last act, if that was all she could do, be saving someone from all this.

A monster knocked at the door.

Her first impression was a ticking-clock of a woman. Her body angular in ways a human spine couldn't sustain. Her face was so big. She was so tall, and long, and those two clicking clock bones jutting from her middle made Grace's stomach roil.

And she knew this monster's name. That was, somehow, one of the stranger elements of this. Like, with The Monopolist, The Lobbyist, and The Oil Baron. They hadn't *announced* it. Neither Chuck nor Cassandra had fully told them. And those three monsters had been so metaphysical, so made of metaphor she couldn't have guessed *exactly* what they were. But she'd *known*. And, as soon as she got a good look at this clock woman, Grace knew her name too.

The 9-to-5.

"Oh! Oh, I see, it's you," The 9-to-5 said. "The Mayor told me all about *you*. You work here. You toil here and make the food. That's what I've heard."

Grace involuntarily took a step back. The way The 9-to-5 talked was stress as a language, as an auditory form. It wasn't even what she said; it was how she said it. Formless stress, panic stress, out-of-time-before-the-plane-leaves-in-another-terminal-and-you-need-to-use-the-bathroom stress. It washed over Grace and actively raised her heart rate.

Grace felt like she was running out of time.

Time to do what? She didn't know. But she needed to get fucking *going*.

"Uh…" Grace managed. "Uh, yeah, that's me, sir."

"Wonderful. That is such a good thing. We love hearing you go, go, and go. We're going to make you work until you die. I think I will enjoy hearing about you being sacrificed a lot."

Grace got her racing heart somewhat under control and got her face as close to neutral as she could.

"Um, thanks, sir," she said.

The 9-to-5 lowered her head, so she was looking right into Grace's eyes. The 9-to-5 smelled like coffee, mostly.

Very strong, partially burned, coffee. But underneath that, more subtle, was the sharp acrid smell of burning rubber. Specifically, the smell that lingers when a car peels out of a driveway.

"You're welcome," The 9-to-5 said.

"Can I take your coat, or anything, sir?" Grace asked.

"I'm quite warm without such things," The 9-to-5 said. "It's hard to be cold when you move as I do."

"Oh, okay," Grace said. "Enjoy your meal, sir."

"Why thank you."

The 9-to-5 walked past, and, as she did, she folded up. Rather suddenly, she looked like a normal woman. One wearing a suit, with pale white skin that looked shiny with sweat. She sat down at the table, and, like everything about this was normal, started chatting with The Ascended Mayor.

Grace took a steadying breath.

Two more to go.

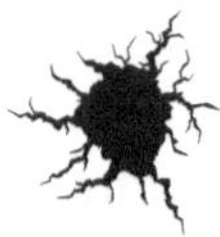

The next arrived with a thunder. Too many knocks.

Grace almost didn't open the door. Her fear response certainly told her it was a bad idea. But that wasn't an option.

We don't have a choice, Grace thought bitterly. *Can that concept stop following me?*

She opened the door. For a moment, it was like she was looking at a boardroom of people. It seemed like at least twenty people. Each of them curious, but dispassionate. Like how a cat might consider a new animal.

They all wore masks.

Old drama masks. Comedy and tragedy masks. Big smiles. Big frowns. Each one was white and looked like it was made of acrylic. Green eyes glowed out from the perfectly round eye holes.

In unison, all the tragedies lifted into smiling comedies. Grace shivered.

The mass of them stepped forward, and a little like The 9-to-5, folded into one person. Their silhouettes shuffling into one another, forming one outline. It reminded Grace of adjusting a deck of cards.

Now that she wasn't looking from one face to another, Grace noticed the rest of how the—

—*The Shareholder* looked.

He wore a dull jacket over a blandly expensive business suit. Had a monotonous business tie on. And wore very shiny, and very generic black shoes.

"Well, look who we have here," The Shareholder said. "Grace. The Grace. How nice to grace your acquaintance. You're on the short-list, you know. A bunch of disrupters. We—"

So fucking quick, the metaphorical deck of cards fanned back out. So many of him stood in a crowd of himself. They could've surrounded the whole building.

Grace mentally flashed back to when she'd been chased into the woods with Declan. The Mayor's Men had felt like the most dangerous thing in the world back then.

They were *nothing* compared to what Greed made.

The crowd collapsed back into one.

"—have been wondering if you were going to shake up anything else before the world ends. If you were going to die earlier than anticipated. We love reliable outcomes— but we also love unforeseen failures—for others, naturally. It opens so many avenues."

Grace was beginning to wonder if there was a single demonic monster in this town who didn't know about her, didn't hold some level of malice toward her. Back before, most of Quill Point knew her as the friendly waitress. She loved that. It helped enormously with loneliness.

This was significantly less pleasant.

"Can I take your jacket, sir?" she eventually asked.

"Ah, yes, I suppose you could," The Shareholder said. "It is rather rude of me to meet with all of the others, and not have the proper form for a grand dinner."

He held the jacket out to her, then dropped it into her hands.

"There. Put it where it can go. I don't much care. I can buy another one."

"Yes, sir. Can do, sir."

The Shareholder walked past her, knocking into her shoulder with such force she crashed into the wall. She didn't shout, didn't wince. She was almost numb to the medium-level pain.

One more to go.

The third and final heralded its arrival with a sound that made Grace flinch. It started as a screeching, scratching noise, then slowly grew more formed. It never quite made it to words, but certainly got across a meaning. Anger. Uncomfortableness. Paranoia. But without direction. The mélange instructed its listener to panic; it didn't terribly matter about what.

Then the knock at the door.

Grace expected a headache from the sight of The Newscaster, but it didn't happen. It was just a strange sight—somehow even less coherent than The Customers. The Newscaster had a face, with a mouth, and eyes, and a nose, but they were all made of shifting paper, or developed photos, or red and green and blue ink. It was like staring into a collage. Newspaper cut outs with layers of television static and a stitch work of tickertape.

When he spoke, words spilled out like they were being squawked out of an old landline connection. She shouldn't have been able to understand, but, like the pixels on a television screen, the mind filled in the gaps.

"Oh, hello there. Are you Grace?" The Newscaster asked.

"Um, yes, sir?"

"Excellent. Lovely to put a face to the name. I've been thinking about how to spin your story. You're well-known enough that we're going to have a feature on you. I really want to get it right—*on the news now, the girl who was killed for her hubris and crimes against*—no, no, that doesn't work. The fear is there. It'll make people feel bad. But it's not memorable."

Grace nodded. "I'm sure you'll figure out something. Can I take your jacket, sir?"

"I'm sure … I'm sure," The Newscaster said. "And you may. You may, here.

He slipped off his jacket. It appeared to be made of green screen. But he didn't hand it to her. Grace waited a moment before moving forward to take it—

Then almost screamed. She was so close to audibly reacting that time. She couldn't stop herself from covering her mouth and taking a half-step back.

A ring of cameras had pushed themselves out of The Newscasters skin, rimming his face. Blood pooled around the holes, growing as splotches, but never falling as drops. The cameras were so much more solid, more unchanging, than the rest of him. They looked sharp, somehow. Each had an aperture that widened and shrunk in tandem, paced like a heartbeat.

From behind both shoulder blades stretched two light stands. At the top of them were very bright bulbs. The stands stretched up almost to the ceiling, shining down on her.

"Oh, she was such a nice girl. Always did what she was told. But then she decided to murder all industry itself! She intended to take down the whole system we hold dear. No, that's too much as well. You have to sensationalize in the right direction, but with a deft hand as well. Grace, you are an enigma, you know that? A problem in a person."

Grace took a shuddering breath through her hands. She glanced up at the glaring lights, then flinched away. It was like looking up at the sun.

"That's…" Grace steadied herself. "That's nice of you to say, sir."

"It's nice until I'm not," The Newscaster said. "You're good ratings, that much is for sure. And now, you should actually take my coat. Thanks for the candid shot."

It wasn't green screen anymore; she had taken a large collection of newspapers in the general formation of a coat.

"Hang it wherever. It's basically dead at this point. An old rag for a different time."

Grace placed it next to the other monster's coat. She turned back to The Newscaster and gave him a smile.

"All ready for your meal, sir?" she asked.

"Yes, I am. I would love to see how the others are doing. I'm sure I can get a wonderful pull quote from them."

Grace stepped to the side to let him through.

He went past her. And with him, the table was full.
The guests had arrived. Five nightmares ready for a feast.

CHAPTER 35

B LISSFULLY, THE FIVE OF THEM DIDN'T PAY much attention to Grace. She brought them their gourmet sandwiches and tea to begin. The food was remarkably normal—just complicated. Declan spent most of his time cooking each steak to their preferences, paired, naturally, with the wine sauce.

In the meantime, as Grace ran back and forth, the monsters talked and talked and talked. The Ascended Mayor didn't even touch his food.

And what they spoke about made Grace's blood boil.

"I am so impressed with how you run The Spire Market, 9-to-5," The Ascended Mayor said, gesturing out with his cup of tea. "It's truly a thing of awe how you pull and push them about."

"Thank you—that's too nice. They are ants. I treat them that way. It's all about the mental bombarding. The wiping memory method is lovely, but I like making it more … relentless. I have this one. I made her a leader. She keeps this walkie-talkie on her. Squawk. Squawk all day in her ears. She hasn't had a good rest in so long. She dreams of it. I can see them."

"How do you think it compares to the back-and-forth model?" The Shareholder asked curiously. "I have them lose all of their memories when they're not working, at least as much as possible. It's nice to leave the tiniest of awareness in them. I think the contrast between work and not is so horrible that both are much worse."

"I like the rush, rush, rush," The 9-to-5 said. "But, again, I see the method's effectiveness."

"How do you avoid them dying too fast?" The Manager asked. "I'd be unable to serve my Customers if I didn't give them some rest."

"I have so many people," The 9-to-5 said. "They go crisp all the time. One every day or so. I have hundreds to burn through."

The Ascended Mayor made a soft sound in the back of his throat. The monsters all looked at him.

"I am sorry about the distinction there. It was on me to designate much of the layout, and I needed to funnel the majority into bigger workplaces. I could only make so many tortures tailored. But, Manager, I have to say that you are doing just as much justice for the cause here."

The Manager nodded in appreciation.

"Besides," The Newscaster added, "it makes for better television, radio, and newsreels, if some people are worse off. It makes the rest feel like they can't complain. You need the showcases, you need the isolating fear, or they might unionize or some shit."

The others at the table grimaced. Grace blinked in surprise. They'd looked genuinely uncomfortable. She gathered herself mentally again and put a tray of sandwiches in front of The 9-to-5.

"Don't say that fucking *vulgar* word," The Manager said. "Don't they know they should work for its own sake?"

"Well, *we* get the reward of their labor," The Shareholder commented.

Four of them laughed. The 9-to-5 only chuckled, then clicked her knife against the table.

The others went silent and glanced her way.

"Forgive me for pushing us into immediate business," she said, "but it is in my nature to not stop working. I've been considering how to improve matters. I think we should discuss it sooner rather than later."

The Ascended Mayor gave her a smile. "Well then, let's discuss."

Grace got the salads as fast as she could. She had a feeling she wanted to hear this next part. Fortunately, Declan had laid them out on a tray. She scooped them up fast enough that she didn't seem to have missed anything.

"Well … there's the issue of the children," The 9-to-5 said. "So far, we've kept them in The Endless Kindergarten and The Unending Middle School, but I feel that's a waste of potential."

"What do you suggest?" The Ascended Mayor asked.

"I have no set plan. I'd hoped we could brainstorm. We could try to suggest The God of Greed allow a full-on anachronism—muck with the Layer's established era. It hasn't been that many years since children worked in textile and coal mines. But I don't think that's the best way of things. It could slow down the process. It would also take resources."

"Couldn't a minor monster handle it?" The Manager asked. "The Mall has three. The Animal Mill is mostly self-regulating. Even Lords of Greed *could* handle matters."

"Perhaps that would work…" The 9-to-5 said.

The Ascended Mayor raised his hand. "How is it being handled currently?"

"That would be mine," The Newscaster said. "The children are trapped in a currently self-fulfilling hell. It's mostly hours of rote memorization, but the architecture does a phenomenal job of generating the right sort of despair."

Grace's skin crawled when The Ascended Mayor asked his next question. Because it sounded *sincere.* Like he was genuinely excited to hear the answer.

"How so? Do tell? This is supposed to be a fun dinner, after all."

The Newscaster chuckled. "Well, for one, I put signs everywhere that tell them the chances of success in their given interests. The theater kids are told the odds of working professionally—and then forced to perform the same play over and over. The artists put their paintings into shredders as soon as they are done with them. The clocks really do tick too slow."

"Inspired!" The Mayor proclaimed.

There were no visible speakers, but canned applause rippled out from The Newscaster.

"Thank you—*at eleven, how your child's hobbies are secretly evil plots to turn them into Marxists!*"

"But they aren't crying out their dreams at the rate we wanted," The 9-to-5 said. "They have hope! What are we to do about that?"

The Mayor put his chin in his hand. "Hmm."

The Shareholder clapped once, sharply. "I've got it."

All the others now turned to him. Even Grace gave The Shareholder her full attention.

"It's simple, really," The Shareholder continued. "We barely need to relegate more magic toward it. Am I correct in assuming the school has no windows to the outside?"

"Well, of course," The Newscaster said. "It is designed to keep kids busy so adults can work. Why would we make it cheerful?"

"Exactly," The Shareholder replied. "Then, with minimal mental magic, we just make it seem like the school day never ends. If the goal is to make this efficient, then we just hustle things along."

The 9-to-5 let out a cheerful giggle. "Perfection! I knew you all would have such excellent ideas."

"That would be phenomenally easy," The Newscaster said. "*Next up, we have an announcement: recess is canceled, and breaktime was never real.*"

Grace focused on breathing through her nose. Rage bubbled through her veins. But also pure adrenaline. It was almost time. She hadn't been sure when one of them would ask, but the menu had called for it. And why else would they want it, if not for—

"I say we drink to this," The Ascended Mayor said. "It only seems fitting!"

"Yes! A great idea," The Newscaster said.

"Wonderful idea," The 9-to-5 said.

"Ah, yes, a superb idea," The Shareholder said.

The Ascended Mayor turned to Grace. Grace looked back at him and tried to keep off her face everything she'd been thinking. Everything she'd been planning for so very long. If he could read minds—if any of the monsters at the table could read minds—she would be dead.

All she had to do was not show it on her face for a few more seconds.

"Hello, Grace. I'm sure you heard already, but we need five flutes of sparkling wine. Bring them *fast.*"

Grace nodded. "Yes, sir."

She spun on her heels so quickly it made her a little dizzy, and then she marched straight for the door. As soon as her back was to them, she couldn't keep the expression off her face.

Please let this work.

She opened the door, let it close behind her, and then said one word aloud.

"Declan?"

Declan looked up from the steak he was tenderizing. He put away the tenderizer, studied her face for half a second, and let out a long breath.

"Is it time?" he asked.

"Yes."

CHAPTER 36

F IVE EMPTY GLASSES IN FRONT OF THEM. Declan pulled out the hidden napkin, wedged between two countertops. He unfolded it. In the center were the few coin shavings that ended up sharp enough to be usable. Created during so many stolen moments, they were each basically needles.

Grace picked up the bottle of sparkling wine. It took some effort to uncork, and when it did, the pop made her heart speed up. Every nerve in her body was on high alert. She kept glancing back at the door. They only had a minute to do this, before they would wonder where the hell their wine was.

She poured each one perfectly—and quickly. Constantly needing to fill coffee mugs and cups of ice water had taught her that skill set. She made sure each one was filled to the same level, give or take a few drops.

The fizzing, bubbly liquid made her think of the oil vat still bubbling in the room with them.

Declan carefully took a pinch of the needles and dropped some in the first one. This was the biggest gamble. Back in the climate change house, they'd learned the most important rule of fighting these monsters: they could be hurt by the things they made, if used correctly. But there was no way to know if it was a small enough amount that the monsters wouldn't notice it in their drinks. There was also no way to know if there were too few needles to actually do damage.

Declan finished the last one. Grace leaned down and examined each one closely. If you were expecting small pieces of metal, they were very easy to spot. They hadn't fully settled to the bottom. The carbonation kept them moving.

But if you were, say, busy with a conversation, and drank it all in one big toast—there was the faintest chance.

Grace stood back up. She was about to pick up the tray of drinks but paused.

"Declan?" Grace whispered.

He looked at her. "Yeah?"

"You know I love you, right?"

"I do know that," Declan said, tears starting to form in his eyes. "I … love you too."

Grace steadied her breathing. "If this is it—"

"Please don't say that."

"—*If this is it*, Declan, we gave it our all, okay? No one can say we didn't fight like hell. I'm so proud of you."

Declan made a small noise in the back of his throat and couldn't help but look away.

"Your father would be so proud of you," Grace said.

"Thank … thank you."

Grace picked up the tray. It felt weirdly light. She felt weirdly light. Like she'd said, they were fighting like hell.

And this was the adrenaline of fighting for something that matters.

A god exists, Grace thought. *That means there's something like divinity. Maybe there's something after all this. Even if I die. Maybe there's some place after death where I'll get to see Declan again.*

She stepped across The Infinite Diner, carrying that tray of wine, and the monsters all looked at her. At her. Not the drinks. She smiled fearfully. Respectfully. The look she used to mollify the most aggressive of customers, back before the world changed.

And maybe, Grace thought while smiling, *there's also a hell where I can send these fuckers.*

CHAPTER 37

GRACE STOOD OFF TO THE SIDE. THEY didn't seem to notice her. They hadn't noticed the metal either. With them each holding their drinks, The Ascended Mayor cleared his throat.

A speech, then.

"We've accomplished so much in such a short time; in the grand sense of things, it's but a blip in our full potential. When I first came to be the mayor of this town, I did it for money, for power, naturally, but I didn't understand just what I was sitting above.

"But fortunately, someone had discovered it. Irena Ink wasted her potential, unwilling to work with all of you, and become something that could've changed the world. She was a Seer, she knew the power of a Rot God, and yet denied herself it. I will never understand her, but she did leave her notes. And for that alone, I must thank her. She left *The Cacophonous Layers*. A book and a glimpse that opened everything.

"And that book taught me so much. That there was a trillion squared and then more Layers out there, and beings that moved about them all. She told me of the god beneath Quill Point, one that she bound there with her death. A Rot God, waiting. And once I heard all of you calling, the grand plan began.

"It wasn't easy. Greed was a true divine virtue, and I had to devote myself to it more than I ever had before. I had to push past those that would stop me. And, oh, they tried.

"The people out in that town rejected greed where they could. They questioned my self-interest above their own interest, even though I *wanted* something more important. Demands streaming in from them as if voting for me gave them any control over me. I had power. They didn't. I kept power. They lost it. That made me *better* than them. But I had to act just enough like I cared about them to never lose my winnings.

"I cannot explain to you how happy I am to be among beings that understand. Empathy is pointless. A lower wrung of human endeavor. Greed is a *god*. Empathy isn't. Community isn't. There's a hierarchy and I know it now. I ascended with such knowledge. The people with the biggest wealth, the billionaires, and the owners, and the violently powerful are mandated to be in charge by the fact that they *have*. It doesn't matter if it was inherited, stolen, or a trick of a dying system. They have. They have it all.

"And we have it all, don't we? Soon enough, people will die in the numbers needed so that The God of Greed can escape this Layer and consume a thousand, million more. He may join the other Rot Gods on the grandest stage. It is my honor to help bring it about. It is my honor to help make it happen. It is my honor."

The Ascended Mayor raised his drink. The other monsters did as well.

"To Greed!"

Seers looking to explore The Cacophonous Layers often neglect to visit the other four Beacon Layers. This is, frankly, a mistake. As a hotbed for newly created Seers, it's often a great place to meet traveling companions.

-*The Layer Tourist* by Stanley Earth-

Interlude Four

Beacon Layer

HAVEN EMERGED FROM A HOLE IN reality. As did their partner, Milda, their partner's dog, Lola, and the wife of their boss at Stylus Books, Cynthia Reed.

One moment, they'd been attending to Thea, who'd seemed to have fainted out of nowhere, and the next, they'd been asked to go through a portal in the skin of reality, because something horrifically bad was happening in Quill Point, Illinois—*again*.

Again, after Murder Sky.

Again, after being trapped in the hotel with a bunch of clay monsters.

Again, after Mayor's Men, mass funerals, a burning hospital, and more. Honestly, Haven should've seen all of this from a mile away. When they'd been pursuing Milda, Haven had ended up reading a lot of horror books. That covered a template of what had happened. And, if that hadn't been enough, all their childhood and adulthood, they'd been reading fantasy books. When aliens and/or demons were on the table already, why wouldn't it be possible for their boss to develop the ability to make portals? Why wouldn't they be able to travel to a different world?

Although, *this* wasn't one of the outcomes they'd imagined. The portal closed—and they weren't in some rolling field with dragons or knights. Nor were they in some kind of faery woodlands.

Even from the smallest glance around, this was sci-fi. A genre Haven had a lot less experience with.

But the principles of genre fiction, they hoped, would carry over rather well. What was the difference between sci-fi and fantasy, besides one having fireballs and the other weird guns? One had teleportation devices. The other teleportation runes.

They started really looking over things.

It's hopefully a utopian science fiction setting, Haven thought, *or this could get really bad.*

The sky was greenish-bluish, but still had clouds, as Haven was used to. There were also a lot of towers. Each about the height of a skyscraper, but the general shape of medieval towers. The towers consisted of clear glass, or perhaps diamonds, and concrete-like stone. Haven spotted a few people standing on various floors.

Okay. Human people. Or at least a species that looks a lot like humans. No idea if we'll be able to talk to them. There's no reason to expect language to be the same here.

At ground level, the area was walkways and large patches of plants. The whole thing wasn't flat. A series of ramps and winding paths, dotted with that myriad life, gently curved through the landscape. It was easily the greenest city Haven had ever seen.

A silvery light caught their attention, and they glanced over to see something like a zeppelin, but not quite, fly around the towers, never crashing into any of them.

Zeppelins are usually a very good, or very bad sign, Haven thought. *Let's assume a utopian future for now.*

Haven spun back to look at the others. The others were in various degrees of visual shock. Milda was holding onto her dog tight, her eyes wide. Cynthia was standing very still.

At least Lola seemed happy, her tongue out, and wriggling slightly in Milda's grasp. Haven imagined she wanted to go running across the huge amount of foliage.

"Do you know where we are?" Milda asked quietly.

"No, I don't. I think this place really is safe though," Haven said. "It looks like we got dropped into the future. Are you okay?"

In true Milda fashion, she shrugged and said her words calmly. "I mean … no, but … I'm okay."

Haven nodded. They expected as much. Only in the direst scenarios—things like running out of money for food, or facing eviction, or, of course, what had happened in the hotel and during Murder Sky—did Milda ever seem phased. Haven loved that about their partner. In the chaos of life, she was stability. Milda was one of the strongest people Haven had ever met.

"How is any of this happening?" Cynthia said, her breathing speeding up. "What did Thea *do*? Why couldn't she follow? What was happening back there? Where *are* we?!"

"I don't … I'm not sure," Haven said. "She didn't say."

Cynthia looked around rapidly. "Is this even Earth? We need to get back to Thea, now!"

Haven held up their hands. "She said she was sending us somewhere safe. I don't think it *is* Earth."

Milda held Lola even closer. "Do you think Murder Sky was aliens? Is this … some other alien's world?"

Cynthia stopped breathing for a moment, then her hands tightened at her sides. "If it is … then they are going to take us right back to Earth. I'm not—they're not going to hurt…"

She stopped talking and tried to catch her breath.

"I think we should ask someone," Haven said. "Find out where we are—what we can do. There's got to be someone that can help. We might have to rely on non-verbal stuff though."

"What?" Milda asked.

Haven gestured out at the strange city—if it even was a city. The scale was huge to them. But maybe this was the equivalent of a small, quaint village to this planet.

"If this isn't Earth, it might not use any language we can speak."

"Oh, okay," Milda said. "Yeah, that makes sense."

Cynthia appeared not to be listening. She'd failed to steady her breathing. Her voice cracked. She seemed to be collapsing in on herself.

"She pushed me here," Cynthia said. "She's still back there. What if she's … what if…"

Cynthia held up her hand like Thea had done to open the portal. Palm out. It didn't work. The air didn't even wobble like it had. After a moment, Cynthia let her hand drop.

Why didn't I think of trying that? Haven thought.

"Please," Cynthia begged. "I need to be with her. I need to know she's safe—"

That last crack in her voice spurred the sensation that Haven had felt many, many times. A firm rock in their chest. An iron coating their insides. It was not of sadness, or grief, but of *action*. It was triggered more often by others needing help, but it had been there many times for Haven as well.

Haven *solved* problems.

When the rainbow-colored flag had fallen during their school dance, they'd been the one to find the custodial staff member and get it back up.

When their uncle had been so sick that he could barely stand, Haven had been the one to care for him. Been the one to learn every damn decent soup recipe you could make on a small paycheck.

When Haven needed a fresh start after their uncle had passed, they'd gotten the loan, moved to Illinois from Oregon, gotten an apartment, and gotten a job at Stylus Books—all in one month.

This. They could handle this.

"Okay, come on," Haven told Cynthia. "Let's take a seat."

Haven guided her to one of the raised sections of the walkway. Cynthia sat down next to a remarkably green patch of grass.

"Can I help?" Milda asked quietly.

Haven gave their partner a warm smile and mouthed, *I got this.*

Then, Haven said to Cynthia, "So, first off, it's going to be okay."

Cynthia's voice arrived as a whisper. "…I knew something was wrong. She'd been having these dreams. Nightmares. She'd wake up screaming, and I never knew what to do about it. But it started before it was … before … the sky… I didn't think it was related."

"I'd heard she was having trouble," Haven said. "She would look really sleepy sometimes."

"Do you think she's alive?"

"I do."

Cynthia went quiet for a long time. It looked like all the energy was leaking out of her. Haven had never seen her even close to this state before. Cynthia was the whirlwind that gave people coffee, a smile, and knew people's names. Cynthia was, as much as anyone, a life blood of Quill Point.

"Do you think something changed in her?" Cynthia asked. "Do you think she changed when Murder Sky happened?"

Haven pursed their lips, thinking.

"How long have you two been married?" they asked.

"What…?"

"How long has it been since you got married?"

Cynthia blinked in confusion. "It's been over thirty years. Why is that—?"

"And you love her?"

"Of-fucking-course I do," Cynthia said instantly. "What sort of—"

"Then you would know."

"…what?"

Haven held her gaze. "If your wife had become not your wife, then you would know. If Milda was changed, then *I* would know. And you've got decades on us."

"I would know too," Milda commented. "I would know instantly."

"So," Haven continued, "was it your wife?"

Cynthia started to nod her head, first slowly, then quicker. "Yes. It was her. I'm sure of it."

"Good," Haven said. "And you know your wife like joy knows love?"

Cynthia kept nodding, an almost aggressive assuredness in her eyes. Haven had seen the exact same thing in Thea. The look of someone who'd ran a business for so long. The look of someone who'd faced down life and won a thousand times because losing was *never* an option.

Haven hoped they'd have the same look when they got older. Hoped there was already the first inkling of it in their own expression.

"Then tell me," Haven continued, "would she *ever* send you somewhere if she wasn't absolutely fucking sure she'd make it back to you? Would she *ever* risk that?"

"Never," Cynthia said. "We'd break down every wall before we'd let that happen."

"Then we're going to get back to her. And she *will* be there."

Cynthia sniffled. She closed her eyes and let out the longest breath. When she opened her eyes, Haven knew they'd succeeded, as much as it could be solved.

"You said that you know what kind of place we're in?" Cynthia asked.

"Yeah, do you have an idea?" Milda added.

Haven stretched their arms above their head, hoping they weren't being wildly overconfident about their abilities.

"Well, if I am right," Haven began, "we're visitors from another world. So, there's every chance that if we just go and talk to someone, we'll draw a lot of attention. I'm amazed we haven't already. Surely whatever government they have would've noticed us."

"So … go up to a random person?" Cynthia said.

"Yeah, I guess so."

Cynthia nodded. "That we can do."

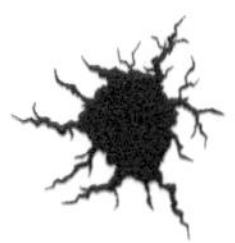

Cynthia led the way. As they walked, all the people Haven could see were indoors and seemingly preoccupied. One person was playing an instrument that looked like a violin made of stone but shrunk to half the usual size. Haven couldn't hear the music through the glass.

Another person had their back to the window and was typing furiously at a device that looked like an electric typewriter, though there was no paper spilling out of it, nor seemingly any section to display a screen.

The group wound through several paths, up and down gentle inclines. If they weren't on a quest with Cynthia and Milda, Haven would've loved to stop and look over some of the flower patches.

Eventually, Cynthia found someone. A man sitting at a metal bench. He looked older by Earth standards. His beard was a snowy white, and the hair on his head was about the same color—and both were quite long. His skin was pale white, with deep lines on his face. He wore a simple red shirt and tan pants. Nothing as futuristic as Haven had been expecting. In one hand, the man held a small device, and in the other, a drink with a metal straw.

Cynthia marched right up to him. She stopped almost too close.

He looked up at her with a calm expression.

"Hi, sir," Cynthia began.

The man winced.

Cynthia paused for a moment, probably thrown by the expression—but she had enough momentum going to continue.

"We need to talk to someone important. Is there a … uh … I guess a mayor we could speak to?"

The man put the device down and shook his head. When he opened his mouth to say something, Haven immediately covered their ears. Cynthia stumbled backward.

Dimly, Haven could hear Lola barking in pain and Milda repeating the word "ow" over and over.

The sound was like speaker feedback. A horrible whine.

The noise slowly pitched into a more bearable range but still sounded almost like static. Like a radio losing a signal, the words weren't quite getting through. Slowly, through what felt like an eternity, Haven started to understand—

"…calibrated. The bylaws clearly state that if you're going to travel out of this Layer, that you need to calibrate your Layer-Filter at a station before you go blasting eardrums."

Haven slowly lowered their hands. "Wait … I'm sorry, I don't understand."

"Have you not even read the bylaws?" the man continued. "Did you not even read the *signs*?"

The man gestured to a pillar of stone sitting in one of the grass areas. Haven looked at it, at a large painted sign stuck to it, and, for a moment, it was like trying to look right into the fucking sun. Green and red lights flashed, and Haven's eyes watered slightly—but then it looked like it was written in plain English.

At the top were the instructions:

Please think of others. All Seers traveling in or out of Deciduous City must recalibrate their Layer-Filter at the designated zone.

Below those instructions was an arrow with some coordinates.

"What the fuck was that?" Cynthia demanded. "What kind of noise was that?"

The man's expression slowly relaxed into a frown. "Wait? Do you not … do not know what I'm talking about?"

"We're … not from here," Haven admitted.

"No, of course we don't," Cynthia added, her hands going to her hips. "We got teleported here—and now we need to find someone who can get us back to where we came from."

"Who … sent you?"

"My wife," Cynthia said.

The man looked between the three of them. "Wait … no, you don't move like … are you not … Seers?"

Haven couldn't quite explain why, but they could hear the capital letter in that word. They'd read enough fantasy books to know a special, proper noun.

"What the fuck is a 'Seer?'" Cynthia asked.

Haven stepped to Cynthia's side. "No, we're not. But I think her wife might be."

The man's eyes went wide. He dropped his drink. It hit the bench and fizzy water spilled out. He stood up and clutched his head.

"Oh! Oh no. Oh no. Okay … okay… Where you were from … was it in the middle of something … big and … umm … what's the world…?"

"Apocalyptic," Milda offered.

"Yeah … that's the one," he said. "That's very much the one."

"And we'd like to get back there," Cynthia demanded.

"No … you don't understand. You need to stay here— and I need to get someone for you. Please don't go any- where. We do have a protocol for this. It was in the bylaws. It *is* in the bylaws. I will get someone who can help you."

The man ran a few feet, then spun around, sprinted to scoop up his device, and ran off again. He didn't look back the second time—or get his cup. He quickly disap- peared behind one of the raised areas.

"Told you that would work," Haven said.

"Are we sure he's not about to get, like, the military to shoot us or something?" Milda said.

"Hopefully not," Haven replied.

"Maybe Thea meant to send us to a different area here," Cynthia said nervously.

Haven pursed their lips. That hadn't occurred to them. Who knew how accurate teleportation was? Maybe this wasn't where on the planet Thea had intended. And, while Haven was going over possibilities in their mind, it occurred to them that Thea might've intended to follow pretty soon afterward. Maybe Thea *had* followed but was somewhere else on the planet. Maybe none of them could be here for too long. There might even be concerns about diseases or radiation or even air quality if they stayed too long. Had Thea accounted for that?

"So, we're not speaking English right now," Milda commented.

Haven turned to their partner. Milda was pursing her lips, deep in thought. She was automatically petting Lola, who still seemed in generally good spirits about things— despite the horrible noise.

"What was that, Milda?" Haven asked.

"These words—right now—they're not in English," Milda continued. "Or Spanish. Or Mandarin, or any Earth language, is it? Or was he speaking something else, and something's translating his language for us?"

A surge of excitement went through Haven. Most fantasy stories introduced some shared language to get around this problem. Science fiction explained it away with some piece of technology. But something like that was really happening here. There was a system in place for this—and it was actively happening.

The world's ending in Quill Point, Haven thought. *Let's not get too excited about other stuff.*

"I sound like myself," Cynthia said. "And our lips are moving with what we're saying."

"Are they, though?" Haven said, thinking about it. "Check my lips, Milda."

Milda leaned a little closer. "Say something more complicated."

"Okay—what?"

"I don't know. Just anything. Uh, tell me the plot of that one book you were reading last week."

"The one about the fire magic?"

"Sure," Milda said.

"It was that one time Xander wrote a fantasy novel. Well, basically a novella. It was a story about this boy who discovered that fire has magic in it, and that you can do spells if you burn very specific things. It turned into a horror book at the end anyhow. He threw his friend into the fire."

"Oh god," Cynthia commented quietly.

Milda leaned back. "That all looked normal. I didn't see anything."

"So, then it translated him," Haven concluded.

"Guess so."

Haven thought for a moment. "Well, we have to wait for that guy, anyhow, so we could test stuff. Uh, I don't know a lot of Spanish, but … um … what's a basic phrase. ¿Cómo te llamas?"

"That was still Spanish," Milda said. "And it didn't do that radio static thing."

"Let me read the rest of the sign then," Haven said. "Maybe that'll tell us something."

Haven went across the grass. The slight movement was enough to kick up sweet, earthy smells. Quill Point was fairly environmentally untouched by American standards, but just moving through this grass opened old memories. Haven's childhood adventure visiting a farm flashed in their mind. The way corn could shush in the wind. How open the sky was without buildings to block the view.

Nature allowed to be, Haven thought. *That's utopia.*

Haven made it to the sign, and though they could read it now, it didn't make it so they could understand it.

Deciduous City Rules.

Haven assumed most of the information was for arrivals. There was a series of numbers that Haven couldn't guess the exact reason for. It looked like coordinates. Maybe where the planet was in the solar system? Maybe where the town was on the planet? The words around it weren't much better. *Technological Level 7, Magical Level 1, Beacon Layer* were the ones that seemed important.

They kept reading.

This Beacon Layer is often visited by very new Seers. It is not uncommon for them to have recently experienced a large amount of stress and trauma. Please be kind to new visitors. It may be the first time they've traveled off their Home Layer, and they may not even know all Seers are drawn to Beacon Layers. Thank you.

Please be mindful of cultures different from your own. Deciduous City is often visited by different beings from many different Layers and has a robust and diverse set of local Layer-Linked cultures as well. Thank you.

Please help us by alerting the nearest Travel Center upon arrival if you've brought any Layer-Linked individuals as guests, objects exceeding Magical Level 1, or technology exceeding Technological Level 7. Thank you.

Please be considerate of other's safety. Thank you.

Please refer to the available documentation for all other relevant bylaws that you may have questions about. Thank you.

Thank you for making a safe Deciduous City for all visitors.

By the time they'd finished reading, Haven felt overwhelmed. They had no idea what most of that meant. The word "Layer" apparently was important, considering how often it was used—and there were apparently two *separate* benchmarks for objects. They shook their head and walked back toward Milda, Cynthia, and Lola.

Cynthia was sitting on the bench, bouncing her foot. Milda still hadn't put down Lola but was petting her as much as possible. Lola was a very chill dog, but the idea of chasing her around a different planet made Haven wince. That would be a nightmare.

"Any luck?" Milda asked.

"It's all sci-fi words. I couldn't make heads or tails of it."

"We need to get out of this place," Cynthia muttered.

Haven looked out at the skyline. Lines and lines of those glass towers stretched off in the distance. There was some kind of dome in one spot. A few more flying vehicles.

Haven sucked in some air, and it tasted clean. Cleaner than they'd noticed before. Quiet and clean and beautiful. Haven was smiling softly to themself when they looked up, blinked a few times in confusion, as—

Two men *landed* in front of Haven.

Haven shrieked and fell on their back, hands outstretched in defense.

Cynthia swore very loudly and scrambled to get behind the bench.

Lola wrestled herself free from Milda's arms and leaped forward, barking loudly. Milda dove after Lola and grabbed her mouth, tugging her back into her grasp and suppressing the barking.

The two new people stood there, side by side, unperturbed. No injuries, no sign of what had just happened. Even the ground was fine.

The man on the left had subdermal tech. They glowed like an LED screen against his very pale white skin. A series of blue lights glimmered across his arm. His eyes were a deep brown, and his short hair was ocean blue.

The man on the right had floating chrome covering him. Sheets of it shifted and moved along his arms and legs, floating just above his burnished orange duster's sleeves and red pants. A much smaller piece of metal stayed right next to his head, not quite flush against his light brown skin. His eyes were brown, and his brown hair was extremely short.

Both of them looked off in the same way CGI can in some movies. Like they'd been superimposed over the world, more real than real.

The one on the left waved. "Hi there. You can calm down. We're not here to hurt you."

"We heard some Layer-Linked people had been portaled in," the other added.

Haven's mind was reeling. Thea had moved impossibly fast right before she'd made the portal, but this was on another level. That landing broke *physics*. It should've left a massive crater. Hell, it should've killed them.

Even that hand wave, innocent in any other context, had looked like an afterimage.

"Who … the fuck are you?" Haven managed to ask.

The one on the left nodded. "My name is Leldon, and my friend here is Bernard. He's overseeing security on this Layer for the time being. I'm just shadowing."

Bernard rolled his eyes. "You know you're not going to be shadowing me forever, right?"

"I don't…" Haven began.

But Haven didn't finish talking. The words left them. It was too much.

"Oh, I think we scared them," Bernard said.

"Oh shit," Leldon said. "Yeah, that makes sense."

Leldon held both his hands up—and Haven couldn't help but be surprised, *again*, at how *fast* the action had been. His hands had blurred and then stopped perfectly still at the end of the arc.

Is that magic? Superpowers? Haven thought.

"Okay, I'm sorry," Leldon said. "This is probably a lot to take in if you're not used to this. Let's start here: who portaled you?"

Cynthia crept around the bench and slowly raised her hand. "My … my wife did."

"Why did she do that?" Bernard asked.

"She … she said it was safer…"

"There was something … demonic going on," Milda added, struggling to keep Lola from escaping. "We were in an apocalypse."

"I think they're from the Isolation," Bernard said.

"Oh, that would explain a lot," Leldon said. "So, this is really all new for you. Okay … um, well, I didn't get your names."

"I'm Cynthia…"

"My name is Milda."

"Haven." They paused to think. "I use they and them pronouns, please."

Bernard nodded. "Of course. And the two of you? What do you use?"

"She and her," Cynthia replied.

"Um, the same," Milda said.

Leldon smiled. "We both use him and he. It's nice to meet you, Cynthia, Haven, Milda—and who's this excited dog?"

Milda shifted again. "Her name is Lola… I'm sorry about her barking at you."

Leldon waved it off. "Oh, it's okay. She's just protecting her human. I can respect that."

Leldon glanced over at Bernard. Leldon tilted his head. Bernard chewed on his lip for a moment, then nodded.

"You'll handle this one," Bernard instructed. "Standard low-level orientation."

Leldon clicked his tongue. "Okay, then. Well … our new guests, welcome to Deciduous City. A Beacon Layer … I suppose you don't know what that means."

"No, we don't," Cynthia said, her voice hardening.

"Right, okay," Leldon said. "So … you are not in your home … dimension … anymore. We use the word 'Layers' to refer to dimensions. We don't need to get into why right now. Just know that you are in a new Layer."

Haven's eyes went wide. Not only a new planet but a new *dimension*. Thea had made a hole in reality to another dimension. And it was a common enough event to have a word for different dimensions.

Haven really wanted to go back and look at the sign.

"There are many dimensions then?" Milda asked.

"Yes. And like I said, there's a lot to that we're not going to get into right now. What is important is that you're safe here from what was happening. You really are safe here. This is a common locations Seers—uh, that's people who can travel to other dimensions, that's our word for it—go to. It's one of the five places that almost all human Seers end up going to as their first portal."

It did not escape Haven that Leldon had specified *human* Seers.

"Why?" Haven found themselves asking.

"We're not sure," Bernard chimed in. "But it's so common that we have a lot of stuff set up specifically for visitors. There are cities like this on all five of the Layers … dimensions."

"We get what Layers are," Cynthia said sharply.

"Okay, good. Then we can get to the next part," Leldon said, picking back up the orientation. "If you're from where we think you are—"

"Quill Point, Illinois. United States of America. *Earth*," Cynthia spat out, crossing her arms. "And I need to get back to Thea."

"Is Thea your wife? The one who made the portal?" Bernard asked.

"Yes," Cynthia replied.

"But she didn't follow us," Haven added. "Or we don't think she did, anyway."

Leldon put his hand behind his head. He let out a long sigh. "She didn't have a weird piece of metal, did she?"

"No…" Cynthia said. "Why would she?"

"Then she didn't follow you. I can explain why that is later. I think I know what's happening." Leldon glanced at Bernard. "We should take them straight to Klein?"

Bernard nodded.

"No—no, no," Cynthia said, her voice cracking. "You're taking us straight back to my *wife*. She's in danger—I can't leave her dealing with … whatever is happening. She's … all alone."

A flash of pain went across Bernard's face. "I get it. I really do, Cynthia. But if your wife is like us, then she's more than able to defend herself. At least for a little while."

"No… I waited long enough," Cynthia said, her voice weakening.

"I'm so sorry," Leldon continued. "But we can't just go back in. Even if we knew the exact coordinates of your Layer—and we don't—we can't go into … the thing that locked down your town. The inside of that ... that phenomena ... makes reality brittle *inside*, but that only helps with using a portal to get *out*. We need to go to the person in charge of dealing with apocalypses."

Cynthia set her jaw. She looked between the two of them. "You're not lying to me, are you?"

Leldon blinked in surprise. "We would never. We really do need his help to take you there. It's not that far of a walk—you just need to follow us."

Haven's mind was still caught on something Leldon had just said. "You have a person in charge of *apocalypses*?"

"They happen way more often than you'd think."

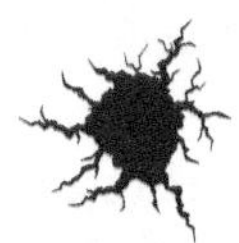

Haven kept trying to figure out more about whatever superpowers these two had. As they all walked, Haven had many examples to study. The way they looked more real than real had to be a part of it, but Haven was mostly interested in the super speed. Bernard was better at hiding it, but even he was moving in that strange, held-tight way. It reminded Haven of someone with a muscle cramp. But occasionally, one of them would slip, and it would be uncannily fast. Their limbs blurring. Or, in one especially fascinating case, Leldon turned his head impossibly quick, but was mid-stride at a human speed.

Haven was so fascinated by this, they almost didn't notice some of the new things in their surroundings. But the surroundings were incredible. The massive buildings made of that strange material. The art pieces that were displayed in glass containers. In one open area, someone was doing street magic that Haven couldn't determine if it was actual magic or not.

Milda kept making adorable little noises of awe as they walked past it all. Even Cynthia, worried as she was, couldn't help but occasionally comment on things.

Haven had been right. This was a utopia.

It was nice being in a utopia.

Haven had never considered how peaceful and clean a city could be.

The biggest thing was the lack of cars. There wasn't any place for them among the winding terraces of pathways and plant life. It was all walkable. A truly walkable city. The only vehicles that Haven saw were the almost-zeppelins that flew by, and, eventually, small personal gliders.

That's why the air tastes the way it does, Haven thought. *There's no smog here—there probably hasn't been smog here in decades, if not longer.*

It was also so quiet. Haven couldn't recall the last time they'd heard patches of nothing. No background noises. No weird ambient hums. No thuds or honks from cars crossing the interstate ramp near Quill Point. Each time there was a sound, Haven could place exactly what caused it.

This place really was in another dimension.

"So," Haven offered up as a conversation starter, "when we talked to that person, it was like—"

"Radio static?" Bernard said. "Yes, that's a thing that happens."

"Why though? Are we being translated, or are you being translated to us?"

Bernard put his hand up to his chin. Or so Haven assumed. One second, his hand was at his side, moving slightly as he walked, and then it was at his chin.

"I was wanting to ask the same thing," Milda said. "It was a little unnerving."

"Sorry about that," Bernard said. "But that's just how the universe works."

"It's a natural process," Leldon explained. "It just happens when you go to a new Layer."

"How does that work?" Haven asked instantly.

"Well, it doesn't happen for us the same way," Bernard said. "Seers don't need to acclimate like that—we're not the same in a lot of ways."

"I'm sorry—what did you just say?" Cynthia chimed in.

Bernard winced and turned to look at Cynthia.

"Sorry, I phrased that poorly," Bernard said. "I keep forgetting you're not as used to all of this."

"Are you saying my wife isn't the same as she used to be?"

"She's still human," Bernard said quickly. "I'm also still human. All I mean is that, by being a Seer, things work a little differently than you might be used to. We operate on slightly different laws of physics and reality."

"She's a superhero now," Haven said. "But she's still who she was."

"Yeah, that works," Leldon said. "Not a bad way to explain it."

"It is a little like being a superhero, I guess," Bernard agreed. "She's still the same person. That's the important part."

Cynthia nodded slowly. Haven was beginning to worry how much more Cynthia could take of this. If Milda had been the one left behind, Haven would've been the same. They were sure of that.

"Anyway…" Bernard continued, "the thing with language is a natural process that Seers can kind of skip. The results are the same—it just doesn't take a moment of those horrible noises. The translation doesn't have to adjust itself."

"But what's actually happening?" Milda asked.

"Yeah, how could something like that be natural?" Haven added.

"Here, I guess we need to do more orientation," Leldon said. "It's a little more advanced orientation, but worth answering. So when something travels between Layers, it's kind of like dropping something into a big amount of water, or any liquid, really—there's a bubble of oxygen around it. Or…"

"Get less technical," Bernard instructed.

"Fine—fine. But there's no way to not be a little technical though. The answer is we're both being translated to each other. You're in a different dimension, but there's a little field around you, at all times, that's operating on your Layer's rules—more or less. We call non-Seers 'Layer-Linked' because they carry around a little bit of their Layer at all times. It's why we're not worried about you not being able to breathe the air … or, I don't know, some issue with background radiation or chemicals. It's also why you can talk to us, and we can talk to you."

That answers one question, Haven thought. *I wonder if it's visible here…?*

Haven glanced down at their own arm. There wasn't any field or anything they could detect.

Bernard seemed to notice. "You can't usually see it. Not unless … no, *that's* a whole other thing to explain… Oh! There's this. You can't see it unless the air is a totally different gas or configuration of gas than your Layer—and in that scenario, there are other worries."

"Like what..." Milda asked nervously.

"The field around you can't protect you from *everything*," Bernard explained. "If the planet is way too hot, too cold, completely irradiated, things like that, it can be overwhelmed pretty quickly. You have space travel on your planet?"

"Limited," Haven replied, "probably not as advanced as what you have."

"Do you regularly go to other planets?"

"No," Milda chimed in. "No, we can't do that."

Bernard pursed his lips. "But do you have space suits?"

"Yes," Milda said.

"Okay. Just think of it like that; it's easiest. If you do end up in the void of space on a different Layer, you actually get a few moments of 'translated' air before it breaks down."

Haven's eyes went wide as they understood better. "And that's what happening with language right now?"

"You got it," Leldon chimed in, nodding. "Your words are going out and they rework themselves into the closest one we've got for it. Words arriving to you work the same. It works for language, dialects, slang, and even accents to some degree. It just takes time for the filter to acclimatize with communication specifically. You need to talk to a local person. We have stations with people who do that as their job."

That means we don't actually know what anyone around us sounds like, Haven thought.

"This is weird," Cynthia offered weakly. "I don't like any of this."

"I'm sorry," Bernard said. "If it helps, I think we're both speaking a language that's marginally similar right now. Only about half of the mouth movements you've been making aren't synched to what I'm hearing."

"No … stop it," Cynthia said, covering her ears. "Now all I can think about is words flying around."

"Once again, sorry," Bernard said with a shrug.

And as soon as Cynthia said that, Haven tried to envision it. Sound waves hitting filters. A strange field around every person—maybe even every object. It was a wholly new thought, but it didn't bother Haven. How often had they dreamed of something like this happening?

All Haven wanted to do now was study it.

"You don't have to worry too much," Bernard said. "We're almost there anyway. Klein should be here—and he can tell us a lot more about what's happening."

"Who is he?" Cynthia asked. "What's his actual title?"

"He's in charge of Logistics," Leldon supplied. "There's a lot happening in a lot of places, and someone needs to keep track of stuff so we can help as many people as possible. I'm sure he knows what's happening on your Layer."

"Our *town*," Cynthia said. "It's called Quill Point, and it's where I grew up, where I got married, and where I'm getting back to."

"Of course," Bernard said.

"We'll do everything we can," Leldon said.

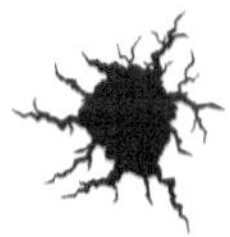

The building's outer façade hadn't been all that impressive, at least by the standards set by the rest of Deciduous City. It was a low, squat dome of a building with a big door at the end of a long stone path. But once they'd gotten inside, it was a different story.

The foyer was vertigo in the most beautiful way possible.

It was a large, circular room with a singular desk at the very back. Between Haven and it, the floor was decorated with rings of glass breaking up a stark porcelain. The rings had perfectly rounded corners and were five feet across. Haven glanced down and got a little dizzy. It went down for miles. Offices. Vehicle storage. Rooms with holograms. And blurs of Seers moving throughout.

Someone tapped Haven on the shoulder. Milda was smiling at them. Haven never could get over how much they loved those eyes looking at them.

"They're getting ahead of us," Milda said softly.

Haven glanced over, and Cynthia was trailing behind Leldon and Bernard.

Haven nodded. "I know we're here because of something horrible … but I can't believe this is real."

"Neither can I," Milda said.

"It's incredible," Haven said. "It's like every story I've ever read."

Lola wagged her tail like she agreed.

"Maybe we can find a way back here, somehow," Milda said.

"Maybe," Haven said dreamily, then glanced at Lola. "You've been carrying her this whole time—do you want me to take over?"

"That would be nice," Milda admitted. "She's heavy."

"Sorry. I should've offered sooner."

Milda shrugged. "It's okay. You've been investigating."

Haven chuckled. "I guess I have. But now it's my turn."

Milda leaned forward and gently laid her forehead against Haven's. Haven closed their eyes. They couldn't recall when they'd started doing that as a couple, but it made the back of Haven's head warm in a way that caused anxiety, worry, or sadness to lessen.

Maybe the reason I haven't freaked out more is because she's here with me.

Milda pulled back, and Haven took Lola. Lola squirmed a little, but seemed to have accepted that she wasn't going to escape from them at this point.

"Okay—let's see what new, paradigm shifting thing happens next," Haven said, then walked over to Cynthia as quickly as they could. Milda followed close by.

Leldon and Bernard were standing at the desk. Cynthia was tapping her fingers against the countertop.

In a sudden blitz of motion, a woman was standing on the other side of the desk.

Cynthia swore underneath her breath.

We're all going to need to get used to that, Haven thought.

The woman had light brown skin and a tight brown hair bun. She wore a pristine, salmon-colored button up with a red tie and had two pairs of sunglasses on the top of her head. Her eyes were a sharp gray color. She moved in a blur, flowing between a few monitors on the desk.

"Hi Wilma. Where's Christopher?" Bernard asked.

"He's busy, so he's having me cover for him," Wilma responded.

"Again?" Leldon said.

"*Again,*" Wilma confirmed.

Bernard cleared his throat. "Well, then—"

"We need to see someone named Klein?" Cynthia said. "Urgently."

Wilma's head snapped to look at Cynthia, then noticed Haven. No, she noticed *Lola.* Her eyes narrowed.

"Is that a non-native dog?"

Bernard cleared his throat. "As we were about to tell you, a seemingly recently created Seer portaled the three of these people—and yes, their bylaw-violating pet—from an active Rot God. Can we please talk to Klein?"

Wilma's eyes widened. "Oh god. Okay."

Haven was expecting it and yet was still startled by how Wilma moved. She was there one second, then she was basically an afterimage of a person. A salmon-colored smear on the air that faded as fast as it formed.

"It'll just be five minutes," Bernard assured them.

That was an overstatement. Within less than two overly silent minutes—Haven had been counting—Wilma was back behind the desk. She ran a hand through her hair, and her eyes were still wide.

"You weren't kidding. This is bad. You should get them to his office, like, right now."

Haven wondered how difficult not using super speed was for Seers. It not only looked awkward but was probably annoying. The staircase they ascended was a long half-loop, stretching to the left in an arc to the upper floor. It had easily over a hundred steps. Each step was austere and made of something that seemed like obsidian. And Leldon and Bernard walked it like their shoes were heavy.

It didn't tire them out though. Haven, Cynthia, and Milda, by contrast, were all panting by the time they reached the top. Haven rolled their eyes as Lola gave out a happy bark.

Easy for you to say, Haven thought. *We need to find something that works like a leash.*

At the top of the steps was a series of mostly glass walls and doors into offices. They almost looked too normal, like something you might find in a corporate setting, except occasionally there would be sword racks against the back walls. Those swords weren't normal weapons, though. Most of the blades were dull gray and jagged. The swords still looked wicked sharp.

I bet they're magic, Haven thought.

Leldon walked to a normal-enough looking door. It was made of what seemed like oak—though could've been some unique wood to the Layer. He gestured at the sign on it. *Chief of Logistical Actions.*

"So, everyone, please be on your best behavior," Leldon said.

"Klein can be a little much for new people," Bernard said. "Especially Layer-Linked people. He doesn't slow down like we do very much. He doesn't really have time to."

"But he's the one most able to help with this," Leldon added.

"As long as someone, please, *finally*, can get me back to my … Layer," Cynthia said. "As long as we're not stuck here any longer than we need to be."

Bernard nodded to the door. Leldon spun the handle.

Inside the room was the type of chaos that was likely secretly organized. The mess of a person on the verge of a breakthrough. Many boards with many papers tacked to them. Stacks of leatherbound and other types of fancy books laid in ways that made Haven worry about the book's spines.

In the center of all of it, there was a desk. A tiny, little desk. It was pure college dorm room style, but it didn't have any energy drinks on it—just more papers.

The dust devil moving around was probably Klein. Wind picked up and moved papers with a level of care that wind typically didn't. Haven managed to spot a flash of skin color.

"Uh, Klein?" Bernard said. "You have Layer-Linked guests."

The blur stopped and resolved into a man. Klein was not terribly tall. He didn't have a lot of muscles, or a big beard. But he still claimed the room. Klein had this seriousness about him that demanded attention. His skin was light brown, and his eyes were a stark gray that peered out from wire-rim glasses. Klein's messy brown hair was pulled back into a long ponytail. He was wearing what looked like some kind of flexible body armor: a rigid red-black thing with lots of little pouches.

"Yes," he said sharply, then seemed to actually notice the people in the room. "Oh, they're here. Great. One second."

With another blitz of motion, he returned with a large screen. He laid it down on the ground—it was easily ten feet wide—and then dropped to his knees to look at it. It displayed a map.

Haven tried to understand how the map worked, but it looked more like someone laying out neuron connections, or the structure of various molecules.

"I've been trying to track down as many fucking Seers as I can—but we're spread so thin right now according to higher ups. This has been a shit show. Ever since…"

Klein looked up at Haven.

"—have you seen a Seer named June?"

"No, I'm sorry…" Haven said.

·Klein pressed on. "My friend, June. Uh … she would've been carrying around a big chainsaw? She was wearing combat boots?"

"I'm sorry, I don't know who that is," Milda said.

"Are you sure? I haven't heard back from her. She's one of the most capable combatants I know, so she's probably just lost her communication device, but still…"

"I'm so sorry," Milda replied.

Klein let out a sigh brimming with tiredness. He closed his eyes for a moment, then opened them with another breath. "Of course … of course. I'm sure she's fine. Besides, we have other things to worry about: you are in the middle of an Emergence, or so I'm told."

"And my wife is trapped in it—who I need to get back to *right now.*"

Klein gave Cynthia a sympathetic look. "Okay … well, I need to know everything you can tell me about what's happening there. We need as much information as we can. I'm planning a full attack, a full salvo, to save everyone in your … town?"

"A town, yeah. It's called Quill Point," Haven said. "It's our home."

"And it's the site of one of the newest, biggest problems we've had in a long time," Klein said. "One that we're not fucking ready for. It's been so much with fucking six."

In a blur, he was at his desk, sitting among all the papers.

"I know it's been a lot for you, but I need you to brief me on this as much as you can. The Layer you live on. It's culture. The history. All sorts of things. I need to know what I'll be sending an entire troop worth of people into. The more we know, the better we can be equipped to handle it."

"And then you'll portal me back in there?" Cynthia demanded.

Klein didn't say anything.

Cynthia's eyes flared. She walked up and slammed her hand on the desk. "I have been marching around in another dimension, bossed around, and when I last saw Thea, there were *monsters* outside, ready to kill us. To kill her."

"She's a Seer … she'll be okay…" Leldon offered.

Cynthia spun around and leveled her finger at him. "Bernard said that already—but you can't know that."

"I should tell you who I am," Klein said calmly.

Cynthia turned back and glared. "Okay. Fucking fine. Then tell me quickly."

"You already know my name: Klein. But you don't know what I do. I am a midlevel person in an organization of sorts. More a large collection of people who all agreed to work together—and have been for a long time."

"Tell me quicker."

Klein nodded respectfully.

"Okay. Shortest version. Gods are real. There were six of them before. They travel through dimensions, killing those dimensions, and everyone on them. Now a new seventh one is in your dimension, and if we don't stop it, *everyone* in your dimension will die. I'm part of a group of people that try to stop that happening as much as we can."

Haven's breath caught.

Gods? Gods!? There are gods? And they are trying to kill dimensions?

Haven's heart sank. This was the problem with all those stories they'd read. It wasn't enough that there was magic. There was always *this* aspect to everything. The stakes. The dangers. Those stories had wonderful worlds, engaging places Haven wanted to visit, but also, more often than not, those fantastical locales had massive, massive wars going on in them.

Cynthia stepped back from the desk. "The whole world?"

"More than the whole world," Klein said.

Haven moved forward; it looked like Cynthia might fall over. But Cynthia steadied herself and sucked in a long breath. Her hand tightened at her side. She stayed still for almost ten seconds.

Klein waited. Everyone waited.

Then she spoke.

"Okay. Okay, I get it. I get it—I get it. Fucking dammit. The whole *world?* But you've dealt with this before? Right? You just said you're an organization that deals with stuff like this?"

"Yes," Klein said. "We've got a background in killing gods."

"What do you need from me to kill this one?"

Klein gently smiled. "I need to understand what is on the Layer where you came from, so I can better understand what I am asking a bunch of my friends to go running into."

"It's a whole world," Cynthia said. "What do you mean?"

"What has the theme been of your world's events lately?" Klein asked. "Any trends? Political? Environmental? Newly born gods always take the bad stuff that's already happening on a Layer—and amplify it into supernatural events."

Cynthia let out a bitter laugh. "We're having like five different crises at all times."

"That's not surprising for a Contemporary Layer," Klein remarked. "But it would be something that was happening in your town, specifically."

Something in the town? Haven thought. *Like something someone did? How big does it need to be?*

"Oh…" Cynthia said quietly. "Oh, no…"

Klein raised an eyebrow. "Yes? Spit it out."

Cynthia clutched at her forehead. "I knew he was evil…"

"What is it, Cynthia?" Milda asked.

Cynthia kept looking at Klein. "Would a corrupt mayor do it?"

"Corrupt *how*?" Klein asked very seriously.

"Raising rent to force people out so he can sell the buildings to investors. Eroding small businesses so he can bring in corporations. He fucked over our lake. Basically, he's being a fucking political asshole."

Klein closed his eyes. "Yes. That's enough rot. That would do it."

"The Mayor of Quill Point is going to destroy the Earth?" Milda asked.

Klein opened his eyes. "He's certainly going to try. Bernard, Leldon, I need you to start teleporting to every Layer where we have any known Seers working for us. I'm done relying on sending messages. Get everyone on it, and I mean *everyone*. And you three, you have interior knowledge of this town. If you want to help your wife, if you want to help everyone there, then I'm going to need you with me. You're going to help me win a war against a god."

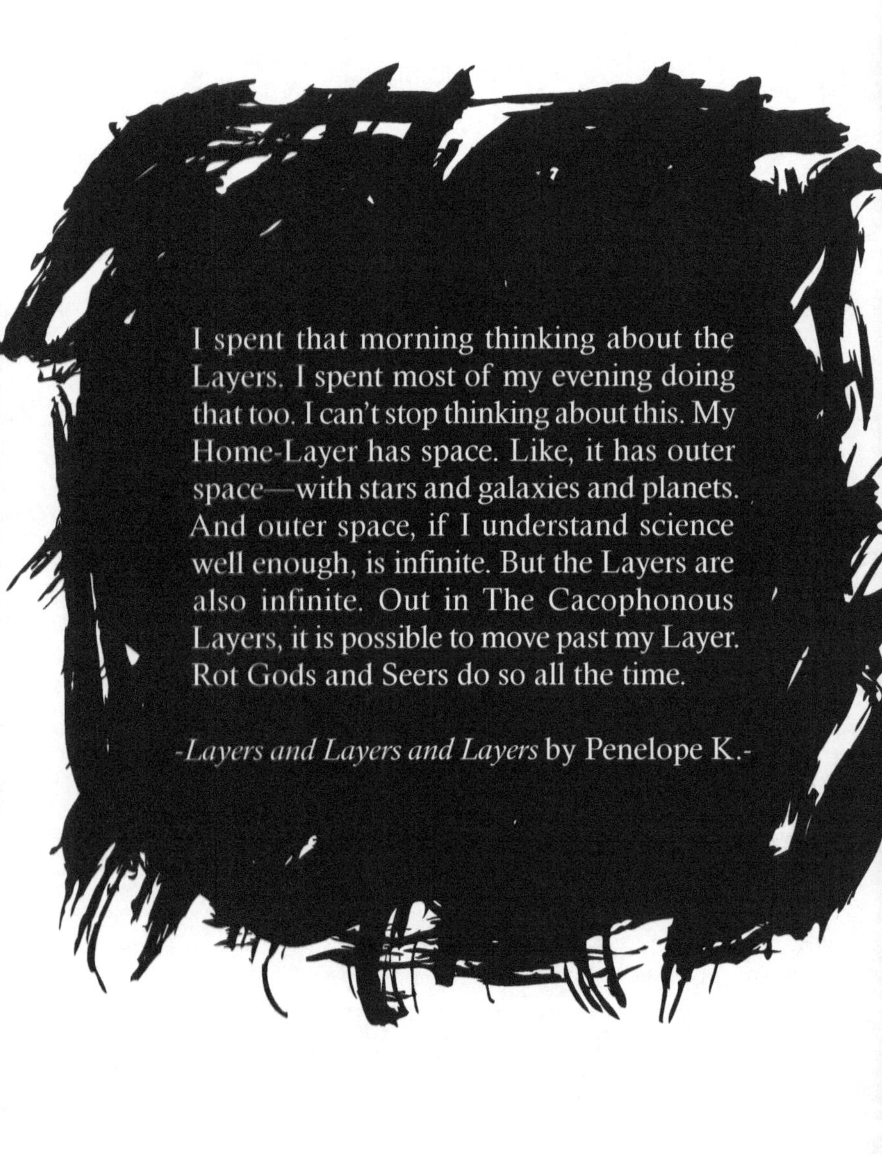
I spent that morning thinking about the Layers. I spent most of my evening doing that too. I can't stop thinking about this. My Home-Layer has space. Like, it has outer space—with stars and galaxies and planets. And outer space, if I understand science well enough, is infinite. But the Layers are also infinite. Out in The Cacophonous Layers, it is possible to move past my Layer. Rot Gods and Seers do so all the time.

-Layers and Layers and Layers by Penelope K.-

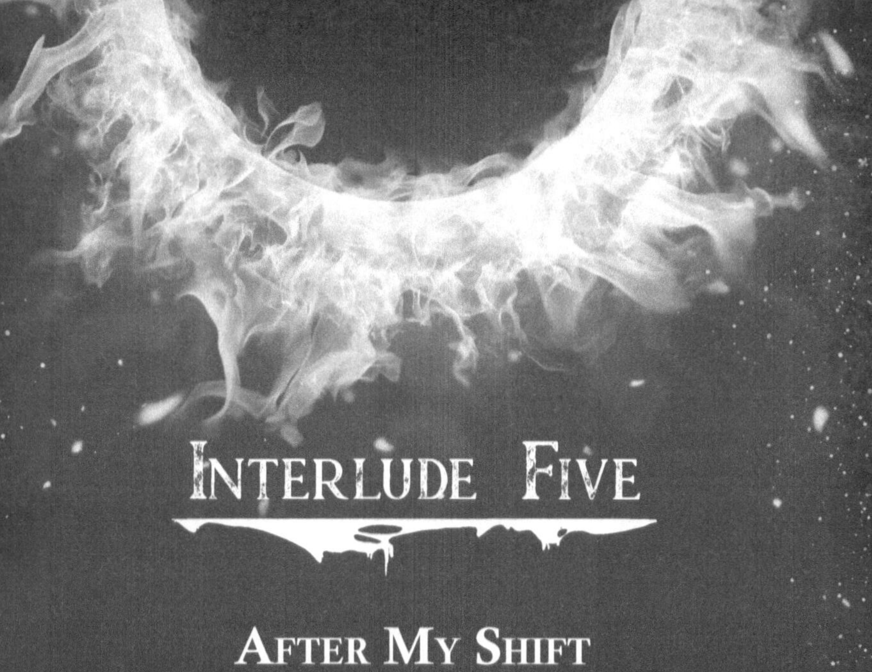

Interlude Five

After My Shift

Of her two degrees, Hope loved economics as a field of study the most. In the page of her college textbooks, it talked of interesting interactions, of laws underpinning the culture she grew up in. Supply and demand. Markets and market forces. It was almost like how people described magic. A system of rules and interactions that, once learned, could be wielded in ways that changed society. It was an electric idea.

It didn't make her college debt feel any better. All those market forces turned their eyes toward her, snarling. It dawned on her more and more that it might be that way for the rest of her life. Sure, she'd known it was a possible danger, but college degrees generally led to better earnings overall. It had been a calculated risk. But the thing about calculated risks is it's so easy to make them assuming you'll win.

And it had started to feel like she wasn't going to win. Quill Point wasn't the cheapest place to live. It wasn't California or New York, and small businesses survived well enough, but minimum wage still stretched thin some months. The problem was, she was overqualified. She was so overqualified that she winced whenever someone actually said they looked at her CV.

Hope had been debating moving to Chicago when the world ended. When Quill Point plunged into something new and strange and awful, where cell phones and cars didn't work, and the Mayor's Men took over, and it had been a struggle to survive at all.

In her dreams, scant moments after waking, and errant flashes when her mind managed to evade the memory alterations magic constantly bombarding her, she tried to understand what was happening to Quill Point, to her, and to reality itself.

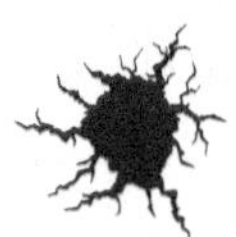

Despite everything, Hope had never found a love for caffeine. Her body didn't process it well. But on the rare occasions she had caffeinated coffee or even tea, it had felt like an average workday at The Spire Market.

A buzz at her hip, followed by a squawk. Hope glanced down at the walkie-talkie. The reception or something seemed to always make her phone not work, but the walkie-talkie never had issues.

"Clean up needed at pillows," squawked out a feminine voice. "Hope, you got it?"

Hope's heart sank. Somehow, this kept happening. Every day for the past week, there had been some kind of issue in that aisle. Hope had tried to check who was doing it. She'd tried a few times. It had led to nothing. The security cameras showed nothing. No group of teenagers. No one even carrying coffee cups. She couldn't even work it backward—no one had bought blankets in the same timeframe.

Here we go again.

Hope unclipped her walkie. "Yep, on it."

Walking through The Spire Market never felt like anywhere else. No matter what, Hope had the distinct sensation she was lost. Even when she knew where she was.

She walked quickly past endcaps for products she only vaguely recognized as real objects. She turned two tight corners. Finally, she was next to the pillow aisle.

Hope went into the aisle.

It was worse this time.

"This isn't a café, you assholes," Hope said to no one. "Do people just assume they can't drop stuff wherever they want?"

At least twenty, maybe thirty, plastic coffee cups sat on every surface that someone could conceivably place them on. They sat next to stuffed animals, pillows, and massive blankets. Most of them still had ice or even some coffee left in them. The slow drip of condensation was already weighing down some fabrics.

Hope did her best to avoid touching the rims as much as possible. Who knew what kind of germs this much random trash would have? She gathered up the first five and carried them to the nearest garbage can. There were only ten garbage cans in the entire store, but at least one was close by.

At least she got that scrap of luck—

—if it wasn't already full to bursting with trash.

The top of the mound was garnished with a paper plate that had once held a slice of pizza. She could tell from the perfect triangular stain.

Hope grimaced, then looked around. The store wasn't as busy as it could have been—and no one was looking at her. Hope frowned at a couple walking by with three lattes, but they didn't notice her either.

Hope lifted her foot. Several of the cups tried to escape her grip. She tightened her grip while simultaneously getting her balance back. A slight hop, a little wince, and then she angled her foot over the circular garbage can opening.

"Fuck it," she muttered.

Hope pushed down on the stack. The garbage collapsed with a little whoomph. And left a little gift. It soaked right through her shoes and congealed on her sock. A shiver squirmed up her spine.

"Oh god—"

Hope stumbled backward, dropping the cups. They danced across the linoleum floor with a clatter. Several customers stopped, glancing in her direction. One of them stared her down with pure-red eyes. The mouths on each of the customers' faces gnashed lamprey teeth.

"Nothing to worry about," Hope said loudly, waving her hand. "Thanks for shopping at Spire Market!"

All the customers nodded at the same time and stopped looking at her. They wandered away—almost dissolving away—and left her alone again. Hope let out a breath, her heart pounding. She didn't understand why they scared her so much.

Hope picked back up the cups and dropped them in. As she was running her hands through her hair, the walkie-talkie let out a squawk.

"Hope, go to the lawn care section, please. We have an emergency."

Hope unclipped the walkie. "I'm still handling the cups. Can you send someone else to do it?"

"No," came the sharp reply.

"Okay … can you send someone to finish up the pillows?"

"No. Hurry up now."

"Okay," Hope said.

She put the walkie back on her hip and let out a deep, *calming* breath. So *fucking* calming. A headache was very quickly blooming behind her temple.

Hope put her face into a rigid smile and readied herself for a day of catastrophes.

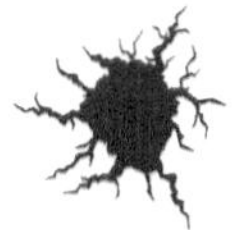

The electronics section sat next to the store's namesake. Whenever someone was working at the linoleum countertop, they stood right in front of it.

It went almost to the ceiling. It was covered in strange symbols. Symbols that boiled the air. Made the air itself seem to unstitch and unravel.

And floating, puppeteer-style, by tendrils, hung corpses. Thirteen people. Their heads opened up; their wet, slowly decaying brain matter being pushed into. Their lips cracked open and emanating the faint chiming tunes of a waiting room.

And above them, at the point where the ceiling met the Spire, was a hole in *reality itself.* Yawning. Screaming. Opened further and further by frequent sprays of blood from semi-translucent red and orange tendrils that crisscrossed the ceiling of the store, hanging almost like bunting, and disappearing out to other places. The smell of it spilled outward, aerosolized, always in Hope's nose when she was nearby, always in the air like a bakery's scent of bread. Gore. Blood sloshed around downshoots. It promised things. It promised whatever this was, whatever it intended, was that of taking and killing and *ripping away all that was good in this fucking world—*

Hope shook her head, scattering away thoughts. She felt weird whenever she looked at it. She knew that the Spire was part of corporate's branding strategy. Something that got people to talk about the store. But it was so annoying having such a big pillar-thing taking up space.

She unclipped her walkie-talkie. "Where did you say it was?"

"Lawn care."

"Gotcha," she said.

She walked through the electronics section, past a coworker looking at inventory on the computer.

A sharp turn, and she was in the lawn care aisle. And she paused. Her face twitched. A soft noise escaped her mouth. She held the rest back. Didn't scream or whimper. Maybe it wasn't real. Maybe this was somehow a prank or fake.

They'd started selling Halloween stuff, right?

And an aisle like that would sell fake blood. Realistic fake blood. Hope bet it could even mimic the smell. And movie special effects were so good lately, right? A whole fake person, body, corpse, would be nothing. A couple of teenagers could fake a person burning from the inside out and smuggle it into the lawn care aisle.

Right?

No, no, no. Fuck no. How could it not be real? It was *real*. That was a coworker. The uniform was for The Spire Market. What other store, what other place, would have a design like that? But who was it? Who had died?

The ring on his finger Hope thought. *There's only one person I know with a ring like that.*

Samuel. He'd gotten that ring for Tanya. A matching set, with two halves of the same design. He'd spent months bringing nothing but peanut butter and jelly sandwiches to afford it. He'd driven a broken car, worked every overtime shift, worked an extra job, to get *that* ring.

What am I going to tell his wife?

Hope took a step back. Her pulse was skyrocketing. A quiver shot up her spine and made her stomach spasm. The scream that had failed to escape her was—

Maybe you're mistaken? Hope thought.

What? No, I'm not, Hope also thought.

Something was clawing at her mind. A little buzzing. A little niggling anti-thought. A skeletal finger tapping at her mind, poking at her brain stem.

It's just a prank—so silly you fell for it, Hope thought.

No, no, stop it! Hope also thought.

Hope brought up walls in her own mind. She tried to find her thoughts within her own thoughts. It was like trying to hold water in a squeezed fist.

The walkie-talkie at her hip squawked.

"My bad. We've got this cleanup handled. Step back, Hope."

Hope did. She wasn't sure if she was the one who made her feet move, but she did step back. A different memory, as elusive as her thoughts, slid through. Dead bodies got disposed of a certain way in Quill Point.

A tendril dropped down from the ceiling. The end of it was a tunnel, almost like a lamprey. It was always waiting for someone to die.

It slammed down around the body, perfectly surrounding it. The body dissolved quickly. Blood particles and skin flakes shot upward with a little tempest of motion. The raw materials went down the channel toward the open wound in reality.

Hope watched it go, her mind split between what she was seeing and what her own mind was telling her—

"Lunch break!" declared the walkie-talkie.

Hope glanced at the device, then checked her watch. It was about that time, wasn't it? Finally.

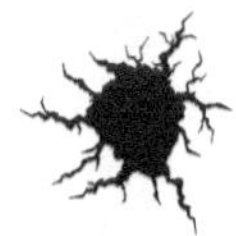

Hope had long ago given up using a fridge for her own lunches. The store had a little employee area, and it had a fridge, but every time she'd put something in that fridge, it was gone by the time she looked.

She suspected it was one of the new hires. Probably Kyle, the nineteen-year-old. Kyle had a hungry look to him—and not in a hustle culture sort of way.

Hope eventually suspected he wasn't always able to afford food, and she started leaving sandwiches when she could. She had no idea if it was helping.

For her own lunches, she eventually defaulted—more habit and repetition than anything else—to the chain restaurant that took up residence inside the store. It had a rotating cast of college graduates to work the thing.

Today, it was a new person. He had brown hair, white skin, and blue eyes. And he already had the worn-out look of someone who realized what kind of job they were doing and had made peace with the boredom. Became *one* with boredom.

Hope approached the counter and glanced at her options. She knew which one she would pick. She'd tried all of them at one point or another. But the meatball sub, despite having no real tomato involved in its production, was the best of the bunch. The cream of the crop. She shivered at the thought of some of the worse options. Avocado mash on spicy ham with rye bread was a monstrosity but was apparently the chain's big offering for the last interminable length of time.

Honestly, who's supplying that demand? Do they have some kind of deal with the pork industry?

"Hello there. What can I get for you?" asked the guy behind the counter.

Hope glanced at his nametag. "Uh, hi, Benjamin—"

"Call me Ben, please."

"Fair." Hope chuckled. "You're new, yeah?"

He nodded his head, then abruptly stopped. "Yeah … I just got hired … some time … ago…"

Benjamin looked past her. Hope glanced behind her, but there wasn't anything there.

"Are you okay?" Hope asked.

Benjamin's pupils kept getting wider. His frame shook, slowly, then so fast. "I'm *not supposed to be* here. I'm *not*."

Hope took a step back. "Uh—"

Ben put his hand to his eyes and kept rubbing at them, so hard it looked like he might hurt himself.

"What is *going* on?" he said quietly. "This isn't real. I don't work here. This *isn't fucking real*!"

Hope glanced around in alarm. Should she call someone? Who, though? The person on the walkie-talkie? Would they help? Was this on her to handle?

She was about to say something when a surging thought broke free. A little of herself made it past the squirming flies of anti-thoughts.

Hope leaned across the counter, grabbed Ben's arm, and pulled it down.

He looked at her with panic in his uncovered eye.

"Quickly," Hope whispered, "write it down before you forget."

"What?" he replied. "What do you mean?"

"You're right. This *isn't real.* We're in something made by a god. Write it down! Write. It. *Down.*"

Ben shivered. He glanced at the paper to the side of him. All that was on the pad were the words *no onions* and a poorly drawn smiley face. But he couldn't get himself to pick it up. To write it down.

The air around him started to shimmer.

"I don't understand. I want my mom. Where's my dad? I haven't seen them since I started *working.* Since … *Murder Sky.* The sky. The sky. Wait. Is there a sky anymore? How long have we been in here? What is it when you look up, and what is it when you look down, and I am so—"

Ben started crying blood. He pulled his other hand away from his eye, and a long string of blood clung to his palms. It kept pouring down.

No, not blood. Blood isn't so many colors.

"What … what is happening…?"

Hope's mind screamed. She knew this, too. She'd seen this happen before—in the shop. To so many people. How could she forget?

Ben didn't seem to be looking at her. His mind was elsewhere, his voice arriving from so far away.

"How is this the world? How am I supposed to survive when the world is like this? I didn't do *this*. How dare they fuck up the world and then not even help us—"

Benjamin went very stiff, his back ramrod straight. The multi-colored slime pushed out from his tear ducts with such force it splashed all over the counter. After a few moments, it stopped, and Ben looked at Hope again.

"I suppose it never mattered much."

Hope didn't say anything. Her heart was in her throat. For a little while, this part of the process had been all that happened. She'd find a coworker assigned to fold shirts, but the shirts were coated in the stuff. The person sometimes even continued working, albeit without any enthusiasm or interest.

But everything always got worse in this version of Quill Point.

And no matter how many times she'd seen this next part, it never ceased to be the most horrible thing in the world. It never ceased to cause a feedback loop inside her head as memories fought fake memories.

This isn't real.
This is real.
This isn't real.
This is real.

Hope clenched her teeth, but that was the most she could move her body. Her muscles spasmed as they tried to relax in calm—because nothing was happening—and get her to run away—because this was death and destruction.

Ben tilted his head backward and let out a flat chuckle. "I suppose it was always going to be like this—"

A faint click. A faint click from *within* Ben.

Ben looked confused. "—wait, no … no, I already gave up my dreams. I already … what more could you *want*—"

Another click, and there was a flash of orange light behind Ben's teeth. It looked like a camera going off, but with a more reddish hue. The area around him got much, much warmer.

Hope managed to take a step back. Sweat poured down her back.

"You can't have…" Ben wailed at the ceiling. "*What more can you take from me?*"

Ben gagged, but it sounded like steam. The smell of charred wood filled the tiny restaurant. Another flash of red happened behind his teeth.

He sagged, leaning hard against the countertop, knocking over a series of generic paper cups. They toppled down on him and bounced off. Ben didn't notice.

He stared at Hope and screamed.

Then a whoosh, and he stopped screaming. But he didn't stop making noises. Firecracker pops went off from somewhere inside him. An orange glow lit up his throat. Followed by a roaring fire.

It surged out of his throat. It flared around his eyes, cooking the sclera.

Another memory hit Hope:

There are no fire extinguishers here.

She cast her gaze up.

And there was never any sprinkler system in this building.

Ben closed his mouth, grimacing, but almost immediately, a hole started to burn through his cheek. Hope wasn't all that familiar with geology, but she knew the thing that was oozing out of his face was lava.

Ben's lips burned open—the lava pouring down his chest. And then he lit on fire. It raged up his head, burning his hair. It engulfed him in a pillar.

Only when his heart burst out of his chest could Hope finally move.

She screamed and stumbled backward until she hit a wall. Hope clutched her own heart as its vibrations soared through her. Her breath sped so much she wasn't always getting oxygen.

The heat was still so unbearable, being this close.

The tunnel, the tube, the red tendril that ran along the ceiling took longer to navigate down than it had in the lawn care section—but it moved past the signage and covered Ben's burning body.

It took away the lava and extinguished the fire. Ben's body—what remained of it—fell apart and disappeared up, flowing toward the Spire.

Almost immediately, Hope felt the anti-thoughts crashing in. She'd gotten the horror; it didn't want her to stop and process it.

It took all of Hope's willpower, but she sprung herself up and ran for the countertop. The fire hadn't damaged anything else, and the pad of paper was still there. There was a pen.

Hope scooped up both and desperately scratched words. *This isn't real. You're in a fake store.*

A staggering headache slapped her temple, and she let out a sharp breath.

I'm being ridiculous, she thought.

No, I'm saving my life, she also thought.

Hope ripped the note away and shoved it in her right pocket. She pulled her hand back before she could crumble it up, and then let the anti-thoughts back in. For a second, relief from the pressure, and then—

What time is it? Hope thought. *I need to get something for lunch.*

Hope blinked in surprise. She was already at the little restaurant. She must've walked there without thinking about it. The stress must've been getting to her.

Standing behind the counter was Adrian. That was what his nametag said anyway. He must be really new. He was in his early twenties. His skin was suntanned white, his eyes a light brown, and his hair was dark brown and gently spiked.

"Hey, what can I get you … today?" Adrian said. "I mean, what can I *make* for you today."

Hope chuckled. She and he both knew that nothing he was going to give her was actually cooked on the premises.

"I'll get the meatball sub," she said.

"Sure, that'll be…"

He trailed off.

Hope blinked in confusion, but then shook her head. She'd clearly heard the price said.

"Damn—that's a little high."

"Inflation," Adrian said flatly. "Can't live with it…"

"Can't live without it?" Hope asked.

"Why would that be a bad thing?" Adrian replied.

"Uh … okay … well."

Hope got her wallet and handed him the card.

"Do you want to cash in your employee discount? You have one use for the month on that."

"Sure. Why not?" she said.

"Okay. Anyway. Let me get you that… I mean, *make* you that meatball marinara subway sandwich, with only the best ingredients."

Hope once again chuckled. And she had the vaguest sensation of wanting to cry and cry and cry.

"That sounds great."

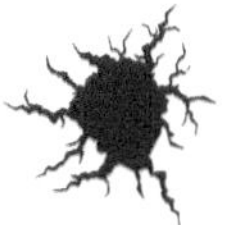

Sometimes, Hope had trouble working out her memories of dating Zaahir. It was almost like the memories were too convenient. They followed a narrative framework that was instantly easy to communicate.

A story in a series of pictures and anecdotes.

She recalled hugging him, touching his arms. Where that had occurred, she wasn't sure. Just that it had. And then … something…

They'd started dating. They went on dates every Friday for three weeks. Then Zaahir had finally gotten up the nerve to ask for a kiss, and she'd obviously accepted that request right away. It was very nice.

And when Zaahir had gotten a job at the same place as her, she'd been excited. They would see each other way more often.

Only … that hadn't panned out. Zaahir had been hired to retrieve the shopping carts. And the task never seemed to end. It was a ridiculous thought, but the parking lot seemed to go on for much further than it should've.

This day was especially bad. Hot and with so many loose carts, it seemed like more than the store should even have. Hope winced from the heat as soon as the automatic doors opened but continued onward.

She went for the bench that had become *their* spot. It was painted blue and was chipped in all the worst places. She sat down, and then wiped off the little flakes of blue paint that always stuck to her hand. Then she stared off into the distance—trying to find Zaahir.

There were a few people getting carts that day. Hope could see five so far, but none of them were Zaahir.

Frowning for a moment, Hope started unwrapping her sandwich. A little stain of red was leaking out from it, staining the paper. She pulled out a napkin from the pile she'd stuffed into her left pocket and put the napkin on her lap—just in case. She hoped that her sandwich hadn't fallen apart before she even got to eat any of it.

"Best part of the day," she muttered around a bite of rubbery bread. "I guess it really is though, huh?"

Because I can at least see Zaahir.

The meatball tasted very salty that day, and Hope wished that she'd gotten a drink. She had no idea why she'd forgotten. Usually, she was on top of stuff like that.

Absent-mindedly, she glanced around the massive sprawl again. After a few more moments, she saw her boyfriend pushing a long line of carts toward her.

Hope smiled. It went up to her eyes. Zaahir always looked nice in his uniform. It was how it clung to his arms, how it seemed to fit him so well. Hope didn't quite understand it, but Zaahir always seemed to be dressed stylishly, no matter what.

Zaahir kept pushing, and soon enough was pushing the carts past her. He glanced at her and gave a little smile, then continued toward the front of the store.

With a soft crash, the long line hit the back of the other carts. He wiped his forehead, then turned to look at Hope.

"Working hard?" Hope asked.

"I think," Zaahir said, slightly out of breath, "that they could … totally … afford … to let me have one of those

electronic pushers. Right? I think they could. This is …
too much for someone … anyone really … to move."

"I can put in another request," Hope said, though
she knew it would go nowhere. "Maybe they'll send us
something?"

"Yeah … sure," Zaahir said with a laugh.

He walked over. Zaahir's shadow slid over Hope. He
stood in front of her, with his back to the sun.

"It's really nice to see you," Zaahir said.

"You saw me yesterday," Hope replied.

"It's *always* nice to see you."

Hope blushed almost instantly. Even after all the times
that he'd said something similar, it was still nice to hear
his voice say it. Zaahir's voice almost always managed
to sound light. Like the weight of the world—and the
struggle of shopping carts—wasn't crushing him.

Hope wished she could manage the same. Maybe one
day she could.

"Thanks," Hope said. "It's very nice to see you too."

"Eh, I'm all sweaty," he said, sitting down next to her.

"Hard day?" she asked.

"Yeah, my rib keeps really hurting. I don't know what
I did to it."

"Banged it into a cart or something?" Hope asked.

"Maybe," Zaahir said. "I should see if my insurance
covers an x-ray."

"It might," Hope offered.

"I guess so." Zaahir cast his eyes down, and something flashed across his face. "I think that's all that's
bothering me."

"Are you sure?" Hope said, pursing her lips. "You
don't sound sure."

"I mean, I guess I'm not," he said. "I kept finding … stuff … on the carts when I went to go get them."

"Yeah?" Hope asked. "Like what?"

Zaahir ran his hand over his trimmed beard. "You know … I'm not sure now. It was really bad though. I was really bothered by it…"

He leaned his head back and stared at the sky. And then tears began to gently spill down his face. Zaahir didn't react to this; didn't sob or cry out. It was almost like he didn't even know he was crying.

Hope opened her mouth to ask, but then a sharp pain hit the side of her temple—just for a second. She closed her mouth. And she could swear there was a faint noise on the wind…

Is that screaming? Hope thought.

No, don't be ridiculous, Hope also thought.

And for a moment, Hope was dropping quickly back into anti-thoughts. But Zaahir spoke. And he spoke with a whisper, the rest of his body so still he was almost not breathing.

"The fire keeps taking the older people," Zaahir said. "There are kids in some of those cars. I can't help them. I want to help them. I have to stop and move the carts. The carts that aren't monsters. The Fuel Things keep stopping me whenever I try to do anything about them hurting people…"

"The … 'Fuel Things?'" Hope managed to ask.

"They're made of … heat," Zaahir explained. "They … don't move the way you would—"

He clutched his head.

Hope let out a small gasp. "Are you okay?"

"We've had…" Zaahir took in a big gulp of air, then winced again. "We've had this conversation before. I can't hold onto it—"

Hope moved to do something—what, she didn't know—when a blast of anti-thought crashed from the top of her head down her spine, and she blinked in confusion.

"Do you want some of my sandwich?" she offered.

Zaahir smiled back. "Oh, sure, thank you."

Hope gestured the sandwich toward him, and he leaned in and took a bite. When he pulled back, a little sauce stuck to his beard.

Hope laughed. "You've got a little something there."

"Oh!" Zaahir checked his pockets. "Shoot, I don't have any napkins."

"I do," Hope said, taking some napkins out of her left pocket. "Here."

"Thanks," Zaahir said.

He took a handful and did his best to get the main front of his beard. "Did I get it?"

Hope couldn't explain why she thought that was so endearing. Why seeing Zaahir do something that mundane made her heart warm and happy.

"You missed a bit in the corner of your mouth," Hope said. "I'll get it."

Zaahir looked a little taken aback by her suddenly leaning in, napkin running at the corner of his mouth. He blushed.

"Thanks," Zaahir managed to say.

"You know I've been a lot closer," Hope said with a chuckle.

Zaahir nodded. "I know that. But it also feels like we just started dating, you know?"

Hope did know. That was part of why the memories always felt somehow convenient. Sometimes … just sometimes, it almost felt fake. Like it hadn't happened yet. It could happen, surely. She loved the ideas, but wasn't there something about Mayor's Men … monsters…?

"So, are we going to do anything this weekend?" Hope asked. "I was thinking we could watch something at the theater?"

"Uh, well, I actually had something planned."

"Oh?" Hope said. "What's that?"

"Well…" Zaahir began. "I had this restaurant in mind. I maybe got us an appointment last week. It's not always easy to get seating. Have you heard of—"

The restaurant's name was a spike of pain in Hope's head.

That's not a real place. Quill Point is trapped. There are monsters here. There's no real restaurant like that. It's a trick. You're trapped, Hope. Zaahir is trapped. None of this is fucking real.

No, that's the lie. Everything is normal.

This is normal.

A normal job.

All of it is normal.

Zaahir was looking at her expectantly. He had those eyes that she couldn't help but fall into all the time. Those brown eyes were grounding. Something that made her less nervous, less stressed.

But lessening *this* fear still left terror.

When did this all happen? I agreed to a first date with him, and I don't … when did we get this far along? Where are the real moments? I want to date him for real; I want to kiss him for the first time, for real. Not have it placed into my headspace. Not be robbed of the real. I want to really be with Zaahir, not pulled along the path of a relationship I won't get the true memories of.

"That sounds lovely," Hope said. "That sounds amazing."

"Yay! I'm glad you want to," Zaahir said.

"Of course I want to," Hope said. "I like having any meal with you."

"That's my line," Zaahir said.

Hope screamed as the slicing sensation and sound of breaking glass resounded and shredded through her mind. She was crawling down a tunnel—toward what was actually happening.

"This isn't *real*," she shouted. "It's a nightmare! They're messing with our perceptions! They're messing with *all* of it. We're being killed and tortured!"

"What—" Zaahir managed.

Then a horrible screech sang out. Hope clutched at her ears. For a second, she didn't know where it was from. But then—

At her hip.

The walkie-talkie.

The voice out of it didn't quite sound like the woman Hope had been listening to before. It was like her voice was layered over itself.

"I think it's time you finished up your break," she said.

Hope unclipped the walkie-talkie and chucked it away with as much force as she could. She wanted it shattered. Though some part of her expected that to fail—for it to crash into the parking lot, bounce around, and end up unharmed. But no. It broke.

It broke against the air.

Mechanical parts splattered across *something* and then cracks formed in the air. Angular distortions of three-dimensional spaces, mostly concave, but a few jutting forward as knife edges. It gave Hope slight vertigo.

A hole that led to pure white appeared at the point of impact. And red-painted fingernails emerged, followed by a hand. Then another. From the other side of some impossible void, someone was yanking apart the frosted glass of reality's skin, and it was such a clean cut.

What stepped out wasn't fully formed yet.

She wore a nondescript blue shirt, with a black blazer over the top of it and gray slacks. Her hair was tied back in a very tight bun. Chunks of her arms, face, and neck were made of rotting, festering globules of all that was wrong with the world. Pus bubbles of existential wrongness. The globules squirmed, stretching like iron filaments reaching for a magnet, before sparkling with prism-light.

Then it stabilized.

Her hair was a simple brown, and her eyes were almost the same color. Her face was utterly generic in a way no human could be. A woman with pale white skin and light pink lipstick.

She lifted a coffee cup that wasn't there before and took a light sip.

"I thought I'd be able to get away without a physical form," she said. "I figured that would be more efficient. But I suppose it does make sense for me to be against remote work, hmm?"

Hope screamed.

Zaahir screamed.

The woman tossed her cup of coffee at the ground.

It crashed with a sound more akin to the sound of a chunk of slate. The meager bit of coffee turned into a massive puddle and sloshed around Hope's feet. She tried to get up from the bench, take a step away, but her legs couldn't lift. Her foot wouldn't leave her now slightly coffee stained shoes.

"What the fuck!" Hope yelled, still struggling.

"Get away from us!" Zaahir added.

The woman unhooked a walkie-talkie she didn't have before. She pressed down a bright red button on the side of it.

You should be quiet around her, Hope thought.

No! What? She's a monster—

YOU SHOULD BE FUCKING QUIET!

Hope clutched her head. She could barely keep her eyes open, but could see Zaahir wavering, struggling to fight as well.

The woman stopped pushing the button. She clicked her tongue.

"You know, sometimes I wonder why we don't just use *this* sort of thing. We could just kill you. We'd get the same amount of death in the end. But that's not how it works. Greed is a many-headed beast, with denying healthcare on one end, and targeted assassinations on the other. We're so much more than commonplace, mundane, simple murder, I like to think. Don't you think?"

She looked at Hope pointedly. And then her finger hovered over the button.

Hope nodded.

"There we go. You've been wonderful, so far, Hope, but you were thinking too loudly, and thinking too thoroughly, and we don't want you to see the truth, now do we?"

Hope shivered but shook her head.

"Because someone like you, someone who under-stands the system, is inherently dangerous. I can't have you thinking. It's so, so isolating, working the kind of job you do. You're surrounded by fodder—I mean people—all *damn* day. So much so that you can't think. But you are, you really are, also alone."

Hope's head buzzed.

She's Productivity Without Empathy. She's The Lonely Rushing. The Days That Bleed into Months.

She's The 9-to-5.

The 9-to-5 tilted her head and smiled. Her voice switched hard to quite cheery.

"Oh! Did what I am just pop into your head? Did you learn my name?"

Hope nodded.

"No, no. What is it?"

She told her.

"Oh, wonderful," she said. "I am over the moon. I was hoping my physical form would coalesce enough from a multi-faceted metaphysical concept that mortals would instantly know my title without being informed by exterior means. That's fantastic."

"Please … let her go," Zaahir managed to say.

Hope glanced at him. He was struggling so much his legs were shaking.

"Oh, wouldn't that be something?" The 9-to-5 said. "Wouldn't that be a paradigm shift? But no. That's not the way forward, or backward, or the way I want. I can never let you go until you die—that's a firing I can get behind."

She pressed the button, and Zaahir shuddered.

"What a blasphemous thought," The 9-to-5 continued. "What would The God of Greed think of that? We're sacrificing—and we've got a lot of people we need to kill."

Hope blinked. A God of Greed? Did she know about that? Hadn't The Mayor said something to that…? No, The *Ascended* Mayor had said something about that…

She would deal with the massive and concerning implications of all that later.

Assuming there was a later.

The 9-to-5 looked down at the pool of coffee and clicked her tongue again. "That was all my coffee. Can't keep going without stimulants. Can't keep up this schedule without fuel. Can't. Won't. No, no, no."

Hope tried to remember that.

The 9-to-5 fixed Hope with a curious look that slowly folded into a glare. "You really should get back to work. I can't have you dilly dallying."

As soon as she said that, the strange coffee started to go away. It was like it was being washed away with invisible water. Runny lines of it went for an open gutter.

Whatever relief Hope got from that faded almost instantly as The 9-to-5 changed, also almost instantly, into a shape that somehow seemed more real, even if it was not anything that existed in the world.

She was more angular. Her stomach segmenting off into three separate sections. Her legs off at one end, holding her up despite an impossible weight distribution. A front, long, zig-zagging chest propping up a face that was twice the size it should've been. Her mouth stretched into a half-moon smile. And at the center of her, the middle stomach section, was an organic clock. Three jutting bones—white and spinal—lay against her shirt, each rotating at different speeds to a meaty ticking.

She spread out her hands, and her arms had gained an additional joint each. She leaned in close, her mouth so wide she could easily devour Hope's brain.

"I said, get back to work."

A bright white light popped like an exploding lightbulb inside Hope's mind—and the monster, The 9-to-5, was gone.

Hope shook her head. She glanced over at her boyfriend, who also seemed to be confused about something.

But then he looked at Hope and smiled.

"So, do you want to go to the restaurant?" Zaahir asked. "I hear they have really good pasta."

Hope nodded. "Of course I do."

"Awesome," he said. "I'm looking forward to it."

"So am I," Hope replied.

"Well, I got to get back to work now," Zaahir said. "There are still so many carts out there. I don't even know where you can get so many carts."

Hope smirked. "I have no idea—but I'm sure you'll get them all today."

"That's the goal."

"Well, love you," Hope said.

"Love you too," Zaahir said.

With a steadying breath, Zaahir walked back out to the parking lot, almost instantly fading into an ambient haze of heat.

Hope watched for a moment, then turned to go back inside. She kept almost stopping, though, and turning around. She absentmindedly touched a piece of paper in her right pocket but didn't take it out. Something was on her mind.

Oh well, Hope thought. *I'll figure it out after my shift.*

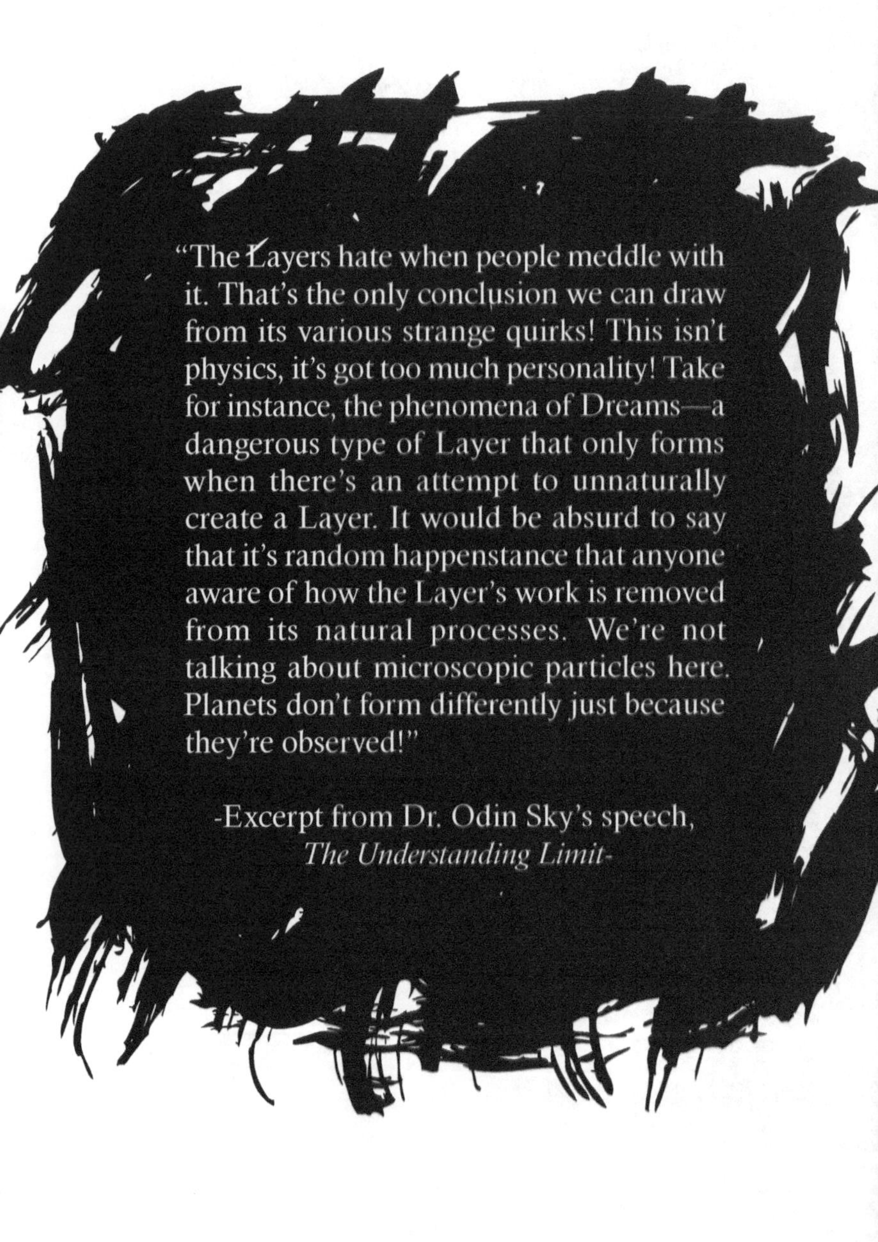

"The Layers hate when people meddle with it. That's the only conclusion we can draw from its various strange quirks! This isn't physics, it's got too much personality! Take for instance, the phenomena of Dreams—a dangerous type of Layer that only forms when there's an attempt to unnaturally create a Layer. It would be absurd to say that it's random happenstance that anyone aware of how the Layer's work is removed from its natural processes. We're not talking about microscopic particles here. Planets don't form differently just because they're observed!"

-Excerpt from Dr. Odin Sky's speech, *The Understanding Limit-*

Interlude Six

The Gold-Plated Woman

When Bree was released from the prison of her own mind, one of the first thing she did was scream.

The next thing she did, as a very natural progression of events, was try to escape. Her wrists almost immediately burned from trying to snap the rope tied around them. Next to her, Grace and Declan both panicked as well.

Arthur was mutating in front of her. Strange fronds of white mold-stuff grew from these horrible gashes in his arms. His jaw distended and turned into something like a wolf's snout, only full of teeth that matched no animal she knew. The air around him grew hazy, and all the air down in that strange place, already stinking with blood, got coppery to the point of inducing nausea as the same thing happened to the others standing around her father.

The golden orb pulsed like it was laughing.

And her father stood with his back to her. Stood in his suit, tall and regal as always, but golden somehow, emanating with strange light. An unearthly shade of the orb's same glimmer.

And he laughed in a voice crueler than Bree had ever heard from him. Then, he gave his speech.

"My Lords of Greed, here is your first assignment: round them up! Kill who you wish, kill when it strikes your fancy, but funnel the rest of them into the businesses, stores, and the Spire itself. They might still give something of their lives before this is done. Force the sick and stab the injured until they comply. Retirement and empathy are both *over*. The world may be ending, but everyone needs to work or spend, *no matter fucking what!*"

That strange golden orb smashed through the ceiling, making Bree scream even louder, before her lungs felt like they'd been squished in her chest. She let out a strained gasp. Massive chunks of the ceiling rained down, spreading a thick cloud of dust.

She could barely breathe for a moment; her lungs felt full of sand. She couldn't see all that well through the haze, but what she could didn't make sense—couldn't be possible.

Around her, the newly changed Mayor's Men were moving too fast. They blurred around the room, chasing after two people Bree only vaguely recognized. A series of taunts and crashing sounds rang out as the majority of them disappeared up the winding staircase.

One of the now-monsters was still standing there though, looking at his hands. A horrible heat haze was flowing from the fresh, moldy wounds on his arms and forehead.

"Wyatt," The Mayor barked.

Wyatt spun so fast, it was more like a section of a video had been cut out in editing. It was faster than a time-lapse.

"Yes-yes, sir?"

"I need your assistance with something now. I have a special task for you, and only you."

Wyatt titled his head—or Bree assumed that was the action that resulted in his head being at that angle—and he didn't speak for a moment.

"What … happened to me?" Wyatt then asked, his voice cracking.

Bree stared at Wyatt. The way his voice had cracked. The way the others had sounded taunting. Their voices sounded *human*. Some part of a person was still in there.

"Oh, my Lord of Greed," The Mayor said. "I know this is a lot to take in. But we don't have time."

With a series of horrible pops and whines, the ceiling above continued to fall apart.

"I need you to *listen*," The Mayor said firmly. "The God of Greed is whispering in your ear, and it will tell you what you need to do soon. But for now, do as I say."

Wyatt straightened up to his full height and nodded slowly.

The Mayor swung out his arm to point. "These two. Declan and Grace—I need them at the diner. Or whatever it will become now. They are going to play a special role. Take them there quickly."

The Mayor looked up at the hole in the ceiling.

"Take them that way."

Wyatt looked confused for only a moment before his blur zipped nearby Bree. Grace and Declan let out yells of protest. Wyatt was nigh immediately right below the hole in the ceiling, holding them over each shoulder effortlessly, and then did something that it took Bree a moment to comprehend.

He jumped out of sight.

She didn't even hear him land. The hole, the night sky, could've been a hundred feet above them, but Wyatt had disappeared into it.

"I did lie a little, perhaps. Let's move things along."

The voice took away all of Bree's confusion. And replaced it with fear. The little girl that was not a little girl, nor human, nor of this Earth had a voice that Bree would never, ever forget.

Bree expected her to leap out from somewhere, or appear next to her, but it was only that voice—and then a cold, clear snap.

The ropes binding her ripped and fell from her.

Bree leaped out of her chair, only for a chunk of the ceiling to fall in front of her and nearly brain her. The edge of the hole in the ceiling kept expanding—kept crashing down in waves of dust and dirt and wood and plaster.

She took a step toward the doorway before a brick slammed down and grazed her shoulder. It was enough force to knock her backward, and for her to clutch at the spot. A thin trickle of blood was already leaking through her shirt. The sensation of actual pain had been suppressed for so long, it was almost confusing to experience it.

"Ah, daughter, so nice to have you participating," The Mayor of Quill Point said, not even turning to face her.

Bree froze, then anger spilled in. "Why would you fucking do this?!"

"You already know what's happening," he replied.

He turned around, and Bree gasped. The gold wasn't only around him—it was *in* him. Long strands of gold, like ore in the ground, were snaking through his limbs. And was behind his teeth.

He was smiling, and it reminded Bree of someone with a flashlight in their mouth.

"Or you should anyway. I assume our mutual demigod friend explained the situation to you? The honor that I have chosen for you?"

"She fucking told me you're selling my soul!"

A plank of wood crashed down right by Bree, and she had to lurch backward, covering her face. She'd still breathed in at the worst time and couldn't help but fall into a coughing fit.

"That's no way to look at it," The Mayor of Quill Point replied. "I am giving you a great opportunity here, Brianna. This town is now under the rule of a wonderful new divinity, another god among many. You will help with its ascension! I cannot think of a better future I could give my child."

"Fuck you!" Bree screamed, then coughed again.

Bree tried to back away, but she was already as far from the door as she could be. The room was circular, and that door was past her father.

"Honestly, Brianna, you've been difficult for so long," he said wearily. "I only want what's best for you. I am going to make you immortal. A piece of something that is grand."

Bree glanced around. Another brick exploded right next to her foot. It took all she could to keep the surge of panic and adrenaline down. Her gaze landed on the chair. It was still intact. She grabbed it and pointed the legs at her father.

"Get away from me. I don't want any of this. You took my *mind*. I've been trapped inside it for days …

weeks … I don't even know how long. You don't want the best for me!"

"A little character-building is all," The Mayor replied. "I can't control every aspect of this—we are working with benefactors that are well beyond all that we can know."

Bree's arms shook. She hadn't been the one controlling them for a long time. They felt almost alien to move now. The exact strength and dexterity they were capable of unknown. But she could still push the chair at him. If he just stepped back a few steps, she could dart around him. She would reach the door.

The Mayor gave her a disappointed glare that Bree knew extremely well.

"I suppose I can't blame you for not understanding how this all works, can I?" The Mayor said. "As you mentioned, you have been stuck inside your own head for a long time. Allow me to show you."

He stepped forward, right in front of Bree. His gold *flared* for a second, growing so bright.

Bree pushed the chair forward.

The chair legs hit him in the chest. The wood cracked, each of the legs snapping and flying off in different directions.

Bree recovered quickly. She scooped up a broken leg, held it like a stake, and stabbed his stomach. The end was sharp. It should've at least hurt. It snapped in her hands. It didn't even wrinkle his suit.

Bree screamed and flattened her back against the wall. She'd seen so many supernatural things. Seen a monster made of a hotel worth of dead bodies. Fought a monster made of clay. But somehow her father calmly looking at her was the most terrifying moment yet.

Then another chunk of the ceiling fell. Nearly all the remaining ceiling. Dust sprinkled down like a sudden blizzard. Fists of stone and wood dropped. There was nowhere she could move to avoid it.

Bree covered her head but expected to die.

A few seconds of noise and dust and loud crashes and that didn't occur.

Bree wasn't even hurt more than she already was. Her eyes and the air were both blurry with particles, but she could see the golden glow. She lowered her arms and found her father standing over her, shielding her with his back.

A brick. The final brick. Red and solid. Struck the side of his head, and the brick shattered. It blew apart into dust and red powder. His gold flared again, sparking like a lightbulb about to burst. The Mayor's smirk didn't waver even a little.

"The God of Greed gave us a gift, Brianna. It's magnificent. I want you to understand how blessed we are."

"What is..." Bree managed. "...how are you doing that...?"

"I could explain ... and for others, I might. But you don't listen to me. I suppose you are an *experiential* study, more ... *focused* on feelings. You and your artwork. Maybe I've gone about this all wrong. Maybe *this* will help you understand."

He put his hand on Bree's shoulder and squeezed. His grip was crushing. Bree let out a scream again and then stopped as something ... shifted.

"I was given Gold-Plating enough for two people. One of my only requests. The demigods may not protect you, but I can't have you dying out there in Quill Point. Even if the monsters and the demigods left you alone, there are many dangers, daughter."

Bree stopped feeling his grip very much at all. It faded. There was a faint sensation like a needle going into her shoulder, and something flowing through her veins, and then…

The effervescent crystallization of perfect peace.

Gravity was with her, not against her.

Entropy was a comical farce, absurd, like being slapped with foam.

She was stalwart against the machinations of…

She was beyond the machinations of…

The heat death of the universe couldn't even … couldn't…

She was a stone in a river that would never erode. A mountain on which all hikers would fail to cross. A diamond not even other diamonds could cut. Her star would never supernova; and her soul would out-glimmer any others.

Her father's voice slowly returned to her.

"…I'm told that all gods have their own unique, individual forms of magic."

Bree clutched her head, leaned against the wall, then let herself sit. All she wanted was to understand what she was experiencing. It was like…

What is this like?

The world was around her, real and there, but she was one step back. One step into her own self. She was a sculpture in a display glass, but aware of all that was happening around her. She was wearing a suit of armor, but comfortable, cooled.

Only then did she look at her arms.

They were just as bright, just as vibrant as her father's. Gold swam down her veins in currents of magma. It didn't hurt. It *couldn't* hurt. Bree was suddenly aware, put in her head as an inarguable truth, that though any injuries she already had were governed by whatever healing process they would've taken, nothing else would ever occur. Neither she, nor any cell in her body, would ever experience damage, pain, degradation, illness, or anything else of the sort. The cut on her shoulder from the brick, it was bruising, the damage from what had happened to her fingers, that would heal as well as it could; it would scab and seal or remain a scar, and every other injury she'd recently endured would follow such a pattern in its healing, but they would be the last changes her body ever undertook for as long as she remained this way.

"What did you do…?" she breathed.

"It's called being Gold-Plated. Is it not incredible?" The Mayor said. "Here, let me truly show you."

He picked up a stone casually. It was easily as big as she was. He dropped it. It crashed down on her stomach. And, for a split second, she could see a vibrant flash of gold around that area.

The stone exploded *upward* into a puff of dust.

It didn't hurt.

She stared at the dust particles that were failing to land on her clothing. It was like a breeze pushed them to either side.

"I must say, I am so very proud of you, Brianna."

Bree looked up and shook her head. The rage quickly spun and soured until it was numbness. He already had what power she now did. There was no point attacking him. And she knew that chastising him was as pointless as it had ever been. Neither would affect him in any way.

Bree spat at her father, and her spittle evaporated on the golden field.

"Whatever you did to me … it doesn't change … fucking … *anything*," she said. "If I *could* hurt you, I would hurt you. You need to get the *fuck* away from me."

The Mayor laughed gently. He glanced up at the hole in the ceiling, at the night sky.

"I did expect this, planned for it, even if it's not what I wanted. Brianna, it doesn't ultimately matter what your opinion is of these things. I chose you, and they chose you, and destiny has been laid with a lot of blood and gold. This isn't a generational wealth that you can just fetter away on art supplies."

Bree stood up slowly and clutched her shoulder. It was extremely tender.

"Fuck you … fuck you … fuck you—"

The Mayor held up his hands. "That's enough of that language. I can see I am not going to get through to you, Brianna."

"It's fucking *Bree*. Get the name *you* picked out of your fucking mouth."

The Mayor shrugged. "Fine then … Bree. I can grant you that much. You are the template for the god's mighty plans—you are *going* to be a part of The God of Greed. So, if you want an unrefined *nickname*, then I can't stop you, *Bree*."

Bree didn't respond to that with even a nod. She walked toward the exit, not looking at him. Piles of debris that were otherwise impassable exploded when she kicked them. It didn't take her long to get to the door.

"I can see that I cannot stop you," The Mayor continued behind her, "but that doesn't mean this isn't what is going to happen. There's no way for you to leave Quill Point. There's no way for you to do *anything else*. You can sit in a hole all you want. You can *sulk* all you want, little miss—but the world is going to be what we made it into. You don't just get to live in it."

Bree flipped him off, and realized with some minis-cule delight that her finger would never get sore, no matter how long she held it up. She kept flipping him off even as she walked around the first lap of the circular staircase.

Then she lowered her middle finger and navigated the mess. Some steps were heavily damaged, and some of them were gone. In front of her was a three-foot gap that dropped straight down. She leaned over and looked into the pile of rubble below. It would've easily broken several bones to fall on it. If she hadn't been Gold-Plated, she never would have tried the jump. At that moment, with everything on her mind, it didn't even occur to her to be nervous about it.

Taking three steps back, then breaking into a sprint, she flung her body across the gap. She didn't get far enough. Her stomach slammed into the side of the plat-form and the stone exploded. At the same moment, she whipped out her arm and caught her fingers around an uneven part of the wall. It was barely a sliver of surface area—not nearly enough to hold up an entire person under normal circumstance. Friction would've torn the skin right off her fingers.

But she still hung there.

Her arms had the capacity to drag the rest of her up. Her muscles should've torn, but wouldn't. Her body was capable of the strength it always could muster—if resulting injuries were never a concern. And with a little extra magic on top of that.

She finished pulling herself over the edge, crawled to the next stable section, then stood back up. She winced. None of that had made her injured shoulder sorer, but it was plenty sore to begin with. Still, after a moment of thought, she smirked to herself. Her father would also have to get out of that pit somehow.

Bree took another step, then glanced back.

"Fuck you!"

The heel of her shoe punched a hole straight through an intact step, and a second hit sent it crumpling down.

"We're going to need to work on your decorum," The Mayor's voice called up from the bottom.

Bree went back to making her way up the tower.

After clearing another jump—much easier this time now that she had some practice—and going up some more steps, she finally emerged from the secret entrance. Or what was left of it. The painting that had hung on the wall had a massive rip through it. Big enough that Bree correctly assumed a person had run right through it.

She didn't actually want to go in the direction the monstrous Lords of Greed had gone. But her choices were to stay in the courthouse, in one of its rooms, and risk her father finding her, or go outside.

So she walked down the hallway. As she was arriving upon a corner turn, it happened. A loud whoosh sang through the adjoining hallway, followed by a meaty thud. It was astonishingly close to her. She looked down, and creeping around that turn was a slowly expanding puddle of blood.

There was also a vague series of almost-words from around that turn. She understood, on some level, that it was someone choking through blood, trying to talk.

She glanced down at her arms. Still running full of gold.

Another phlegmy sound from whoever it was, and then it stopped.

Bree let out a long breath. She rationalized that she'd seen dead bodies now—lots of them. That she could stand to see one more horrible thing if it meant getting away. It was probably only one dead person, not a hotel full.

She paused again when the horribleness of that line of thinking occurred to her.

I want to be sickened by this. I can't become desensitized to cruelty.

Every muscle in her body tense, she rounded the corner.

It was, indeed, a dead body. Freshly dead. Bree didn't know who this person was, only that he was a man, probably in his forties, with fraying brown hair on his head, badly sun-tanned white skin, a roughly done shave on his chin—with those little pieces of paper where he must have messed up—and empty, empty, empty brown eyes. He looked like he was covered in red paint splatters. A craft project gone wrong. His clothes had soaked up a lot of it, but the rest was stuck in globules and streaks.

And his upper and lower halves were barely connected. A chunk was missing, and there were internal organs. Stomach, liver, large intestine, small intestines, gallbladder—

Bree had a strange sensation spill through her. It wasn't nausea, exactly. Nausea without a preexisting, pre-Gold-Plating cause apparently couldn't happen with her new abilities. Her stomach didn't constrict in anticipation of expelling vomit; that would've hurt. The disgust and revulsion were entirely mental, and she stood there, showing it only in her expressions.

It was the spine that really bothered her.

Past the mess of sloshed organs was the spinal column, still intact, still connecting the two pieces of the person. It was slick with blood and bent slightly, but she could see it, at the back of all of that gore—and it tore at her mind.

Her hands went to her head, and she started to breathe fast. She couldn't hyperventilate—because that would hurt. But she forced herself to breathe as fast as she could.

Well, she wasn't desensitized.

The body felt too close. Everything felt too close.

Forgetting how it had been with the debris before, she kicked out at the body. Her foot crashed into the side of the man's chest and with an erratic spin—the lower half flung about by the momentum of the top—the body moved. The corpse flipped through the air. Then crashed into the wall. The "paint" on him also decorated the wall. His body landed in a new, more bent position, the vertebrae straining.

A fluid leaked from the corpse's mouth across the floor.

Bree didn't stay to identify it.

She ran. Bree barely noticed that, like her strength, her speed was increased. Her legs would never get sore, or tired, or injured from full-tilt running.

As she did, something, almost out of her vision, moved along the top of the hallway. A tendril of—

Is that from the sky?

The doorway out of the courthouse wasn't attached anymore. She went past it quicker than she expected to and—

Quill Point was different.

The tendrils that had taken over the sky—the red and orange streams of light—weren't just in that hallway, they were visible all over, even though it was night. And they were down among the earth. They were in clearly defined shapes. Off in the distance were little buildings that hadn't been there. And on a hill that hadn't been there: a broad-cast tower and building. Further away, multi-story con-structions were where they weren't before. Big buildings had risen from nothing at all.

Bree stopped sharply, stood still for a moment, trying to process all this. Trying to—

It turned out that she couldn't properly cry either. Tears didn't run down her face; she couldn't sob; her nose didn't run; it didn't pinch her face or make her chest hurt.

She picked a direction and ran.

Nothing would be able to stop her. Nothing would even be able to slow her down. If she met a wall, the wall would eventually lose.

She almost closed her eyes so many times during that run.

It felt like she was going down an alleyway. A hill. A pit. It felt like the world was actively boxing her in.

She didn't cease. Until the ground changed.

The ground beneath her feet decided it didn't want to be the same as it had been before. She stopped in her tracks as the grass and sidewalk and road became an ever-stretching parking lot; each section spinning over into its new look like she'd been secretly standing on game tiles. Yellow and white lines traced themselves in real-time, forming boxy spaces for the cars that were simul-taneously being dragged there from where they'd stood since Murder Sky.

A crackle of moving pieces drew Bree's eye, and she nearly fell over with alarm. Rising like a massive beast cresting from the ocean was a theater building. Its win-dows bulging octopi's eyes; its long stretching hallways tentacles ready to envelop a ship; its height like a massive skull glimpsed above the sails. The gunwales of reality were being overtaken.

Bree couldn't help but experience massive vertigo from standing in the wake of it. She screamed out so loud that it should've hurt her vocal cords—if they were capable of being hurt. Her sense of space and where she was in that space shifted. The front of the building was closer, closer, closer—but it wasn't stretching at her. Nor was she being pulled. It was more like the distance existing between her and the building was being taken out of the holistic equation. The geographic proportions of planet Earth were being rendered about a hundred feet less.

Bree fell over. The golden field around her sparked fiercely. She held her hands up on instinct.

"My father is … is The Mayor…" she managed to say. "I'm under the protection of The God of Greed."

The frosted-glass doors to the theater creaked open slowly. Three sets of them all leading to a shadowy lobby. From inside, there were faint sounds of shuffling. Of whispers. It sounded like the inside of a museum she'd visited. A palpable sense of quiet.

Bree glanced up at the rest of the building.

It was around five stories tall, with a somewhat asymmetrical architectural style. Pillars of differing heights sat on either side of the doors, and a large awning would've kept out the rain. Around halfway to the top of the building, there were glowing letters that didn't appear to be electric lights.

The Greed Theater.

Bree pushed herself to her feet. A quick look around found that she was in a sea of parking spaces. The courthouse was the only other building she could feasibly walk to. The bent, strange skyscrapers were all off in the distance. She had no desire to go to either of those places.

"You … want me to go in there, don't you?"

All but one door gently closed. A click sounded somewhere, and what was promptly illuminated wasn't the lobby anymore. It was a tunnel of a hallway, with a stretching red carpet.

Bree took a single step back, away from it.

The parking lot around her feet started to surge and bubble. A small pit formed to the left of her—and then another, a little closer. A car about ten feet from her lurched to one side. It slowly sank down.

"Okay … okay…" Bree said. "I get the point."

The car disappeared down, and all the pits closed.

Bree walked into the theater.

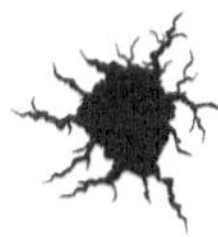

The hallway was impossibly long and smelled like popcorn. Vegan-friendly popcorn, to be exact. Her *favorite* vegan flavored popcorn to be even more exact. She hadn't had it in so long, not since Murder Sky. Her father got it shipped from a special vegan grocery store in California.

It was a strange memory to call up again. Not something she thought about much. She'd told a caterer that she was vegan one time, then off-hand mentioned she liked popcorn another time. And a week or so later, when she'd gone into the living room to watch a true crime documentary, she found a bowl of freshly popped popcorn by her lounge chair. She'd absentmindedly eaten about half the bowl, and from then on it was always an option.

The smell made her nervous. Not that it was the wrong smell or growing into some sickly version of itself. Just that it was there at all. There were only a few ways anyone could know about her popcorn, know that memory, and she didn't like any of the possibilities.

She spent a little longer walking before the faint sound of popping kernels drifted toward her. She waited a moment for something—she wasn't sure what. Maybe a little popcorn machine to roll toward her on its own? Maybe a clay monster to walk over and hand her a bag?

None of that happened. She looked down the hallway, down a long path of plush walls and lights inlaid into them. It stretched a while and then ended with a wall that seemed like it should've had a door. It did not have one though.

The popping slowed down, then stopped, and the popcorn smell faded. Bree took a single step forward, and the inlaid lights pulsed. It reminded her of an airport runway. Only growing faster—so fast. If she wasn't Gold-Plated, it would've given her a migraine.

An obviously quite loud series of rumbles and crashing sounds were far off. It built to a crescendo. A metallic, discordant orchestra.

What the fuck is happening? Bree thought, still afraid, even if she knew she couldn't be hurt. *Is this place not finished yet?*

The sound got quieter; the light flickered slower. Everything more or less calmed down. Wound down. Everything stopped.

And a bright voice yelled out.

"Quiet please! It's almost time to begin!"

Bree jolted. It had been the little girl's voice.

And there was, as there should have been, a door at the end of the hallway. *Hello* flashed on a screen above it that also hadn't been there before. The floor—no, the entire hallway—slowly angled downhill toward it. The front of Bree's feet wanted her to drift forward. The hallway wanted her to drift forward.

And open the door.

She complied.

It was heavy.

And it led to the theater.

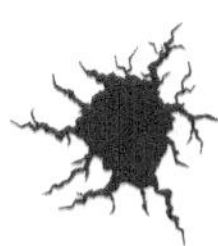

The room was bowl-shaped and titled downhill even more. Rows and rows of seats fanned out in a crescent. Everything was overwhelmingly red plush. It was on the chairs, accented with black, shiny leather. It was up the walls, along with white, sound-dampening panels.

But it ended with the stage.

The stage was easily the width and length of a building, and high up above the seats—so high there was no way the front row would ever be able to see the show. The curtains were halfway drawn back.

"It's almost time!" sang out the little boy's voice. "Please take your seats!"

Bree frowned.

"Please, why don't you take your seat?" the voice insisted. "We will be starting in *THIRTEEN SECONDS*."

The top of the theater silently crackled with lightning, and for a second, she could see those massive Murder Sky shadow hands waving in the storm clouds.

Bree froze up, fear crashing into her brain. She managed to spin back for the entrance. She would run down that endless hallway for as long as she had to—and she could run forever now—rather than face this new horror.

She almost made it when two ushers stepped out from nowhere. They were tall, thin, made of lines. Made of clay. They looked like a human nervous system without any bodies.

One shut the door as the other stepped in her path.

"It's time to watch the show, Bree," the little boy called out. "We're putting it on for you. As a special gift to the new template girl, we wanted to let you see how special things really are."

The clay monster reached out for her arm. Its tentacles wrapped around her limb. She—for a second—expected it to shatter her arm, to proceed to squeeze more and more of her into bloody pieces.

Then she yanked her arm back, and the clay tentacles exploded into particles with a hiss of gold.

"You're not trapped here," the little girl called from somewhere. "We're here to give you a show, Bree. It's for you."

Bree didn't listen—she flung her body into the nearest of the clay monsters, and it was like charging through a wet particle board. The monster burst apart around her. The other one didn't move to intercept. It slunk to the side of the door and stood there.

"I don't want anything to do with you," Bree screamed out across the massive theater. "I've had enough of you!"

"I'm not in your head anymore, Bree."

Bree went to the door, gave the other clay monster a glance, and pulled with all she had. The door groaned. But it didn't open.

"Only a god, or a god's tool, can hurt you, Bree. You've become Gold-Plated. I couldn't kill you now, even if I wanted to. And to be clear, I don't."

Bree kicked the door as hard as she could. The door cracked. She kicked again, and it collapsed into little splinters. Revealing another door behind it. She kicked that one twice too, and it cracked in huge lines. But it didn't quite burst like the original one. She kicked it twice more, and it finally snapped down the middle. Behind it was a third door.

"Bree…?"

"Shut up. You and my father and the gods, they can all shut up. I am not going to be trapped again. I am not."

"Bree, what did I tell you about magic? What is the one universal rule, do you recall?"

Bree didn't respond. It didn't even hurt to throw herself at the doors over and over. She could just keep doing it. There was something nice in knowing that she could bang her head against a wall—and the wall *would lose*.

But some part of her did remember. Even though the little girl had said all sorts of strange things, a lot of it sounding like concepts from philosophy, physics, or sociology, she did recall the core of it.

All magic demands death.

And then, as a follow up, she recalled that the little girl could absolutely read minds.

"That's right, Bree. And we've got the whole town. Creating like this takes a lot of calories, fuel, and though we can make *some* things before we kill, we do need to kill. So, can imagine how many people I'm squashing into blood chunks just because you want to break doors?"

Bree stopped. She made fists. But she stopped. And turned away. The horrible Murder Sky cloud was gone when she looked up—and the stage looked different. The curtains were pulled together.

"Are you ready to see the show?" the little boy asked.

Bree didn't deem that worthy of a response. She just sat down in the nearest chair and crossed her arms.

"Excellent," the little girl said.

"In that case," the little boy added.

"*Then we can tell you the tale of how you'll help us change the whole of reality as you understand it*," they said in unison.

The curtains drifted apart. Beyond them, the stage had been set up elaborately. It was four layers of structure made of thick planks of wood. Big wooden columns held the whole thing up. It looked very much like four massive tables balanced on each other.

And standing on the very top layer were two demigods that were currently disguised as children. The little girl with her clay skin and clay hair and clay eyes and gray clothes and the little boy with a missing tooth in the middle of his smile and an electric blue outfit. The little boy looked a lot more human, but his shadows made by the houselights were much, much too big. And his eyes glowed yellow.

"*Hello, esteemed guest*," they both said at the same time.

The little girl stomped her foot, bowed, and then started into her monolog.

"You're soon going to be a part of a being born of greed. We need a template that doesn't waver, so that when we travel across the Layers, we'll still keep to our metaphysical reference point. Without you, we'd be whatever context was appropriate to that Layer entirely, unable to maintain cohesion. And that wouldn't be having one's own distinct identity, now would it?"

The little boy bowed. "It would be like if you were whoever happened to be named Bree in a town whenever you visited."

"And that's not any fun," the little girl said.

"But what's a 'Layer?'" the little boy asked. "I bet she's not even heard that word yet."

They both looked over at Bree and smiled with smiles that lacked any emotion at all. Bree stared back at them, trying to wrap her head around what they were saying. And trying not to give them the satisfaction of her seeming afraid. Even if she was. Even if she knew the little girl could peer into her mind and see. It was better than cowering.

"Do you know?" the little girl asked.

Bree almost refused to answer.

"No," she said bluntly.

The little boy laughed.

"Ah, so … we should explain that. A Layer is a form of reality. It's a whole reality. Your solar system, the galaxy, your quarks, all the molecules and atoms, and everything else, all of it. It's *one* Layer."

"But how do Layers work?" the little girl asked.

"Well, sister," he said, "I suppose we can explain."

The little girl was suddenly holding a large, thin, hardcover book. She flipped it open to the first page. "Once upon a time, a man was walking along, minding his own business…"

Then, right below them, on the third section of the scaffolding, the air started to shimmer. A second later, a man was walking slowly across the platform. He was an older man, with pale white hair, suntanned white skin, and was wearing a red shirt and denim overalls. He looked around the space, confused.

"…and then he had a heart attack," the little girl said.

The man suddenly stopped and clutched at his chest. He fell to the ground, screaming out with frantic, desperate cries.

"Then what?" the little boy asked.

"Well, he survived—sadly. And while he was on what *would* become his deathbed, he told a story to his wife that he'd told her a thousand times. He'd always wanted to write it as a book. He was always telling stories about this ex-supernatural warrior who lost his powers and was trying to reclaim a normal life. This story, his favorite story, was about when the warrior had gone fishing with his friend right before his friend died."

The section below the third changed. Bree watched as two men stood on a boat and fished.

One of them was larger, with muscular arms barely contained in his black shirt, and wore dark blue jeans. He had black hair, blue eyes with deep bags underneath them, and pale white skin. A massive, golden sword was strapped to his back. The other person was a little taller, with a pinkish complexion and long, blond hair. He was wearing cargo shorts and a tee shirt with a picture of a fish on it.

"Wait…" the little boy said, "are you telling me…?"

"Yes, brother?"

"Are you telling me that whenever someone tells a story, to *anyone*, it makes a new reality where that story is *true*?"

"Yes, that's how the *whole* thing works, brother. Though there are some rules. Layers are all started as stories being told by someone, but they have to be fictional stories, with no existing people included. You can't duplicate a soul. Lies, half-truths, over-exaggerating, don't have the energy, the engagement of the soul, to count. They will not generate a Layer. Intent, though, intent—to tell a story, to relay a message, to impart a lesson—*matters*. Imagination is the lifeblood and source code of every cosmos except the first ever. This is why they are called 'Layers.' They are ever-expanding, stacked upon another. A person imagines and creates a Layer, and then its inhabitants will create more. But it's barely hierarchical. The order of creation doesn't make anything more or less real—except the first. It is also not at all limited in scope or frequency. One telling of a story generates an entire Layer. The story doesn't have to include other people than one, other places than its immediate setting—it's all created within the storytelling, based on the assumptions and implications that are stated or unstated by the teller. It's automatic world-building, bound only by the rule that its creations cannot transcend their Layer without outside interference by Rot Gods, demigods, or even higher powers. Now, why is it a full universe every time? Well, I could say that's just the physics of the Layers—and it is. I could say that's the rule that was put in place—and it is. But then you'd ask, *how* did the Layers start? Whose rule would that be? And that's a different story. That's a whole other ballgame. And there's plenty of more immediate Layers already for us to concerns ourselves with."

Bree sat in her chair, trying to make sense of what she'd just heard. That *couldn't* be how it worked. To even consider the full scope of something like that would be … she was feeling a little dizzy.

Bree's mind raced and wouldn't stop racing. She felt like she was drowning in her own thoughts.

Every fairy tale, every fiction book, every campfire story, every half-finished novel, all of it are real worlds out there. All of it is happening. I've made worlds. We've all made worlds. How many universes are there in the whole—?

A horrible growling sound snapped Bree out of it. The little girl was standing at the edge of the platform, smirking down at her.

"I know you're having trouble with this, but we do have more to explain. Do you think you can keep your mind from running away long enough? Maybe what I have to say will make you feel better."

I fucking doubt it, Bree thought.

"Hmm, well, it's still worth a try," the little girl said.

"Well, I have a question," the little boy said. "Maybe you could tell me something?"

"Okay, what is your question?"

"If the husband likes to tell the same story, doesn't that mean that there are hundreds of nearly identical realities? All of them based around this one fishing story?"

"Oh, see, isn't that interesting?" the little girl said.

Bree held her breath, staring up at the stage. She *needed* to know the answer to that very same question.

The little girl sat down at the edge of the stage and swung her legs back and forth.

"Let's say," she began, "that we have two Layers from the same storyteller, but he's told it two slightly different ways. Or even a few people tell the same story roughly the same way, give or take some details. Maybe it's a story passed down through history, even."

The fourth and final section of the scaffolding, closest to the stage, went hazy for a moment, and then there was the same boating scene. The two of them mirrored each other perfectly. It was uncanny to watch.

"The Cacophonous Layers—the full name for the whole expanse of dimensions—has rules for this, too. For instance, it abhors taking up what it considers unnecessary space. And if two or more Layers are almost, or exactly, identical, they collapse into one Layer, containing as many qualities as possible from both that don't cause a paradox."

The little girl snapped her fingers—and the entire structure collapsed down slightly. The third section fell down, boat and all, and crashed into the fourth.

Pieces of wood and splinter-shrapnel shot out.

As well as a squirt of blood.

In the wreckage, Bree could see two mangled bodies, each copy dead in different ways.

It rippled away then—replaced by only one scene, on one section of scaffolding.

"It's, unfortunately, not actually so violent. No one dies from it. And Layers do eventually become stable. The population doesn't typically notice this or that being altered in small ways. And even that eventually stops. And we call those 'True' or 'Stable' Layers. Fly eggs, god eggs, are never laid on Layers that aren't."

"What decides the final outcome?" the little boy asked.

"That's another story as well."

"But we do know?" the little boy said.

"We're born of a god—of course, *we* know."

The air shifted, and all the scenes disappeared. The little girl hopped down and landed without issue. Her brother followed and stood next to her. They both snapped their fingers at the same time, and the scaffolding disappeared.

"And that's why we're going to use your mind to keep to this Layer's version of Greed, Bree," the little girl said. "This is what I mean about immortality. Whatever you think about wage theft, rent hikes, hoarding of resources, all of that—or whatever we show you and teach you about it—is what'll make sure we bring that *exact* version to all the Layers we visit. We will be *this* Layer's definition of greed, even if we end up on some Layer populated entirely by a totally different species. We'll be bringing it to the whole of creation."

The boy giggled. "And you'll help us kill their populations too. Calories for spreading rot."

Bree didn't outwardly, verbally disagree this time. Every single time she had; it had only resulted in pain. She tried to keep her thoughts quiet.

"We hope you've enjoyed this educational show, Bree. Because now, now we're going to let you wander in a hellscape. You'll turn into a sculptor that'll help craft the visage of the end of worlds. A high, high honor."

Bree couldn't keep back a thought of pure revulsion.

The little girl smirked.

"Shouldn't we give her a small primer?" the little boy said. "Some examples of what she'll find out there?"

"I suppose," the little girl said, the smirk not faltering. "We *are* in a theater. And we do have an audience. We may as well let you get to know the performers in this little story that you're going to witness, Bree. The things that are going to happen to these people."

The seat next to Bree had been empty. Now, sitting there, was a woman. She was hyperventilating silently. Crying. Staring at something Bree couldn't see.

"*The entire town is caught in this, Bree*," the children intoned together. "*It's everyone you've ever known. A hell for each.*"

More seats filled with faces.

Grace and Declan, both looking exhausted, pained, their eyes filling more and more with anguish.

A guy with lava pouring out of his mouth.

A girl in a suit, stuck listening to a death toll.

Exhausted. Worried. Fearful. Beaten down. Beheaded. Burned. Sliced. Flayed. A town has a massive population. A town can have hundreds of thousands of people. Quill Point had lost many—but nowhere near all. And their images, their possible futures, filled the theater, and when the theater seemed too small, the walls stretched in both directions. To look at either, to look beyond, to see the dimensions of the theater was to see a crowd stretch off into the distance until they dropped away, and to hear their screams roll in like a rollercoaster of people careening overhead. A lamentation of a town having a collective nightmare that didn't relinquish to any other outcome.

They were trapped in Quill Point. They were trapped in what The God of Greed demanded.

"Now go meet them!"

Bree's chair surged backward beneath her. She let out a shrill yell as she was flung through the door, down the hallway, and then sent tumbling through the entrance and across the parking lot. The chair burst apart around her. Bree's head slammed into the ground and made a crater.

"*Have fun, Bree,*" the voices called on the wind.

Bree didn't get up for a long time. She stared up at the sky, aware that she could stay there forever. Aware that hunger or tiredness were a form of physical pain, and thus banned from her new existence.

She thought a long time about what she'd just learned until her head felt foggy. Stories were real—and she was a story. But everyone was a story.

Bree thought, and she thought, until the wideness of her thoughts was too much to keep. It was like considering the dimensions of a solar system in relation to a home. She struggled within her thought's own context.

Instead, another thought-pattern emerged.

Her mind returned to here, to Quill Point.

A part of her—growing by the second—*could* understand the suffering around her. That was within the scope of mental capacity. And even if this played into the demigod's plans, she couldn't bring herself to ignore the world and the violence being inflicted on it.

She sat up.

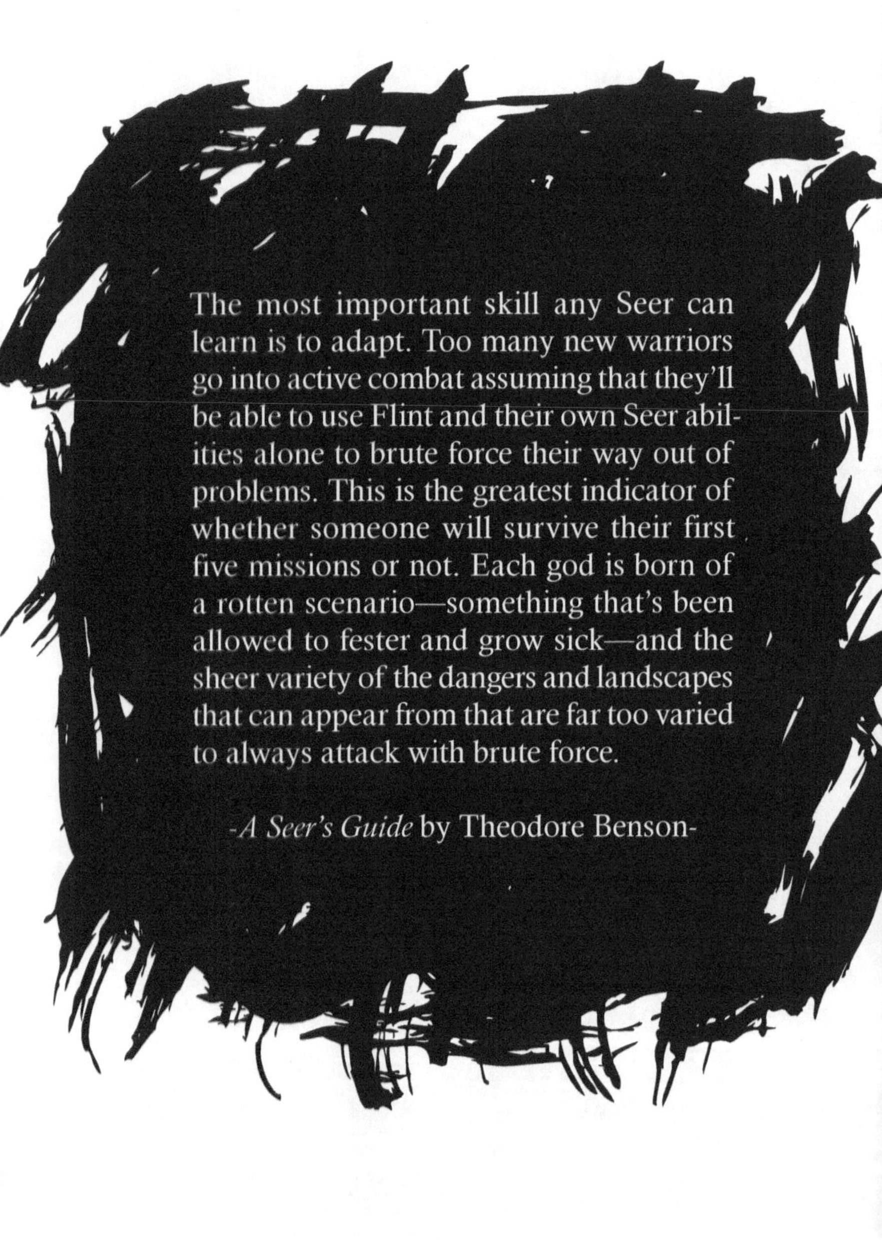

The most important skill any Seer can learn is to adapt. Too many new warriors go into active combat assuming that they'll be able to use Flint and their own Seer abilities alone to brute force their way out of problems. This is the greatest indicator of whether someone will survive their first five missions or not. Each god is born of a rotten scenario—something that's been allowed to fester and grow sick—and the sheer variety of the dangers and landscapes that can appear from that are far too varied to always attack with brute force.

-A Seer's Guide by Theodore Benson-

PART 3

OUR TURN

CHAPTER 38

L ITTLE PIPER WATCHED THE NEWS IN HER *parents' house. The television was a boxy thing, sitting in the alcove of a cabinet made of tan wood. The volume had been turned almost all the way down, and a faint murmur of conversation flowed out from it.*

Little Piper was practicing reading lips.

She'd gotten better at it over the past few weeks. When a few of the boys in her class had started to very quietly talk to each other, and then laugh in her general direction, she swore that she would find out what they were saying. Even if it was mean, she would find out. Little Piper thought it was much meaner to not say it to her face than whatever those boys had to say about her.

And besides, if they talked to her face, she could tell them all of their flaws in a few moments—if she wanted. Little Piper wasn't mean. But it didn't mean she didn't know exactly what to say to upset people. Egos were balloons easily popped. Self-confidence was more prone to crumbling than cookies.

The screen flipped from the man with white skin, silver hair, and tired gray eyes to a woman standing by a big blue wall with little clouds and a cartoon sun. She had white skin, too, and was wearing a green dress. She had blond hair.

The weather was boring, but Little Piper had never tried to read this person's lips before.

The woman gestured to the number by one of the clouds.

"…seventy-five," Little Piper muttered. "Partly … rain…"

She squinted. The woman was moving her hand a lot, and the background was altering as she talked, and some part of Little Piper's mind kept latching onto those motions. She'd taught herself to pay attention to as many things as she could. But that wasn't useful here. It was almost a different muscle entirely to focus on just one aspect of a face.

"High chance of…" she said alongside the woman.

The screen flipped to a seven-day forecast. No person for her to study. Little Piper let out a disappointed sigh. Her eyes hurt a little from looking at the screen so intently.

The slight sound of her mother's feet on the carpet was behind her, and Piper turned to look.

Her mom had the same brown skin as she, as well as the same type of light brown hair. But her mom's hair was curlier than hers, more springing around her head. And her mom's eyes weren't brown. Her mom had gray eyes, like the guy on the television. Her dad's eyes, Piper's grandfather's, were also gray. Piper's grandmother had brown eyes—Little Piper assumed that's where she got it from.

Her mom was wearing a T-shirt with a band's picture on it, sweatpants, and a really big bathrobe draped over her shoulders. It reminded Little Piper of a wizard's robe.

"What are you watching there?" her mother asked.

Little Piper glanced back—and tried to hide her frown. The news had shifted over to something new. Pictures of some big building somewhere. She looked around the bottom third and found that it was talking about something in downtown Chicago. Something about a bank robbery.

The image jumped to a man with a microphone. She could read his lips really easily. The words "twelve dead" weren't the words Little Piper would've liked to have read though.

"Oh!" her mother said. "No, let's not watch that, honey."

She walked past Little Piper and scooped up the remote.

"You should be watching something for kids. One of these cartoons."

Little Piper just nodded along. She would turn it back soon enough. She'd wait until her mom was back at her desktop computer and deep into whatever college schoolwork she had. Little Piper didn't yet know what getting a second degree was exactly, or why an adult in their thirties would willingly do more schooling, but she knew that it kept her mom very distracted.

"I swear to god, do they have to show all this horrible stuff?" her mom muttered. "The world is scary enough."

She flicked it away to some cartoon that Piper didn't care very much about and raised the volume. It was a baby show. If she couldn't practice anymore, she at least wanted to watch some mystery show.

"Here, watch this," her mom said.

Then her mom let out a large yawn and walked back into the home office. Little Piper waited until she heard the squeak of her chair that meant she was leaning back. Her mother started humming. That meant she'd put on her headphones.

Little Piper got the remote, turned the volume all the way down, and returned to the news.

The marionette sat in his chair. The wires that held him were loose and swaying gently in the air-conditioned room. They connected to the joints of his arms, his elbows, and the top of his head.

The marionette's glossy face reflected a red sign. He didn't speak either. His mouth was a hinged creation but stayed shut for the moment.

Above the mouth, above a thin line of black paint that mimicked a mustache, were two staring eyes, painted with big blue irises. They didn't have pupils, just wide, blue circles.

The marionette was wearing an outfit that looked tailored to his thin, lanky frame. A tan suit, with a large tie that lay below the desk where the marionette sat. A name tag was pinned to the front of the suit, but all it said was "Mr. News." So that didn't clarify much.

The light reflected in his face turned green.

A soft chime emanated throughout the room.

The marionette moved then. The connecting strings tugged by unseen fingers. First, his head shot upward, straightening his posture. Second, both hands shot up into the air, palms outward. Shining from the light, jutting out from his palm, were hundreds of tiny needles. He kept his hands on either side of his head for a moment.

"Hello," Mr. News said. "Welcome to Quill Point News. The only news."

His hands dropped, and he leaned closer to the camera with every sentence.

"In today's news, we'll start with our usual news. We'll be reading the list of everyone who died. Every. Single. One. And then we have even more important news, provided by our corporate owners. Won't that be exciting?

And, as always, reporting with me is my unwillingly and lethally threatened co-host, Piper."

The camera panned to Piper. She was wearing a nice suit and had her light brown hair pulled back. Her makeup had been done perfectly. Inside, she wanted to scream until she vomited, and then cry until she passed out. But that would have to wait until later. It was still the morning shift.

"That's right, Mr. News," Piper said as cheerfully as she could. "We'll be going over the whole list of causalities, and then we have a few think pieces that Mr. News will be telling us. Can you give us a sneak peek?"

"I sure can, Piper. Today, we'll be talking about how starvation is a great motivator to apply for more jobs we won't hire you for."

Piper's eye twitched. "…Yep, that and more is on today's show."

"And after that," Mr. News continued, "we'll be sending one of the Lords of Greed to interview some people on the streets of Quill Point and ask them how they're handling the end of their world."

"Sounds like a change of pace," Piper said.

"It sure is Piper. It sure is."

"Wow," Piper said flatly.

"So, don't go away," Mr. News said. "We've got a lot today on Quill Point News. The only news in Quill Point. The only news you should ever listen to ever again. We want to make sure you hear it. We put speakers and radios everywhere, in every building, so you'll be sure of one thing: you're *going* to die. We'll be back!"

CHAPTER 39

A T THE END OF THREE HOURS, ON HER first major break of the day, Piper felt immensely guilty about being relieved. Partially because, compared to what some people were dealing with in Quill Point, she had it fairly cushy. But more importantly, she felt relieved because Mr. News hadn't read out Sean's name among all the names.

Twenty-seven people had died today, some of them she knew, but none of them had been her brother. One person, a girl named Erin who'd worked for Cynthia at The Quill Point Café, had died of an enforced caffeine overdose. Another had been ripped into pieces by deliberately unsafe manufacturing equipment.

Piper leaned back in her chair, her mind cataloguing it. It was her largest source of input on what was happening out there. Arthur had taken her to this weird radio station as the town was first changing. But she was good at working with implications.

And there were a lot of those.

A god underneath Quill Point, formed of human sins, had been secretly growing in power and had just woken up. The mystery of why The Mayor had been gathering cash and kicking people out of their intact homes solved: because this particular god was of money and greed. And that god was, mostly, warping Quill Point and killing its citizens through very metaphorical representations of the most horrible aspects of greedy actions.

And that was, like, twenty revelations in itself.

But now that she knew some of it, there were bigger gaps brought to light. *Multiple* gods. The universe had a confirmed instance of polytheism, and at least three within the pantheon, if not more. One of the others represented violence. What was that one like? And why had she never heard of such a god, or the other one, doing something on this scale to the world? They were—presumably—older than The God of Greed. They were, *presumably*, just as able to end the world.

Presumptions and assumptions.

There was one other thing though. One other datapoint pinging at her mind. And this one seemed the most pressing, the most immediately important. For the majority of the time she'd spent in this news-hell, she'd had a boss. The Newscaster. A being made of shifting mass media. If Piper had been unsure how much metaphor truly played into how this apocalypse worked, The Newscaster and Mr. News threw it into sharp clarity. The Newscaster was so thoroughly made of what he represented that she'd known his name and his whole deal on sight.

And he was missing.

Gone.

He'd said that he was going to a dinner with some of the other monsters. He'd been excited about it.

He never returned from it.

Perhaps it was the environment she was in, the news she constantly heard, but her mind went to death. She had almost nothing to back it up, but that was where her thoughts went. The Newscaster was dead.

Which meant the monsters could die.

She glanced at the Mayor's Men—no, "Lords of Greed" now—and wondered. She glanced at Mr. News. A small smile flitted across her lips.

I haven't figured it out yet, but I'll get you eventually.

CHAPTER 40

AN HOUR WASN'T THAT LONG, ESPECIALLY with days like hers, but Piper worked through what conclusions she could make for now and found a lot of time in her break remaining afterward. Her mind was a little exhausted; a distraction seemed in order.

There wasn't much in the way of distractions though. Except one. Because she and Mr. News didn't read out the news the whole day, the rest of the airtime needed something.

Piper stretched her arms above her head and went to the small, adjacent room. It was a box of a room with a doorway but no door and a large front glass window. Flanking either side of the window were two very large speakers. Inside, it was cramped with its equipment.

Piper walked quietly. She didn't want to interrupt Izzy.

She was working. Her hands pressed to her headphones, counting to herself silently. She was going down from thirty. Her shoulders went up and down to a rhythm, but she clearly didn't like the song.

It didn't take Piper's skills at reading people to work that part out. Izzy had a massive frown.

Piper leaned against the doorframe and waited, examining her further.

Izzy had been the most self-realized person Piper had ever met. There was a fierceness and a softness, all at once, that emanated out of her. Anger and empathy in a constant dance that didn't contradict. She had medium brown skin, shiny black hair, and her eyes were a dark brown. Her fashion sense was Punk; leaking small rebellion even as death loomed over them both. Currently, it was only a leather jacket and a piercing on her lip, but Piper had seen her before the end of the world. She'd seen her at music concerts.

Piper wondered if they would've been friends before all this. Probably. If they'd met in high school, absolutely.

Oh well. At least we get along, Piper thought. *At least my only coworker in hell is a nice person.*

Izzy finished her countdown. She flipped a switch, then leaned forward to talk into a microphone.

"And that was our newest song, 'Corporate Jingles and Calming Drone,'" Izzy said. "We've got a few advertisements for you, but then we'll be back with 'The Sounds of Distant Construction.' We hope you're having a terrible time."

Izzy pulled off the headphones and let out a long sigh.

"Bad day?" Piper asked.

Izzy threw her head back. "When is it not?"

"Good point," Piper said. "Would you like some company?"

"If you want to," Izzy said.

"I could use some human company," she replied.

"Yeah—that sounds good. There's a stool underneath the console."

Piper nodded. The stool was almost flush with the top of the console, and it almost stuck as she pulled it out. But she managed to settle it next to Izzy.

"Sorry," Izzy said, "I don't want to encourage a Lord to sit in for a while."

"Oh yeah, that's sounds horrible," Piper said.

"Yeah, it is."

A silence passed for a moment. Piper was not a fan of silence, at least not lately. She wracked her brain for what she knew about Izzy.

"So … how's the girlfriend?" Piper asked.

"I don't see her that much," Izzy replied. "I'm not sure what part of this place she's been assigned to, actually."

"Doesn't she tell you?"

"Probably. The other me probably knows. She's had that conversation."

"Oh. But you can still recall she's good?"

"She's not dead, if that's what you mean."

"Yeah," Piper said. "…I guess that it what I mean."

That was another piece of information Piper chewed on sometimes. Piper was never allowed to leave; she had to sleep in the building. Mr. News would even wake up from his otherwise inanimate slumber and force her to do bonus, three-in-the-morning broadcasts on weekends. But Izzy could leave. She *had* to leave. She had set shifts. And when she did, she lost her ability to know what was happening to her. It was a weird dream state; a half-recalled nightmare. Most of the people out in Quill Point were like that, apparently. Walking through a Greed-based phantasmagoria only vaguely aware that people were lost, gone, mulched.

Piper didn't know if always remembering all that was happening made her lucky or not.

"How are you?" Izzy offered abruptly.

"I'm … not looking forward to the next shift."

"Yeah. That makes sense," Izzy said.

Another horrible stillness. The top of Piper's head felt staticky. Her mouth was dry from all the talking she'd had to do, and yet she still wanted to speak.

"How much longer is your shift?" Piper asked as if she didn't already know.

"Too long—but then too short," Izzy said.

Piper raised an eyebrow. "Why too short?"

Izzy let out a long sigh. She squeezed her eyes very tight, and then released them a second later. "It's something I've been thinking about."

The tone of that statement made Piper flinch a little.

"Okay…" Piper began.

Izzy gestured at the way out of the news station.

"When I leave, they take some of my memory … and…"

A light on the console turned red. Izzy abruptly stopped talking and snatched up the headphones.

"Still listening out there? We assume you are. Next up, we have a five-minute long epic we call 'Someone Sick in the Cubicle Next to You.' We hope you're having a terrible time."

Izzy clicked another switch, pulled off her headphones, and looked back at Piper.

"Sorry about that."

"It's okay," Piper said gently. "You were telling me something?"

"Right…" Izzy clicked her tongue. "Right."

When she didn't talk for a moment, Piper felt the urge to push her. Once upon a time, her ability to find out people's thoughts was more casual, more accidental. But when she decided to sharpen the skill, it turned into almost a hunger. She didn't know *why* she had such a disposition, but it felt like an adrenalin rush when people started to tell her things. It made people less mysterious, somehow less unknowable.

But she also knew how effective a light pause could be for prying out information. Sometimes, the vacuum created by silence had a hardcore gravity.

Izzy sighed. "I go out that door … and they take my memory. But … what am I without memory? It's more like I…"

The reaction that passed across Izzy's face was almost hard to categorize. It was fearful, yes, but also pained. Piper tried to form a reference point for it.

It's like how people are right before they go into surgery. That apprehension that they might not ever wake back up…

"It's like I die. This me *dies*. And then I come back to life."

"Oh…" Piper said.

"Yeah … so, like, does that mean that when I kiss my girlfriend … it's not the person she started dating? Is that cheating? If her memory is also being wiped all the time, does that mean she also died? Does that mean my girlfriend *died?*"

"…I don't know," Piper said.

Which was the honest truth. She didn't know.

"How could fucking *anyone* know?" Izzy replied. "It's not something that is supposed to be possible."

Piper tried to think through this new puzzle. Surely there was some solution to it.

Okay… there isn't a real answer to this… but maybe I can make it a little easier on her.

"This is kind of morbid…" Piper began.

Izzy let out a bitter chuckle. "Oh no, not *morbid* things. How will I cope with something nightmarish? My life is so full of hopeful fucking jubilation right now."

Piper flinched, but quickly scanned her face. Oh yeah, she was angry—but she wasn't angry at her. Piper glanced at the Lords of Greed. Hopefully, she was aiming her rage at them. That was at least an appropriate target.

"So, then," Piper continued, "if you *do* die … like this place kills us…"

"Oh, you weren't kidding," Izzy said.

"No, I was not."

"Well, go on then—it's not like I don't think about dying a lot."

"Right, so, if you *do* die here, then you're definitely gone. No one walks out of here. No one will go back to where you live. And if that's true, then that's *real* death. Meaning the other thing is a fake death."

"Yeah, I don't think that's how that works." Izzy looked up at the ceiling for a moment, then sharply back down. "There's more than one way to die."

"But no matter what happens to your memories, it's still the same body."

Izzy frowned slightly. "Assuming that we can prove even that. Maybe they fucking melt me down the second I step through that door. There's no way to know. All I have are my memories."

Piper's next words dried up in her throat. Now Izzy was mad at her, specifically. The slight tightness of her lips there proved it.

"Okay … maybe we should talk about something else," Piper said.

Izzy rolled her eyes and looked up at the ceiling again. Piper was debating walking away; she'd clearly botched this conversation. But just as she felt the awkwardness balloon too large, Izzy cleared her throat.

"I'm sorry … this isn't your fault."

"It's okay," Piper said immediately.

"Yeah, but still, that was rude. We've all got existential terrors to deal with. I can't imagine being stuck here all the time. Spending all day, every day with…"

"A puppet?"

"Yeah, that." Izzy shook her head gently. "A big puppet."

"It's not a lot of fun, I'll admit," Piper said. "But, um, hey, Izzy?"

Izzy looked over and nodded. "Yeah?"

"It really is okay. We're under a lot of stress."

"Stress is … it's not a big enough word."

"Yeah," Piper replied, "I feel that."

Izzy glanced at the clock and took a deep breath through her nose. "You know you have like ten more minutes before you have to get back to work."

"Yeah, I do…"

Izzy gave out a small chuckle. "Well, let me set up another song, and then we can talk about … whatever you want to talk about."

Piper nodded. She had a weird feeling in her chest. Something like gratitude, but also guilt. Part of her really wanted to keep going with that argument. Surely, with enough prodding, she could convince her friend that she wasn't dying every day. Even if Piper didn't believe her own words, she wanted to comfort her friend. Even if she felt it hubris, Piper figured she could undo an existential crisis.

But doing that could so easily backfire too. Freaking Izzy out unnecessarily was a really bad idea. None of them could afford to fuck up. Piper had heard the names of too many dead people to risk something like that.

As she waited for Izzy to finish, Piper remembered a nightmare she had. She had it a lot. Or so she assumed. Most nights now Piper woke up from some horrific dream at least once, and sometimes recalled it. And in the nightmare she knew, her own name rang out, was decreed. By some unknown way, she'd died.

Oh, who was she kidding?

Lying to Piper was almost always pointless, even when she, herself, was doing the lying. She might not know the exact methods, but she knew exactly the three monsters who could've killed her.

One was a puppet.

And the other two were walking toward her.

Chapter 41

Out of everything in that radio station, Piper was probably most scared of the Lords of Greed. They weren't the most visually unsettling—that "award" went to Mr. News—but she'd seen them transform. She'd been there when The Ascended Mayor had turned them into the monsters that they'd become.

And something like that tended to stick with you.

She'd had time to acclimatize to the sight of unearthly mold and massive mouths full of teeth—she got daily chances—but it hadn't really happened. It never stopped disturbing her. They were unnerving in a primal sense.

The two of them, Brook and Wyatt, stood on either side of the doorway. Brook leaned on it. Wyatt stood a little stiffer.

"You're needed for the next newscast," Brook said.

"Okay," Piper replied simply. "I'll go do that."

She tried to be as respectful as she could with them. As calm and as unassuming as possible. That was usually the most effective tactic. Piper had dealt with her fair share of angry people working at the grocery store.

Piper gave Izzy a little wave. Izzy returned it. Piper got up from her stool and walked to the doorframe. Her heart rate was already climbing.

"Maybe you should have shorter breaks," Wyatt said. "What do you need breaks for?"

"I don't know," Piper said evenly. "I could ask about that ... if you want."

She continued past the two of them, all too aware of the horrible mold growing from their open sores. All too aware of how effectively they had been killing people before. She focused on trying not to let them see how tense she was.

That ended up being pointless.

Brook appeared in front of her, moving that unearthly quick way, that way that felt more like teleportation. Piper let out a little gasp and clutched her chest.

Brook didn't seem to notice her reaction—or more likely, just didn't care.

"I sometimes wonder why you got to live," he said. "We're his Lords. We're the ones that accepted his power. I understand there are operations at play here, but why did it have to be *you*?"

"I don't know," Piper said simply.

"You don't know?" Brook said, leaning in. "You, Piper, don't know *anything*?"

"I ... I don't. You can hear The God of Greed, right? I bet he'd tell you."

Brook raised his hand. He didn't make a fist. He didn't touch her. Just let it hover there, by her head. Piper had seen a Lord of Greed's hand go right through solid stone.

"Are you trying to insult me?" Brook asked.

"No … no, of course not…"

Wyatt let out a chuckle, and the sound of it made Piper shiver. Another thing she'd not gotten used to was how the Lords of Greed sounded. For the most part, they'd kept their original voices—and that was odd enough—but also there was their *laugh*. When a Lord of Greed laughed, it sounded like something burning.

"Are you sure, Piper?" Brook asked.

"I would never… I just don't know how to answer your question."

"Well, why don't you try and think of one? You seem to know things," Brook said. "Like how you just magically knew that I'd gotten some help on that final."

A knot formed in Piper's stomach; she tried not to show it on her face. She'd almost forgotten about that. It had been so long ago. She didn't even know that Brook had known she told the teacher.

"Sometimes," Brook continued, "I wish that I had been the one to run into you—to get the order. You shot Arthur, and all he did was hurt you a little. He could've at least seen how many bones he could snap without you going into shock."

That blow from Arthur had been one of the most painful things Piper had ever experienced.

"I'm sorry," Piper lied.

Brook made a faint crackling sound in the back of his throat. The image of a wolf made of fire popped into Piper's head.

"Oh, you're 'sorry…'" Brook repeated. "That's a funny thing…"

"Uh, Brook?" Wyatt chimed in.

Brook looked over impossibly fast. It practically left an after-image.

"Yes?" he asked, his voice strained.

"The broadcast is about to start again. We need to get ready."

"Just a second, Wyatt," Brook said sharply.

"She *needs* to be on air."

Brook let out one more, quieter, crackling sound. He glared at Piper for a moment, working his elongated jaw back and forth like he was thinking of something. Then, he tilted his head slightly, like he was listening to a noise in another room.

"Okay … yes. Fine. It's time."

He and Wyatt both disappeared from view, then reappeared by the camera setup. Piper's hair fell back down from the faint wind that had picked it up. She let herself take a calming breath, a moment of peace before horrors, then went over to her desk.

On the desk were the records of the dead. Piper didn't look at them yet. Mr. News went through his wake-up routine. A soft, happy hum emanated from him.

The light for the camera turned on.

CHAPTER 42

"AND THAT'S THE NEWS FOR THE DAY," Piper said. "We here at Quill Point News hope you listened to all of it … because that's what you are able to do."

"Yes, that's right!" Mr. News replied. "When you're not working yourselves to death, or even while you are, you should be hearing about all the bad things happening in the world. Right, Piper?"

"Right…"

"Thank you for agreeing," Mr. News said with a laugh. "I really appreciated it. After all, the viewers know— we *all* know—you're only here because I haven't murdered you yet."

"That's … right," Piper said.

Mr. News laughed again. "Thank you so much for looking over the news with me, Piper. It's been a pleasure."

"Sure … you too," she said.

"Is there anything else you'd like to say for all our captive listeners out there?"

"Uh … no. I think I said all I wanted to."

"Oh, come now," Mr. News replied. "Surely you, Ms. Observant, have one or two more closing thoughts for everyone. I'm sure you can come up with something to say."

Piper wracked her mind. She never knew when Mr. News would throw something like this at her. She suspected it was entirely just to amuse himself.

"Well, Mr. News, I'd like to say that you should all listen to the great music we have for you tomorrow. Our D.J., the amazing Izzy, has all the best hits planned for you."

"Oh! Yes, that's a great point, Piper," Mr. News said. "We *will* have some great songs. Thank you, Piper. And thank you, listener. We hope that you're having just a horrific time out there in Quill Point. Have a bad night!"

The lights shut off. Mr. News went slack again in his chair. Piper let her shoulders relax, just a little. She sat so stiffly during the news—the anxiety and tension of, well, everything, getting into her muscles.

Brook stepped away from the camera. For a moment, he looked right at her. Piper shivered. She didn't have a lot of examples to know what open malicious intent looked like, but it wasn't hard to place it now.

But Brook gently shook his head.

He will change his mind one day, Piper thought. *There's no way he won't eventually just slash your throat.*

"Alright, shows over," Brook announced. "Time for all of the people who get to leave to go home. Piper, have fun staying here. I'm sure Mr. News will love the company."

Piper nodded.

From the D.J. station, Izzy let out a faint groan as she got up from her seat. She ran her hands against her knees, then the back of her legs. Piper could sympathize. Her legs were also often sore from sitting too long.

"Aren't you forgetting something, Izzy?" Brook called. "We have a protocol here. We can't deprive Piper of her entertainment."

Piper hid her wince. She had been hoping Brook would forget about that. Sometimes he actually did.

Izzy didn't even look. She just reached out and flipped a switch.

The two speakers sparked on. Sometimes they played dull corporate music. Sometimes they both pushed out a low, bass tone. It was the sort of sound that could easily fade into the background—but it wasn't calming. The opposite, actually. It made her slightly anxious. Her body couldn't help but tell her that danger was *around*. No place specifically. Just around.

Though that could've also been the voice that announced, quietly, randomly, "Everything is getting worse."

It was the bass tone this time. Piper did her best to shove the sound out of her perceptions. The sooner it was background, the better.

Izzy walked past her for the door. Piper tried to give her a little wave as she passed, but it was pointless. Worries presented themselves freshly on Izzy's expressions as she went. Piper's attempts to dissuade her fear of existential death hadn't worked.

Piper still got up from the desk and followed along. Maybe her being nearby would help.

Brook opened the door slowly, at a speed that didn't break reality—or the door—and smirked at Izzy.

"Have a lovely rest of your time," Brook said.

Izzy noticeably paused right at the threshold. Her shoulders were so tense.

"Waiting for something there?" Brook asked, his voice tinged with amusement. "It's *just* a door."

"Um…" Izzy started to say, then pursed her lips.

"Hurry up," Wyatt said. "We have places to be."

"I … uh … can I actually stay here for the night?" Izzy asked. "I can get more songs ready—or clean up. Or something."

Brook rolled his eyes. He didn't even deem her question with a response. He pushed her over the threshold.

Piper couldn't quite see Izzy's full facial expressions— she'd only half turned back before it started—but something did shift. If there was some form of death happening, it happened in a few distinct phases. It was a little like the face someone might make when you're going up to them and saying hi, but they haven't recognized you yet. Only reversed.

Izzy then walked off into that changed Quill Point, down the hill's winding path, past the beds of roses.

"You're not the only one who can observe stuff, Piper," Brook commented. "I can hear what you two talk about over there."

Piper frowned slightly. She wanted to say something; find some way to make him leave them alone. But even the attempt would surely fail.

"Well?" Brook continued. "What do you have to say about that?"

"Where was The Newscaster today?" Piper asked calmly.

Brook blinked in confusion. Piper tried to hide her smile. Sometimes, it was that easy. Sometimes, assholes and bullies drifted into a script and weren't prepared for interruptions. People who feel powerful often feel like that extends to their ability to control the topic.

And Brook was exactly the kind of person to assume he had power unless directly proved otherwise.

"That's not your business," Brook snapped.

Okay, that means it's a bad thing, Piper thought. *He'd gloat if it was a positive thing.*

"Oh, okay," Piper said. "I just…"

Soften up the words. Verbal weakness encourages openness. Brook's a dickhead and privileged. It has to seem like I'm trying to cater to his needs.

"I wanted to make sure that I was doing a good enough job," Piper continued. "He's been away. I'm sure he'd be happy to return to something good."

Brook's eyes narrowed.

Oh, okay, too far. Izzy's attempt messed this up a little. He's a little more self-aware than expected, Piper thought. *Okay, then. Make it seem like it's fear then. He likes fear.*

Piper didn't have to try very hard to seem nervous. "I mean … I don't want to … if he's unhappy…"

"Or if *I'm* unhappy," Brook replied, a slight huff in his voice.

Oh, there it is. He's sensitive about his place. Okay … that means … that means The Lords of Greed aren't The Mayor's most powerful soldiers. Or at least most high-ranking. He serves the monsters.

"Oh, right … sorry … yes… I don't want to make either of you unhappy…"

Oh, this bit is risky. Please be right.

"So, should I ask you both about what you'd like and … uh … and mix the instructions together?"

Brook blitzed right in front of her. He looked like he wanted to tear Piper's head off.

"Fucking stop asking so many questions!"

Piper went silent, watching the rage bubble. She hoped that, even if the anger cooled a little, he would eventually—

"You answer to *me*," Brook continued.

Gotcha, Piper thought. *The Newscaster is gone for good then. You wouldn't risk the reprimand otherwise.*

"And if you want to make it so I don't snap your neck soon, Piper, you will do everything you can. I want you *smiling* as we read out all the pointless people murdered. I want you cheerfully engaging with Mr. News like you *love* all of this."

Piper nodded.

"Fucking say it!"

"Okay. I will do that," Piper replied. "I will do that, sir."

Brook almost seemed frozen for a moment. Piper only had some idea of what he might've been thinking. His chest rose and fell sharply from the rage.

Then he snorted and turned to Wyatt.

Wyatt regarded Brook for a moment, then shot a faint glare at Piper. Both of them didn't say anything more. They went out into the night.

Piper waited a moment, until the door swung back shut, until she was fairly certain they'd gone, then took a long shaky breath. She couldn't contain the smallest smile for just a second. The surge of adrenaline, and, more importantly, victory, danced through her. Then, just as quickly, she hid it from her face.

She glanced at the sleeping Mr. News. He hadn't reacted. Just a stiff, terribly creepy marionette.

Piper walked away, letting her mind work with the new information.

The big, important information.

The Newscaster is gone, and it was a bad thing. Which means he died or was badly hurt somehow. Presumably at or around the time of that party. I doubt The God of Greed would attack its own aspects—or that a god-created monster got hurt by accident—so that means...

That means a person or persons did it.

That means there's at least one way to hurt the monsters. Maybe, just maybe, that even means there's a way to kill the monsters.

Piper's eyes narrowed and a familiar sensation crystallized in her chest. An assuredness. A type of confidence that had carried her through so many bad experiences before. It had felt too insignificant to face the current hell, but ... maybe it *would* serve her once more, as well as it always had. There *was* a way to win; she felt sure of that.

And if anyone could figure it out, I can.

CHAPTER 43

M R. NEWS DIDN'T TEND TO DO ANY-
thing, but he made Piper nervous. She couldn't
help but imagine waking up to him there, hovering over her.

The fear wasn't enough to give her insomnia though.
Sometimes she even managed to sleep right away—but it
wasn't the usual anymore. The adrenaline in her from a
day of news didn't fade for a long time.

Usually what would happen was a few hours of languid, bored nighttime. The quiet of the news station a
cloth over all sensations. It stretched, and it sat, and it
reminded her of the gentle fall of dust.

Often, she spent that time as far away from Mr. News
in the building as she could. The break room never felt
like much of a break, but it was far away, and it did contain a fridge that always had food. Bland, horrible food
in containers that looked like they wanted to fall apart,
but was food, nonetheless. The sink in the break room
worked and running it—the continuous hiss of water—
sometimes helped quell the anxiety.

But tonight was different. Piper didn't expect to sleep much at all. She had some time without the Lords of Greed observing her. And that meant she could snoop around.

She'd visited the room with the light streaming out from under the door before, and she hadn't learned anything those times. But fresh, new, effective context often breeds discovery.

Inside the room, there wasn't much. There was a long wooden table with mic stands, microphones, paper, and a few other sundry items, like headphones and a circuit board. And freestanding, toward the back, was a printer, and a shredder next to it. Piper had examined both of those objects in detail before. The shredder looked stained with blood, but she never knew how that happened. The printer was generic. It was an office-style printer, eggshell white, and had ineffective wheels at the bottom.

There were some weird things about that printer though. For one thing, it was always on and running.

For another, it never scanned anything—at least not in a way Piper could see—but it kept shining out a bright white light and made the usual operational noises. She'd opened it once, but it was just an intense light. It had hurt her eyes for almost ten minutes afterward.

And, finally, at about the same time each day, the printer would start spitting out paper. No one reloaded it with ink or paper, but that didn't seem to matter.

Usually, the contents of that paper just depressed her. Today, she pulled what it had already printed out. She didn't turn on the ceiling light, but the printer's glow was sufficient.

It was a list. The other times she'd examined this list, outside of when it was read out during the news, she'd always skipped to one spot. She'd find her last name. She'd find her brother's last name.

This time, she started reading from the top. There had to be information here—something she could use. It wasn't data from someone's face, from their motions, but it was still raw data.

They didn't bother with the full list's contents for broadcast. The full list was for every person in Quill Point—tens of thousands of names. Some with *survived another day* written next to their name if indeed they had.

The others had different descriptions. Date, time, name, location, and horrific death.

Her eyes prickled from soon-to-be tears, and her stomach felt queasy within a few pages. There were horrifically unique ones—and horrifically repeated ones. She'd found two of the entries for Murder Sky already.

She kept reading. She wanted one specific location.

By the time she found it, one name out of so many, her entire body was tired. The printer had stopped printing, but it still scanned nothing, over and over. A metronome. Even with what that horrible machine reported, Piper could see herself falling asleep to that noise.

But she kept reading the passage over and over.

It had happened two days ago—technically three, since it was past midnight.

The rest said:

Greg Feldman. The Infinite Ink Well Diner. Cooked in oil until dead.

She heard it during the news, yes, but it had been lost in the sea of morbid declarations. But now it held significance. One day before, The Newscaster went to a dinner at that location. One day before, The Newscaster never returned.

"What would it be?" Piper whispered. "What happened there?"

The first time she'd had access to the list, she'd checked in on Declan, Grace, and even Bree to see if they were still alive. They had been, at least before.

"Did they stash Grace back in the diner?" Piper mused. "I don't know what they'd do with Declan, but it's possible they would with Grace."

She flipped until she found her name. Grace was still marked as alive. So was Declan. That didn't say much about how they were doing—but if Grace was at the diner … then she'd survived the thing that killed Greg.

She'd survived the thing that had happened to The Newscaster.

Is that too big an assumption? Piper mused. *Just because she always worked there before the end of the world doesn't mean they'd place her right back there again.*

Piper worked her jaw a little—and then winced. It still hurt sometimes from when Arthur had hit her. She shook her head and thought of an idea.

The fastest—but not fast—way she could think of to get a better grasp of things would be to read all the names. People were dying all over Quill Point. Piper had a decent idea of the core locations, the most populated areas, just by the frequency of the deaths. But she hadn't seen the diner mentioned anywhere else yet.

That still wouldn't confirm Grace was there.

Piper tapped her finger on the table a few times. She stared down at her hand like it would give her some better idea. Her pool of information was so small.

It still might tell you something important.

She flipped to the first page again.

CHAPTER 44

P IPER WAS RIGHT: IT HADN'T TOLD HER the secret. Pages and pages and pages and nothing that direct. After all, why would the document the evil god made give her direct clues about how to solve this? But Piper was also right: it did give her more information.

And Piper could do a *lot* with a little information.

Her initial hunch, for one, had been confirmed. Only Greg was listed dying in The Infinite Ink Well Diner. Thousands of deaths, and not a single other passage about that location. That was an extremely unlikely scenario except…

Except what Piper suspected.

Going strictly off the frequency of locations appearing, Quill Point was laid out in two distinct ways. There were clustered areas, like something called The Spire Market, with lots and lots of deaths—and then there were places with only a few people, like where she currently was.

That suggested the diner had a small staff. Extremely small. Or the monsters were somehow being dramatically less willing to kill the people there.

That seemed extremely unlikely.

A more likely problem *had* occurred to Piper though. The list could contain some lies. But, if it did, they were subtle lies. The list appeared comprehensive. Or, at the very least, it had deaths stretching back to the early days. Every single loss Piper knew about was accurately documented. Albert Turner was even listed, despite not living in Quill Point.

Piper decided that the calculated risk of trusting it was the best option. It was certainly better than no conclusion.

But she still hadn't found out *how* The Newscaster died.

For that, she would need to gather more information.

Or, more likely, *pull* information out of someone. She wasn't sure she could effectively trick Brook into revealing more. But she hadn't really tried Wyatt yet. That might be an effective tactic.

But that could wait for morning. It needed to wait until morning.

Because, after hours of thinking, reading, calculating, she was truly exhausted. Perhaps the *most* exhausted Piper had ever felt. Her brain was sluggish, and her internal sense of balance was wavering. She needed sleep. Even knowing Mr. News was around ... even with the increasing threat of Brook killing her out of rage ... she could feel tiredness take over.

Piper didn't have a set bedspace inside the station. They'd never even entertained giving her one. She made do with various chairs and even spare soundproofing foam before, but with the hum of the printer and the false safety of a closed door behind her, Piper didn't bother to go somewhere else. She scooted closer to the table covered in junk, used her own arm as a pillow, and let exhaustion take her into the next day.

CHAPTER 45

IZZY ALWAYS ARRIVED BEFORE THE LORDS of Greed. Usually, an hour earlier. She'd walk through the door and cross over the threshold. For a moment, then, she'd have memories shift across her face. It was always odd for Piper to see. A human mind doesn't usually boot up like a computer, and it certainly doesn't usually within the span of a few moments.

Then, she would—as quickly as possible—go to her little room. Piper could see inside from most angles. Izzy usually just sat there, doing not much of anything, until the Lords showed up.

The expression on her face signaled to Piper that asking anything during that time was a bad idea. It had taken Izzy a week to basically say the reason why—and it had been mostly unprompted.

"I have to listen to fake silence all day," she'd told Piper that day. "All this corporate bullshit. I hate it. If I have to have *silence*, then let it be actual silence. That's the only thing that keeps me from…"

She hadn't finished that sentence, but Piper could hazard a guess what sort of things she would do.

It was with *all* of that in mind that she still found herself walking to the doorway. During the brief period of waking up with drool on her arm and a crick in her neck, and Izzy arriving, Piper had thought of maybe a decent solution to one problem. It wasn't the most *important* problem at the moment, but it was *a* problem.

With extreme trepidation, Piper knocked once on the doorframe.

Izzy turned and looked at her like she'd just sworn at her, called her the worst insult. Then she raised an eyebrow. Piper noted that she still hadn't actually given her any indication that she could come in.

Piper nodded, hoping that would be enough.

Izzy worked her jaw for a moment. Her shoulders dropped, and she nodded ascent.

Piper walked in slowly. "Hey…"

"Hi," Izzy said. "I uh…"

"I know this is your, um, quiet time," Piper responded. "But can I talk to you about something?"

"What?" Izzy said sharply.

Piper flinched back slightly, not managing to keep the shock off her face. Not that she hadn't, on some level, expected Izzy to react a little negatively to things.

Regret flashed across Izzy's face almost instantly though. "Sorry…"

"It's okay," Piper said instantly. Any other response would've delayed the main conversation—and they only had a little more time before the Lords hovered nearby. "I just wanted to talk to you about … yesterday. I've been thinking about stuff."

Annoyance flashed across Izzy's face.

This is really pushing things, Piper thought.

"You mean about me dying every fucking day?" Izzy asked.

"Yeah, that…"

"I don't think you can do anything about that, Piper," Izzy said.

"I don't know…" Piper began, "I … maybe thought of something."

Izzy stared at her for a moment, but when Piper looked right back, Izzy let out a little sigh. Izzy nodded.

"What is it?" she asked.

"What kind of music does the other you listen to?" Piper asked quickly.

"I don't know … that…"

"I mean, I know you don't know exactly what she does," Piper continued, "but I'm sure she leaves out records or tapes or … I don't know how you listen to your music."

Izzy took out her phone from her pocket. She looked at it with a glance that hinted at much deeper sadness.

"I mean … this thing has some songs saved on it…"

"But you streamed the rest, huh?"

"Yeah," Izzy said, pinching the bridge of her nose. "I had a list of over three thousands songs in general rotation. This has, like, twenty on it."

Piper winced. "Shit."

"Yeah," Izzy said. "It fucking is."

Piper shifted her weight from one foot to the other. She was slowly regretting this conversation. But she also didn't feel like she could bail out on it now. Hopefully, it would have the desired result.

"I mean … at least they're your favorite songs."

"*Were* my favorite songs," Izzy said sadly. "Even the best guitar solo in the world can get old."

"Yeah, okay… I get that."

"What does it matter, anyway?" Izzy asked. "What do my terrible music options have to do with … other stuff?"

"I mean … so, you *do* know what songs, roughly, you listen to, out there?"

"Yeah," Izzy said. "I do."

"And they're songs you would listen to, yeah?"

"Yes."

"The *same* music?" Piper pressed.

Izzy raised an eyebrow. "Yeah, it's the same. Pop Punk stuff. Bands like *High-Speed Nihilism* and *Fuck Your Understanding.* It's the stuff I've been listening to since I was a teenager."

"Important stuff, then?" Piper asked.

"Uh, yeah."

Piper took a deep breath. These next few sentences needed oomph. And one of the very circumstantial tricks Piper had found to get people to really consider something she said was, paradoxically, to reply with it fast.

"How important is music to you?"

"What?"

"Is music special?" Piper pressed.

"Yes…" Izzy said, looking slightly confused. "It matters—"

"Does your soul hear the music?" Piper said.

Izzy didn't respond for a moment, then sighed. "I see what you're trying to do, Piper. And, like it's nice of you, but … I don't think…"

Piper had too much momentum now. She couldn't stop herself from finishing her counter argument if she wanted to. There was energy to it. There was power in knowing what you wanted to say.

"Izzy, if you're telling me that music has no soul, then so be it—"

Izzy balked. "Wait a minute—"

"No, I won't," Piper interrupted. "If you want to tell me that music isn't held by the soul, isn't heard by the soul, then fine. But you know what it's like at a concert. Are you going to tell me that someone else can listen to all of the same songs as you, as much as you know they did, and call them soulless?"

"But she could just be going off a pattern!"

"But, right now, this version of you, does she only love those songs because memories say that she does? Or is it the soul that's always been here, who loves the art, because that's *you*?"

Izzy didn't respond. She'd started crying.

Piper blinked in surprise. She took a single step forward, then stopped herself. "Oh, shit... I'm sorry..."

Izzy let out a huff and wiped at her eyes. "No, you're not, Piper. Fuck, you wanted to win."

"I ... I just wanted to make you feel better," Piper said.

Izzy let out a half-laugh that only someone mid-crying could produce. A little sharp breath that somehow was on the knife's edge of grief and sarcastic self-defense.

"Sure. Like that's possible in this hellhole."

"I mean ... we need to keep our spirits up... and I didn't want you to worry about more than ... all of this..."

"Well, thanks for that, for the thought, I guess," Izzy said, "but you're not going to *logic* me out of this... I'm not a puzzle, Piper. I know you're good at, like, reading people, but it's not..."

Izzy pulled her arms and legs in tighter. The thought of her curling into a ball flashed in Piper's mind's eye.

"Ugh, fuck... I hate crying," Izzy added.

"So sorry," Piper muttered. "I really am sorry…"

Izzy rubbed both of her eyes a little too hard, leaving the skin around them slightly red. She breathed in through her nose and out through her mouth.

"Look, okay, I'll grant you that you might be right, Piper. I don't *not* believe in souls. I don't know much else about the universe, but I do believe in souls. So fine…"

"That's all I—"

Izzy cut her off. "No. Stop. Piper, stop. Fine, fine, fine: maybe I don't die from that *one* thing. But I have enough shit to deal with here. And I don't need you attacking me with philosophical questions during my only break."

"I just wanted to make you feel better," Piper repeated, though even weaker this time.

And internally, Piper felt a surge of guilt. She hadn't even thought about it, but as she said that last sentence, her body language, tone, volume: she'd said it with the full intent to get Izzy to forgive her as quickly as possible.

And, of course, it worked.

Izzy's gaze softened a little, and she let out a more organic half-laugh. The kind that emotions wearing off could easily produce. The type of noise anger makes as it evaporates.

"If you really want to make me feel better, I just need a few minutes to myself before work starts, okay?"

"I…"

"Piper, please," Izzy said quickly. "I'm not mad at you—not really. But please. Just *enough* for now. Don't try to solve me just so you'll feel better about things."

Piper bristled slightly. She shouldn't have. It wasn't the right thing to feel. But she did. It was all well and good for her to read people. She was fucking good at it. But other people weren't allowed to read her. Piper's mind, emotions, thought-processes, were supposed to be hers, and hers alone.

She managed to hide the slight frown that wanted out. She nodded. Now was not the time for her own emotions.

"Okay. I'm sorry. I'll let you do that."

"Thank you," Izzy said. "I do know you're trying to help."

Piper nodded again. She took a step back out of the room. She spun away. Her shoulders dipped, and she shook her head slightly. Her mind itched in a way that she couldn't quite give a name—but hated whenever she felt it.

I'll have to figure out something else, Piper thought. *That was the wrong approach. I'll need to do something more subtle next time.*

Then, as she glanced at the door and thought about her upcoming plans, she winced.

Assuming, of course, that we don't die before then. That I make it that long.

Chapter 46

"**. . . A**ND THAT'S WHY WE SHOULD only be building luxury homes!" Mr. News concluded. "It just makes the most sense for everyone. Right, Piper?"

Piper jolted slightly. "Yes, of course. Sure…"

"Do you not agree?" Mr. News asked, leaning toward her.

"Does it matter?" Piper said awkwardly.

Mr. New's shoulders bounced up and down, but no actual laughs made it out of his mouth. Then, a moment later, the sound of a studio audience cackling rippled out from around him. It sounded more mocking, jeering, than any sitcom Piper had ever seen.

"No, of course not. You've been quiet though, Piper. I want a little more oomph from you."

Piper's heart sank slightly. She glanced at Brook. He held up three fingers, gnashed his massive jaws, then put down one of his fingers.

Piper winced. "So sorry, Mr. News. I … uh … the news was very informative and horrible, as always."

"I'm flattered," Mr. News said. "I hope all of you out there feel the same as Piper. It is horrible out there for you. There's no hope for anyone not already in power—like our corporate connections—and you should feel very alone."

"I feel alone," Piper said weakly.

"See! That's the spirit! That's what I like to hear! And, when we return, that's what you'll hear more of. When we return, I'll tell you about how, if you don't have money, you shouldn't be allowed to have a social life. That it's only fair to define that by income. Isn't that fun? Talk to you then!"

Mr. News gave a wave, then settled back in his seat. For a moment, Piper assumed he was going to be dormant until the next broadcast, but his head rapidly swiveled toward her.

Piper jolted.

"Were you not interested enough in things, Piper?" Mr. News asked. "Is fear of dying not *stimulating* enough for you?"

"No, of course not," Piper said. "I'm terrified."

"You don't sound terrified," Mr. News said. "You sound like you're thinking about other things."

"I swear. I'm not," Piper said, trying her best to sound convincing. "I … I just can…"

Piper wasn't a big fan of outright lying. Usually, she didn't need it. People could detect lying way more easily than what she did. But if she had to lie…

Then you make it so true it hurts.

"I'm worried you'll kill my brother. He's out there. That's what I was thinking of."

"So, you weren't terrified—you were anxious," Mr. News said.

Piper put a slight hitch in her voice. Getting it to rumble, like ice cracking; it didn't take much effort to bring up the very real fears she had.

"I'm *terrified* you'll kill my brother," Piper insisted.

"Is that why you were looking over the names last night?" Mr. News said, his voice sounding colder than normal. "That was very odd of you."

"Yes… I wanted to make sure…"

Piper let her gaze fall. Her stomach hurt. Her eyes prickled from tears. Those, too, were truth brought forward. Ever since Murder Sky, it wasn't hard to muster existential concern, all-consuming fear. It had taken so long to make those feelings stay in the back of her brain, let alone not invade her every waking motion.

"I wanted to make sure…"

"Well, well," Mr. News said, "it will happen soon enough—and we will report it right to you. Shout it at your face."

"I know," Piper said.

The sitcom laugh track erupted again.

"Can I take my break now?" Piper asked.

"An hour, yes," Mr. News said. "But then I expect you to be horrified about the things I am talking about. Brook isn't the only one that can kill you on air. Imagine what it will do to my audience when I cleave your head off."

"I can imagine it," Piper said.

"Good," Mr. News said.

Then he finally seemed to go dormant. Piper waited a moment, staring at the monster. Her pulse was racing. She internally chastised herself for letting her guard down that much. Yes, she needed to solve the problem—but she couldn't muck things up just because she had a plan now.

Chapter 47

THE TRICK TO HER PLAN, PIPER REALIZED, wasn't just that she needed to talk to Wyatt. It was finding a way to talk to *only* Wyatt. Brook and Wyatt always seemed to be around one another.

It was almost like they knew, on some level, that Piper couldn't be allowed to get him talking.

As she got up from the desk, she glanced at them. Once the broadcast had ended, they'd blitzed over to the other side of the room. She wasn't entirely sure what they talked about when they weren't directly threatening her.

When they were talking at all.

Sometimes, they simply stood there, heads tilted to the side, listening to whatever godly horribleness they could hear that Piper couldn't.

Not that she would *want* to hear it.

Well, probably not.

Today, though, they were chatting about something.

Piper walked over to the printer room's door and leaned against it. She closed her eyes and rubbed at her temples. Unlike most days, she didn't actually have a headache.

As she ran her hands down her face—she looked over at them. Held her gaze on Brook's mouth for as long as she could get away with. Openly staring would be too obvious.

Dammit, Piper thought. *Not enough time.*

She tilted her head against the door and closed her eyes again. After letting her body relax again, she let one eye creep open.

This time, she caught a few words from Brook.

I'll be the one to find her.

Piper let her eye drift closed. She let out a long breath—hopefully looking full of stress—and pushed herself off the door. After her disastrous pep talk, she had no intention of actually talking to Izzy, but she started walking that way. It was what was expected of her. Piper moved sleepily, like the act of moving was taxing. Some days, it was.

And she kept glancing their way.

Rip her head off.

Piper walked to the doorway. Fortunately, Izzy was in the middle of a song and didn't look over at her. Piper reached out like she was going to gesture to her, then slumped with disappointment. She took a step back from the doorway and shuffled toward another wall. The two Lords of Greed didn't seem to even be watching. But if they did or had, all of it should've looked organic enough.

After another moment, Wyatt did say something useful.

There are only so many places to hide from there.

Piper got a little excited. Did he mean the diner? Were they talking about Grace? It only made sense. If something bad had happened to The Newscaster, and it certainly had, then Grace would've had to run afterward. It wasn't good that they were searching for her—but it was great they hadn't found her.

Piper spun away. She was out of ways to spy on them. Now she walked to the breakroom—and her mind was abuzz. There were a few missing puzzle pieces, sure, but a picture was forming.

It had been a dinner, right? More than one monster. Lots of monsters, probably. But whatever had happened bought Grace enough time to escape. What on Earth could be that effective?

As she stood in front of the stocked fridge, full of bland food, she still couldn't work it out in her head. She needed just a little more data. A clue to unlock the next puzzle piece. Her mind churned with bad options about how she might get it.

Everything she could think of doing was a stunt. Very dangerous ones. If she did it wrong, then … well. One of the Lords of Greed might just gut her on the spot.

But wasn't every second now inherently risky, inherently full of looming death?

Oh god, please don't let this be how I die.

CHAPTER 48

HER HEART RATE WAS IN HER EARS AS she walked over to the two of them. Whatever they were talking about was clearly important—because they didn't seem to notice her for a bit. She was almost right in front of them when Brook glanced over.

"What the fuck are you doing?" he asked.

"Uh—"

Brook closed the gap between them. "What the fuck do you want, Piper?"

"I just … I had a question…"

"What could you possibly need to ask?"

Despite having thought through most of her options, the most likely motions this conversation could take, Piper still felt off balance. It was one thing to plan a conversation. It was another to actually have one.

One trick—much more requiring acting than Piper's actual skill set—was convincingly introducing information like it had organically happened.

"I saw something…"

Brook's expression shifted. The haze that always rolled off the Lords of Greed's mold seemed to get more oppressive. Piper had the distinct sensation that the rest of the world was disappearing and she was trapped with Brook.

This is what it would feel like right before he kills you.

"What did you see?" Brook pressed.

"Uh … well, I think it was a … girl? Running by? Outside? I saw it by a window."

She flicked her gaze to Wyatt. His expression was less intense. Almost … curious. Yes. Curious. The kind of look when you're invested in acquiring more information. She knew it well enough.

Piper literally was betting her life on that calculation.

"There was … maybe two of them, actually," she added quietly.

Brook didn't even respond to her. He took a second, presumably thinking, then the door slammed. Piper assumed he had opened and walked through that door— but he had been too fast to be sure.

Piper blinked in half-genuine surprise. That had worked remarkably well. But the task was half done. The task had another step. Wyatt was alone.

One of the easiest tricks to get information out of someone is to piggyback on information you already have. A full secret is a solid wall. A half-known secret is practically gossip.

"Do you think it's Grace?" Piper asked. "It looked like Grace … and … Declan?"

Wyatt didn't respond for a moment. His posture shifted a little. Piper was just about to chime in again— pushing things even more—when he let out a faint hiss.

"If it is them, they'll be dead in a minute."

"Oh…" Piper said, hoping she sounded afraid enough. "Because they escaped?"

A flash of anger in Wyatt's eyes. "Those two didn't *escape*. There's no escaping The God of Greed."

Piper cleared her throat. "…Okay."

"Go get ready for your next shift," Wyatt said roughly. "This doesn't concern you."

Piper debated, once again, pushing it. If she wanted to, she could certainly get a little more out of him. But he also might just knock her across the room.

"Right … sorry…" Piper said, looking down at the ground. She spun around and started walking to her desk.

"And … don't ask any more questions," Wyatt instructed.

Piper nodded without looking back. Despite the apprehension bubbling in her stomach, she tried her best to keep a smile off her face. As far as she was concerned, she'd just gotten all the confirmation she needed.

There were only two major issues left to face for this particular project of hers. One was a consequence. And one was a singular question. How had Grace hurt those monsters?

And how pissed would Brook be after finding nothing?

She got the answer to that one a moment later.

CHAPTER 49

IN A RUSH OF WIND, PIPER WAS KNOCKED off her feet. She tumbled across the floor, skidding across the carpet. It didn't so much hurt as startled her. Her mind didn't quite catch up to what had happened yet.

"Lying little piece of shit," Brook spat. "You sent me looking for *nothing*!"

Piper put a hand on the ground, letting it stabilize her a little. She looked over at Brook. He was huffing slightly, rage in all of his expression and posture. It would've been terrifying to see that look on his face even before he became a Lord of Greed.

"I … what…?" Piper asked.

"You sent me looking for *nothing*."

A bloom of racing panic was already forming in Piper's chest. Her fear kept ratcheting higher. This was the major danger. This was the least planned-for part. And she wasn't entirely sure how to talk herself out of it.

"But … I saw them!" Piper insisted.

"Did you? Did you *really*?" Brook said. "Or are you fucking with me?"

"I … I saw … Grace run by. She was going through the roses outside. Declan was with her. They looked really scared."

"When did you see that?" Brook asked, his voice sharp.

"When I was on my break!" Piper said. "Just a minute ago! That's why I walked over to tell you. I don't know how else to explain it."

Brook went quiet for a moment. His next sentence felt like the first serve in a game of tennis. A projectile screaming across the court, ready for Piper to fail.

"Why would you sell out someone?" Brook asked.

Shit. Fuck. Dammit.

"I…" Piper swallowed a buildup of spit in her throat. "I didn't…"

Brook was suddenly right above her. Piper's entire body had a cold, disconnected feeling wash over it. Adrenaline seemed to replace her blood. Too energized to not move, but too scared to even flinch.

"I hope you enjoyed your little prank," Brook said.

Piper's jaw hurt as she forced out words. "It … wasn't … prank…"

Brook held up three fingers. He put down two. The final one had a nail that could easily cut open her throat. He placed it against her forehead.

The nail moved, breaking skin. Piper could feel a thin line of blood trickle down the side of her head. He dragged his nail down almost an inch, ripping skin as he went.

Piper forced her words around a gasp. "I didn't … I saw her…"

Brook studied her face for a moment. He didn't believe her. Piper could tell. But the rage was rapidly cooling.

"When I kill you, I want to enjoy it. This will kill you far too fast, Piper."

Piper gasped again. Her heart rate felt too rapid for her to form words around it. It took too much air. It took too much concentration.

"I … please."

"Am I more powerful than you, Piper?"

"Yes."

Brook smirked, then let out the smallest chuckle. He stepped back at normal speed. Somehow, that made it all the worse.

"I think I'll start looking for our next co-host. You have a show to go do, Piper, but one more slipup—and I know you will so soon—and I will kill you in the most painful ways I can imagine."

Piper's neck muscles were so tense, but she forced her head to nod.

Brook rolled his eyes. Then blitzed away.

Piper lay there, looking at the ceiling. She focused on breathing. Breathing meant she hadn't died. Oxygen flowing down her arms, through her tight chest—those were signs of a living person. At some point, felt like an hour, was probably only a minute or two, something loosened in her brain, and she felt like she could stand. The blood from what was a shallow wound still poured down her face. She got her elbows underneath her and pushed up. Her stomach muscles screamed. Her entire body shook. She felt like she might vomit.

But underneath it all, she *knew*. She held onto the thought as a victory. She'd gotten away with it. They'd given her so much information. So much fucking information.

Now she just needed to know *how* Grace did what she did.

Chapter 50

T**HE NEWS HAD BEEN ESPECIALLY HARD** to hear that day. She found herself flinching more, wincing more.

"And in today's final story, we have a massive treat for you. We hear someone's final moments!" Mr. News announced. "We've got a live audio recording of someone from The Spire Market. He was there late. The 9-to-5, one of our newest additions to Quill Point, doesn't need to eat, but sometimes does. Let's listen!"

Mr. News gestured to Izzy, who very begrudgingly flipped a switch. Lights flickered on toward the bottom of the dual speakers, and a second later a faint electric hum flowed out.

Piper expected to hear basically horror movie audio. The buildup to the kill. Tension. But no. Mr. News had literally meant they just had an audio recording of someone dying.

It started with a sharp, pained scream.

Piper couldn't help but remember when the Lords of Greed had first transformed. When they'd run out into the crowd that Zaahir had gathered.

The sounds of slaughter.

But one person dying doesn't take that long when monsters are involved. After that, it was just a wet sound. Somewhere between someone chewing on a steak and tearing open a watermelon.

Mr. News let it play for a whole minute before he gestured for Kamas to turn it back off.

"His brains, I'm told, tasted incredible. That's what awaits some of you! I hope you're looking forward to it," Mr. News said. "And with that, we're done for the day. We hope you enjoyed the only news there is to hear. Because that's what just happened. Goodnight!"

Mr. News dropped back into seemingly just being a puppet.

Piper didn't get up from her chair. Her doing so was somewhat performative. Her sitting there in abject despair was likely what Brook wanted out of her. He likely wouldn't do anything else for now, as long as he thought she was distressed. But it wasn't like that noise *hadn't* sunk into her stomach.

She kept her head down, pressing it to the cool desktop. She moved her knees up to her chest—as best she could. It was uncomfortable, but she hoped she didn't have to wait long.

She eventually heard Izzy switch back on the speakers and play its horrible dull noise for the night. She heard them leave through the door. It was faint, but she heard the printer start its grim reporting.

Piper waited another moment after all that before lifting her head. The news station was dark, mostly silent. Her neck was really sore. She rubbed at it as she stood up.

A quick glance at Mr. News showed what it usually did. It wasn't a weekend day. He should just stay there.

As far as Piper could tell, the next stage of her plan was a go.

Chapter 51

S HE WENT BACK INTO THE PRINTER ROOM. Not to read the print-out again—although she did quickly make sure Sean, Grace, and Declan were still alive—but because it felt the safest place to think. Only one door in; assuming a Lord of Greed didn't just punch through a wall.

But slight, maybe fake, safety was better than nothing. It gave her room to think through things.

Piper's sleep deprivation wasn't helping though. Her head kept feeling warm from thinking—like a computer overheating. She could get herself some water, but even that felt like too much of a distraction. There was a glaring solution to all this, surely? She refused to accept that there was nothing she could do about things.

She started with some speculations. That felt like a good way to get the mind working in the right direction.

A knife?

Unlikely. How could she have managed to survive in a room full of monsters with just a knife?

Poison?

More likely. But what could poison monsters made by a god? She could've slipped it into something with the dinner, but that would be a gamble.

A fire?

Environmental stuff might be good. Milda talked about that; she'd been in the hotel and the clay things died to water. Maybe they can't handle fire. Maybe they can't handle some kind of cold?

"God, I can't think of what to do," she whispered to herself.

She sat down and pulled the paper closer to herself with a faint rustle. Maybe reading—*again*—the notes on the Kraken Hotel deaths would give her some new idea.

"Please," she muttered, tracing her finger down the paper. "I just need to figure this out…"

Piper was interrupted by a soft noise. She couldn't place it at first through her tired mind, but then her mind made the connection. The noise of—

She spun around. The door was already open. She frowned and stood up from the chair, then took a single step toward the door.

How long had it been—?

The doorway had nothing in it.

But Piper had seen this in movies before—and immediately looked up at the ceiling.

Mr. News perched on top of the doorframe; his knees bent up. His fingers were dug into the ceiling, each finger having punched a hole for him to grip.

"News at night," he whispered. "My co-host appears to be scheming."

A shiver passed up Piper's spine. "Uh, hi, Mr. News. It's not a weekend. What are you doing up?"

"You went in here before. And it *seemed* innocent enough once. But twice? And messing with the papers? That's a scheme. I suspect you're planning something you shouldn't be planning, Piper. That's what I think. I smell a different sort of story."

"I don't know what you're talking about," Piper said. "I'm just resting for our next broadcast."

Mr. News let his legs unfurl. "No, no, Piper. You might be able to trick some humans, but you can't trick me. I know snooping when I see it. And I know leading questions when you ask them. Together, it is too much. We don't do investigations. We report. We report what our corporate owners want us to report."

He can be hurt, Piper thought frantically. *You can hurt him.*

Mr. News dropped to the ground. He rose by his wires, even if Piper wasn't sure what they were attached to. A faint rattling sound echoed through the room.

"I know Brook won't mind much," Mr. News continued, stalking forward. "As long as I make it painful."

One door in wasn't safe when it was a *blocked* door.

Piper kept backing up until she bumped into the table. A little gasp left her throat, and she glanced behind her. There wasn't anything useful. Just a bunch of junk. She couldn't even imagine using most of it as a weapon—

She scooped up the microphone and held it mostly by the wire. It was a frayed wire. She wasn't sure how long it would last if she tried to swing it. But it was either the microphone or try to use an old circuit board like it was a brick.

"Oh! I love that idea, Piper," Mr. News said with a chuckle. "We can record your voice, too, as I rip out your heart. That way Brook still gets you hear you die."

Piper tried to keep herself from shaking. She held up the microphone higher.

Mr. News chuckled again. "You're going to fight me, Piper? You're going to fight the news? You can't fight bad news. There's always more and more of it."

"We don't have to fight…" Piper breathed.

"It won't be a fight."

Mr. News lunged forward; his hands full of needles.

In a panic, Piper flung the microphone in a sharp arc. Mr. News's wires pulled him sideways, avoiding it. The wires then tightened, reversing his momentum so he could immediately leap at her, his hands outstretched.

Piper let out a scream and more fell than ducked. She collapsed underneath the table, her head clipping the side on the way down. Mr. News went over her, landing on the table.

Gasping, Piper pulled her legs closer to herself as she blinked away stars. The part of her jaw Arthur had dislocated started hurting again. She pushed herself back up to sit and yanked the microphone back to her.

Mr. News's face, upside down, peeked out from over the table.

"Do you know what your bones snapping sound like?"

Piper gave her best yell of defiance and swung the microphone up at his head. Mr. News ducked back out of sight. The microphone bounced off the edge of the table and fell to the ground—and she gathered it up again. Piper heard a series of rattles right above her, but he didn't jump down yet.

Piper's breathing was so loud in her ears, but her mind caught on something. Mr. News kept *dodging*. She'd attacked—he'd dodged. It made sense. A basic rule of how fighting worked.

A rule, though, for humans.

Why is he acting like this can hurt him?

Mr. News's hand darted out and grabbed one of her legs. She always suspected he was strong, but Piper barely had time to gasp in pain before Mr. News flung her across the floor.

Piper crashed into the other wall. The door out was both extremely close and way too far away.

Quickly running out of what adrenaline she had, she used the wall to push herself up to standing. Blood lightly pooled from where needles had stabbed through her pant leg.

Mr. News didn't crawl off the table. The wires lifted him slightly up, then deposited him on the ground in a standing position.

"Alright. News is over for the day," he announced, striding toward her. "We hope you enjoyed it, Piper. Because this is all you'll ever get."

He swung his right arm. Piper pivoted left. The microphone was in her hand, held like a club. The microphone's front mesh cracked into the side of Mr. New's head.

The wood cracked open, letting free a torrent of flickering red light in an otherwise hollow shell. Mr. News let out a faint gurgling sound. He stepped back.

"That was uncalled for…" Mr. News said.

"Die!"

She snapped the microphone out, this time hitting Mr. News straight in the chest. It knocked him off his feet with a resounding crack. He landed with his arms splayed out on either side.

"I don't…" Mr. News hissed. "You weren't supposed to…"

Piper hit the underside of Mr. New's chin with the microphone. It carved a divot from wooden jaw to wooden forehead. The red lights faded away.

Piper stood over the body.

I killed a monster.

Piper let out a little sound she couldn't quite attribute to any single emotion, then ran her hands through her hair more than a few times. The rush of realization, of solving the puzzle, of winning a fight, of surviving, was still so electric that she almost couldn't sort out her thoughts as they passed by.

I fucking killed a monster.

She suddenly felt a little off balance and sat down against the wall. She cycled through little laughs, swears, "Oh, my god," and a few other reactions as she stared at Mr. News.

When she felt fairly sure he wasn't going to move, she closed her eyes. Piper let her arms and legs relax, adrenaline and pure fear melting *slightly* from her.

That was until she could think straight again. It took a few minutes, but once she could work through what had happened, less pleasant emotions rushed through her—as well as acidic worries. Because, *yes*, she'd killed a monster. A victory, for sure. Good job, her. But she'd won a *singular* fight in a town afflicted with a god's dominion. And her *other* bosses, Brook and Wyatt, so eager to kill her before, wouldn't hesitate to chop her into pieces as soon as they knew that she'd murdered Mr. News.

Which meant, oh fucking god, oh fucking hell, which *meant* … she had one night to figure out a plan to kill two more monsters. And they had super speed.

CHAPTER 52

S**HE LET HERSELF HAVE ONE MORE HOUR** to calm down. It wasn't enough—but it would have to do. Her heart rate went up, up, up, until it was making her feel lightheaded. Then it slowed down, down, down, until the contrast from before made it seem like she didn't have a pulse at all. She checked her wrist. She had a pulse.

Somehow, that felt like a signal.

She stood back up.

The best option, Piper decided, was research. Really fucking morbid research. Her stomach rolled at the thought of it. Anyone else but a murderous monster: she would've vomited.

The rule was clear enough to her now: you could hurt the monsters with things the god made. She was sure Grace or Declan had figured that out somehow. In fact, considering they made it back from the forest—a feat never achieved before—they probably had survival skills Piper could only dream of.

But what were the limits of the rule?

A microphone, swung hard enough, would hurt a human too. Blunt force wasn't that special. Did using objects in that way translate to normal force—or was it special?

You broke a wooden face with a single swing.

Okay, so … possibly the damage was magnified. But Piper wasn't going to take that on faith. She would at least try out something.

God … this is going to haunt me for a while.

Piper took the circuit board and found a chunk of Mr. New's wooden head that wasn't totally destroyed. She nudged it gently with the circuit board, then took a look. Just grazing didn't seem to break the wooden skin.

Nothing for it. Here we go.

She smacked it down as hard as she could in that spot. It caved that spot in.

She took a step back and ran a hand through her hair. "Damn…"

Okay, so, theory confirmed. It hits harder than it should.

Piper let out a faint breath. Test one done. But it didn't answer the question of what she could do about The Lords of Greed. Who cared if she could hurt them if she couldn't hit them? She would need to be more creative.

She paced beside Mr. News's body, thinking.

I could make some kind of trap, she thought. *Something for when they walk in the door.*

She shook her head, discarding the idea. What could she do? Plant a fucking bucket over the door? Have it drop some water on them? They just be slightly more annoyed as they murdered her.

Her mind did stick on the idea of water, though.

Solid objects work. What about…?

She shrugged her shoulders. Trying something was better than dying. She gave one last look at Mr. News, making sure he didn't get up somehow, and walked out of the room.

In the breakroom was a sink. And there was a microwave. And mugs. Any other time, they would be perfectly normal items. Nothing worth thinking about. But Piper's mind whirred as she walked.

Halfway there, she stopped for a moment. She wasn't entirely sure why. She glanced behind her, then around, then tried to listen more carefully. But there was nothing. Just the horrible speaker noise, gently rumbling.

I'm the only one here, Piper realized.

The building was made by Greed, but none of his minions or monsters were inside right then. It felt inert because perhaps it was. Piper had a dollhouse when she was a little girl—her dolls very quickly became serial killers and skilled combatants—and the dollhouse itself had felt like that when she had all the dolls on some other adventure. A building with a purpose it currently wasn't fulfilling.

She shivered a little, thinking about the purposes of buildings out in Quill Point. This one at least didn't have blood on the walls.

She finished walking to the kitchen and surveyed her options. The sink did have a hot water tap, but she wasn't sure she could get hot *enough* water from that. The microwave would have to serve dual purposes then. Two experiments.

But first, she should probably drag Mr. News's body into the kitchen.

CHAPTER 53

THE MICROWAVE DINGED. PIPER POPPED the door open and wished she had some kind of oven mitts. A mug could handle a lot of heat—her fingers, less so.

But she couldn't let it cool too much either.

So, as quickly as she could, she pulled off her suit jacket and grabbed the mug's handle. It was still so hot; the water inside was boiling. But she yanked it to the edge of the counter. Then poured it down in a massive splash on Mr. News.

Some of the water hit her legs, and she jolted backward with a yelp. But it wasn't enough to distract her. Piper's gaze fell on where the water had landed.

The boiling water melted through Mr. News's face like she'd used some intense acid on him. Steam rose off as the wood bubbled.

Piper wasn't sure how to feel about the grin that spread across her face. The sight was disturbing. But the implications were … amazing.

She stretched her hands above her head and cracked her fingers. "Oh … they might just be fucked."

She went back to the microwave and pulled it down to the floor. It was a cheap, mostly plastic thing. Something she'd expect in any company building. Which, she imagined, was entirely *why* it looked that way. Piper hadn't quite worked the minutia out yet, but the magic going on clearly worked through some level of metaphorical logic.

She'd figure that all out later.

Piper yanked free a chunk of Mr. News's jaw. The boiling water had turned the material soggy, like he was made of cardboard.

The chunk went in the microwave. She paused. There was a chance this might be slightly explosive. She might not want to be standing next to it right as she did this.

She put it on for five minutes. Highest setting—

—then fucking sprinted to the other side of the room. She squatted, resting on her ankles. Watching. The chunk of wood *was* wet. It might not react as quickly as she imagined. It might take a little while—

The chunk caught on fire.

A bright orange flame sparked to life inside the microwave. The sharp tang of burning wood, paired with a horrible rotting smell, flowed out.

Piper didn't know if there was a fire alarm, but she ran back to the microwave like there was. She unplugged it, picked it up, poured out the still burning wood into the sink, and then turned on the sink. A hearty rush of steam rose up.

As the steam cleared, Piper could see the fire had stopped.

Piper let out another nervous laugh. She let out a faint swear afterward. Then she turned away and walked out of the room.

She clutched her forehead with both hands as she walked. Thinking through what to try next. She felt propelled, somehow, by her own thoughts. Like she couldn't keep her body still if her mind was going to work this fast. They had to both be rushing.

Piper wished she had a science book with her. She wanted to double-check what she was thinking.

Boiling water, sure, made sense enough—but a microwave used some kind of airborne wavelength. It altered the air, and usually the food too, when it was running. That was her understanding of how microwaves worked, anyway.

It would have to be enough.

It mattered that a common, mundane alteration in the air, if produced by something Greed made, worked as a weapon. That mattered. That fucking super mattered.

"Vibrations … cold … warm … sound waves…"

Piper stopped so fast in her tracks she almost toppled over. Her head wanted to continue forward. Her mind felt like it was running down a track.

Piper had an idea.

She just needed Izzy.

CHAPTER 54

PIPER FIGURED A LITTLE SPECTACLE WAS the most effective way to get Izzy onboard with her plan as quickly as possible. They'd had their fight. A disagreement. But there was no time for that anymore. Izzy arrived earlier than the Lords—but not by that much.

So, nerves jittery, and feeling that special kind of tiredness that seemed to both give her energy and make her body's outline slowly fade from her perceptions, she went to work. She set up everything she could do, then pulled up her chair. She couldn't sleep—but she did rest. Piper would let herself have one more moment before everything went to hell.

As she did, the sun began to rise. Weird shadows pushed against the blinds. Shapes of buildings that shouldn't be there—shouldn't exist here. Skyscrapers. Sprawling box stores. Those weren't Quill Point.

Piper wondered if the feeling she had was rage, defiance, or hope. She wondered if, in this case, they were even different things.

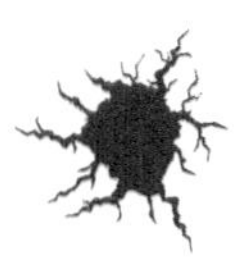

Izzy walked through the front door and immediately let out a stream of colorful swears. Piper, dozing slightly, jolted in her own chair, sitting up straight.

"What the fuck?" Izzy added. "What the actual fuck?!"

Piper rubbed her eyes and then grinned. "I got a few things done since you were last here."

"Fucking shit, Piper! What did you *do*?"

What she had done was set up proof. She'd put Mr. News in his chair. She'd put the microphone she'd killed him with in his hands.

"I won," Piper said. "We have an hour."

Izzy blinked in surprise, taking a step back. "Is he…"

"Oh yeah, as far as I can tell, he's really dead."

"You … you killed a monster?"

Piper shrugged her shoulders. "Yeah, I sort of did."

Izzy took another second to think. Even Piper wasn't entirely sure what Izzy was going to say. Even Piper wasn't sure what was going through Izzy's head.

"Fuck," Izzy said. "Do you fucking know what this means?"

"Which part?" Piper asked, tilting her head. "The part where I know how to kill the monsters? Or the part about how we have to kill Wyatt and Brook now—basically as soon as they get here?"

Izzy blinked in surprise. "Uh … the second one."

Piper nodded, then sprung up from her chair. She clapped her hands together over her head. "Don't worry, Izzy—I've already thought about that. I've got the plan laid out. Made the weapons too. I just need some help from you."

"Wait, what … *what?*"

"You know lots about sound systems, yeah?"

"Yes…?"

"Good. Then you'll get to kill a monster too."

CHAPTER 55

PIPER FINISHED SETTING UP EVERYTHING she could for now. She'd shoved Mr. New's corpse into the printer room, with the list. The water would have to wait until the last moment to be effective.

To call Piper nervous would be disingenuous. Nervousness was nothing compared to the sensation she was feeling. She was somehow both impatient—for there was still a little time left and not much left to prepare—and terrified.

She went into the room and checked on the final part of this.

Izzy was working, fiddling with the wires. She sat in her usual spot by the soundboard but looked more alive than she had in a long time.

Piper stood off to the side then, holding her weapon. It was a horrible thing; it *looked* violent. And soon enough, she would use it.

Piper wondered how many nightmares she'd have for the rest of her life after this.

If she lived.

"Okay," Izzy announced. "That's about the best I can do."

"Will it work?"

"I mean—it might only work for a minute or two. I'm not going to test that part. But, yes, everything is rigged the right way."

"Okay … I guess we wait."

"I guess so…"

Izzy took a long breath. Piper didn't need her skills to tell that Izzy was stressed.

Izzy leaned forward, looking at the dials she'd adjusted. The title of the song she'd picked flowed across the tiny display screen.

"Do you want to check it again?" Piper commented in the silence.

Izzy moved back, sitting up straight. "No, I'm sure now. I used to do something similar back in my own room, only less intense."

"Remind me not to come over," Piper teased, trying to break the tension.

It didn't quite seem to work. But it did do the thing that Piper seemed to be very good at getting people to do. Piper could almost feel it before it happened.

She'd said the cue, whatever cue it was this time: the other person was about to tell her about themselves.

Izzy let out a small almost-chuckle. "Honestly, I'm not sure if my old house *exists* anymore. It was back when I lived with my parents. My apartment would never let me get away with something like this."

Piper paused, her mind doing its thing. Then she raised an eyebrow. "Do you still think of your childhood bedroom as your room?"

Izzy looked at her. "Do you know how spooky that is?"

"What?"

"That," Izzy said. "I told you *one* sentence, and you just went for the jugular."

Piper almost said something, then paused again. She thought for a moment. She didn't want them to have another fight—not right before a much more important fight. They couldn't afford to be emotionally distracted.

"I'm sorry… I just noticed the wording you used," Piper said.

"Oh. Huh," Izzy said. "What did I … what word?"

"You called it 'my own room.'"

"I did?"

"Yeah, that was your word choice."

"Huh. I mean … yeah. I moved out a long time ago, now. Basically, right when I was eighteen. I had a decent job and a decent amount of savings. And it was cool. I wanted that independence."

"You didn't have roommates?" Piper asked.

Izzy nodded. "Not one. I got a little studio, instead. Really little. I didn't want to share, you know?"

"Yeah, I get it."

"I figured if I was going to be independent, I was *going to be independent.* The very first night, I bought a whole pizza, and ate it in one sitting, and then felt a little sick and vomited in my own damn toilet, you know? I kind of miss those days."

The next thing Piper thought to say just kind of popped into her head. She didn't plan it. It was almost an instinct. The right words to keep the other person talking.

"But it got lonely," Piper commented.

"It got *so* lonely," Izzy said. "I didn't realize how lonely, until … it's just, people are made to be communal.

I worked from home. I could go days without seeing anyone. Time would go … weird on me."

"What happened to your old room?" Piper asked.

"Oh, they turned it into a guest room. Most holiday visits I ended up sleeping there. It was nice to hear my mom and dad move around as they got ready for bed."

Piper gave a small smile. "That sounds nice."

"Why are you asking all of this stuff, anyway, Piper?"

"I … I'm trying to keep myself distracted, mainly," Piper said. "I don't want to be in my head right now."

"I wish we had some good music," Izzy said. "It fills time. Lyrics can drown out my thoughts."

"I guess that makes sense…" Piper said, trailing off.

Izzy went quiet too. Her eyes went to the front door. The place where their potential murderers would emerge.

Another surge of adrenaline and fear rattled through Piper, somehow even worse than it already was. Piper felt like it was squeezing on her stomach. She glanced at the weapon again.

"Are you sure you don't want to check again?" Piper asked.

Izzy looked over at her. She seemed like she was about to say something—but just glanced down at the console. She muttered a few words underneath her breath, hovered her fingers over a few things, then sat back.

"It's set," she said.

"Okay."

Another moment of silence passed. Piper was slightly worried she wasn't breathing. She forced some air into her lungs.

"Okay … I have an idea," Piper said.

"What?" Izzy said absentmindedly, her eyes fixed on the door.

"When this is … all over," Piper elaborated, "let's … let's have a concert."

Izzy turned her head sharply. "What?"

"When Quill Point is … better … let's get everyone for a concert. Everyone will be invited. We can celebrate."

Izzy made a slight noise in the back of her throat: a little, bitter chuckle that could easily turn into a ragged sob.

Oh, dammit, Piper thought.

"I don't think things are going back to normal, Piper," Izzy said, her voice cracking. "I don't know what … The God of Greed did, exactly… but we're not going to fix things."

"I'm hoping we can figure something out. Operating word being 'hope,'" Piper said.

"That won't fix this," Izzy said.

"No, but it's what we've got," Piper replied. She looked out at an imaginary crowd, somehow all in that room with them. "I can see them. People we know. Everyone … everyone together again."

"Piper…"

Piper looked at Izzy.

Izzy stared back at her. Izzy's shoulders suddenly dipped.

Piper held her gaze. She tried to, anyway. Piper didn't quite know when she started crying, but she was already deep into it by the time she noticed. Her chest felt like it was encasing itself, trying to protect her breaking heart.

"Piper?" Izzy repeated, quieter this time.

"Yeah?" Piper asked. "What is it?"

"I…"

"Yeah?"

"I just … I'm trying, okay?"

"I know you are." Piper managed a smile. "I know you are. Thank you. I need you."

"You're welcome."

Izzy didn't say anything more. But a change flowed over her face. Her eyes got angrier, her expression more serious. After a second, she slammed her hand down on the turntable. Once, then twice.

"I've been singing about this," Izzy said.

Piper didn't quite know what she meant by that—but she didn't ask for clarification. It would resolve itself in a moment.

"I've sung so many songs about this," Izzy continued. "Do you know how many songs are about fighting back against injustice?"

"Hundreds," Piper said automatically.

"Much more," Izzy replied.

"And…?"

"And, as long as there have been artists, there's been someone fighting. I've cried with rage over those lyrics. On some level, I knew what I was saying. I knew the meaning behind them—but…"

"This is different."

"No. It's not," Izzy said. She looked at the door again. "It's just our turn."

CHAPTER 56

WHAT HAPPENED TOOK TWO MINUTES. All told, from start to finish: two minutes. But adrenaline can slow things down. But the mind can hold moments, even very short ones, in an almost stasis.

Piper would remember this for the rest of her life. However long that might be.

Izzy stood in the room with the soundboard. She was ready with all she had set up. Piper stood just to the side of the front door; her own weapon held. They'd managed to make two, Izzy had one as a backup.

The Lords of Greed arrived.

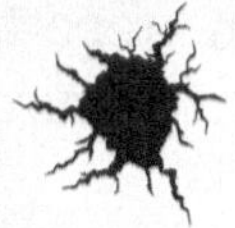

The door opened, and Wyatt was finishing a joke. Piper didn't try to parse it. All of her mind was focused on the plan.

Brook walked in first. Wyatt trailed behind. They didn't look over at her. They wouldn't expect this. They wouldn't expect anything out of the ordinary. Both were too distracted with their own power to pay attention.

Wyatt closed the door. Piper's gaze fixated on Brook's back. The back of his neck. Could she hit the back of his neck cleanly? Or would it be best to go for the back of his knees, let him fall, and then attack?

She didn't move yet. Her heart hammered in her chest even harder when the two of them paused. They were likely confused slightly. The smallest margin of their pattern interrupted. Usually, Piper would be easily in sight. Usually, Izzy would be out of the little room.

Piper could hear in the back of her head what Brook would've usually yelled at them.

Alright, you pieces of shit! Time for work!

Usually, the window to Izzy's workstation wasn't shattered.

Piper made the planned cue. A quick thumbs up. It wasn't necessarily, though: the timing was clear. Now was the moment. If it was going to work, it would have to be now.

The speakers hummed ominously, loud even when they weren't playing anything.

They'd picked the most chaotic, most layered of the songs in the news station's repertoire. A droning, concordant tune that was meant to mimic nearby construction.

It started.

The speakers played the music so goddamn loud Piper felt like it was shaking her eyeballs.

And it hurt the Lords of Greed.

Brook and Wyatt both stumbled, fell, collapsed backward into the door—at a normal human speed.

Piper walked around the side of them. She could see their eyes roll up in their head. The blood pop from their mouths. Stalks of their mold rose up, shaking in pain.

The music was so loud that it still hurt Piper's ears through the headphones—but it was bearable. She could think through it. She could attack.

The water in the mugs had barely cooled, they were still scalding. Piper poured one on each of their heads, then smashed down both mugs on their skulls in tandem. The porcelain broke into flying shards.

Brook and Wyatt yelled out as sections of their mold melted. Piper couldn't help but wince from how quickly sores formed on their skin. It didn't slow her down.

Kill them. Or die.

Piper scooped up her weapon. It was a cobbled together thing, but Piper had done her best with the time. She'd broken the window for a reason. She'd snapped off legs from the table in the printer room. She'd stuck the glass into the wooden legs. Piper's hands were covered in small cuts from its construction; the glass stained with her blood. But the glass would stay in the wood.

It *had* to stay.

It was the only way this would work.

Piper picked Brook first. She swung for his head. The first smack sent a shot of blood across Piper's face like Brook had sneezed. Some of the glass shards remained in his face as Piper pulled back and hit him again. Each blow had less and less windup.

The seventh blow snapped the leg in half, sending a chunk flying across the room. Brook's face was soaked with gore. Through the massive cuts, the white mold pushed itself outward, tearing open skin as often as it entwined itself with the wounds. Glass shards, embedded in his skin, started to fall away.

A voice emanated from Brook, from the wounds as much as his mouth. It sounded like rushing fire.

"Greed always wins…"

Piper glanced, for just a second, at the weapon in her hand. The club now ended in a jagged spear of wood. Then she stabbed Brook through the throat. It didn't quite feel like stabbing skin—it was more like breaking through wet cardboard. A rush of blood pooled over her hand; it splashed down on Brook's shirt. The mold in Brook's face—all of it—started to fall off. It looked like snow. What was left of Brook was incredibly dead.

Piper didn't have time to process that fact much. She'd *killed* someone—and there wasn't time to face that reality. The battle was still going. Because, out of the corner of her eye, Wyatt reached out for her. His motion was slow, his entire frame shaking—but he could still kill her.

The speakers gave a horrible whine around the music as smoke poured out of them. Piper's already elevated stress skyrocketed—they'd been worried about that exact issue. There was only so long it was possible to force a speaker to play that loudly.

Piper stepped backward, pulling the weapon back out of Brook's throat.

One of the speakers blew. It let out the loudest pop that Piper had ever heard—and then sparked and stopped playing. The other speaker let out a horrible whine.

Wyatt's mold stopped reacting, and he started to gather himself. He was still moving at human speeds, but that could change very quickly.

Piper stabbed his chest. Wyatt didn't manage to dodge it—but him pulling back in pain also pulled the weapon away.

Wyatt composed himself somewhat. He snarled at her. His mouth was full of those teeth. Those teeth that could easily rip someone's head off—

Out of the corner of Piper's eye, Izzy sprinted with her own bat.

Wyatt didn't have time to react before Izzy slammed several shards of glass into his side. He stumbled, knocked off balance, blood pooling down from the cut.

Piper darted forward and yanked free her spear from his chest, leaving open a rapidly bleeding wound.

Wyatt looked between the two of them, the murderous rage fading slightly. He seemed almost confused. That second of stillness was what killed him. Izzy slammed the club into his stomach, knocking him to the ground.

Piper and Izzy both attacked him as one. There wasn't any strategy to it anymore. They didn't even aim much. Each time he tried to attack one of them, the other would hit him again. Stab him again. Sink chunks of glass into him.

At some point, the other speaker blew out. But it didn't matter anymore. In almost silence, punctuated only by heavy blows and breaking skin and the ringing in Piper's ears, they ensured that Wyatt and Brook were dead.

CHAPTER 57

IZZY EMERGED FROM THE BATHROOM. Piper had been standing right outside. She didn't want to get too far away from Izzy. If she was alone, if she let herself, Piper could feel echoes of the blows in her arms. The water had cleaned up the blood—but none of it did anything for the shock.

They'd shoved the bodies in the printer room with Mr. News. Piper had thrown up while they moved them— which made Izzy throw up.

They didn't speak to one another after that. They simply hadn't. Perhaps it was because Piper hadn't fully expected for them to survive at all. But here they were. Piper's own thoughts were so loud in her head. She tried her best to keep her focus on reading Izzy. Somehow, even that felt off now.

As Izzy left the bathroom, her breathing was still irregular. She seemed on the verge of a panic attack. She kept taking in long, sharp breaths. It seemed to help her. To pull some of the tension out of her. Piper tried to mimic the way she breathed. It didn't help her nearly as much.

Izzy gave her a long look, then. Piper couldn't quite figure out what was going through Izzy's head.

Izzy cleared her throat. "We should…"

"Yeah?" Piper asked a little too quickly. "What?"

Izzy stopped talking again. She ran her hand across the back of her other hand's knuckles. She gripped her wrist so hard it looked painful. Another long pause.

"How about…" Izzy managed. "How about we talk later?"

"Sure," Piper replied.

"Okay. We'll figure something out. But … I want … to be alone for a little while, Piper. I want to … I want to be alone."

A surge of fear passed through Piper. *Alone?* But alone meant…

I can still smell the blood.

"I … do you need to…?" Piper started. "I don't know if I can be alone. I … maybe we can just sit quietly?"

"No."

Piper flinched. "But—"

Izzy held up her hands, and they quickly started shaking. Her breath hitched faster. Every few words cracked. "No. Piper. I need—fucking hell—I need to go and not be for a while. I think I need to sleep."

Piper felt like she might drop right through the floor. But she still nodded along. She still stood there as Izzy walked off.

The space between them was massive. Piper stood in a void; her muscles were locked with yet more emotions. Eventually, she managed to walk over to the desk and sit down. It was the exact same spot she'd been when Mr. News had read aloud horrors.

She leaned back in the chair, stared at the ceiling. She looked at it without thinking, and then thought about random things, and then thought about the sound of glass shattering and mold and the temperature of blood, and then she went back to not thinking—the cycle lasted what felt like days.

She pulled out her phone, even though it lacked power. She tried to imagine the pictures saved on it. The games she used to play as she was falling asleep—before everything.

She looked at the door to the printer room. She wondered if it now printed anything about Brook, about Wyatt. If she could see how Greed chose to present her murdering them.

She clutched her head.

Sean's still out there. Grace is still out there. Declan is still out there.

She looked down at her hands. As the shock wore off, as the horrors crept into her mind, she focused on *why* she'd done this in the first place. Was it only survival? Certainly, that was part of it.

But it was also because of Quill Point.

The list of the dead was long. The crimes of The Mayor, and his patron, were innumerable.

She had the knowledge now. A way to win. Maybe not every fight—but more than before. It was her responsibility to take the next step.

Her stomach roiled at that.

Why me?

Because she was there. Because she knew. To not do something in a world gone cruel when there is so much cruelty was to not face the world at all. If cowardice existed—that was it.

But why do I have to be the one?

She looked at the door again.

There might not be a good reason. And maybe there never would be. The trauma of all the things inflicted didn't mean anything besides Greed was evil. It wasn't some culmination—it was just horrible times, forced on people who didn't deserve it. There wasn't glory. She was simply here.

That was why.

She was in this because she'd won. Because she should've lost but hadn't. That was why.

It's a ledger of the dead.

It's also a ledger of people worth fighting for.

It's a ledger of what could be lost if you don't do something.

But it had taken all of her, all of her will and her thinking and her observations, to beat three monsters in a town with more monsters than she knew.

The hydra had so many heads. And she had not even a true sword.

What can I do?

The monsters could be hurt by things they made. That was the rule. Lords of Greed or monstrous metaphor, every fight in a changed Quill Point would be improvised, desperate, relying more on creativity than anything else.

What fucking hope did they have? What, was she going to fight every monster with a spiked bat?

A ledger of the dead and soon-to-be-dead.

But had that really been her weapon? A simple bat?

Or had it been what she knew? Hadn't it been, truly, information?

A ledger of people who have every reason to fight. If only they knew that they could. If only they knew a way that would work. Now, then, who does know what would work?

Piper closed her eyes.

Why me?

Chapter 58

I N THE MONSTER'S GLEE, MR. NEWS TOLD Piper more than he'd meant to. Throughout their time as "co-hosts," he'd spoke of what it was like out there.

The town of Quill Point, warped as it was, had radios in every office. Had speakers above the doors.

Izzy had agreed to Piper's new plan without argument. Even if, as soon as they did it, more things would find them. More monsters and Lords of Greed would arrive, ready to kill them.

But she agreed. Perhaps, Piper reasoned, Izzy had been having the same thoughts as her. Perhaps anyone decent would, in their situation.

Once it was set up, Piper sat in front of the microphone and thought for a moment. The new printout would tell her tonight—if she lived until tonight—the results of what she was doing. The outcome of this choice. She knew that there would be so much death, one way or the other. That was unavoidable.

She wished it wasn't such a foregone conclusion.

"You ready as soon as I finish talking?" she asked Izzy.

"Yep. I hope it works."

"So do I."

Piper had hoped for a better world than this. She wished that the path leading to this hadn't been walked in the first place. Those people of the past had allowed greed to flourish. There *had* been a way where this didn't have to happen.

But Piper wasn't going to hesitate any longer.

She pulled the mic close. No prepared speech. This wasn't quite that anyway. The Mayor gave speeches. She spoke the truth.

Piper saw things.

"Hello. I'll just say the most important thing first. You can hurt the monsters. Anything made by them can hurt them. Anything you can grab, any object you can use as a weapon, will work. Whatever you have. Keyboards, nails, or pieces of glass. Whatever you can. We don't have to die like this."

Her breath caught for a moment, and it felt like electricity was moving up her spine, through her mind. Tears sprung to her eyes. But she kept talking. She kept telling them what needed to be said.

"We … never … had to die like this. Do you hear me, Quill Point? Do you fucking hear me? I have sat, and I have listened to a newscaster talk shit about people I care about. I have heard good people … great people … people I saw every day … suffering. And I have heard the lie that we are all fucking facing these things alone. We are not. And we are not. And we are not. We. Are. *Not*. And these things don't get to *just fucking happen*. The god that has killed so many of us is a god of greed, and he will take everything of us, blood and lives alike, if we don't do something. I am terrified. I think they're going to kill me for this. But I am talking *anyway.* Fighting anyway. I hope with these words, a thousand battles start. Because this must happen now. Because that's the only way. I'm so sorry that we are the ones that have to do it. I'm so sorry that we *have* to be the ones to do this. But we're in rot. We're in hell. It's hell out there. You have to fight back. Quill Point … this is what we have to do to survive now. We must…"

Piper leaned in close to the microphone.

"We must fight back."

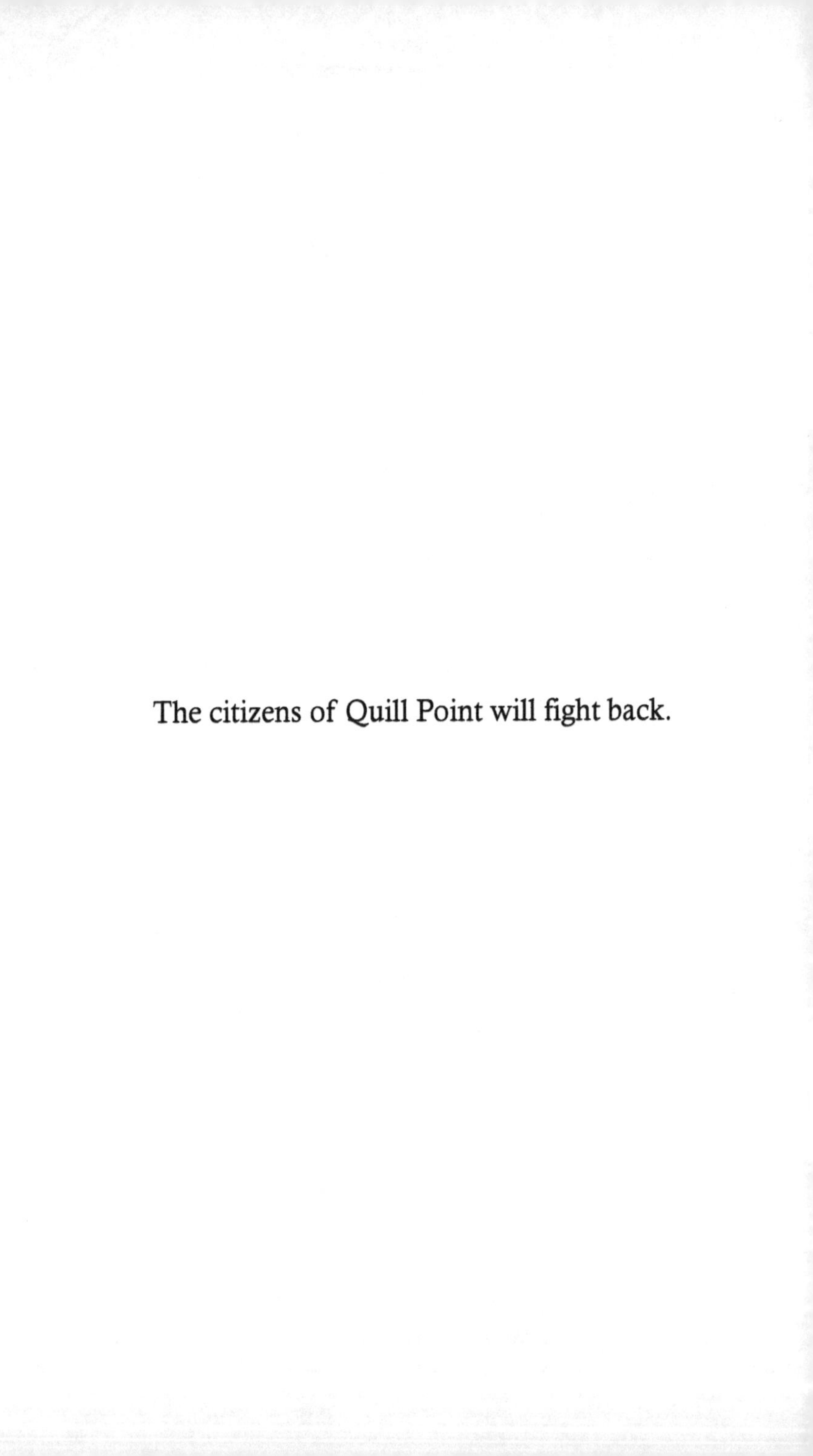

The citizens of Quill Point will fight back.

Afterward

T HE QUILL POINT CHRONICLES WAS always meant to be complicated. But I didn't realize how complicated it would be by the time I got to this book. It sometimes feels like it has slightly grown out of my control, and it's an active effort to keep it going toward the endings I envisioned.

But I made it complicated for a few reasons.

The biggest one was I wanted a story that rewarded people for looking for the tiny clues, the foreshadowing, and who worked out the timeline. There are small moments in these books that are there to set up whole plot lines. I heavily used landmark events (Murder Sky and The Emergence are the most obvious ones) so that readers could track when things happen, but I still wanted it to feel like the story moved around on the timeline a lot.

I also wanted a story that was based on social connections, which I consider rather complicated—but also fascinating. I try to make these books have an undercurrent theme of how communities and people care about each other, and that it takes active malice, like the Mayor's Men, to even weaken those ties. And the easiest way to get that across was to have a massive cast and to have characters know most other characters. I even went so far as to try to make tracking those social connections a big part of how readers engage with the series.

And, as I continue with the *Quill Point Chronicles*, I hope that this complicated format remains engaging and entertaining. That each character's story, journey, and ending add up to something that people will really love.

And I hope that—for all you horror fans out there—I manage to scare you a few times. These are cosmic horror books, after all.

Book Club Questions

1. Irena Ink left information for future mayors that ultimately gave the current mayor his chance to end the world. But, if you were her, and didn't know that—do you think it was a good decision on her part to even let other people know about the room underneath the courthouse?

2. Irena Ink says: "History will want records. It always does." Do you agree with that?

3. Chuck and Cassandra work well as a team. What aspects of their personality allow them to work well as a team? What makes someone a good teammate?

4. Chuck has plans to find an army to fight back. Given what you know of the new Quill Point, how might he go about doing that?

5. Charley and Dereck learn from Lotty that "Emptied People" tend to be those with specific types of jobs. Why do you think that is?

6. Buddy the dog is able to detect the emotions of the humans around him easily. Have you ever had a pet who seemed to know what you were feeling?

7. Thea escapes two different monsters who try to kill her. They both represent something to do with greed. What do you think they represent?

8. Grace manages to not react to a lot of horrible stuff said to her. How well does that mirror how people sometimes treat service workers?

9. The story cuts away before we can find out if Grace and Declan's plan works. What do you think happened right after The Ascended Mayor finished his speech?

10. The Layer that Haven is in doesn't appear to use cars as vehicles. How much do you think the prevalence of cars affects your life and where you live?

11. The 9-to-5 informs Hope that her understanding the system makes her dangerous. Why is that? And why would a monster be that concerned about her?

12. Bree invokes The God of Greed's protection when she feels threatened. Why do you think that was her first instinct?

13. Piper uses a lot of small tricks to get people to tell her information. Do you have any tricks that you've found useful for finding out things you wanted to know?

14. Piper asks herself why she has to be the one to help save people. Do you agree with her conclusion?

Author Bio

OCTOBER KANE IS A NOCTURNAL HORROR author and general fan of spooky things. Once he discovered cosmic horror could be blended with a lot of other genres and subgenres, his love of monsters and existential themes found its home and he's been writing books about that ever since. He also enjoys cooking, taking walks, and reading books in a lot of different genres. You can find him around Florida.

Discover more at
4HorsemenPublications.com

10% off using HORSEMEN10